THERE'S SOMETHING ABOUT MERRY

CODI

sourcebooks
casablanca

Copyright © 2022 by Codi Hall
Cover and internal design © 2022 by Sourcebooks
Cover illustration and design by Monika Roe/Shannon Associates

Sourcebooks and the colophon are registered trademarks of Sourcebooks.

Published by Sourcebooks Casablanca, an imprint of Sourcebooks
P.O. Box 4410, Naperville, Illinois 60567-4410
(630) 961-3900
sourcebooks.com

Originally published in 2021 as an audiobook by Audible Originals.

Cataloging-in-Publication Data is on file with the Library of Congress.

Printed and bound in Canada.
MBP 10 9 8 7 6 5 4 3 2 1

For Allison.
Thank you for being as excited for this series
as I am and for all of your awesome insights.
Merry shines brighter because of you.

CHAPTER 1

MERRY

IT CANNOT BE NOVEMBER FIRST.

Merry curled up on her U-shaped couch with a sherpa blanket covering her lower half, her fingers working the knitting needles in her hands absently as she stared out the window. Tiny flurries swirled through the air like glittering wisps on the wind, obscuring the trees beyond. After a string of lackluster relationships that had taken her from Washington to Colorado, she'd decided the outside world wasn't quite as green as the rows of Douglas and Noble fir trees across her family's Christmas tree farm and she'd come home a year ago. A year of swearing off men and enjoying the peace of being single—

Someone pounded on her front door and she jumped a foot in the air, her knitting needles clacking together.

"What the hell?" she hollered.

"It's Nick. You decent?"

Merry set her knitting and blanket aside, climbing to her feet. "Yeah, come in."

The door opened and her brother came through the door, his Navy beanie covered in dots of melting snow. "Don't sound so cranky." He held a tray of coffee cups in one hand and a white pastry bag in the other. "I come bearing goods."

"Awesome, I'll forgive you for practically breaking down my door. I haven't mustered up the strength to make any coffee yet." Merry took the bag from him and set it on her kitchen counter, peeking inside. "Chocolate chip scones. Yum."

"Mom and Dad bought everyone breakfast since it's all hands on decorating duty."

Merry glanced out the window at the falling snow. "Really? In this?"

"Don't be a wimp. It's barely coming down."

"But it's cozy in here. I've got my blanket, my pellet stove, and now delicious hot coffee." She reached for one of the cups but Nick held it away from her.

"Ah-ah! This is for working people only. You want to stay inside, you can make your own coffee."

Merry gave him the stink eye. "Fine. I'll get changed."

"Hustle up! Everyone is waiting on us."

Merry walked through the kitchen of her tiny house to the drawers in the wall under the loft where her bed was. Her family and friends had helped her build the four hundred square foot home on the back of her parents' property in late spring, just across the gravel road from the foreman's cottage. She pulled out a thermal shirt, jeans, and her wire-free bra and popped into her bathroom. Merry glanced at her small claw-foot bathtub longingly, but that would have to wait until tonight after decorating was done. Usually it was just the main house and yard, and then a string of lights around the flocking tent where people paid for their trees. But it was the seventy-fifth anniversary of the Winters Christmas Tree Farm's grand opening and her parents were determined to make it magical.

She finished changing and brushed her teeth, tossing her long blond hair up into a haphazard bun. Her brother was drinking his coffee and watching out the window when she came out of the bathroom.

"Is the snow getting worse?" she asked, grabbing her thick winter headband off of the jacket hook and sliding it into place.

"Nah, still the same, but we're supposed to get a few inches. That's why everyone wanted to get an early start."

"Is Noel at work?"

"No, she's up at the house. I told her she didn't have to come out here on her day off but she insisted."

"That's because she's family." Merry shrugged into her jacket with a smirk. "The two of you just need to make it official."

Nick leveled a hard stare at her. "Don't say anything like that around her. We haven't even been together a year and I don't want her feeling pressured."

"Relax, I'm not going to. I know her almost as well as you do." That wasn't exactly true. Nick and Noel had been inseparable since infancy and when Noel's parents died, she'd moved in with the Winterses. Noel loved the rest of them, but no one had ever cracked through her barriers the way Nick could. Merry always expected them to date and when they'd crossed the line to more than friends last Christmas, she couldn't have been more thrilled.

Just because Merry didn't talk about the two of them getting married didn't mean Merry wasn't hoping for it.

Nick held out the second coffee to her and once she'd shrugged into her black down jacket, she took it. "I know, I just can't help reminding everyone. Don't want anyone scaring off my hippogriff."

Merry quirked her right eyebrow, setting her coffee cup on the counter. "You compare the love of your life to a large mythical creature that is both scary and freaky-looking?"

"Hippogriffs are beautiful, majestic animals."

Merry sat down on the couch to put her socks and boots on, snickering. "Good God, how did you ever woo a woman?"

"Noel thinks I'm romantic."

"Or she pretends you are. She probably doesn't want to hurt your nerd feelings."

"Grab your breakfast and come on," Nick grumbled. He opened the front door and stepped outside, leaving it wide for her to follow. Freezing wind whipped inside, bringing swirls of glittering flakes with it.

"Hey, were you born in a barn?"

He didn't respond and she muttered several colorful names as she tied her boots. Before she stepped outside, Merry grabbed her coffee cup and the pastry bag. She told her Alexa good-bye and all the lights in the house shut off.

Merry closed the door behind her, not the least bit surprised Nick had headed up to the main house without her. Siblings were a blessing and a curse, depending on the day.

She walked along the textured walkway her father helped her create, which was still visible beneath the thin sheen of snow. Her grassy yard had died once the weather turned, as had all of the flowers in the white raised beds closest to the house. The only green in her yard was her Blue Spruce bush she'd bought on sale at the end of the summer, but in the spring her yard would be bursting with color, including several different irises. The four-foot vinyl fence with the latched gate was the finishing touch to make it feel like a real home.

Merry passed through the gate and traveled across the gravel road behind her parents' house, straight toward the foreman's cottage. The dark-brown log cabin exterior and green roof blended in with the woods behind it. She nibbled on the scone as she hummed a few bars from "Let It Snow", watching the snow fall all around her as she passed by the shiny Jeep in the driveway.

Up until a few months ago, Hank Cuthbert had lived there with his two chocolate Labs, but when he'd decided to retire and move further north, her dad had put out feelers looking for a new foreman. She'd honestly thought he'd train her to fill the position. Instead, he'd told Merry if she really wanted to take over the farm one day, she'd want a great foreman by her side.

Merry argued at first, because she'd come back to heal but also for her father to teach her all the ins and outs. If something ever happened to her dad, she'd know how to cut and haul a tree but none of the day-to-day stuff. He'd waved off her argument with some ridiculous statement about living forever, and after seeing her mother's warning look, Merry had shut her mouth.

Several weeks later, her dad hired Clark Griffin via Zoom. Clark was twenty-seven, her brother Nick's age, who'd moved away for college and hadn't been back since. She remembered him as a teen working weekends on the farm, but they hadn't run in the same circles. He'd been quiet and skinny with long hair, and when he wasn't working, his face was always buried in a book. Merry had done well in school, but she'd preferred being around people at dances, parties, and camping rather than being alone. Although after one day of working with him, she'd thought there might be something more to the broody Clark. He'd seemed to loosen up and when he laughed, his whole face transformed. She'd harbored a small crush on him for a few weeks after, but he'd avoided her like Merry had a disease he didn't want to catch. She'd moved on and he'd left town a few months later.

When Clark arrived with a seven-year-old son, she'd tried to bite back her frustration and engage Clark in conversation, but his personality was somehow worse than when he was seventeen, awkward on his good days and taciturn the rest of the time. Or it could be her projecting. Her parents adored him and his son, Jace, and didn't seem to have an issue getting along with Clark. Just her.

She cut to the left of the cottage, up the hill to her parents', finishing off the rest of the crumbly, sweet scone. The pumpkin latte chased down the remainder of it, warming her belly, while her face had gone numb under the blasts of chilling air. She'd planned her day around decorating at ten this morning, but getting the jump on it three hours earlier should open her day up for a relaxing afternoon. As long as there were no hiccups in the process.

When she rounded into the front yard, she found her family and the farm employees bustling about. Carrying lights and boxes of blow-up decorations, they whizzed around through the dancing flakes like Christmas wind-up toys.

"Hey, Merry!" The small, high voice belonged to Jace Griffin, Clark's seven-year-old son. He was bundled up in a red jacket, Spider-Man beanie, and gloves, his hazel eyes bright.

"Hiya, kiddo." Merry returned his wide smile and motioned to the box in his hand. "What have you got there?"

"A blow-up Mickey." The little boy's small round face had a sprinkling of freckles over an upturned nose, and she had the fanciful thought that he'd look like an adorable Christmas elf with the right clothing.

"Nice. Where's Minnie?"

"On the porch still. You can grab her if you want."

"I'll do that."

"I got her," Clark said, coming up alongside them.

"Morning." She took a drink of her latte. "Still finishing my wake-up juice."

Clark gave her a small smile, his trademark when he was around her. *Does he even have teeth?* she wondered.

"I could have used an extra cup today."

Wow, more than a three-word sentence? Clark hadn't been much for open conversation with her and usually kept his responses short and closed.

"Late night?" she asked, although he didn't look tired. Lack of sleep left her with bags under her eyes, but Clark's bronzed skin was smooth, his brown eyes bright. She wished she tanned like that, but her skin only knew two shades: alabaster and lobster. Thank God Idaho stayed cool nearly ten months out of the year.

"We went trick-or-treating until almost nine and then watched

It's the Great Pumpkin, Charlie Brown." He tilted his head to the side with a wince. "Fell asleep on the couch at a weird angle."

"You're quite the night owl, aren't you?"

Clark's lips tipped up in that half smile, almost as though he was afraid to look too happy. "Gotta go to bed early to get up early."

"I once crammed for a test until four in the morning and was up by seven a.m. to kick its a—butt!" She caught herself, glancing down at Jace. She already owed a couple bucks to the pint-sized mercenary's swear jar. "But you might try a hot compress on the sore side and slowly keep working it the opposite direction. It will feel so much better, trust me."

"I'll give it a try, thanks."

"Dad, this box is getting heavy," Jace griped, adjusting his grip.

"All right, all right." Clark shrugged good-naturedly. "The impatience of youth."

It was on the tip of her tongue to remind Clark he wasn't old by any means, but they were already walking toward the other end of the yard. Her gaze drifted over Clark's retreating back. Time had definitely been kind to him. Gone were the skinny, stooped shoulders and straggly hair hanging down his back. His brown hair was cut above his collar, and he actually filled out the blue flannel he wore rather nicely. Ever since his return to town the local women, even the married ones, had been overcome with lusty intentions. Merry noticed at least two or three casseroles a day and quite a few pies that first month being delivered to Clark's front door, each of the ladies dressed from their Sunday best to next-to-nothing cocktail chic. Word spread quickly that Clark made it abundantly clear to every woman who'd pursued him that he wasn't interested in dating. Period. Breaking the hearts of every hopeful female in Mistletoe.

Up until last night, Merry related to his feelings. Dating and relationships equaled a lot of work that didn't pan out. But standing at the bar last night until last call watching happy couples sway in tight embraces, a rush of loneliness had swept through her. The overwhelming emotion left her tempted to break her year-long abstinence with the next rando who offered to buy her a drink, but in the end she'd gone home alone. It was the right choice, but certain parts of her anatomy disagreed with her.

But sex wasn't the core of a great relationship, which was her ultimate goal. To find someone who made her as happy as her dad made her mom. A man she'd consider her other half, the way Noel felt about Nick.

Merry caught sight of her brother, setting the ladder against the house. Noel stood next to him with a lasso of Christmas lights hanging off her arm, her brown hair knotted on top of her head except for a few stragglers dangling around her face. Nick brushed Noel's hair back tenderly, gazing at her like she was beyond precious to him. It was nauseating, and yet Merry winced at the stab of jealousy in her gut.

"Merry," her mother called. "Come here, I have a job for you."

"Of course you do," Merry said without any real bite, but her mother still snorted.

"Such a smart-ass." Victoria Winters held up bundles of lights, visibly mangled. "Can you untangle these for me?"

"Sure." Merry took the mass from her mother and headed for the patio furniture at the end of the covered porch.

"Where are you going?"

"To sit while I work on these. As wonderful as your faith in me is, I can't walk and untie these knots at the same time."

Her mom huffed. "Fine. I'm going to make sure your father doesn't get any ideas about climbing one of these ladders. If he falls and breaks his neck, I'll kill him."

"That seems a bit redundant, Mom."

"You know what I mean," Victoria said with a wave of her hand. "Don't take all day with those. We have a lot to do, and I need your help."

"I know," Merry grumbled. Sometimes her mother talked to her as though she was still the precocious eleven-year-old hiding in the trees to avoid her chores.

Her fingers weaved and untwisted the green light strands, the task not unlike when her yarn snarled up. She looped and wrapped, watching the employees and their significant others work together. Her envy crept to the forefront again as one of the farm hands, Martin, grabbed his adorably pregnant wife around the waist and kissed her, swiping the box she was carrying as though it was too heavy for her to manage. Whatever he said to her was disregarded when she grabbed the burden back from him and waddled away, smiling at him over her shoulder.

Merry yanked on the light string a little too hard and a pink casing popped off. She got up, chasing it across the porch as she ticked off the list of available men in town in her head. It was short and those on it didn't exactly snag her interest. Every relationship she'd ever had started with an instant shock of attraction and progressed from there, but her track record was evidence enough that her judgment was not to be trusted. Between her first boyfriend, the thief, to her last, the cheater, she really knew how to pick 'em.

Holly had told her more than once she picked the same type of man, but in a different suit. It would make more sense if she'd fall for an outdoorsy guy with a big heart like her dad. Instead, she'd spent a year with a marketing major who'd been caught plagiarizing and then left school without a word. Two years she'd wasted shacked up with a borderline alcoholic who'd asked her home for his brother's wedding but dumped her the minute they returned because his mother didn't see a future with her.

The final catalyst was her last boyfriend, Killian Peters. He'd had her fooled for sure, convincing her to move from Washington to Colorado with him so he could work at his dad's medical practice. He'd been older, had his life together, and Merry thought she'd finally found a decent, honest guy.

Until she'd caught him giving one of his nurses a gynecological exam. With his penis.

She'd packed up her stuff that day and driven home, telling herself the whole way back to Idaho there would be no more uprooting her life for any man. Merry would take all the time she needed to figure out what would make *her* happy.

After a year, Merry knew she wanted a man completely crazy about her, passionate about family, and who wouldn't lie, cheat, or steal. That wasn't asking much, right?

Jace raced up the porch steps and slid to a stop in front of her as she straightened up with the light casing in her hand.

"Need some help, Merry?"

"Sure, that would be great." She went back to her perch and pulled a short bundle of lights from the box, holding it out to the kid. "Thanks. I appreciate it. My mother gave me a herculean task."

"What's that mean?" he asked, sitting down in the chair across from her.

"It means hard."

"Yeah." Jace held the lights up in front of his face, so only one eye was visible through the knotted mess. "I think Miss Victoria should buy some new lights and throw these away."

Merry laughed and mimicked her mother's tone. "Waste not, want not, my child."

Jace dropped the lights to his lap, his brow furrowed. "My dad said it isn't nice to make fun of people."

It was such a sullen reaction to harmless teasing that Merry fought back a grin. "That's true, but sometimes kids tease their parents. Don't you ever give your dad a bad time?"

"I don't think so."

"Wait until you're a teenager and get back to me."

"Uh-oh," Clark said, leaning over the porch railing. "What about his teenage years?"

Merry hadn't noticed Clark approach, surprised once more at his congeniality today. "I was just telling him that sometimes kids gotta tease their parents and get 'em to lighten up. It starts right around the time they turn thirteen. Didn't you razz your folks?"

"We didn't have that kind of relationship."

His curt tone startled Merry, and her mind raced for something to say. Clark gave her one of those closed mouth smiles before she could get her bearings and added, "I didn't mean that to come out so bluntly."

"I'm sorry. I guess I take for granted my parents will give me as much guff as I dish out."

"No need to apologize." One of the hands called his name and he waved. "Excuse me, I'm being summoned."

Clark walked away, leaving Merry perplexed. She hadn't meant to stick her foot in her mouth, especially when he'd finally given her a glimpse of the man her parents raved about.

"Dad doesn't like to talk about my grandparents," Jace volunteered.

"Oh yeah?"

"No. I think it makes him sad. He gets the same way when I ask about my mom."

Merry didn't know much about Clark's life and her curious nature urged her to pry, but she bit her tongue. Clark's complicated relationships weren't any of her business and she definitely wasn't going to pump his seven-year-old for information.

She noticed Jace's melancholy expression and leaned over, whispering, "What do you say we get these untangled and sneak inside for a cup of hot cocoa?"

Jace perked up. "Yes, please."

"Then less jabbering and more working." She started singing "Rudolph the Red-Nosed Reindeer" and Jace sang along with her, the tension leaving the boy's tiny body.

Merry felt eyes on her and looked up, discovering Clark kneeling in the middle of the lawn watching them. He was hovering over a flattened blow-up, his face a mask of intensity.

Why is he looking at me like that?

Warmth licked along her skin until her cheeks flushed.

"Can we sing 'Jingle Bells'?" Jace asked.

Merry turned her attention away from Clark. "Absolutely. You kick us off."

Jace launched into the jolly tune, and she involuntarily glanced at Clark, but he was focused on blowing up a ten-foot Santa. She couldn't get Clark's facial expression out of her mind. Had he been irritated with her for letting his son help her? Had he overheard his son and thought she was gathering dirt? It wouldn't surprise her if some of the more manipulative women in town had tried using Jace to get to Clark, but she would never. Besides, based on the rumor mill, Clark wasn't interested in getting involved with anyone, and she was done with emotionally unavailable men.

Mr. Clark Griffin had nothing to worry about from her.

CHAPTER 2

CLARK

CLARK GRIFFIN WALKED THE ROWS of Douglas Fir trees on his way back to the main house, his arms aching from hanging Christmas lights around the flocking tent. After the first few hours of decorating, Jace had begged to stay with Victoria, who was making cookies, and she'd been happy to take his son, despite it being a Saturday. Although now that he thought about it, Victoria never passed up a chance to spend time with Jace, which left Clark to get his work done without worrying about what Jace was getting into.

The snow left a light dusting across the tree needles and the Winters Christmas Tree Farm was picturesque, a Christmas-card quality scene. The country setting combined with the elements of winter, his favorite season, gave Clark a sense of peace, something that had been lacking while living in California. He'd moved to the west coast for college when he was seventeen and rarely escaped to the mountains while living there the past ten years. The smells of the city didn't compare to the woods. Clark breathed in the scents of pine and soil, his face splitting into a wide, satisfied grin. Mistletoe, Idaho, really was a breath of fresh air.

He could see the blow-up Micky and Minnie deflated on the ground beneath the big red sign for the Winters farm. Although Christmas was still eight weeks away, the weather turned fast after mid-October, and with trucks coming in before Thanksgiving to collect the pre-cut trees to fill local orders all over the region, the holidays would be over before he knew it. Since it was his first season with the farm, he'd wanted to get a jump on everything and prove he belonged here, that he was the best man to keep this farm running smoothly.

Although he'd been an agricultural science major at UC Davis, he'd been most interested in plant pathology. When he'd finally finished his graduate program, he'd ended up working for EcoLeaf, a biotech company where the hours were long and migraines at the end of the day from peering through a microscope hours on end were severe. He'd worked hard to put himself through school to get a great job to take care of Jace, but he realized rather quickly that financial security didn't make up for not seeing his son.

"Dad!"

Clark grinned as Jace came racing down the hill towards him, his gangly legs churning so fast Clark held his breath, waiting for his son to crash and burn. Clark dropped the empty tub he'd been carrying and rushed forward. He caught Jace as he launched himself into Clark's arms, swinging him high into the air before hugging him. Jace laughed against the side of Clark's neck, holding him tight, and Clark breathed him in. He still remembered standing in the hospital room the day after Jace was born, staring at the empty bed where he'd left Patrice sleeping. He'd gone back to their apartment to get the car seat and thought maybe she was in the bathroom until he opened the door and found it empty. But it wasn't until he called her cell and discovered she'd blocked him that the reality sank in. She was gone and Clark was on his own.

Being a single dad before his twenty-first birthday hadn't been in his plan, but he wouldn't change it for the world.

"Were you good for Victoria?" he asked, picking up the empty tub with one hand and balancing his son on his other hip.

"I'm always good. I helped her bake cookies and I even cleaned up my mess."

"I'm proud of you." Clark carried him up the rows, realizing that soon enough Jace wouldn't let him do things like this. He was growing up so fast and Clark planned to enjoy his kid cuddles as long as he could.

"I was thinking tonight we'd do breakfast for dinner. Waffles." Jace's hazel eyes brightened. "Eggs. Maybe some fresh cut straw-berries? What do you think?"

"Yes! I love breakfast for dinner."

"Me too."

Suddenly, Jace pushed against his shoulder. "I want to get you a cookie to try. They're really good."

Clark set him down. "You know I don't like cookies, buddy."

"I promise you will like these!" Jace took off at a run for the main house with Clark trailing behind, smiling contentedly. Their first five years together were rife with struggle, but he'd been deter-mined to finish school. He'd found services and grants, pushing himself through his last year and a half while working nights and weekends. He'd taken all of his earnings, and what didn't go to supplement daycare, food, and housing, he invested. Clark studied the stock market, IRAs...any way to make his money go farther so they would never have to struggle again.

Clark caught up to Jace as he took monster steps up the stairs, clearing them in seconds.

"Remember to knock! Don't just barge—" Jace pushed inside the front door and Clark finished with a groan, "in."

Clark climbed the front porch steps and set the empty tub to the left of the door with the other empty red and green containers they would be putting back into the shed tomorrow. He followed after his son, knocking politely against the open red front door, waiting for Victoria Winters to acknowledge him. She stood in the kitchen smiling at Jace, who was hugging the family's big bloodhound, Butch, and she waved her hand at Clark to come farther in. Her blond hair was clipped back from her face, falling just past the hood of her red button-up sweater. She pointed apologetically to the phone pressed against her ear and he shut the door behind him with a shake of his head to silently convey it was no problem.

"Yes, I understand that. It really is hard, especially when these things happen unexpectedly. I'm sure she'd be happy to help out. Do you have a pen?" Victoria rattled off a phone number and nodded her head as she spoke. "Absolutely. You take care, Dana. Bye." She set her phone down on the counter with a tired smile. "Hello, Clark."

"Hi. Everything okay?"

"Oh yes. Dana Kirk isn't able to do the Festival of Trees this year and she tried to get me to take over, but I can't right now with everything going on here. I told her to ask Merry."

Merry. The middle Winters daughter. Funny, kind, and helpful—at least, that's what people said about her. Besides a few brief interactions when he'd worked on the farm his senior year, they hadn't spent much time together before he left for college. There was one day when he'd thought there was more to her than the bubbly, popular girl, and he'd worked up the courage to ask her out, but that brief infatuation had been squashed under her boyfriend's pickup tires as he'd peeled out of the driveway with Merry in the passenger seat.

When he came back to town, Merry hadn't been rude to him but there was a definite aloofness. She'd never come out to Clark's face and said anything, but a few weeks after he moved in, he'd been coming around the side of the house and Merry and her sister had been on the porch. He'd pulled up short when he heard his name.

"Why do you care if he's here?"

He'd recognized Holly's voice, which was slightly higher than Merry's husky one.

"Because I feel like Dad doesn't trust me to run the farm. Why else would he hire a new foreman?"

"Maybe he's playing matchmaker. Hot foreman who knows his stuff paired with his eager daughter—"

"Okay, no, that sounds like the start of a bad porno. Besides, Dad would never. Mom might, but they both know how I feel about dating right now. It's just...why him?"

Why him, indeed. He'd been in a lab since graduating college, even though he preferred the outdoors. He might have the education, but he didn't have the hands-on knowledge, which was why this first season was so important. Clark needed to prove the Winters family chose the right man, and keeping Merry at a distance insured she wouldn't witness him making a mistake, giving her ammunition to go to her dad. The way the people of Mistletoe talked, he half expected Merry to walk on water, but humans were flawed and could do some crappy things to each other, especially when they wanted something.

Despite his reservations, his son adored her and was always finding a reason to run next door to see her. Working with a mostly male crew who gossiped worse than prep school girls on TV, he'd learned Merry moved home a year ago after a bad break-up, and despite multiple offers, she'd turned every one of them down. Didn't stop the guys from talking about how beautiful she was, and he couldn't disagree. Watching the two of them this morning laugh and sing while they worked on the snarled Christmas lights created a dull ache in his chest, bringing attention to the hole in their lives he tried desperately to ignore. People to love. Family.

This year had been the hardest one so far, with Jace asking a lot more questions about his mom and his grandparents, and the answers...well, they weren't something Clark thought his seven-year-old needed to hear.

"My daughter may not appreciate me volunteering her," Victoria continued, "but I really can't do everything, no matter how bad I want to."

Clark chuckled. "Sometimes you gotta delegate."

"Yes, and to be quite honest, I like to enjoy the festival, not deal with the details that go along with it."

Butch broke free of Jace's affections to greet Clark, leaning his whole body against him.

"Hey, big guy," Clark whispered, patting the dog's side before responding to Victoria. "I'm looking forward to checking out the festival as an adult. We didn't really attend it when I was a kid. I was going to go with the other farm employees as a teen, but I think I got sick the day of."

"Hopefully you'll stay healthy this time. It is such a great event that helps out so many people and programs. You and Jace will enjoy it. Maybe they'll have a superhero tree."

Jace bounded into the kitchen and wrapped his arms around Victoria's thighs. "You think?"

Instead of getting irritated or shooing him away, she chuckled, brushing his sandy hair back off his forehead. "Maybe that new gamer shop will do one."

"That would be cool. Can my dad have a cookie?"

"Of course he can. Do you want another one too?"

Jace nodded.

A lump clogged Clark's throat. Victoria treated Jace like a grandson and they'd only been there a few months. Clark's parents cared enough to send Jace a birthday card and that was it. He'd made the effort, hoping their initial disapproval of Clark's life decisions would fade as they spent time with their grandchild, but that hadn't happened. He'd blown up at them a few days into the last trip after his father berated Jace for spilling his juice on the floor. Clark packed up their stuff and booked a hotel, dipping into his savings so they could spend one day at the Magic Kingdom. Clark sent a Christmas card once a year with a recent picture of Jace inside, but nothing more. It took him too many years to realize they would never be the kind of parents he wanted, and it was useless to be angry with them for it. They weren't going to change.

The only family member he cared for besides Jace was his brother Sam. Sam was eight years older than Clark and had practically raised him until he'd moved to Oregon a few weeks after he'd graduated high school. Sam put his artistic talents to use as a tattoo artist and the first time he'd come home for a visit on a motorcycle with full tattoo sleeves and a tongue ring, Clark thought their parents were going to have a stroke.

Appearances were everything and they'd had no problem telling Sam to get lost. Clark remembered chasing his brother out the door, begging Sam to take Clark with him, but his mother screeched at him to get inside. Sam hugged him hard, told him he'd call, and headed out of town the way he came. The next seven years passed at a snail's pace, with secret visits from Sam and his year at the Winters farm bringing brief stints of happiness in the solitude. Clark only had a few acquaintances, but they never spent time together outside of school. His shelves of books were his only escape and he consumed nearly six books a week. It worked out well for his parents and for him. They'd never been involved, unless either boy did something that could make them look bad. Sam and Clark didn't exist unless they needed to parade them around as a perfect little family.

The day Clark left for college, he'd packed up his Subaru with everything he treasured and didn't look back. Didn't visit. Called for major holidays, but they were usually too busy for more than a brief exchange.

Watching the loving way Victoria and Chris Winters were

with Jace brought the futile anger to the surface all over again at the people who raised him. He hadn't expected Chris and Victoria Winters to treat them like family when Clark took the foreman position at the Winters Christmas Tree Farm. Victoria had even offered to pick up Jace from school and watch him so he didn't have to hang at the after-school program. Clark didn't want her to think he was taking advantage of her, but she'd insisted. Now Jace didn't think twice about bursting into the main house, treating it like a second home.

Victoria picked up the head of the cow cookie jar and reached in to grab Jace a cookie, leaving the body of the black-and-white cow wearing a red-and-blue-striped scarf decapitated.

"That poor cow loses his head anytime someone has a sweet tooth," Clark joked.

"Oh!" Victoria squatted down, laughter bubbling out. "I never thought about how morbid it looked! My mother got it for me years ago during my cow phase and I rotate it in when the weather turns cold and put the cow in the bathing suit away. Now that I think about it, that one does the same thing. You want one?"

Clark chuckled. "No, thank you."

She replaced the top of the cookie jar with a sigh. "I wish you would. Otherwise, I find myself eating too many of them!"

"But Dad, I want you to try one," Jace protested.

"Would you like a container of cookies for your place so your dad can try them later?" Victoria asked.

Jace nodded his head enthusiastically and Clark gave in. "Thanks, that would be great."

Victoria pulled out a clear container and filled it nearly to the brim with chocolate chip cookies before snapping the red lid in place and handing it to him. "This will get you home so you can put them in your cookie jar."

"We don't have a cookie jar. We always buy the prepackaged cookies because we don't make fresh ones."

"Well, you're going to need one if Jace becomes the master baker he's aspiring to be," Victoria said with a wink.

Butch, who had been politely sitting next to Jace, watching him take bite after bite of his cookie, finally whined and lifted one massive paw into the air, his long, droopy ears swaying with the motion.

"You can't have these kinds of cookies, Butch." Victoria pointed to a jar in the corner in the shape of a hound wearing a Santa hat. "Jace, will you get Butch a cookie?"

Jace shoved the remainder of his cookie into his mouth with a nod and hopped like a frog across the floor, making Victoria laugh. Then he stood on his tiptoes and set the lid on the counter. Butch turned his attention to Jace, trotting next to him, his tail whipping through the air furiously. Jace pulled out a biscuit and held it up above the dog's nose, which was a struggle since Jace wasn't much taller than Butch.

"Sit, Butch."

The dog flopped his butt on the floor, his tail thumping against the tile. The dog took the biscuit gently from Jace and lay down, enjoying his treat.

"Tell him he's a good boy."

"I should get Jace home and start dinner. Thanks for letting him hang with you."

"Anytime. He was such a big help this morning decorating

and he did most of the work on the cookies. I sat back in a chair with my feet up, barking orders."

"No, you didn't! We worked together."

Victoria hugged him hard. "You are sweet to give credit when it's due." She let him go and patted Clark on the arm. "You know you two are always welcome to come up here and eat with us. I still cook like my kids are at home instead of grown and living on their own."

"I appreciate that." Clark cleared his throat when his son tried to sneak a second cookie. "Jace." His son froze at the deep warning tone. "Come on."

Jace slunk back toward him, obviously disgruntled, but Victoria called out to him, halting his pouting.

"Jace, do you think you can convince your dad to come up here for dinner next Saturday? We want to thank him for the great job he's doing."

Clark didn't have time to react before Jace whooped. "I can do that!"

"And if you two don't have any plans for Thanksgiving, you get your tushes up here. I've got a lot to be thankful for this year. My family is healthy, our farm is thriving, and you came back into our lives, bringing my favorite kid with you."

Jace beamed.

"We'll be there," Clark said, taking the cookies from Jace. "Thank you again, Victoria."

Jace tugged on his arm. "Dad! I'm hungry."

"All right, we'll go home and eat."

"It's no problem at all. See you tomorrow, Jace."

"Bye!"

Jace grabbed his free hand, dragging him out the door and down the steps. When Clark didn't match his speed, Jace raced ahead around the corner of the house and out of sight for a moment. Back in California, Clark would never have let go of Jace's hand, but being among the evergreen trees created a bubble of tranquility he hadn't experienced in the years he'd been away.

Clark followed a little way behind Jace as he burst through the door of their home and ran straight to his bedroom, bouncing with every leap. Clark peeled off his gloves with a chuckle, slipping them into the pocket of his jacket. The cozy three-bedroom cottage had a small kitchen and dining room that opened into a comfortable furnished living room. Down the hall was a Jack-and-Jill bathroom between two of the bedrooms and at the far end was the master. It was more spacious than the one-bedroom apartment they'd lived in and you couldn't beat the yard outside.

Clark hung up his coat and blew out a breath. The temperature in the house was colder than it was outside. The stove in the corner helped with keeping the house warm so they didn't have to run the heater all the time and Clark had spent the summer gathering firewood to keep them stocked until the spring.

Jace came running back into the living room, dancing behind him as Clark started a fire.

"Dad!"

"One second, buddy. It's cold in here."

"Dad, it's almost Christmas."

Clark put the guard back in front of the mouth of the fireplace and stood up, facing his son with a smile. "I seem to remember that. Vaguely."

"I know what I want."

"What's that?"

"A puppy."

Clark groaned. "Jace, I don't think Mr. and Mrs. Winters are going to want a puppy in here."

Jace's face fell. "Why? They have a dog."

"Yes, but it's their house and so is this. We are just living in it while I work for them."

Jace's lip quivered. "Oh."

Clark sighed, pulling his son into his arms. "Just give me a little time to find us a house and we'll get a dog."

"Any kind?"

Clark squeezed him tight before dropping him back onto his feet. "We'll see. You want to help me make dinner?"

"Yep!" Jace raced into the kitchen and pulled his Avengers apron off the peg. "Matey Jace reporting for duty, Captain."

Clark tied his own apron around his waist with a ferocious scowl. "All right, ye scallywag. Get me eggs, pancake mix, and bacon. Off with ye, or ye'll be walking me plank, says I!"

"Aye, aye, sir!"

While Jace ran to the fridge, Clark pulled out their waffle maker, baking sheets, tinfoil, and a large frying pan. He'd never learned to cook as a kid. His mother would pitch a fit if they disturbed her kitchen. It wasn't until Patrice was pregnant with Jace that Clark taught himself how to make healthy meals for his pregnant girlfriend.

Clark grimaced, remembering the longest nine months of his life. He'd been twenty, about to finish his second year in college when he'd met Patrice at a party. She'd been confident, wild, and kissed him without even asking his name. She was unlike anyone Clark had ever met and he'd become addicted to her. Her body. Her spirit. He'd fallen down a hole for over a month of partying and screwing every night.

Until the stick turned pink.

They'd both been scared to death, discussing their options, agreeing to have the baby and raise it together, only to have her fly off the handle days later about leaving. Clark tiptoed around Patrice's ever-changing moods for the entire pregnancy, doing his best to keep her happy. One day she'd be dragging him through the baby section of the store, pointing out all the things she wanted. The next he'd come home from work to find her on the bathroom floor crying in a fetal position.

"Patrice! What's wrong?"

"It's a boy."

Clark lit up. "That's great. I wish I could have been there, and I know you wanted a girl, but—"

"No! I made a mistake. I can't have a baby."

He'd never felt so helpless and confused in his life.

"It's too late for anything else."

"Then I'll give it away. I cannot have a boy."

Clark froze, a cold sweat breaking out all over his skin. "No."

Patrice sat up, glaring at him. "Excuse me?"

"If you don't want him, that's fine. But that is my son, too. And I'm not giving him up without a fight."

After screaming at him for over an hour, she'd finally broken down and let him hold her, crying in his arms until she'd fallen into a fitful sleep. The next few months rolled by calmer and Clark thought Patrice was happy. That they were finally connecting.

And then she disappeared.

"What about the strawberries?"

He cleared his throat, trying to dislodge the lump his memories created. "Sorry, I forgot."

Jace frowned at him. "Captains don't forget things."

"Argh, are ye challenging me, matey? Maybe ye'd like the bite of me steel!" Clark waved his black plastic spatula at Jace and his son giggled. Grabbing a wooden spoon from the utensil drawer, he waved it at his dad.

"Avast!"

They clashed the utensils against each other, dancing around the small kitchen. When the oven went off with the pre-heated alarm, he let Jace stab him right in the gut.

"Argh, a fatal blow, to be sure. Ye are the new captain, 'twould seem."

Jace dropped his spoon with a shake of his head. "No thanks. Too much responsibility."

Clark ruffled his hair. "Smart kid. All right, I'll put the bacon on while you crack three eggs into a mixing bowl."

The two of them worked with a rhythm born of many homecooked meals together. Jace had been helping his dad out in the kitchen since he was three, as they'd cooked instead of getting take-out to save money. Clark preferred living simply and buying everything with cash. No loans. Teaching Jace that want and need were two different things.

But his son never lacked for the one thing Clark missed growing up: love and affection. He was a damn good father and they were doing fine on their own.

Which was just one of the many reasons he didn't date. Even if he found someone he was interested in for more than a few hours, the idea of bringing someone else into their lives who could potentially screw with their well-oiled machine sounded like more trouble than it was worth. Since the day Jace was born, he'd always put what was best for Jace first and foremost. Maybe that was extreme, but growing up with parents who used him and his brother like props, he swore he'd do better with his own child.

After dinner, they followed the same routine as every night. Bath, pajamas, setting out their clothes for the next day. So far, Clark had been working only weekdays, until today. From now until Christmas, it would be six, sometimes seven days a week. Luckily, Chris said Jace tagging along on Clark's rounds wouldn't be an issue and Jace loved exploring the farm with Clark.

They watched a half-hour show together every night before bed and tonight, Jace picked *A Charlie Brown Thanksgiving*. They watched it every year, but Jace seemed a bit disenchanted with the cartoon this time.

"I don't understand why they always have Charlie kick the football and hurt himself."

"The writers thought it would be funny, I guess," Clark said.

Jace scowled at the flat screen. "I think it's mean."

"Yeah, it is."

"Lucy is the worst."

Clark chuckled. "It's a cartoon, buddy. It's not real life."

"Girls at school chase me. I don't like it."

"Tell them to stop. Or don't run."

"But when they catch me, they try to kiss me." Jace wrinkled his nose and covered the lower half of his face, muffling his voice. "I put my hands over my face like this and tell them to stop, but they keep coming."

"You should tell the duty aide, then. She'll make them stop."

"I don't want to be a tattletale."

"Well, looks like you're stuck then, buddy. I'm out of options."

Jace released a sigh. "Girls are so gross."

"Someday you'll change your mind about girls."

"You don't like them."

"What? I like girls!"

"You do?" Jace cocked his head, studying him. "Do they like you?"

"Sometimes. Why would you think I don't like girls?"

"'Cause I never see girls chasing you."

Solid logic for a seven-year-old.

"Adult women don't chase men. At least, not in that way."

"What way, then?"

Clark rubbed the back of his neck, searching for an explanation. "Adults go out to dinners and movies. We date."

"So, why don't you date?"

"I guess I haven't found someone I want to spend my time with."

Jace turned to stare at him with brows knitted together and a deep frown. "I think you should try. I know you get sad sometimes. Maybe finding someone nice will make you happy."

"First rule to happiness, buddy, is you gotta find it in yourself before you can be happy with anyone else."

"Why wouldn't you be happy with yourself? You're awesome, Dad."

Clark hugged Jace tight. "Thanks. I think you're awesome too."

"I know," Jace said, leaning against Clark's side. "I think it would be nice to have other people, is all. It's always just us."

"We've got Uncle Sam."

"But he isn't here and…"

"And what?"

"He doesn't smell good."

Clark would have laughed if the words didn't sting. "What about me? Do I stink?"

"No. It's just…never mind."

Jace didn't say anything more, but the conversation lingered, echoing in Clark's head. Jace wanted Clark to be with someone nice, but there weren't a lot of nice women who caught Clark's interest. Independent women who didn't need him were the only women he'd ever known romantically and sexually, starting with Patrice. He wouldn't even know what to do with a sweet girl; she'd probably run screaming at his brutal honesty.

Still…if Jace wanted someone in their life, he could at least consider the possibilities.

Clark pulled out his phone just as Snoopy donned his pilgrim costume. Clark scrolled through the app store, his thumb hovering over the pink square with the two letter Ms entwined. The

MeetMe app commercials had popped up a few times while watching videos on YouTube, and while he usually skipped past them, he watched long enough for it to stick in his mind. Maybe that was a sign he wasn't as closed off to finding someone as he thought.

His conversation with Jace brought to light some hard truths. Clark's life consisted of work, Jace, eat, and sleep. He'd never gone out bar hopping with friends like other guys his age and hook-ups only occurred when he could find a trusted babysitter for a few hours, always at her place or a hotel. He never stayed long, but the women he chose knew the score.

Clark stared at the screen, tapping on the box titled *username*. Woodsman27. Even if he weren't a single dad, he'd want a little anonymity. Especially considering his past experiences. He typed up a short bio and uploaded a picture of one of his woodworking projects.

Before he could second guess himself, he clicked all of the boxes below the section titled *what are you looking for* and hit submit—including FWB. Maybe it wouldn't be so bad to find a "friends with benefits" situation at least. Someone who wasn't looking for forever or didn't want to complicate his life, but could stave off the sadness his son sensed.

And if it grew from there—

"Dad! You're not watching!"

Clark practically dropped his phone, every cell in his body screaming to take it back. "Sorry, buddy."

"You always say no devices during our time."

"You're right. Won't happen again."

They continued watching the show, but Clark's heart didn't

slow as his phone dinged once. Then twice. And a third time as he carried his sleeping son to bed ten minutes later. When he came back to it, the app had found three matches in the area, all looking for FWB to dating.

He clicked on the first match and immediately scrolled past her profile. Clark wanted someone that was at least old enough to legally get a drink.

The next woman's profile pic was a set of handcuffs and a crop. *Not my bag, but good luck to you.*

The third had a profile picture with a ball of yarn and two knitting needles. Her screenname was KnottyGirl25. Clark smirked at the use of k-n-o-t.

Clark clicked her profile and scanned her bio.

> Hi. I am not sure what I'm doing here, but I thought I'd give this a shot. I'm twenty-five. I work a lot. I love crafting, sleeping in on my days off (not a morning person!), and my favorite drink is a Malibu Sunrise. The song I play on repeat is "Adore You" by Harry Styles. The movie that lives rent free in my heart is *Notting Hill*. I want to find someone who doesn't lie or cheat and shows basic human decency. Oh…and must love all things Christmas.

The corners of his lips tugged at that last line. Although they had sent out the perfect family Christmas card, his parents hadn't bothered with Christmas trees or presents unless they had friends visiting. Clark dreaded the day after winter break ended when they were in school and the other kids would talk about all the fun they had. When they'd asked him about the holiday, he'd snapped at them. It hadn't exactly endeared him to his classmates.

The one bright spot about Christmas time in elementary school was his teachers. Every year on the last day before the holiday break, his teacher would leave a brightly wrapped gift on their desks. Although some kids groaned about getting a book for Christmas, he treasured every single one of the books he'd received from kindergarten to fifth grade. It wasn't until his senior year of high school when he'd attended the Winters Farm employee Christmas party that he'd had a real holiday celebration. The year after, he'd sent a gift to his brother Sam and to his surprise had received one in return. Sam invited him to stay the holidays with him the next year and they'd gone all out with spiked eggnog, decorations, and a huge Christmas dinner they'd bought from the local grocery store.

The next Christmas with Patrice, Clark went out and bought matching stockings for them and planned to embroider them with Daddy, Mommy, and whatever name they decided on. After she left, he'd had the third stocking monogrammed with his brother's name and hung them every year. Although some Christmases had been leaner than others, Clark adored the holiday and wanted to make sure Jace experienced all the magic the season had to offer.

He read the profile one more time before Clark tapped the message button with his thumb.

Hey KnottyGirl25…

CHAPTER 3

MERRY

MERRY STOOD IN LINE AT Kiss My Donut Monday afternoon, staring at her phone screen as she waited for her turn to order. The message on MeetMe had come out of nowhere, because she'd forgotten she'd even signed up. She'd downloaded it on Valentine's Day, after too many Malibu Sunrises and a second box of Dove chocolates, longing for any kind of attention. Of course, she'd regretted her decision the next morning when she'd woken up to fifty messages from men and women all searching for something different. Somewhere between *"Can I see your feet?"* to *"Are you into couples?"* she realized her mistake and deleted the app. If she hadn't been in her spam folder looking for something else, she never would've seen the notification email.

> Hey KnottyGirl25,
>
> This is my first attempt at online dating and you popped up as one of my matches. I am also a fan of Christmas, which brings me to my conversation starter...

What is your favorite Christmas movie?

Woodsman27

Merry clicked on his profile picture, smiling at the image of a wooden snowman. She read his profile, which was pretty simplistic. Twenty-seven. Interested in woodworking, outdoor sports, and reading. Not an exact match of interests, but at least he hadn't started the correspondence with *"How big are your boobs?"*

The person in front of her finished ordering and Merry requested a large iced white mocha with sweet cream. Once she finished paying, she sank into a seat at a table by the window. Mondays were always a little chaotic at Mistletoe Elementary, especially after a holiday based on candy and costumes. Kids were dropping by the front office all day to tell her about their costumes and how much candy they hauled home from trick-or-treating. She loved the excitement on their faces, but she was ready to be home, soaking in her bathtub with a glass of peach sangria instead of meeting Dana Kirk.

Her first instinct had been to call back when she'd gotten Dana's voicemail and decline. Between two jobs and all of the holiday events coming up, she didn't want to be in charge of the Festival of Trees, one of the biggest charity fundraisers of the season. But when Dana explained she needed to fly out to California because her youngest daughter was on bedrest due to a high-risk pregnancy, Merry couldn't bring herself to say no. She told Dana she was happy to help, but silently acknowledged it was a massive undertaking with only a little over a month to organize. Dana had been running the event for twenty years and Merry didn't want to be her chosen successor when she decided to step down from it. Being the organizer meant when things went wrong, she would be the one to blame and she hated confrontation.

Merry looked at the time on her phone screen, her lips compressing. "Come on, Dana," she mumbled to herself. Tardiness was her pet peeve and she was early to everything.

At least while she was waiting, she could give Woodsman27 an answer. She liked that he'd actually read her profile and reached out about her interests instead of being worried about what she looked like.

She tapped the MeetMe app and clicked the icon to reply.

Hello Woodsman27,

I honestly forgot all about this app until I saw an email in my spam yesterday and checked out your message. To answer your question, I love *Elf*. "Baby it's Cold Outside" is one of my favorite Christmas songs and Zoey's rendition brings on the goosebumps. What is yours?

P.S. I like your snowman. Did you make it?

She'd noticed he'd checked all the boxes, including Friends with Benefits, and if that was his main goal, he was barking up the wrong tree. Still, approaching her like a human being instead of an object to screw scored him the courtesy of a reply at the very least.

Besides, maybe her parents would like some of those wooden snowmen for the farm.

The door opened and Dana came through waving, her black hair cut in an A-line, framing her round face.

Merry hit send and set her phone down so she could wave back. Dana sat down across from her, dropping a red binder on the table and setting her purse on the floor with a *slap*. The binder was decorated with a rhinestone Christmas tree and glittery puffy paint that scrawled across the plastic, legibly spelling out *The Festival of Trees*.

"I am so sorry I was late! Between packing and scheduling flights, then talking to my son-in-law for updates, I lost track of time. Thank you for doing this. I know you're probably plenty busy without me adding to it, but I have to go."

"Absolutely, Dana. Your daughter and grandbaby need you."

"They really do. I hate her being so far away, especially having her first child, but they needed to move for her husband's work. I'm half tempted to move closer to them, but I hate California. It's expensive and hot and—" Dana cut herself off with a wave of her hand. "You didn't come here to listen to me gripe!"

Merry chuckled. "You're fine, Dana. I've got plenty of time. I'm going to pop in to see my sister after this and then I'm going home. Tell me what I need to know."

Dana patted the top of the red binder. "This is my Festival of Trees bible. Everything you need is in here, including order forms for businesses to fill out to reserve their trees. Your father guarantees us fifty, but you'll have to talk to him about how many you will actually need. Usually it isn't even that. People would rather donate a raffle basket or gift card instead of a tree, less time consuming I guess."

"That's ridiculous. It's the holiday season and this town needs to step up. I'm going to make it my goal to get a tree from every business in Mistletoe."

"Ha, good luck with that! There is no way you're getting the Gallaghers to buy and decorate a tree. I think Declan is ornerier than his father and I've wanted to knock Liam upside the head a time or two."

Merry smirked as she flipped open the binder, studying each page. "They aren't the nicest men, but I am a firm believer that enough Christmas cheer can melt even the iciest of hearts." She stopped on the schedule page, her eyebrows shooting up at the lengthy list. "I love how detail-oriented you are."

"It's taken me twenty years to get to this point and a whole lot of frustration, but this is my baby. It feels strange passing it off to someone else to organize, but I trust you. I've done my best to make it easy for you and hope there won't be any hiccups."

Dana's sweet tone dripped like sugar-free maple syrup and Merry resisted the urge to audibly gulp at the pressure. "I'll do my best to make you proud."

"I know you will. And you can message me if you have any questions. I'll be available unless I'm sleeping or holding a baby."

"I will."

"That's it, I suppose." Dana hopped back up out of the chair. "I have an early flight in Boise, so I need to get back home and finish packing. Thank you, Merry. This event is very important to the town and I feel better knowing it is in such good hands."

"Safe travels, Dana."

Dana gave her a wiggle of her fingers and ducked out the door eagerly. A little too eagerly.

Merry picked up her coffee in one hand and continued to flip through the pages, studying the color-coded schedule. Tree orders were due to her family farm in two weeks. Vendor booth deposits needed to be paid in full by the end of November. Paper snowflake garland collected from the elementary school the week before the festival. The list went on and on, all the while working, helping her parents, and trying to have a life of her own.

Merry pursed her lips, her breath rushing out in a sigh of resignation. *I need to stop being a pessimist. As a Christmas lover, this event is my jam and I got this!*

After throwing her purse strap over her shoulder, Merry gathered her coffee cup and the binder, giving herself a pep talk as she pushed out of Kiss My Donut. She'd been volunteering all year wherever she was needed for town events and although this was the first time she'd headed one, there was no reason to freak out. She'd follow Dana's schedule and it would go off without a hitch.

A Shop for All Seasons would be open for another forty minutes and at least if she collected Holly's order and deposit, she'd be one step closer to making this festival a success.

Merry passed by the Bank of Idaho, admiring the fall window they'd painted across the glass. Last week it had been bats and skeletons and today it was pumpkins, turkeys, and scarecrows. The day after Thanksgiving, it would change again to whatever Christmassy theme they planned this year and Merry couldn't wait to see it.

Although some businesses went the traditional route of decorating for each holiday, Scrap and Sew Craft Store had a wood sign in their window display that made her snort.

Happy Hallowthanksmas!

Felt pumpkins sprinkled the fake snowy ground, and to the

left, classic monsters made out of yarn were sledding down a hill of white cotton. Gorgeous Christmas wreaths made of sparkling ribbons and bows hung above like multicolored stars, and smack in the center was a stuffed, quilted turkey, complete with a large paisley fabric tail. It was absolutely adorable, and she considered popping in to find out how much it was, but she didn't decorate for any holiday but Christmas. There wasn't enough space in her house to display much anyway, so she kept it to one tub of Christmas stuff. She could get a small shed for storage, but her heart didn't leap for any other holiday the same way. Once the greens and reds of the season started popping up in stores, she'd be humming and smiling until January first. Heck, if it was socially acceptable to keep her holiday décor up and listen to Christmas carols all year, she would.

Merry opened the door to her sister's shop, and when she stepped over the threshold, the obnoxious call of a turkey exploded above her head, making her nearly stumble into a display of wooden porch signs. It made sense her sister would change the sound celebrating all the major holidays, but that door alarm was enough to give patrons like Merry a stroke.

"You all right?" Holly called from around the rather large frame of Declan Gallagher. They were facing off in front of the checkout counter, Declan's posture rigid and imposing, but Holly didn't seem fazed by the big man's irritation.

"I'm good, but you gotta get rid of that door alarm. I think I lost ten years off my life."

"I agree with your sister," Declan griped. "You need to take it down a notch with all this holiday cheer."

Holly rolled her eyes. "Nobody asked your opinion, Declan."

Merry busied herself with exploring the store instead of listening to the two of them snip back and forth. Shelves of trinkets stretched across the store, full of fun and eye-catching items. Stuffed foxes holding sunflowers. Extra-large mugs with adorable fall puns. Floral wreaths of maroon, brown, orange, hunter green, and yellow leaves adorned the walls.

The only thing out of sync with the fall ambiance was the music. A cheery rendition of "We Are Santa's Elves" played through the speakers, which might explain why Declan Gallagher stood with his flannel-clad arms crossed over his chest, scowling at Holly.

"It's too early for this ear-bleeding crap."

Holly in turn held a stuffed turkey like she wanted to bash Declan over the head with it. "Christmas music is cheerful and uplifting. If your ears are bleeding, maybe you should see a doctor. Or an exorcist! Is it black ooze coming out, by any chance? If you're possessed by a demon that hates Christmas, that would explain a lot."

Merry snorted, ducking behind shelves of fall garland.

"I am not possessed, I'm just not a Christmas freak! It isn't even Thanksgiving! Can't you play smooth jazz like a normal human instead of this holly-jolly garbage?"

The man hated Christmas, the whole holiday season, Merry thought. She grinned at her silent paraphrasing from *How the Grinch Stole Christmas*, but it was true. Declan had taken over his father's hardware store next door last year when his dad semi-retired, and apparently the walls between the businesses were thin. He'd complained about the music more than once and hadn't stopped there. He'd been rather vocal that the tree lighting ceremony in the town square was a fire hazard, the light parade equated to a public disturbance, and that Evergreen Circle would cause a full-blown community power outage one day with its animatronics and blow-up displays. If he'd been a seventy-year-old curmudgeon, it would have been one thing, but he was the same age as Merry.

And boy, did he get on her sister's one last nerve.

Holly held the stuffed turkey by the neck and Merry smothered a giggle. If that thing had been alive, her sister's grip would have broken its neck.

"Who hurt you, Declan?" Holly cocked her head to the side. "Why are you the man who hates Christmas?"

"I don't hate Christmas. I think there is a time and place for Christmas music and décor...like December."

"That is your opinion. You have voiced it, I hear you, and now you can take your Grinchy behind back to your whosits and whatsits store."

"It's a hardware store!"

"I know!" Holly shouted, launching onto her tiptoes to stand nose to clavicle with him. "It's from *The Little Mermaid*."

"I've never seen it."

Holly placed a hand on her chest and gasped. "No wonder you are such an angry-pants."

Declan bent over Holly, his eyebrows snapped together. "I swear to God, Holly, I am going to dismantle your sound system if you don't turn that shit off."

"Go ahead and try, but my speakers will come back bigger and louder!" Holly finally whacked Declan with the turkey on the shoulder. "Now git, before your negative energy ruins Bublé for me."

Declan roared, a guttural low growl that grew as his hands went up in the air. "Impossible woman!"

"Obnoxious miser!"

Declan slammed out of the shop and marched past the window where two scarecrows were kissing.

"Whew, I would not want to be his next customer," Merry mused.

Holly smirked at Merry. "I swear, fighting with that man is the best foreplay."

Merry sputtered. "You're sleeping with Declan?"

"Of course not!"

"Thank God! I was going to commit you."

Holly tilted her head at an angle, staring off. "Maybe if he shaved off the beard and had a personality transplant." She shook herself, frowning. "Nope, never mind. Not gonna happen. I could never be with anyone that cantankerous. But arguing with him boils my blood until my whole body is tight and I just need one really good—" Her eyes rolled back in her head and she twitched as she let out a loud, high-pitched "oh!"

"You are disturbed."

"You're telling me you don't have the best sex when you're pissed off?"

"What's sex?" Merry deadpanned.

"You haven't been with anyone since that horse's ass from Denver?"

"Killian. And no, I haven't been with anyone since."

Holly grabbed onto the side of the counter, as if the shock of Merry's lack of bedroom antics had somehow knocked the wind out of her. "Are you sure it still works? It might squeak or crack from lack of use."

"Har har. You're so funny. It's fine. I said I haven't had sex with another person, not that I haven't been checking my own oil. Not having to worry about another person's wants and needs has been nice, actually. Less complicated."

"It's only complicated if there are emotions. The only thing a man wants and needs is a place to—"

"Can you not finish that sentence?"

"What? Do you know how many men have actually worried about whether I got off or not? One. That is twenty-five percent of my sexual partners to date that gave a rat's ass about my satisfaction. Sad, right?" Holly clucked her tongue and slammed the turkey down on the counter. "Just one of the many reasons I prefer to leave feelings out of it."

Woodsman27 and his box checked "friends with benefits" popped into her head, but as a serial monogamist, she didn't know how to have sex without emotions. You should at least like someone before you turn your body over into their care.

"I've never been the casual encounters type."

"Maybe you should try it. You've done the whole year of singledom and figuring out who you are. Now you need your cleansing lay before you can move on to another relationship."

"A cleansing lay? Where did you get that?"

"Just something that makes sense to me. Your ex cheated. You needed to heal your heart, but now, you need to boost your confidence with someone who cannot wait to rip your clothes off. Once those two things have been accomplished, you are ready for *the one*."

"I didn't say I wanted to be ready for *the one*."

"Then if you aren't actively searching for Mr. Right, you've got time to make some more items for my shop."

Merry's jaw dropped. "I gave you a laundry basket full of hats, blankets, and stuffies for Halloween and Thanksgiving a month ago."

"What can I say? Frankenbear and Fall Fox were a big hit with the kiddos. Honestly, you should just open your own online store. Your stuff is so cute, you could make a decent profit. Maybe even quit the front office at the school."

She'd been thinking of opening an Etsy shop for a while, but things kept cropping up and she'd get distracted. "It's not like working at the school is a bad job."

"But it isn't where your heart lies. You want to grow Christmas trees like Dad. God knows why."

"You seriously don't care about the farm?"

"It will always be my childhood home and I'll help out when I'm needed, but that place is all yours when Dad retires. Neither Nick nor I want it."

"Thanks," Merry said sarcastically. "I love being the default child."

"Whoa! I only meant we won't step on your toes. I thought you wanted to run the farm."

Merry swallowed back her irritation. "I do want it, but sometimes I think Dad doesn't trust me."

"Now you're talking crazy. The farm is Dad's baby, like this store is mine. He doesn't want to give up the reins to anyone."

"Or he doesn't want to give them up to me. If it were Nick asking—"

"Oh, don't go there. Dad isn't sexist. But he can't boss you around the way he can Clark. Just give it time and I swear he will come around."

Holly's unshakable confidence didn't convince Merry, but it wasn't worth pressing the topic. "I'll drop some more by tomorrow. I made the cutest fall leaves baby blanket, but I'm tempted to keep it."

"For all the future grandbabies you're giving Mom?"

Merry rolled her eyes. "I am missing a key element for children."

"Not really. They make them in frozen pops now."

"Okay, subject change. I need something from you." Merry paused as she pulled the order form out of the binder. "Fill this out and give me your deposit."

Holly set the turkey down on the counter and took the paper, the skin between her eyes wrinkling. "This is for the Festival of Trees."

"I know. I'm organizing it this year while Dana is in California."

Holly whistled, widening her eyes and raising her eyebrows before turning her back on Merry.

"What is that?"

Holly rustled some of the papers behind the counter before coming up with her check book. "That is my *good luck with that* reaction."

Merry put her arms on the counter and leaned over to smack her sister's shoulder. "You cannot say something like that and not expand on it."

Holly ripped her check from the book and straightened up, waving it toward Merry. "The Festival of Trees is like planning one wedding for two thousand people. I'm pretty sure Dana only organized it because she self-medicated with a bottle of wine every night from November to December."

"I thought Dana sounded a little too gushy. If that's the case, why would she do it for so long?" Merry asked, taking the check from her and slipping it into the clear zipper pouch in the binder.

"Because she couldn't find someone to pass the buck to. Until you."

Merry's eyes narrowed. "Mom gave her my number, because she was too busy."

"Sold out by your own mother. That's cold."

"You're enjoying this."

"Only because it isn't me. You have to learn to say no, sis. You can't save everyone." Holly tapped a finger to her lips. "Maybe that's why you pick so many male fixer-uppers. It's part of your pathology."

"I don't think that means what you think it means."

"Inconceivable!" Holly hollered, shaking her fist in the air, and Merry laughed.

"Well, I am bound and determined not to screw this up, no matter how many difficult people I have to deal with. I love Christmas. I love the Festival of Trees and nobody is going to ruin that! In fact, I have a plan to get every single business to buy a tree this year. Hmmm, I should have grabbed Declan's check while he was here."

Holly snorted. "That Scrooge wouldn't buy a tree."

"You want to help me convince him?"

"I do not."

Merry responded with her very best puppy dog face, complete with sad pout and teary eyes. "But...you love me. And I'm the only sister you have."

"Still a 'no' from me."

"I see." Merry pretended to be resigned. "That's fine. I suppose I'll just have to relay your lack of cooperation...to Mo-therrrr."

Holly's brown eyes narrowed. "You wouldn't dare."

Merry smirked.

"Evil," Holly grumbled.

"Maybe so, but I get the job done." Merry waved the binder at her triumphantly as she headed for the door. "Thanks for helping me out, sis. You're a trouper."

"Bite me!"

Merry pushed out of the shop, grinning from ear to ear when her phone chimed. It was another message from Woodsman27.

KnottyGirl25,

That's a good favorite to have. Mine is *National Lampoon's Christmas Vacation*. You can't go wrong with a classic and the squirrel in the Christmas tree was hilarious. I did make the snowman. In fact, I have three of them in various sizes I plan to put out for the holidays. I enjoy woodworking, it relaxes me. My favorite Christmas song is "Run, Run, Rudolph".

I've got to make dinner, but I'm curious, what knitting projects are you working on? I'm making wood coasters with a tree line across the surface. I've burned myself at least half a dozen times, but I'm determined to master wood engraving.

Woodsman27

He was asking her about her crafts now? Who was this guy?

Chapter 4

Monday 5:57pm

Woodsman27,

I crotchet and knit, and right now I'm making a lap throw for my mother with green, red, and white granny squares. You should get some of those heat-resistant gloves that come with hair straighteners and crimpers! Save your fingers. Unless you're trying to burn off your fingerprints in order to easily get away with murder...I mean... Moving on.

Do you ever make those snowmen for other people? I'd love to buy some for my parents. Too cute!

I'm going to turn on a Hallmark movie and enjoy the enchilada I picked up on my way home. I swear I could eat Mexican food morning, noon, and night!

What food could you eat forever?

KnottyGirl25

Monday 7:48pm

KnottyGirl25,

    That blanket sounds nice. I have a sherpa-lined one I've been sleeping with now that the nights are colder. What Hallmark movie are you watching? As for my favorite food, I like Thai. When I was in college, there was a great Thai place near my apartment and although I didn't eat out often, it was my go-to when I did.

    I'm going to knock off for tonight, but I have a very important question.

    For Christmas dinner, do you serve:

      a) Prime Rib

      b) Ham

      c) Turkey?

Sweet Dreams,

Woodsman27

Tuesday 6:32am

Woodsman27,

    I'm going to cheat and say all of the above! As someone who comes from a big family, we tend to do all three, especially since I'm not a real big fan of red meat. Blasphemy, I know. Besides, I'm all about the mashed potatoes, preferably loaded, but I can hang with gravy.

I was watching *Christmas Next Door*. Super cute movie and just what I needed.

Now I have a very serious question. You can only have one of these sides for Christmas…which do you choose?

a) Mashed potatoes and gravy

b) Rolls

c) Yams

d) Roasted Brussels sprouts?

Your answer will determine whether I speak to you again. ;)

KnottyGirl25

Tuesday 12:11pm

KnottyGirl25,

Wow, that's a lot a pressure to put on a man. But I'm going to have to go with potatoes and gravy. I don't have much of a sweet tooth, so the yams are wasted on me. And potatoes pair nicely with prime rib, which is my favorite, but I usually make a ham because it is cheaper. I'm curious if I passed your test and if I did, which side would have a been a deal breaker.

As for my next poll, let's talk presents. Do you…

a) Open one on Christmas Eve and the rest on
   Christmas day

b) All on Christmas morning after breakfast

c) All on Christmas after dinner

d) One a day starting the 12 days of Christmas?

Personally, I love gift giving and cannot wait to watch someone open up something I chose for them. And I am an excellent gift giver.

Woodsman27

Tuesday 4:02pm

Woodsman27,

Oh, if you'd said Brussels sprouts we'd be done here. I get the dilemma of prime rib vs. ham. Even if it was my first choice, there is no way I would buy it unless I was charging for admission. Although you not liking sweets is unnerving. Oh well, more for me!

And who the heck waits until after Christmas dinner to open presents?! That is pure torture. Evil personified. Sadistic to the max!

All right, so I'm a bit dramatic, but to answer your question, I am all about the night before Christmas present. We'd open ours at around five in the evening because it was always a pair of pajamas with matching slippers, flavored cocoa, and a bag of our favorite popcorn. We'd all vote on what movie to watch, and then get up early to open presents BEFORE breakfast. We usually have biscuits and gravy or cinnamon rolls, which pair nicely with coffee and Baileys, I might add.

Oh, so that's your love language? Gift giving? Mine is acts of service and gifts.

What is the best gift you've ever given and received?

Now, if you'll excuse me, I am going to make dinner and devour it along with a glass of wine in my bathtub because that is my favorite place in the whole world. (My second favorite place is my bed because I love sleep!)

KnottyGirl25

Tuesday 8:26 pm

KnottyGirl25,

I don't mind Brussels sprouts, with enough butter and seasoning. And yes, I will pass along all my sweets to you… except pumpkin pie. That one I'll keep.

I'm glad I am not one of those foul demons who waits until after dinner for Christmas presents because I'm a little scared you'd come after me with a shotgun and salt rounds…maybe some holy water. I bet you used to jump on your parents at five in the morning for presents, didn't you?

Your night before Christmas present sounds awesome. My family didn't celebrate Christmas growing up. Not for religious reasons, but because my parents didn't want to. My brother and I started celebrating when we became adults, but the best present I ever received was a copy of *Where the Wild Things Are* from my kindergarten teacher. It was my first Christmas present and I still have the copy on my shelf.

As for the best present I've ever given, the year I gave my brother a monogrammed stocking filled with his favorite candies and snacks he cried. I'm going to go out on a limb and call that the best present I've ever given.

My favorite place is the woods, followed closely by sitting in front of a fireplace. I hope you're not a spoiled brat, but even if you are, at least you're a funny one.

I'm off to bed, but I hope I have a message from you in the morning.

Woodsman27

Tuesday 10:43 pm

Hey Woodsman27,

Wow, you go to bed really early! I'm a total night owl. Usually I don't go to bed until eleven and wake up at six-thirty...in theory. Sometimes I hit the snooze a couple times, dry shampoo my hair, and take off. Don't judge me.

I'll let you keep the pumpkin pie unless it's the last piece, then we may have to square off. But I'll gladly slip my BS onto your plate (see what I did there...B.S. LOL) They look like plant brains and that gives me the creeps.

Did you just slide into my messages with a *Supernatural* reference? 'Cause I freaking love that show, and not just because the leads are hot. I mean...they are, but they're also funny and the show can really hit me in the feels.

I was never the first one up on Christmas (even as a child, I liked to sleep). You didn't celebrate Christmas as a kid, but as an adult you are all about it? And I love that you put your brother's name on his stocking. That is so cute! My mom made us stockings out of our favorite character fabric from when we were toddlers and they are twice as big as a normal stocking, so they hold more goods. My mom buys stocking stuffers all year long, except the candy. That's fresh...I think.

I am not a big reader, but my favorite gift was my hope chest. It's a little old-fashioned, but my dad made it for me out of cedar and my mom filled it with one of the prize-winning quilts my grandma made, a dish set she'd started collecting when I was born, and some of my childhood mementos. I keep it below my stairs.

My eyes are getting droopy. TTYT.

KnottyGirl25

p.s. I really like chatting with you.

Wednesday 5:59am

Hi KnottyGirl25,

I like talking to you, too. It's funny because I down-loaded this app a few months ago, started my profile and never finished it. I assumed with it being such a small town, I wouldn't have very many options so what was the point?

Now I'm really glad I did.

I like that your favorite gift is something given from the heart, instead of an iPad or something like that. I love the smell of cedar, so good choice of wood on your dad's part.

Just call me a zombie, because I like plant brains. Slurp. ;)

I'm not much of a fighter, but I am an excellent negotiator. Maybe we could split the pie in half? I don't mind sharing with you.

And yes, I was talking about *Supernatural*. It is a fun show and although I like the actors, they aren't really my type.

What character fabric is your stocking made of?

I love to read. In fact, my spare room has three bookshelves stuffed full of my favorite books.

I need to hop in the shower. I wonder if you're awake yet.

Woodsman27

Wednesday 7:34 am

I was definitely not awake! This was one of those days when the snooze button was a blessing and a curse. Thankfully I was able to get to work on time.

I feel like I should elaborate about the dry shampoo. I still shower. I just don't get my hair wet because it takes so long to dry. But I don't show up to work smelling moldy.

Veggie zombie, huh? That's a new one. I am good with compromise and splitting the last pie slice with you. If I like you enough, I'll even give you the last bite! And my stocking is Princess Jasmine from *Aladdin*.

All right, you love to read. What is your favorite book?

I hope you have a great day at work!

KnottyGirl25

Wednesday 10:42am

My favorite book is *The Hobbit*.

I'm glad to know you smell good. I sometimes shower twice a day because I hate climbing into bed with the day on my skin.

I'd probably take you up on the last bite of pie. Love me some pie.

If you could be another person, alive or dead, for one day, who would it be?

Talk to you soon.

Woodsman27

Wednesday 3:22pm

Fantasy, huh? My brother made me watch the *Lord of the Rings* movies. I liked them, but I'm more of a romantic drama fan.

I think I'd like to be Audrey Hepburn. She was so classy and brilliant.

What about you? I'm surprised you're messaging me in the middle of the day. Aren't you usually at work?

Driving home!

KnottyGirl25

Wednesday 6:07pm

Yes, usually I'm busy during the day at work, but I had a little break and thought I'd message you. I hope that's okay.

I don't mind romantic dramas, but modern movies and books that perpetuate an ideal don't really hold my interest.

You go into a fantasy movie knowing it could never happen, but a romance misleads people that somewhere out there is a perfect someone waiting for them.

Maybe I'm a pessimist, but relationships aren't my strong suit.

I think I'd like to be Billy the Kid. There is so much mystery around his death and who he really was. A leader? A villain? A scared kid? He fascinated me ever since I saw *Young Guns* for the first time. (My brother is eight years older than me and introduced me to all that the '80s had to offer).

I know it's strange for two people who have never met to get to know each other this way, but I hope you're having as much fun as I am.

Awaiting your response,

Woodsman27

Wednesday 9:05pm

I just got back from my sister's and I wanted to shoot you a message before I went to bed. I'm sure you're already asleep. Your bedtime is eight, right?

To be frank, I'm a relationship failure myself. I don't know why, but I seem to fall for men who ultimately break my heart (or steal my savings—long story.) I sometimes think I can't trust my instincts when it comes to falling for someone and it's made me gun-shy to get involved again.

I realize I'm telling you this and we met on a dating site,

but it's true. You could be anyone, but I want you to be exactly who you are in these messages. Funny. Honest. Smart. I know movies roll credits as soon as the couple admit their feelings and that isn't reality, but my parents have been happily married for years, so I know long-lasting true love exists. It just seems to evade me.

Wow, I went a little serious on you, didn't I? Please disregard everything I said here except this...

I'm having a great time. Talk soon.

KnottyGirl25

CHAPTER 5

CLARK

CLARK GRABBED HIS THICK JACKET off the coat rack and stepped outside before slipping into it. The temperature had dropped twenty-degrees in the last hour and he could tell by the curling clouds in the distance that snow was rolling in. He wanted to check out the north side of the property before it started coming down. The trucks would be here the end of next week for those trees and he needed to mark them for replacements in the spring on his chart. There was no point in trying to dig holes to plant now; the ground was frozen solid for the next several months.

He whistled as he trotted down the steps of his front porch. Things had moved along this week without incident and he sent a little prayer up to whoever was listening that they would continue to do so through this first season. Clark couldn't have asked for a better situation for him and Jace. As long as they made it through the busy season without any major trouble, the Winters Farm would keep him on, and he wanted to be here. Not having to pay rent every month, having only essential bills, allowed him to put away money every month in savings and add more to his portfolio. Goals like saving for a house, building a college fund for Jace, and retirement were looking really good.

On top of all that, his correspondences with Knottygirl25 had increased exponentially the past four days. They'd been firing off messages last night until he'd passed out on her at eleven o'clock. He'd sent her an apology this morning and she'd shot him a message an hour later.

> **Good Morning, Woodsman27,**
>   I suppose I can forgive you, since you get up at the crack
>   of dawn every day. Makes sense you can't hang.

Clark had smiled at her teasing, wishing he didn't second guess everything he typed. The last thing he wanted was to come off like a creeper, but meeting her had been at the forefront of his mind since her third message. It was strange to have had all of these discussions about their likes and dislikes, but not even know what color her eyes were.

The fear of moving too fast niggled, stalling his thumbs from responding.

If we'd met in person, I'd have asked her out on a date already, he thought.

Coffee was non-threatening, right?

No, not coffee. That implied meeting in the morning and it would be easier to find a babysitter at night. However, what if she said no to dinner or drinks because it was at night? He was a stranger on the internet and she was a single woman. She was probably terrified to reveal her identity, just like he'd hid his to protect Jace. And there was a chance she'd find out he was a single dad and lose interest. Some women didn't want to date a single parent.

It would be ironic if the first person to catch his interest in years turned out to be everything he'd been avoiding.

He didn't believe it though. There was something about KnottyGirl25 that came through the messages, warm and inviting, and he couldn't imagine her being able to fake that. While a small part of him was willing to wait to meet her, the majority wanted to talk to her face to face. Even if they didn't end up being anything more than friends, he really, really liked talking to her.

With a steadying breath, he typed,

I can hang in person, if you're up for it.

The minutes ticked by like hours as he waited for her to answer; even if it was to tell him to go to hell, he didn't think KnottyGirl25 would ghost him.

Finally, his phone chirped and he clicked on the message.

I'd like that.

A whispered "yes" escaped his lips.

How about tonight? Brews and Chews? 8:30pm. We can get a drink and talk?

That was the last message he sent and he hadn't checked his phone since, mostly because he'd been too busy making and taking calls, getting ready for the harvest.

Clark stepped onto the peg of his quad and threw his leg over, settling onto the seat. As he turned the key and it came to life, he took off up the trail passing by the main house. He couldn't wait to get off work, not only because he was bone-tired, but he had a good feeling he'd have a message from Miss Knotty.

He heard his name over the roar of the engine and pulled the quad to a stop, turning in the seat. Merry was tearing down the hill toward him, dressed in a pair of jeans and a butter-yellow sweater, her black jacket open and flapping behind her. He shut the engine off and waited for her to reach him.

"I'm so glad I caught you," she panted, her cheeks red with exertion. Her blond hair was pulled back from her face in a single French braid, drawing attention to her hazel eyes and lush lips.

The fresh-scrubbed look reminded him of the Merry he'd met while working at the farm his senior year of high school. One afternoon, they'd been swamped and she'd helped him haul trees out to customers' cars. He'd stared at those lips the entire time she chatted with him—well, more like chatted *at* him. He'd been painfully shy back then, but she'd made him laugh so much his face hurt. They'd never talked much until that day, but by the end of it, he'd screwed up the courage to ask her out. It would've been his first date and he remembered the way his heart pounded in his ears as he searched for her when his shift ended.

Of course, before he could catch her, she was climbing into the cab of a lifted white truck and driving off with some jerk from the football team. As Clark watched the truck turn the corner in the distance, he remembered why he'd never spoken to her before. Girls like Merry were busy every weekend with dates and parties, mingling with people who either ignored him or tormented him. He'd been crazy to think she'd look twice at a guy like him.

From that day until he left, he'd put the notion of Merry Winters as anything more than his boss's daughter out of his mind.

She blew an escaped strand of hair off her forehead with a puff. "Sorry, had to catch my breath. Note to self, do a little more walking and less sitting this winter."

"I think you look great," he said, immediately regretting his observation. Merry was stunning, but that didn't mean he should be commenting on it.

The red in her cheeks deepened to a violet hue. "Thank you. I've gained some weight this year enjoying too much good food, and—" She stopped abruptly with a laugh. "You know what, not important. I wanted to talk to you about the tree numbers. I'm organizing the Festival of Trees this year and I need at least eighty."

Clark's brow knitted. "Are you sure? I don't have the numbers in front of me, but I thought the festival was fifty."

"We're getting some new businesses participating, which is why I'm requesting the increase. It's really exciting."

"That's great. Can we talk about the details tomorrow though? I want to do my rounds and get back before the weather hits."

"Oh, sure. Sorry to keep you. Just wanted to make sure it was doable. I didn't want to promise something I couldn't deliver."

"Understandable and yes, I can do that for you." He turned the key and revved the engine once more. "See you tomorrow."

"Yeah, sure, see you." She made a move to leave, but suddenly swung back. "Actually, can I go with you? It's been a while since

I've taken a look around the place and honestly, I'd love to see what you do. I've been trying to get my dad to teach me more of the day to day operations, but he keeps putting me off."

How can I say no to that without feeling like a jerk?

"Um, sure."

Her uncertain smile widened and she did a little hop of excitement he couldn't help finding adorable. "Great! Thanks."

She climbed up behind him and her arms slipped around his waist, locking against his abdomen. He could feel the warmth of her pressed against his back and, unbidden, a semi stretched the front of his jeans.

Shit.

If that wasn't evidence it had been too long for him, he didn't know what was.

"I'm ready," she sang, traces of laughter in her voice. Her excitement was infectious and with a smile, he pressed the throttle. The quad took off at a steady pace on the outside of the trees, the rows whizzing by like labyrinth paths. As he took a hard bump, she gripped him tighter, her body bouncing against him and he slowed, wondering if he should turn around to get the riding helmet he'd left behind. He didn't usually wear one for property checks unless Jace was with him.

"Want me to go back and get the helmet?" he asked loudly.

"No, I'm good! I don't scare easily."

The urge to gun the engine a little to test her mettle shot through Clark, but he resisted. If they'd been friends, he might have teased her a little, but he couldn't let his guard down.

If I'm so worried about Merry Winters, then why did I let her come out here with me?

Because her earnest request to come along touched that raw ache of loneliness he'd been trying to beat back? Even if she resented his presence, he wanted her to know he wasn't her competition. He'd given up avoiding her; especially with the holidays fast approaching, they were going to need to find a common ground.

Clark took the long loop around, pointing as several deer bounced further ahead into the pines to their left. He'd been planning on taking a peek at his MeetMe messages while checking the property, but he couldn't do that with Merry along for the ride. He'd hurry with his rounds, then drop Merry off and grab Jace at the same time. If Knotty said yes to tonight, he'd need to find a babysitter fast.

He parked the quad at the end of the row of planted trees, near the start of the natural growth surrounding the farm. In the distance, craggy mountains cut through the gray clouds like the jagged teeth of a saw. Clark shut the quad down with a smile, watching the wispy bottoms race across the top of the ridges, playing peek-a-boo with the peaks.

"I never get tired of this view," she said, reading his mind. "I mean, I left for several years, but the beauty of this place makes me wonder what I was thinking."

He waited until she climbed off the back before dismounting, running a hand over his face to feel for bugs. "Sometimes you don't know how good you have it until you let it go."

"Very well said. I definitely learned my lesson."

Merry stared at the mountains, short strands of hair escaping her braid and curling along her temple and neck. His gaze trailed over her profile, lingering on her flushed cheeks and curved lips.

Stop looking at her like that and say something!

Clark cleared his throat. "I take it you didn't find it."

"What?"

"You didn't find what you were looking for out in the world."

Her mouth twisted in a wry smile. "You'd be right. Turns out the missing piece I couldn't locate was me. I needed to leave, do everything wrong, and then come back to realize who I am and what I want. My family. The farm. My friends. Mistletoe itself. There is something about your home town nothing else compares to. I hopped from state to state after college but never found the sense of community anywhere else like I had here."

They had that in common. He'd picked a college away from his parents, hoping to find somewhere he belonged. The Winters Farm was the place he'd been looking for and he didn't want to lose it. He wasn't sure why Merry had wanted to come out here with him, but her easy, warm demeanor was slowly chipping away his resolve to keep his distance.

"What about you?" she asked. "Why did you come back? Your parents aren't local anymore, right? Where did they end up?"

"Florida, but we aren't close. They liked the idea of kids more than they actually wanted us around."

Merry winced. "Sorry, that's got to be rough."

"It wasn't."

"Do you always give short answers when someone shows an interest in you?" she mumbled.

Clark startled. "You really want to know about my life?"

"I wouldn't have asked otherwise."

"All right, let's say I didn't know any different until I started school. I rarely went to friends' houses because my parents didn't want to have to drop me off and pick me up. It might interfere with their plans for the day. By the time I got my license and could drive myself, what friends I had spent their weekends playing video games and I could do that with them from my own room, so…"

He trailed off, hating how sad his childhood sounded. The last thing he wanted was pity.

"Do you still talk to your friends?" she asked.

"No, they all left Mistletoe after graduation too. We're Facebook friends, but you know how that goes."

Merry scoffed. "Oh, yeah. I have those. It's funny, I thought I was close to so many people in high school, but I only stayed close with two of them. Although they recently got boyfriends, so I'm kind of the fifth wheel. I'm single by choice, but it's not much fun watching everyone around you making out."

"That must make me the flat tire." He caught her confused expression and laughed. "Sorry, bad joke. I only mean people stop asking you to go get a beer when you need to plan ahead for a babysitter."

Why am I telling her this?

"You know that if you ever need anyone to watch Jace, you only need to ask. My mom adores him."

"I already feel like I'm taking advantage of your mom. I'm her employee."

"Don't tell her that. She thinks of you and Jace as a part of the family. So does my dad. He speaks highly of you." Several seconds passed as they walked together in companionable silence, until Merry said, "You can ask me too, you know."

"Ask you...to watch Jace?"

"Well, yeah. Your son is the sweetest kid I've ever met and I may not have much...okay, any experience with kids, but I'm pretty sure I could keep him alive for a few hours."

Clark hesitated and Merry laughed. "Why do you seem thrown by that?"

"Because I didn't think you wanted me here."

Merry froze. "What do you mean?"

"I overheard you talking to your sister when I first arrived. You were upset your parents hired me."

Merry's face flushed. "I'm sorry. None of that was about you. I'm frustrated with my dad. I've asked him to teach me everything that goes into the daily workings on the farm, but he brushes me off."

"I didn't realize you wanted to take over someday."

"It may be many years in the future, but I'd at least like to be prepared, you know?"

Why did the catch in her voice trigger the urge to touch her? Flexing his fingers, he took a step to the side, putting a few more inches between them. "What do you want to know? About the farm, I mean."

"Really? After what you heard, you'd teach me?"

"This is your home. I just work here." As true as the words were, they sank like a stone to the bottom of Clark's stomach. He may love it, but it was too new to get comfortable.

Merry walked up to one of the Douglas Firs up ahead and fingered its branch. "What are you looking for out here?"

"There are lots of answers to that question, but the main thing is that the tree needles are green and pliable. Swollen nodes and white masses usually mean an infection. I'm not worried about root rot, but these trees on the outer edge of the property don't get as much attention as the ones closest to the main house. Disease spreads fast and the last thing we want is to lose too many mature trees because we missed something."

"You went to college for plant diseases, right?"

"Plant pathology. I was hoping for a job that would take me outdoors, but I ended up in a lab for a few years. Great pay, but the long hours kept me away from Jace and I wanted to be home with my son. Your parents needing a foreman was a lucky break."

"I feel worse now."

"Why?" he asked.

"For being such a jerk about my dad hiring you. He told me that a good foreman is a necessity and I'd be happy to have you by my side."

"I hope that's true. It would suck to move back here and have you forever hate my guts."

"I didn't ever hate you. I was upset at first, but my parents can't say enough good things about you. I couldn't get a handle on you because anytime I came around, you found something else to do."

"Staying out of your way seemed the best option, considering what I knew."

"Please don't do that anymore. I was venting my feelings, but I'm not some soap opera villain looking for ways to discredit you. I hope you believe me."

"I do." He walked along the row, fingering the branches as he passed. "Is that why you wanted to tag along out here? To get to know me? Clear the air?"

"I wasn't sure what I wanted. I just saw you on the quad and thought a ride around the farm sounded fun. Now I'm glad I came along and got to really meet the great guy my parents keep raving about."

Clark slowed to face her, touching her arm as he smiled. "Thank you, Merry. That means a lot."

She stared at him strangely before she released a little laugh. "You're welcome. And I really am serious about Jace coming over. Although you might not agree when I feed him ten pounds of sugary snacks before sending him home."

Clark stumbled back in mock horror. "You wouldn't!"

"Chances are slim, but not zero."

"I guess I'd better stay on your good side, then."

"Probably best. Although I feel like I should be the one on my best behavior from now on."

Clark looked up from the tree he was studying, his gaze locking with hers. "I admire your candidness. I always have."

"Thank you. I don't remember the two of us having very many conversations, even before you left for college."

"That's because you were out of my league."

"Ouch. Please tell me I didn't come off like a giant superficial jerk."

Clark held up his fingers apart a tiny bit, smirking. "Only this much."

To his surprise, she shoved him gently on his arm, the gesture friendly and familiar, as though this wasn't the first real conversation they'd had in years.

"I'm only teasing. You were easy to be around. The people you hung with, I can't say the same."

Merry looped her arm through his. "I'll give you that. My entire dating history includes every flavor of asshole. I think back on my life sometimes and wonder what the hell I was thinking. Do you ever do that?"

The weight of her arm in his took Clark back to the one day he really got to spend time with Merry, how she lit up the room, treated everyone like they were her best friend. Merry had a way about her; easily approachable, with a personality warm and inviting that people flocked to. She didn't think twice about teasing a stranger or taking the arm of a guy she was getting to know.

He'd never had that natural ability to connect with people, maybe because he'd had such a disconnection in his own life. It wasn't until Jace came along that he'd finally learned to speak up and ask for things, usually with less tact than most, but he couldn't stand pussy-footing around things.

"Not particularly. I only ever dated one person and although that didn't turn out the way I wanted, if I hadn't met her, I wouldn't have Jace."

Merry released him and walked backwards so she could face him, her expression bright and earnest. "He is such a funny, special kid." She stopped, cocking her head sheepishly. "I should really thank you. Jace will keep my mother occupied for several years."

"Occupied?"

"Grandkids. My mother says they are the reward for raising children, as if we aren't good enough for her."

"You don't want kids?" he asked.

"I do. I want a passel of kids, but not any time soon. I want to meet someone and have a few years to just discover us before we add another person to the mix."

"No single dads for you, huh?" He'd meant it as a joke, but there was a sharpness to his tone he couldn't mask.

Merry's face flushed. "I mean...I've never dated a single parent, but I would be open to it."

"You would?"

"Well, yeah. Like I said, I want a bunch of kids."

"Even if they aren't yours?"

"Just because they don't share my blood doesn't mean they wouldn't be mine. My parents never officially adopted Noel after her parents died, but I consider her my family. My sister. And I'd feel the same way as a co-parent."

Clark hesitated, surprised by her passion on the subject. "I didn't mean to offend you. In my experience, some women aren't as enthusiastic about dating single fathers."

"You're telling me you've never been with anyone else except Jace's mom?"

"Depends on what you mean by *been with*."

"Dating!" She cleared her throat. "I was talking about dating."

"Then no. I haven't dated anyone."

"That's a shame," she said.

"Why is that?"

"You seem like a nice guy. I already know you're a good father, or your son wouldn't have turned out to be such a great kid. You're employed, which is always a bonus." She shrugged and added rapidly, "And you aren't hard to look at."

She turned away from him, missing his slack-jawed expression. "Hard to look at?"

"I said what I said. Don't make a big deal about it."

Clark laughed. "A definite improvement over the gawky teen I used to be."

"Actually, I thought you were cute then too. All wiry muscle and mysterious."

Shock waves shot through him, freezing him in place. "No you didn't."

"You had no idea I had a crush on you?"

He shook his head, his heart slamming in his chest.

"I did. It was during peak season and the place was swamped, so I helped out. We spent the whole day together and I was enamored with your dark eyes and broody soul."

Clark scoffed. "Broody soul?"

"Yeah, like Angel on *Buffy*. Swoony."

"I remember who I was in high school and *swoony* is not the term I would use."

"Well, you were never a sixteen-year-old girl, so you don't get a vote."

"Fair enough." Clark's thoughts drifted back to that day. The laughter. The disappointment when he realized Merry had a boyfriend. "Why didn't you say anything?"

"Because every time I came around after that day you avoided me. I figured I wasn't your type."

"I thought you had a boyfriend."

"Oh yes, Johnny, one of the many jerks I dated. I actually broke up with him after working with you. Not because of...well, not fully because of you, although I figured if I was crushing that hard, I probably shouldn't be dating him."

"Why did you break up then?"

"Someone had been taking money from my wallet for weeks and I thought it was Holly, but I caught him when I came back from the bathroom that night. Had to apologize to my sister, which she was merciless about. Like I said, I know how to pick 'em."

Clark almost told her he'd had a crush on her too, but it felt too close to the realm of flirting and he shouldn't go there with her. Not just because she was his boss's daughter, but they lived next door to each other. If things went south, he'd still have to see her every day.

And he still had KnottyGirl25 consuming his thoughts.

"I'm sorry, did I make you uncomfortable?" she asked.

"No, of course not. I'm flattered that a beautiful girl found me mysterious."

"I mean, I still find you mysterious, but I no longer fantasize about you reading me poetry or anything."

"You would have been very disappointed. Not only do I not like poetry, but I don't have a romantic bone in my body. A woman like you would be wasted on me."

Merry laughed. "I don't have unrealistic expectations anymore."

"It's not unrealistic to want a man to treat you like you're the best thing that ever happened to him, Merry. Don't settle for anything less."

CHAPTER 6

MERRY

IF THE TREES COULD TALK, they'd call Merry an idiot.

Everything coming out of her mouth made her sound like a jackass. She'd wanted to melt into the soil when Clark brought up the single parent thing. It wasn't that she wouldn't date a man with children. With the exception of Clark, she didn't know any other single dads so she didn't think about it.

Over-explaining in my own head is making me feel worse.

Then the *not hard to look at* comment. She'd meant it as a compliment, but he'd seemed offended by it, so then she told him about her little crush. He'd tried to be nice and let her down easy, but she kept on until he said something he obviously regretted. It didn't take a genius to pick up that Clark thought she was a swell gal and that was all there was to it.

Now they'd been walking silently for the past several minutes and it was all because she'd rambled!

Merry hadn't even thought about those two weeks of mooning around the farm in years, because it was embarrassing. Popping up when he was working, only to have him disappear with his book rather than talk to her. He'd been so far removed from the guys she usually went for and it had been unnerving that he hadn't been interested.

God, I sound like a vain twit in my own head. I can only imagine what he's thinking.

As a teen, she'd thought he was scrawny under his baggy sweatshirts, and then she'd watched him lift tree after tree with ease. His hooded dark eyes would stare into hers as he listened, hardly saying a word, but when he did, his voice had a surprisingly deep timbre. She'd imagined him saying her name with that low register, but instead, he'd kept his distance and she'd moved on.

When he'd given her that very real smile this afternoon, the first one she'd seen from him since they were teens, it knocked the wind right out of her. Clark was hot. All dark-eyed and outdoorsy, with hair she could get a grip on when she kissed him. His broad shoulders filled out that jacket and she could imagine him replacing the Bounty paper towel man if he decided to grow a beard and—

"Merry? You all right?" he asked.

She cleared her throat, keeping her face turned away so he wouldn't see her blushing. She'd never been a shy person, but when flustered, her face turned redder than a rich, ripe strawberry. Especially around attractive men.

"Yes, I'm good. Just thinking."

"That's what I do when I come out here. It's my quiet time. I go through my mental to-do list, think about life and the meaning of it all. You can really sort everything out among the trees."

"I didn't mean to encroach on your alone time."

"Honestly, I don't mind your company."

"I feel like I keep saying things I shouldn't."

Clark shrugged. "Better an awkward honest answer than a smooth lie."

"Yes, but we really haven't had any one on one time together and I should be fixing the *wonderful* impression I made when you first arrived."

"You made an impression years ago and my opinion hasn't changed."

"Good or bad?"

"Good."

Why did that one word, said in that deep, gravely voice of his, tickle her giddy?

"Well, thank the Lord for that. I would hate to run you off now that we're getting along."

"Even if you chased me with a rabid grizzly, you'd have a hard time getting rid of me."

"I'm fresh out of those," Merry teased. "If my dad ever lets me take the reins though, I promise not to let all that power go to my head."

"Are you really planning on taking over when your parents retire?" He sounded skeptical.

"Why is there a tone when you ask that?"

His face stretched in a sheepish smirk. "I can count on my hand the number of times I've seen you out hauling trees with us."

"Hey, I can get dirty if I need to."

There was that smile again, taking out her knees like a linebacker. "I didn't say you couldn't."

The alternate meaning to their conversation registered and she burst out laughing. "Oh, boy! This took a strange turn. Let's get back on track. Me taking over the farm. I didn't think I would. I always loved it out here, but I guess I assumed my brother would take over. Then he joined the army and fell in love with programming, and I realized I wasn't being honest with myself because I'm not big on going after what I want."

"I'm the opposite. I've known what I wanted since I was seventeen, and when your dad's foreman post popped up in my feed, I knew I had to apply. I was really surprised he hired me."

"Why is that?"

"I'd been working in a lab since graduation, with some field work, but I don't have any experience running a farm. I did a lot of research and I'm a fast learner, but I need this season to go well."

Merry reached out without thinking and squeezed his hand. "It'll be an awesome season. I have faith."

His eyes crinkled at the corners and he returned her gesture, compressing her hand in his larger one. "Thanks."

The heat of his skin warmed hers, flutters erupting inside from her stomach to her chest. His eyes were a touch lighter than her sibling's, and she could have sworn she saw flecks of green in their depths.

Merry's phone went off with Beastie Boys' "Girls" and she released his hand with a start. Digging her phone out of her pocket, she groaned. "I forgot my friends were coming over for dinner tonight."

"It's no problem, I'll take you back."

"We can finish your inspection."

"Are you sure?" he asked.

"Yeah, just let me answer this." She slid her thumb across the screen. "Hi."

"Where are you? We're standing outside your front door freezing our asses off," Sally said.

"It should be unlocked. Just go inside and I'll meet you there in half an hour?" The last was said with a question and Clark nodded. "Half an hour."

"What are you doing?"

"I'm inspecting the north side of the property with Clark."

"Oh, your hot foreman?" Tara piped in and Merry rolled her eyes. She should have known Sally would put her on speaker phone.

"Yes, but it isn't like that. We're working."

"Uh-huh, working that body. Uh-uh-uh—"

"Okay, I'll see you soon."

"Love you!" they hollered.

Merry ended the call without returning the sentiment and glanced at Clark, who continued his rounds, disappearing into the rows of trees ahead. Hopefully he hadn't heard them, or her humiliation would be complete. Clark probably thought she was chasing him with all her talk about being single and crushes and fifth wheels. Did she just have dating on the brain because of the Woodsman's last message?

She clicked on the MeetMe app and opened the message, her stomach knotting.

Tonight?

Even if she wasn't hanging with her friends, it was too soon, right? He could be anyone. He could be lying about his age, his hobbies...which would be on par with her track record.

On the other hand, they'd had so much fun chatting this week, they could have an even deeper connection in person. And they were meeting in a public space. If he did turn out to be a creeper, she'd ask one of the bouncers to walk her to her car and she'd never have to see him again.

Woodsman27,

I actually have plans tonight, but I could do 8:30pm tomorrow at Brews and Chews. Would that work?

XO,
KnottyGirl25

Merry slipped it into her pocket as Clark headed back toward her. "Your friends okay with waiting?"

"Oh yeah. I never lock my door, so they can go right in."

"You need to be careful." It was said sharply, taking her aback, and Clark's face flushed as he added, "I just mean as a woman living alone and a lot of strangers visiting the farm, you should keep it locked during the day."

"I lock it when I'm at home, but there isn't anything of value. You may be right, though. I've been thinking about getting a dog."

"Can I send my son over to play with it if you do? He's been begging me for a puppy."

"Absolutely. You're both welcome. If you need to borrow a cup of sugar or some other neighborly item you run out of, I've got you covered."

Clark stepped around a tree, his mouth tilted up in the corners. "You're saying I need to make up an excuse to stop by?"

"No, I mean you can come over anytime!"

"Anytime, huh?"

Her eyes narrowed. "You're messing with me, aren't you?"

"A little bit. I didn't expect you to get so flustered."

"Why not?" she called after him as he rounded the next row of trees.

"You don't seem easily frazzled. The way you're always jumping in to help people, taking charge. Unflappable."

"Who do I help?"

"Do you normally plan the Festival of Trees?"

"No."

"Didn't think so. Since I've been back, I know you've helped out at Father's Day Frittatas, the Fourth of July parade and the fireworks display. I saw you filling drink orders at the Labor Day concert, not to mention running the front office of the school. For a woman who spent years away from here, you didn't miss a beat fitting right back into the fold."

She really hadn't. She'd come home last fall and it wasn't long before her mother roped her into performing at the Christmas concert. After that, it had come naturally to volunteer when someone dropped out of an event or they needed an extra hand.

"I guess coming back here was like riding a bike. I go where I'm needed."

"That's why people love you."

Merry tossed her head, shooting him a playfully haughty look. "And why wouldn't they? I am completely lovable."

"Ooof, humility and graciousness are also lovable."

"You're saucier than I expected, has anyone told you that?"

"They haven't used that word exactly."

"I like this side of you."

"All part of growing up, I suppose." He pulled his gloves out of his jacket pocket as the first few snowflakes started falling. "We should be heading back."

Merry followed along behind him and climbed onto the quad first. When he settled back between her thighs, she entangled her arms around his waist again, breathing in the scent of cedar and soap as he fired up the quad. Today was the first time she'd been aware of Clark as a man, mostly because he was so standoffish and cordial. With her mom and dad, he was polite, friendly, and professional, but he seemed to hold himself away, as if keeping some invisible barrier in place. Considering how he'd talked about his parents and childhood, it made sense he'd have trouble with attachments, but then he doted on his son. He really was a conundrum.

There had been a few moments among the trees where he'd let his guard down and surprised her, but that didn't mean he was interested in her. No sense in disintegrating the ground they'd covered by getting hung up on how good he smelled.

Still, there was that smile. His voice. How funny he was when he lightened up. If women thought Clark was a catch before, wait until they got a load of him relaxed and in his element. They'd be breaking down his door and carrying him off like cavewomen.

I might have been one of them, if he'd shown even one iota of interest.

Despite his playfulness on their walk, he hadn't pushed the conversation further than idle flirting and she'd respected him for it. He seemed like a nice, honest guy not looking to lead anyone on.

He parked the quad next to his Jeep and Merry could see Sally and Tara watching them through the window of her house. She climbed off the quad and brushed her hair out of her face, wincing as she felt the flyaway strands everywhere.

"Wow, the wind really did a number on my hair."

"You can call it quad chic. Start a new trend."

Merry laughed. "I'll give that a try and let you know if it works. Thank you."

"It's not a problem." He dismounted and took the keys out of the quad. "I'll make sure you get your eighty trees, and if anything changes, you know where to find me. I'm going to go collect my son from your mom and start dinner."

"I bet he misses you when you're at work."

"It's better than it was. At least now we have a routine down." Clark nodded behind her and she turned as Sally and Tara ducked. "You have fun with your friends."

"Thanks. Have a good night, Clark."

"You too, Merry."

She turned, self-consciously wondering if he was watching her walk away but didn't want to get caught checking. When she opened her front door and looked back, he was nowhere to be seen.

Tara popped into the doorway with a glass of wine and wide blue eyes. "Holy hell, you did not tell us you had a thing going with the sexy foreman."

"I don't!" Merry pushed her way into the house and closed the door. "It was work."

"Oh, it *looked* like work, straddling his backside like that. Tell me the truth," Tara said, waggling her dark brows. "Does he have abs under that workman's jacket?"

Merry rolled her eyes at Sally, who was unloading take-out containers onto the counter. "What is wrong with her?"

"She got dumped."

Merry spun around to face Tara, who was glaring at Sally.

"What happened? You two were all hot and heavy last week."

Tara's blue eyes blinked rapidly and Merry knew from years of heartbreak her friend was trying to keep it together and not cry. "He said we had sexual chemistry, but not lasting chemistry."

"Douche bag," Sally sang.

"Oh honey." Merry held out her arms and the taller woman fell into them, her brown hair tickling Merry's cheek. "Forget him. We'll make a voodoo doll and stick pins right in his favorite area."

Tara choked out a wet laugh. "Forget the doll. Just give me a voodoo peen. It will look like a pin cushion by the time I get my feelings out."

"Tell her what he said about your boobs!"

Merry glanced over her shoulder at Sally with a grimace. "What did he say about her boobs?"

"They were saggy!" Tara sniffled.

Merry hugged her tighter. "What the fuck?"

"Asssssshollllle!" Sally dragged out the word this time, hitting a deep note on the hole.

"Do you actually think your boobs are saggy?" Merry asked.

Tara pulled away, wiping at her wet cheeks and eyes. "No, but I don't understand why he had to go there."

"I believe I've explained the why in two different terms. He's a—"

"Come on, Sally," Merry cut in, pulling Tara to the couch to sit. "Honestly, Tara, did you really like him?"

"I don't know. He could be fun. Outside the bedroom."

Merry held up a hand, waving it back and forth. "Wait, time out, are you telling me he sucked in bed?"

Tara nodded.

Sally carried three shot glasses and a bottle of Fireball up the steps and sat across from them. "Hold on, you've been crying all day over trash D?"

Tara giggled and Merry's lips twitched as she joined in on the razzing. "Nah, those aren't sad tears. Those are the tears of a grateful woman who knows she never has to endure his minute man antics again."

Tara laughed harder, whisky drops flying over the full shot glass Sally handed her.

"Whoa, don't spill that on my rug! If I drag that up to my parents', my mother will start asking me why my rug smells like a distillery."

"Tell her to mind her bidness." Sally held her shot glass up in a toast and Merry clinked her glass to hers.

"I'm not saying that to my mother and I know you don't say it to your mother either."

Sally chuckled. "Maybe not, but I'd love to see your mother's expression right before she murders you."

"All right, let's do this toast so we can eat something." Besides, Merry's arm was starting to ache from holding up the shot glass. "The last thing we need is getting hammered on an empty stomach."

"To good friends, new experiences, and no more trash D," Sally said.

Tara tapped her glass and knocked it back, wheezing. "He really was the worst, but I thought he was sweet."

"That's how they get you." Sally gathered up the shot glasses. "They all come at you with the good guy routine until they hook you."

"Uh-oh," Merry said, climbing to her feet to help with the food. "Did Pike do something?"

"Nope, he's a good egg. I'm speaking in general. Men are shifty creatures."

Tara hopped off the couch and grabbed the bottle of Fireball, "I agree! I'm going on a guyiatus! That's a guy-hiatus, for anyone confused."

Tara filled up the shot glasses again, while Merry grabbed her container of enchiladas and rice and beans. "I did that this year and it was liberating. I finally feel prepared to get back into the dating pool."

Sally sat across from her on the sofa with her feet tucked up under her, green eyes on Merry as she took a bite of her taco before mumbling, "And you've set your sights on your neighbor?"

"No. He isn't ready to date and I am done with people who aren't looking for the whole shebang."

"Still, you know what they say about the quiet ones," Tara called from the kitchen. Instead of bringing the shots in to share, she took all three in succession. "They're all about the control in the bedroom. Anyone want another shot?"

Merry nodded absently; an image of Clark naked lounging in her bed rippled through her mind. What she imagined he looked like, anyway.

Tara set the shots on the side table and went back for her food.

Sally leaned close, whispering, "It's gonna be a long night."

CHAPTER 7

CLARK

CLARK SAT DOWN NEXT TO Jace at the Winters dinner table the following night, keeping his head down while Chris Winters said grace, his right hand held by his son. The family had lengthened the table so Chris and Victoria sat on the ends, while Holly, Nick, and Noel were situated across from Clark, Jace, and Merry, her soft hand fitted into his.

Clark's knee bounced under the table, checking the clock again. It was ten after six and in just over two hours, he'd be sitting down with KnottyGirl25 over drinks.

"Amen."

Everyone released hands and he sat back, running his hands over his thighs to calm the motion. He didn't want to give the Winters family the impression their invitation to family dinner wasn't appreciated. Erica, his babysitter, wouldn't be there until eight and if he'd skipped dinner to stay home, he'd probably be pacing the living room and changing his shirt again. He'd sweated his way through a T-shirt and polo already and he needed to remember to reapply deodorant before he walked out the door.

He turned his head to discreetly sniff just as Merry reached to pick up the bread basket. Her wavy blond hair fell forward, obscuring the upturned nose and Cupid's bow mouth. He pretended to crack his neck so she wouldn't realize what he'd been about to do. She was another complication he hadn't seen coming. Although he was eager to meet KnottyGirl25, Merry had occupied a number of his thoughts last night and he found himself analyzing everything she'd said to him. He repeatedly told himself it was a bad idea to get involved with her, for a number of reasons, but a tiny voice at the back of his mind kept whispering, *"What if it works out, though?"*

After taking a roll, she tucked her hair back and held the basket out to him with a smile. "Want?"

Clark's gaze dropped to her lips. "What?"

"Do you want a roll?"

"Yes, yeah, of course. Thanks." Clark took one for himself and set another on Jace's plate before passing it along to Chris, his face burning. The ease he'd experienced in her presence yesterday was replaced by a jumpiness reminiscent of the teenaged boy he used to be.

It could also be that his date tonight already had him on edge, but he didn't think so. Something changed after their chat and Clark didn't like it. He wanted to go back to thinking Merry was a nice girl who lived down the way, instead of the funny, sexy woman who smelled like Christmas cookies.

"How's planning going for the festival, Merry?" Chris asked.

"Great! Sixty-six businesses in Mistletoe have put down a deposit for trees. My goal is eighty, but that's sixteen more than last year and I still have a few weeks. I'll get there."

"I knew I suggested the right woman for the job," Victoria murmured, winking at Merry, who snorted.

"Yeah, thanks for that. No more volunteering me for things this year, please. I'm up to my eyeballs in responsibility."

Nick snapped his fingers. "Damn. I was hoping to convince you to help me deliver premade meals for Thanksgiving and Christmas."

"Me?" Merry squeaked.

"Well, all of you. I agreed to help out, but we had a lot more people sign up for meals than we were expecting and I need more drivers to help out."

Clark held up his hand. "I'd be happy to help."

Nick shot him a grateful smile. "Thanks, man."

"When do they have to be delivered?" Holly asked.

"Day before, by eight p.m."

Holly nodded. "I can close the shop a few hours early. Where do I need to pick them up from?"

"Mistletoe Reformed Church. I'll put your name and arrival time on the volunteer sheet."

"Might as well make it a family affair," Chris said. "How many meals are going out?"

"The last count was seventy-five," Noel answered.

"But the number is going up." Nick chuckled. "I guess people don't want to cook this year."

Merry grabbed the potatoes from the center and dropped a spoonful on her plate with a clack, drawing everyone's attention. "I'm in too, if you still need people."

"Thanks, sis. I knew I could count on you all to help out.

And Clark—" Nick held his beer bottle up in a toast. "Glad to have you here. If anything, you're keeping this workaholic—" Nick nudged his dad with his arm. "—from driving the rest of us nuts."

Clark tipped his water glass in response. "Happy to help."

"It's been a blessing having Clark and Jace," Victoria gushed, reaching out to ruffle his son's hair. "He helps me bake and is becoming quite the chess player."

"When you get finished wiping the floor with my mom, Jace, come find me. I'm the chess champion in this house." Chris cleared his throat and Merry continued with a grumbled, "Only because my dad doesn't play anymore."

"Although I may come out of retirement for the right player." Chris winked at Jace from the end of the table and Jace grinned.

Clark took the potatoes from Merry and put a small scoop on Jace's plate.

"Dad..." Jace whined.

Clark raised a brow at his son's whine, delivering a silent warning. They'd had a long discussion before coming over for dinner that Jace had to try a bite of everything to be polite. Even au gratin potatoes.

Jace stabbed a fork at the white ovals smothered in orange cheese sauce without another word.

Merry leaned closer to Clark, her hair brushing the skin of his arm as she addressed Jace. "You don't like potatoes?"

Jace looked at Clark before answering her. "Not really, but I have to try it."

"Do you like ketchup?"

Jace perked up. "Yeah!"

"You want to try some on those bad boys?"

"Sure."

Merry hopped up from the table and went to the fridge. Clark ignored the warm glow in his chest at the kind gesture. All of the Winters family seemed to be inherently good with kids, even if Merry swore she didn't have much experience.

Merry came back to the table, handing Jace the bottle. "There you go, Jace."

"Thank you." Jace popped the lid open and squeezed a mound on top of the dollop of potatoes. Clark checked on Victoria to make sure she wasn't offended, but she simply smiled at Jace as he took a large bite of ketchup-coated potatoes.

"This is really good," Jace announced.

Merry grinned, holding up a bite of her own reddened potatoes. "I'm glad."

Clark turned to Merry, who was also watching Jace take another bite.

"Thanks for that. We are working on eating at other people's houses. It's not a normal thing for us."

Her hazel eyes locked with his, her mouth twitching. "It's no trouble. I was a picky eater and these potatoes aren't my favorite."

"They're mine though," Nick said, taking a massive bite.

"We know, golden boy," Merry shot back.

"You say that like it's a bad thing."

"Lord love a duck, you two are going to drive me to drink," Victoria muttered.

"I've got the ticket for that!" Holly jumped up from her seat and went to the kitchen, coming back into the room with a wine bottle in each hand. "Red or white, because I brought both."

Clark smothered a laugh with his napkin as Victoria looked up to the ceiling. "I know you never send us more than we can handle, but you might have miscalculated."

"Rude." Holly set one bottle on the island and opened the other with the corkscrew. "Just for that, I'm not sharing my wine with you."

"Noel, would you please wrestle that bottle of red from my daughter and pour me some?"

Noel got up from the table with a smirk. "I'm on it."

Holly handed Noel the bottle with an eyeroll. "Suck up."

"Can you guys stop goofing off?" Jace hollered. "I'm trying to enjoy my potatoes."

The adults laughed and went back to eating, the conversation turning to more casual topics like the upcoming tree harvest and how Holly's shop was doing. When the meal finished, Clark took his and Jace's plates into the kitchen, coming up alongside Victoria.

"I can wash if you want to go sit down."

Chris stepped up, elbowing his wife out of the way. "Both of you get out of here. Dishes are my domain. Holly! Get in here and help your old dad."

"I'm coming."

Victoria patted Clark on the back, leading him into the living room. "Best let the Dish Master do his work. Come sit with us."

Clark found himself on the couch next to Merry, who had her feet tucked up under her.

"Mrs. Winters, can we play chess now?" Jace asked.

"Absolutely. You know where it is."

Jace took off down the hallway with Butch trotting along behind him.

"Your son is so good with Butch." Victoria lowered her voice and whispered, "Jace's mentioned once or twice that he wants a puppy."

Clark shook his head. "I'm sorry he brought that up. I already told him maybe when we get our own place—"

"Nonsense! The man in the cottage before you had two big Labs through the course of his employment and I think it would be good for Jace to have a pal." Victoria seemed to realize she may have overstepped and added, "I mean, of course it is ultimately your decision, but if you want to get a dog, we have no issue with it."

"Thank you, Victoria," Clark said quietly.

Jace came running back in with the game clacking is his hands. He sat down on the other side of the coffee table across from Victoria and the two of them chatted as he set up the board.

Clark checked the clock on the wall. It was almost seven, so he still had forty-five minutes. He looked over at Merry, who was watching her mother and Jace, a bemused smile on her face.

"You look nice," he said softly.

She whipped his way, her cheeks burnished pink. "Thank you. I'm going out with a friend after dinner."

"What friend?" Victoria asked, peering at her daughter over Jace's head.

"Hey, concentrate on your game. This is an A and B conversation, so C your way out of it."

"Jace, do you hear how she talks to her mother?"

His son turned and shot Merry a disapproving look. "You should be nice to Mrs. Winters. I wish I had a mom like her."

The room fell silent. Clark's chest twisted up in knots at Jace's admission. It had been just the two of them for so long and it wasn't until recently Jace started asking questions about his mom. Clark told him Patrice wasn't ready to be a mom, but she'd done the best thing she could do for him, and that was letting Clark raise him. He didn't know what else he could say, but Jace had simply shrugged and moved on to a new topic, so Clark thought it wasn't a big deal. He'd always been afraid that as he got older, Clark might not be enough for him. That he might crave that maternal bond he was missing.

"That was a wonderful thing to say, Jace. Thank you," Victoria murmured, her eyes shimmering.

Merry leaned over and tapped Jace on the shoulder. "I wasn't being mean, I promise. Remember when I talked about teasing your dad when you get a little older? That's what my mom and I do. I love her very much and we like to play."

"My dad and I pretend we're pirates when we cook dinner. He's the captain and I'm his first mate."

Clark coughed when Victoria and Merry sent him amused looks.

"That sounds like a blast," Merry said. "Our parents raised us to believe that the more families play with each other, the more love there is between them."

"Then my dad loves me a lot."

The adults laughed.

"I am sure he does." Merry leaned over his shoulder and spoke in a stage whisper, "Now, get your game face on. I wanna see you kick my mom's butt so I can take you on next time."

"Forget it. I am the chess master!" Victoria crowed.

"Nuh-uh," Jace said.

Merry climbed to her feet. "I'll be right back to watch. I'm going to grab something from my car."

"Speaking of your car, I need you to go to the grocery store for me tomorrow."

"I knew there had to be another reason you wanted me living so close." Merry crossed her arms over her chest, shooting her mother a scowl. "It couldn't just be because you love me and missed having me around."

"Of course I missed you...doing my grocery shopping."

"Nice, Mom."

Victoria let out a wicked laugh and Chris turned from the sink with a grin. "Why is my wife doing her witch laugh?"

"Excuse me? I do not sound like a witch!"

"You kinda do, Mom," Holly said.

Victoria pointed a finger at her. "Watch it, my pretty, or I'll put a spell on you."

"Do you need help?" Clark asked Merry, surprising himself.

Merry's smile still had a crazy effect on his heart rate.

"Sure, that would be great. I bought an espresso machine, but it's too big for my counter space, so I figured I'd bring it up here and it's heavy."

"Oh, an espresso machine," Victoria chimed in. "I've always wanted one of those, but your father says we don't need it."

Merry sent her mother an arch look. "Well, it's a good thing your daughter didn't want to drive all the way back to Twin Falls to return this one. Just remember who paid for it."

"Rude," her mother said. "You should remember who kept you alive for eighteen years."

"And while I appreciate you doing so, I know how you like to commandeer things."

"The way you commandeered my favorite boots when you were in high school and then ruined them?"

"See? Like mother like daughter." Merry grabbed the doorknob and pulled it open, grinning at Clark. "Let's skedaddle before she remembers everything else I borrowed."

"Lead the way," Clark said, following her out the front door. They stepped onto the porch, the brisk air smacking him in the face. Even though the Christmas lights blinked around them, casting colorful flashes of light across the yard, the lack of moonlight created a deeper darkness beyond the giant blow-up Santa waving in the middle of the front lawn.

"Whew, it got cold out here."

"Winter is coming."

Merry shot him a smirk. "*Game of Thrones* fan?"

"Yes, until the last season. That ending was weak."

Merry covered her ears with a squeal. "I'm only on season four! Do not tell me!"

"How have you avoided spoilers?"

"I stay off Reddit and ignore all things GOT."

"What's taking you so long to catch up?"

"I binge it for a bit but then it becomes so exhausting, I have to take a break."

Clark winced. "I can't believe you said that."

"What?"

"You're talking about one of the most epic shows of our time!" Her noncommittal shrug sent all the air from his lungs and he started spluttering. The heartless woman thumped him on the back with a laugh.

"You all right there, Sparky?"

Clark caught his breath with a wheeze. "You...may have traumatized me."

"You've definitely become more dramatic."

"Only when it comes to my fandoms."

"I do apologize for insulting such an epic show and giving you a coughing fit."

"It's fine. I was surprise—ahhh!"

Clark knew what was happening the minute the bottom of his boot hit the ice. Both feet scissor-kicked out from under him, his arms circling in the air.

I must look like a goose taking flight.

The wind whooshed around his ears for several seconds before the impact of landing on his back knocked all oxygen from his lungs. Still less painful than her belittling *Game of Thrones*.

Merry's face filled his vision, flashes of green and red lighting up her knitted brow. "Are you all right, Clark?"

"Missed the ice."

Merry grinned. "Really? Seems like you hit it dead on. Ten out of ten for the fall, by the way."

"Shouldn't you be checking for a concussion instead of busting my chops?"

"Sure." She held up her fingers. "Count 'em."

"Three."

"What's my name?"

"Merry."

"Where are you?"

"Currently on my back in the Winters front yard."

Merry reached down and grabbed his hand. "I think you're good."

Clark gripped her warm palm in his and got to his feet, his back and ass throbbing. "Thanks for the lift."

"You're welcome." She released his hand, frowning down at the cement. "It's weird that there's any ice. Dad's usually good about salting the walkway."

"Probably some of the snow from the lawn melted onto the cement and refroze."

"And you found the only patch on the whole stretch. I gotta say, I'm impressed."

"At my gracefulness?"

"No, that you didn't use falling as an opportunity to give me a cheesy line like 'Looks like I fell for you'."

Clark winced. "Guys really do that?"

"Oh yeah. Corny, insincere…" Suddenly her eyes widened. "Not that I think you're interested in me or that you're a jerk or… Shit, I didn't mean to say that or even allude to that! I was being incredibly presumptuous and I am so sorry. I am such an idiot sometimes."

"You're not an idiot, Merry."

"If you say so, but between yesterday and tonight, I'm really not sure."

"What happened yesterday?"

"Telling you I had a crush on you back in high school. I feel like I made you uncomfortable—"

"No, you didn't!" he blurted.

"I didn't?"

Clark ran a hand through his hair, all the reasons he'd had not to be honest eluding him with her standing so close. "I almost asked you out."

"When?"

"That day we worked together."

"Why didn't you?"

"Because you got into a truck with another guy. Figured I didn't stand a chance."

"I see." She opened up her car door without saying anything else and Clark shuffled his feet, wondering what was going on inside her head. He looked away when she bent over and pulled the lever to the trunk. He did not want her catching him staring at her ass.

When she straightened up, she shut the door with a shrug. "Machine's in the trunk."

As he rounded the back of the car, she came up alongside him, her shoulder brushing his. "It's funny, isn't it? We liked each other at the same time, but still missed our chance to do something about it."

Clark reached into the trunk for the machine, his heart pounding. What was she getting at?

"Maybe nothing happened then because we were supposed to end up back on the farm. Together."

Clark hit his head on the trunk and lost his grip on the espresso machine box, rubbing his already sore head with one hand. "Shit."

"Are you okay?"

"Yeah, just a complete klutz tonight." He went back into the trunk for the machine box, wishing she wouldn't stand so close. Her Christmas cookie scent pervaded the area around him, making his mouth water and he didn't even like them. Too much frosting.

It took a moment to get a grip on the box because his hands were slick with sweat but finally he hefted it into his arms.

"Thanks for the help."

"It's no problem."

"Why didn't you say anything yesterday when I told you I'd liked you?"

"I...didn't want you to get the wrong idea."

"Which is?"

Clark's brain sputtered like an old junker engine as he collected his thoughts. What was the wrong idea? He was attracted to Merry and the more he got to know her, the harder it was to come up with viable reasons why they wouldn't be good together.

God, someone save me from the ninth circle of hell I'm in.

The roar of an engine broke the awkward silence and they turned in unison as a monster of a motorcycle pulled into the Winters driveway. The rider turned off the bike and swung a leg over before removing his helmet.

Clark's older brother, Sam, grinned at him.

"Hey, bro, I'm home."

Son of a bitch, that is not what I meant.

CHAPTER 8

MERRY

MERRY SAT ON HER MOTHER'S couch across from her sister Sunday afternoon, looping her crotchet hook through the project in her lap. Holly hadn't stopped talking about Clark's brother showing up for the last fifteen minutes and Merry wished she'd find a new topic. Between her embarrassing scene with Clark before his brother's timely rescue and Woodsman cancelling their date last minute, she did not want to talk about men on an empty stomach.

"I don't care that he's ten years older, Sam Griffin is *foine!*" Holly crowed from her perch on the love seat, twisting a red curl around her finger.

Merry shook her head with a smirk. "Since when are you into bad boys?"

"Hey, just because he drives a motorcycle and has tattoos doesn't make him bad. He could be a cinnamon roll. Ooey, gooey, squishy and sweet. Loves puppies and kittens."

"I think I'm going to get a dog," Merry said, trying to

change the subject but her sister was determined to streamline the topic.

"If Sam were a dog, he'd be a Doberman...all sleek and protective."

Merry rolled her eyes. She couldn't say much about Sam, because their meeting had been relatively brief. Clark carried in the espresso machine and collected Jace within a matter of minutes, whisking his brother and son down the hill to the cottage. Merry should have been grateful for the interruption, as it saved her from further embarrassment.

The real shock had been Clark's admission he'd liked her too.

It was painfully obvious he didn't feel that way about her now, and she wanted to kick herself for the fumbling attempt at suggesting there might be something between them. On top of all of that, there was also the matter of Jace. She'd never dated anyone with a child before and it came with its own complications.

Wow, she was really getting ahead of herself. Clark hadn't shown her a shred of interest, so all of the runaway thoughts rushing through her head were unnecessary.

And then Woodsman...

Hey KnottyGirl25,

I have a family emergency and need to cancel. I am so sorry to do this last minute, but I hope you'll give me another chance to make it up to you.

Yours,

Woodsman27

A family emergency could be anything from *I got cold feet about meeting you because I'm married* to *I've lied to you about everything, even the snowmen I supposedly made.*

The tiny voice in her head chided her that he could be telling the truth, but her track record with men outweighed her benefit of the doubt.

"Whoa, where did you go off to?" Holly asked, waving her hands in the air.

Merry shook off the dreary thoughts with a shrug. "Nowhere, just thinking I want a cinnamon roll now."

"No argument here. Oh, speaking of things you want, it's still a no go with Declan. He is adamant he doesn't need to order a tree. I even offered to decorate it for him."

"Damn. I really wanted to end up with at least seventy trees and he was the crown jewel on making this year's festival a success."

Holly held up her hand and in a British accent, announced, "Fear not, dear sister, I have one last card to play before I fold."

"What the heck was that?"

"Practicing my stage voice. I convinced the Mistletoe Theater Troupe to donate a tree by agreeing to be their on-call understudy for the year."

"What the heck is that?"

"If they have a last-minute drop-out before performances start, I fill in."

"Why you?"

"I'm assuming it has to do with my following on Instagram and YouTube. And I am quite the actress."

"You are a daredevil elf on social media, not Julia Roberts."

"Just you wait, sister Merry, just you wait," Holly sang with a terrible Cockney accent.

"Stop butchering *My Fair Lady.*"

Holly sniffed. "I thought I nailed it. I also called in favors at The Pipe Doctors, Light Bright Electrical, and Games and Gadgets, that new nerd store on 5th."

"That puts us at seventy trees!" Merry dropped the needle-work project in her hands and tackle-hugged her sister, falling on top of her with a squeal. "How did you do it?"

"I own a holiday store where they can get ornaments at cost *and* I offered to decorate for them...with a nominal fee attached."

Merry hugged her again. "You are awesome." Merry stood up and after going back to her seat, added, "But I still want Declan."

"Oh, you can have Declan. He's a poop."

"Not like that. I still want you to work on him."

Holly cracked her knuckles with an evil smirk. "I'll work him over, free of charge. I'm sure there's a metal pipe lying around that store of his."

"You're terrible."

"Yes, but only because it's him." Holly whipped out her phone and tapped away at the screen. "By the way, whatcha making there?"

Merry held up the project she was working on with a grin. "A present for Tara. She got dumped by that mechanic and I thought the perfect voodoo doll would make her smile."

Holly burst out laughing at the pink plush penis with x's for eyes.

"A voodoo peen?"

"That's what Tara called it, but I think we can do better. I need to go to the craft store and get some stuffing for him and I was going to add a red button for a mouth. What do you think?"

"That Mom's going to have a fit when she sees it."

"I'm not letting her see it until I put the pins in. Besides, Mom isn't as sweet and innocent as she pretends to be."

Holly arched an eyebrow. "Do you know something I don't?"

"Nope. Just a feeling I have. Plus she keeps threatening to tell us where we were conceived."

Holly groaned. "Please don't bring that up. I am still recovering from the confirmation that our parents are sexual beings."

"Okay, new topic," Merry laughed.

"Have you checked her hoarder closet?" Holly asked.

"For what?"

"Stuffing for your peen."

"Why would Mom have stuffing in there?"

"What part of hoarder closet do you not understand?" Holly hopped up from the couch and disappeared down the hall. Merry set her project down and followed behind. Holly opened the hall closet and Merry marveled at the collection inside.

"Holy crap! I think Mom needs an intervention."

"Don't even think about it. This thing is a life saver when I get invited to a last-minute party or forget to shop for a birthday!"

"You own a store!"

"But then I have to eat the cost. This is free!"

Merry chuckled as she watched her sister rummage through the shelves of candles, cellophane-wrapped baskets, and other miscellaneous products her mother picked up at whatever dynamite sale she found.

"Aha!" Holly popped up with a hideous gnome throw pillow in her hands. "We can dissect this puppy and use the innards."

"Mom will be pissed."

"Are you kidding me? She'll never miss it. Plus who is she going to give this to? It's fugly."

"I agree but still—"

"Sis, she will not care. Gotta save money where you can."

"We still need to ask Mom."

Holly pulled out her phone with a huff and dialed, holding a finger up when Merry tried to speak. "Hey, Mom. Yeah, can I have that ugly gnome pillow from the closet? For an art project." Merry couldn't make out what her mother said, but Holly shot her a wink. "Thanks, Mom. Love you." Holly ended the call and slipped her phone into her back pocket. "She said yes."

"What exactly did she say?"

Holly mimicked her mother's voice: "I don't care, honey."

Merry grinned. "All right."

Holly walked into the kitchen and pulled a pair of scissors from the junk drawer. "Care to do the honors?"

"Nah, I want complete deniability in case she changes her mind."

"Fair enough." Holly cut through the seam and reached inside, removing a fistful of white fluff. "Jackpot."

Merry held open the bottom of her plush penis. "Give it to me, baby."

Holly sat down next to Merry and handed her the fluff, while Merry stuffed it inside. When it was filled up, she stitched the bottom closed and held it up for her sister's perusal. "What do you think?"

"Oh my God, he's cute." Holly took it from her, holding it up like a baby. "I want one. But I want mine bigger. Something to cuddle with. Oh, can you make it look like an elf?"

Merry burst out laughing, her mind already picturing it. "I can try."

Holly handed it back with a rueful laugh. "It will be the only D I've gotten in...ugh, too long."

"This is a weird conversation."

"Why?"

"Because you're my baby sister."

"I am almost twenty-four. Not a baby. Mom had Nick when she was younger than me."

"Do you think about that?" Merry asked.

"Didn't we just say a few minutes ago we wanted to avoid thinking about mom, sex, and procreation?"

"Not that, I mean...do you think about having kids right now?"

Holly blinked at her. "Well, not now. Eventually, I'll have at least two. After I'm done with my adventures."

Merry groaned. "You need to stop with that YouTube channel!"

"Hey, it isn't just YouTube now. I have over 200,000 followers on TikTok and another 70,000 on Instagram."

Merry rubbed her temples. When her sister started her channel as the Adventure Elf, they thought it was funny. Holly had always been into skydiving, rock climbing, and other extreme sports, but when she added the elf costume, her first video went viral. Her following blew up and she'd used her earnings from the channel to buy her shop, which was amazing, but they'd all been concerned about her doing something extreme for views.

"You're nuts and are going to end up in a body cast someday. They are going to find your body broken at the bottom of a mountain, in an elf suit."

"And they'll say I died doing what I love." Holly shot her a dirty look. "I'm insulted you don't watch my videos. You're my sister. Where is the love and support?"

"Hey, I follow you on social media! I just hate thinking of you putting yourself in dangerous situations for views."

"Listen, you might like playing it safe with boring corporate types and being a sweet little helper, but I am a risk-taker. I am not afraid to jump in and get my feet wet, so stop projecting your hang-ups on me."

"What hang-ups?"

"Oh, come on!" Holly groaned. "You are the queen of scaredy-pants everywhere!"

"I am not! I have had plenty of adventure."

"Being a serial monogamist isn't adventurous. You can't be alone."

"I've been alone for the last year!"

"I bet you anything you'll dive back into the dating pool and fall for the first jerk who smooth-talks his way into your panties. You call me nuts, but you're the crazy one! You date the same guy repeatedly and expect a different result."

"How can you say that? You never met most of my boyfriends."

"Yeah, but I know the O.G. boyfriend and he sucks balls. Based on that and the way your relationships end, I think you need to change it up a bit. Date someone not on your radar."

"Or I can remain happily single and not date anyone," Merry grumbled.

"Solid plan, one which I have been following for several years. I just thought there might have been a little spark between you and Clark the foreman."

Merry could feel the blood rush to her cheeks. "When did you see a spark?"

"Last night. When you two walked outside. Alone. In the dark under the glow of Christmas lights—"

"Nothing is going on with Clark!"

Holly sat forward, cupping her chin in her hand as she studied Merry intently. "Then why are you blushing?"

"Because I have pale skin and it's warm in here?"

"Uh-huh."

"You do know you're annoying, right?"

She sat back again with a smirk, spreading her arms over the back of the love seat and crossing her legs. "That is in the little sister job description."

"You have that down pat."

"Flatterer."

Merry left her stuff on the couch and got up. "I'm going to call Mom and see when they are getting back from the store so I can get lunch started."

"Oh good, I'm starving."

"Who said I'm making you any?"

"Rude."

Merry chuckled and opened the fridge, rummaging through the drawers, but nothing sounded good.

"Uh, Merry?" Holly said.

She closed the fridge with a grunt. "What?"

"Butch has your penis."

Merry's gaze flew to her parents' bloodhound and sure enough, clenched in his massive jowls was her voodoo peen.

"Butch! Drop it!"

She came around the kitchen island and Butch scrambled down the hall toward the laundry room, his paws tearing across the floor for traction. Merry slid to a stop in the doorway, but the dog was already through the doggy door and outside.

"Crap!"

Merry opened the outside door and took off after him. The last thing she wanted was for her dad or Clark or...oh, God, Jace, to find a stuffed penis floating around the property.

Butch was having a ruckus of a time and as she jumped at the dog and he slipped through her hands, she noticed her sister standing off to the side with her phone up.

"You'd better not be recording me!"

"I would never," she said insincerely.

Merry didn't believe her for a second but one problem at a time.

She raced after Butch, wincing as her bare feet connected with something pokey but she kept going. Almost. So close.

Merry caught hold of the head of the penis and slowed to a stop. She bent down eye level with the hound and in a deep voice growled, "Drop it."

Butch opened his mouth and stepped back, his long muscular tail sawing through the air excitedly.

"No, I'm not throwing this for you." She grimaced as wetness coated her palm from the sopping yarn. "Freaking drool monster. You're pretty spry for an old hound, you know that?"

Merry spun back towards the house and found not just her sister, but Clark standing at her side, watching something on her phone.

Oh please God no…

"Holly! What are you showing him?"

Clark looked up from her sister's screen, an amused expression on his face.

"He only caught the tail end of the show, so I thought he'd like to see it from the beginning."

Merry closed her eyes, imagining all the ways she could kill her sister and get away with it, but her parents were fond of the red-headed brat.

Damn it.

"I think I've seen enough," Clark said, obviously taking pity on her discomfort. She was grateful for it.

"Where's your brother and Jace?"

"At the house. I needed some air and heard the commotion, so thought I'd come see what was going on."

"Just me chasing a dog around, trying to retrieve my…" Merry squeezed the object in her hand so he couldn't see what it was. "Project."

Holly leaned over and used a stage whisper. "It's a voodoo doll of her friend's ex's penis."

As much as she loved her folks, Holly had to die.

CHAPTER 9

CLARK

CLARK COVERED HIS MOUTH WITH his hand, hiding his smile. He'd come around the side of the house to see Merry chasing the dog and at first he'd thought they'd been playing. Then he'd noticed her bare feet and the desperate look on her face.

Plus Holly standing there recording the whole exchange was something a younger sibling would do only if it was blackmail gold.

Merry looked ready to fly through the air and tackle her sister. Pine needles and leaves stuck out of the golden strands of her messy bun and streaks of dirt lined her cheeks and forehead.

She was an adorable mess.

Merry took a step toward Holly, her fists clenching and unclenching.

"Careful, Mer. There's a witness," Holly cheerfully sang.

Merry cast him a disgruntled look. "You gonna testify against me if I murder her?"

"Nah, just don't get any blood on my trees."

Merry's lips twitched, obviously fighting a smile, and his pulse kicked up a notch. His resolve to stay away from her was wavering, especially with their unfinished conversation taking up permanent residence in his head. He was almost positive she was going to ask him to get to know each other better, and it seemed like all of his very good reasons for not getting involved with her had twisted into arguments on why they'd be an excellent match.

Which was insane in itself, since he'd taken the walk away from his place to type out another message to KnottyGirl25. He had been ready to tap send when he'd seen the shenanigans in the side yard and stopped to check it out. The sisters were bickering again and he took the moment to read through his message.

> KnottyGirl25,
>
> I know you're probably imagining the worst of me, but I swear I had an unexpected visit from my brother and I couldn't leave him. I'd been anxious and excited about our date all day. I was prepared with prewritten jokes in case I got nervous. Please know I was just as disappointed about not meeting you as I hope you were about not seeing me.
>
> Can we try again?
>
> Woodsman27

He pressed send before he lost his nerve and slipped the phone into his pocket. Two messages in less than a twenty-four-hour period may seem desperate, but he could only imagine what she was thinking with him cancelling on her last-minute. He couldn't leave last night, not until he knew why his brother was there.

They'd had plans for him to come the week of Christmas, so showing up almost six weeks early threw Clark into a tailspin of worry. Even though Sam was older, Clark often felt like the doting parent to a rebellious teen instead of the younger of the two.

Although they'd spent a few hours talking and catching up, his brother kept assuring him there was nothing wrong. That it didn't make sense to live a state away from his only family anymore and would Clark mind if he crashed with them until Sam found a place?

Clark said yes, but deep down, he knew there was more to it, but Sam wouldn't tell him the truth until he was ready.

"Where's your brother?" Holly broke in.

"He's watching a cartoon with Jace."

Butch let out a howl and ran for the front of the house.

"I think Mom and Dad are back, so I'm going to see if they need help." Holly took off at a jog, with Merry glaring at her back.

Clark grinned. "Not gonna go after her? Get some revenge?"

"I'll wait until she least suspects it and then pow!" She opened her hands to mimic an explosion and Clark watched as the ball of pink in her hand elongated into a roughly seven-inch penis.

Balls and all.

"I thought she was joking."

Merry's face flushed and she clutched the stuffed shaft to her chest. "It isn't what you think."

"It's not?"

"I-I—" Merry visibly swallowed before blurting, "My friend

was dating this jerk who said some unkind things, and she jokingly suggested I make a voodoo peen. And I thought, hey, that would be funny and she needed a laugh, so I gave it a try. I finished it, left it alone on the couch for a few minutes and then, boom, Butch was running off with it, and the last thing I need is my parents to find a plush penis chilling in the yard."

She was talking a mile a minute and when she paused for breath, he asked, "Did it work?"

"Did what work?"

"Did she laugh?"

"I haven't shown her yet. I wanted to stick the pins in it before I sent her a picture. They're two inches long with little red hearts at the end."

Clark laughed. "Remind me not to piss you off."

"As long as you don't chip at my friend's self-esteem, you won't get one of these."

He sobered. "Damn, sounds like she dodged a bullet."

"She did, but in the moment, we don't think of it that way. We wonder what we did to deserve it."

Clark's stomach clenched as a shadow passed over Merry's face and he reached out instinctively, cupping her chin in his hand. He stepped closer, staring into her shimmering depths of gold and green, and murmured, "I'm sorry if I was being insensitive. I only meant that men who treat women that way don't deserve tears. They need a swift kick in the ass."

They don't deserve you, he thought.

Merry briefly leaned into his touch, her lips tilting in a small smile. "Or testicles."

"I'd say both." His hand shifted, tracing along her jaw. "Any man you're with should worship you, not make you cry."

Merry's eyes widened, her lips parting slightly. "I don't need to be worshipped. I only ask for honesty and respect. Love."

The way she said that single word, with such reverence and longing, settled like a heavy stone in his chest. He knew what love for his child and his brother felt like, but to fall in love? To find someone who could be his partner, his person? He wasn't sure he was capable. He'd wanted to love Patrice simply for being the mother of his son, but in truth, once the initial lust wore off, she'd exhausted him and he'd been relieved not to have to cater to her tailspin of emotions. Love had never factored into their relationship.

Love meant letting his guard down, allowing someone to really know all of his insecurities and fears. The power to break him when they decided it was over. The benefits of romantic love didn't seem worth the cost.

With KnottyGirl25, maybe they could build something comforting based on friendship and common goals.

Merry was a romantic soul and anything less than a love like her parents had wouldn't satisfy her. Clark didn't think he was capable of it.

After a moment's pause, he stepped away and held up his phone. "I'd better get back to Jace and Sam. You'll have to let me know how it goes with the..." Clark waved his hand toward the object she held.

The intensity of the moment eased as she held it up, amusement lighting up her eyes to a brilliant shade of amber. "Are you having trouble saying penis, Clark?"

"No, I am not having trouble saying penis."

"Uh-huh. I think you are."

His eyes narrowed. "Are you challenging me? 'Cause there is a long list of anatomy names only guys know."

"Oh yeah? Prove it."

Victoria called out Merry's name and he shrugged. "Maybe another time."

"Perfect save." She shot him a saucy grin as she took a step backwards toward the house. "I better get inside before she starts counting to three. You have a good rest of your day—ouch!"

Clark took two steps forward when she jerked her left foot up off the ground, slipping a hand under her elbow to steady her. "Hey, you okay?"

Her heart-shaped face pinched with pain as she twisted her leg forward, trying to see the bottom of her foot. "I stepped on something sharp."

"Hang on. I'll take a look. Lift your foot this way and a little higher for me."

Merry swung her foot up behind her so the sole faced the sky. He saw the blood already smeared from the ball of her foot to the heel. A deep cut ran horizontally across the arch and he grimaced.

"You got a nasty slice across the bottom of your foot that looks deep. I'm going to pick you up, all right? Probably faster than you hopping along beside me."

"I can hobble, really."

"I'm sure you can, but I don't want you to lose your balance and make the gash worse." Clark bent over and lifted her into his arms before she could protest further. She wrapped her arms around his neck, a rush of air escaping her full lips.

"Hang on tight to me and the little guy. Don't want to lose him again."

Merry buried her face in his chest with a snort of laughter and Clark's grip tightened on her. He strode around to the front of the house and up the steps, kicking the door gently with his boot. Holly opened the door, stepping back with a startled expression.

"Merry." Victoria rushed around the kitchen island, worry etched in the fine lines of her face. "What happened?"

Merry lifted her head, a sheen of tears in her eyes. His heart stuttered at the pain etched in her pale features. "I cut the bottom of my foot on something in the yard. Clark insisted on helping me inside."

Clark hated the wobble in her voice and held her tighter as Victoria launched into mom mode, motioning him to follow her. "Bring her to the couch and I'll take a look."

Clark carried her over and set her gently onto the cushions. Victoria lifted Merry's foot, inspecting it with a cluck of her tongue.

"Why in the heck would you go running around outside with no shoes on?" Victoria squinted, then barked. "Holly. Grab my glasses from my purse, and the first aid kit. I've gotta clean this up. You might need stitches. Clark, can you hand me a towel from the corner cupboard?"

Clark did as she asked and when she wiped at the blood on Merry's foot, Merry winced and reached for Clark's hand, still clutching her little johnson against her chest. He kept waiting for Victoria to ask about it, but she was laser-focused on her daughter's injury.

"Oh, baby, I'm sorry. You sure did a number on this. I'm going to send your dad out to look and see what in the heck you cut yourself on. I don't want anyone else getting hurt."

Merry hissed when her mother probed at her wound, and tightened her grasp on Clark's hand until his bones creaked.

"Easy, Tiger, you're going to break my writing hand, and your dad likes my reports legible."

"Sorry," she said, easing her hold. "I'm not good with pain."

When she tried to release him, he held tight. "I'm only teasing, Merry. You kung fu grip me as hard as you need."

Holly came back in with the kit and handed her mom her glasses. She slid them up over her nose and stuck her head down a few inches from Merry's foot.

"I was right. We're going to need to take you to get a few stitches."

Merry groaned, her face going sheet-white. "Really?"

"I'm afraid so. I'm sorry, honey. I know you hate needles, but they're probably going to need to give you antibiotics. You don't want to get an infection."

Merry must have realized she was still holding his hand because she glanced up at Clark, extracting her palm from his. "Sorry for crushing your fingers. I appreciate the ride, though."

"It's not a problem. Sorry about the stitches. Just think about your favorite show and play it in your head when they poke you." He felt awkward and stiff standing there with the three Winters women watching him. "That's what I tell Jace to do."

Merry gave him a small smile. "I'll remember that."

Now I'm giving her advice for my seven-year-old? What is wrong with me?

"I better get out of your hair. Do you need me to help you to the car?"

"Chris will be out in a minute. Thank you, Clark."

Clark nodded at Victoria and Holly. Before he turned away, he shot Merry a reassuring smile. "I'll see you around."

"Bye."

He headed for the door, feeling like an ass for hanging around like a concerned boyfriend. His arms still hummed from the warmth and weight of her there and he wished he could just turn off these conflicting emotions.

Before he closed the front door behind him, he heard Victoria sputter, "Merry Elizabeth Winters, is that a penis?"

Clark laughed the whole walk home. There was never a dull moment with the Winters family. He liked all of them, although Nick and Noel he didn't know as well, but they seemed nice. Nick invited Clark to the bar with him once, but it was when he'd first moved to town and he hadn't found a reliable babysitter yet. He'd thought about inviting Nick to get a beer now that he'd settled in, but Clark thought it would be weird to cold-call him.

Why did making new friends seem like dating?

When he stepped through the door, Sam and Jace were sitting on the couch, credits rolling on the show they'd just finished. His brother's sun-kissed brown hair was still mussed from sleep.

"Hey, what took you so long?" Sam asked.

Clark shrugged out of his jacket and hung it up. "Merry hurt herself and I helped her inside the house."

"Ahhh. The blond from last night? I hadn't seen her since she was a kid. She grew up nice."

Clark's jaw clenched at the way his brother drew out the *I* in *nice*.

"She's not available."

Sam snapped his fingers. "The sexy ones are always taken."

"What's sexy?" Jace piped in.

"Don't worry about it," Clark said, waving his hand. "Why don't you go grab us some fruit snacks and I'll make us lunch."

"Yes!" Jace jumped up from the couch and raced into the kitchen.

When he was out of earshot, Clark shot his older brother a dark look. "You gotta watch what you say around him. He hears everything."

"Sorry, wasn't trying to expand his vocabulary. Just used to adult talk."

"Just be aware, he knows all the swear words and if he hears it, he'll charge you for them. The price for each word is on the side of the swear jar."

Sam picked up the jar on the side table, reading the chalkboard label. "A dollar for an f-bomb? Seems a little steep."

Jace came back, hollering, "Catch, Uncle Sam!"

He tossed the fruit snack pouch through the air and Sam dived dramatically, cradling the package in two hands and falling to the floor.

"Touchdown!"

Clark shook his head as his son handed Clark a blue packet, running for Sam and high-fiving him.

"Hey, Dad? Uncle Sam said he'd take me for a ride on his motorcycle if it's all right with you. Can I go?"

Clark's smile dissolved and he shot his brother a narrow look.

"Not today, buddy. Why don't you go listen to an audio book while I talk to Uncle Sam?"

"Okay." Jace worried his bottom lip, then turned to Sam. "I'll see you, Uncle Sam."

"All right, my dude. Have fun." Sam wrapped Jace up in a bear hug. "What audiobook you listening to?"

"A Goosebumps book."

"Awesome. I love scary movies. I'll have to introduce you to some of my favorites—" Sam paused when Clark cleared his throat and added, "when you're a little older."

"We can stream a Goosebumps movie tonight if you want," Jace offered.

"I'm down."

Jace walked past Clark, paused and ran back to hug him. "Don't be mad at Uncle Sam, Dad. Please?"

Clark ran his hand over his son's head. "I'm not, buddy. I promise."

Jace kissed his leg and took off down the hallway. Clark didn't say anything until he heard the door close.

Clark crossed his arms over his chest and scowled at his brother.

"I thought you weren't mad."

"I'm irritated."

"Ah, subtle difference."

"He's seven. Too young to be on the back of that bike of yours."

Sam stood up with his hands in the air. "I don't mean to overstep, but you were about his age when I took you for a ride on it."

"That's because we had parents who didn't give a shit if we crashed and burned."

"Damn, you don't trust me with my nephew?"

Lines formed around Sam's mouth, the hurt on his face deepening his sun-weathered skin. Clark crossed to his brother and gripped the taller man's shoulders. "I trust you. But I've seen the way other drivers are on the roads out here. They don't look. All it takes is one of those idiots to cross the line on a curve. I never want to get that call about Jace or you."

Sam's crestfallen expression dissolved into a wide grin and he pulled Clark into a hard, back-slapping hug. "I appreciate you caring, brother. You're the only one who does."

The edge of sadness in that statement got Clark thinking about Sam's life. Thirty-five, never married. Nobody to come home to. Clark knew he'd been wanting to start his own tattoo parlor, but other than that, he lived a solitary existence.

"I'm glad you're here, Sam."

Sam pulled away, all traces of melancholy gone. "So, you're still okay with me crashing here?"

"You can stay here as long as you want, brother. My home will always be your home."

"Thanks."

Clark headed into the kitchen. "I'm going to make lunch. You want in?"

"I never turn down food." Sam sat at the kitchen table and leaned back in the chair, stretching his legs out. "So, back to the girl...how big's her boyfriend? Could I take him?"

"Merry?" Sam nodded. "She doesn't have a boyfriend. At least, I don't think she does."

"But you said she was unavailable."

"She's not really your type, is she?"

"That's never stopped me."

Clark snorted. "I believe it, but she'd also my boss's daughter. I don't need you coming in here, screwing your way through all the local women until you piss everyone off and there's a line of angry husbands and fathers ready to run me out of town."

"This is not the 1950s. If a woman wants to roll around in the sheets with me, who am I to tell her no."

"Just make sure none of those women have the last name Winters. And that you don't bring any of them back to my guest sheets."

"I wouldn't bring a one-night stand back with a kid here. You think I'm a complete asshole?"

Clark pulled the sandwich fixings out of the fridge with a sigh. "No, I don't. I just want to be clear."

"You're wound awfully tight. I think you need to get laid more than I do."

Clark didn't respond, preferring not to discuss the topic when his son could come walking out anytime. "You still haven't told me the real reason you're back here. Not that I don't want you here, but I know it's more than you missing us."

"It's not even worth talking about. I'm just happy to be back in the fold. Maybe with me around we can get you out and get a life."

"I have a life."

"You have a purpose, but you aren't living. Look at me. A wandering artist with dozens of broken hearts trailing behind him. A lonely soul, just searching for the one woman to complete him—"

"You should have been an actor. You've got the whole melodramatic angle down," Clark cut in.

Sam shrugged, a sheepish grin on his lips. "Maybe. But seriously. How about next weekend we find a sitter for Jace and hit the bar. A couple beers, maybe meet some women. What do you say? Wanna be my wingman?"

It had been a long time since Clark had been out simply to have fun. Mingle with other adults.

And if KnottyGirl25 ever messaged him back, he could plan their meet up for the same night. Once his brother found a woman to go home with, he'd ditch Clark without a backwards glance.

"Just call me Goose, Maverick."

CHAPTER 10

MERRY

MERRY SAT ON ONE SIDE of the booth in Lord of the Fries Diner, listening to Ryan Welsh bitch about vendors for the festival. The punny restaurant had been a staple in the town since the eighties, the walls decorated in artwork related to the classic book *Lord of the Flies*. The menu had a cartoon french fry on the front wearing a top hat, tail coat, and a monocle over his left eye. As cheesy as the décor was, the food was outstanding.

It was a little after ten in the morning on Wednesday and she'd taken the day off to catch up with a friend from college who was passing through. Unfortunately, the friend had called from her hotel room in Boise with a horrible case of food poisoning and canceled. Since the day was already hers, Merry had popped a couple of aspirin to dull the pain of her stitches and decided to do a little Christmas preparation shopping. All that had been delayed when she'd agreed to meet Ryan to talk about his concerns, but the conversation was putting a damper on her day.

That was unfair. She liked Ryan. He was the only boyfriend she didn't regret, because he hadn't been awful. He'd been very sweet, actually. They'd become friends freshman year of high school after meeting in Home Economics class and had dated a couple of months, until he'd come out as gay. They'd remained friends up until they graduated and went off to college. It surprised Merry he'd come back to Mistletoe as he'd always complained about the cold, but like hers, his family was tight-knit and amazing.

As part of the festival committee, he'd offered to handle vendors, but he'd called her three times since Sunday and when he'd found out she wasn't working today, asked her to meet him here to chat. Only it had turned into more of a rant than a friendly conversation.

"Mrs. Carlson doesn't want her craft booth next to the bookstore's booth, because they display *nasty* books." He said the last with a high-pitch falsetto, followed by a scoff. "I want to tell her she doesn't have to look if she's offended by shirtless men, but dear God, she could probably learn a thing or two from those books. Like some relaxation techniques because the woman is wound tighter than a top and she's about to blow."

Merry picked up her coffee, cradling it between her fingers as she took in Ryan's perfectly sculpted brows shooting up and down with every word. When Ryan got excited, every facial feature got into the action, including his vibrant blue eyes, and she usually loved watching him talk.

Today, though, she just wanted to eat, shop, and not think about her lengthy to-do list and the emotional whirlpool that had become her brain. Not referee adults with ridiculous demands.

"So move her to another spot. What's the issue?"

"The issue is I've organized the booths according to their

category. Books, crafts, and other goods are in one section. Food and beverage in another. And half the vendors have a beef with someone else. I swear, I never knew how dramatic people could be over the littlest thing, like who bought the last flat of canning jars! This isn't *Little House on the Freaking Prairie*! If you want a jar of jam, buy it! You don't have to boil it yourself, Nellie."

Merry bit back a laugh. It wouldn't be productive to tease Ryan that all of the dramatic canning enthusiasts could be matching his energy. His exuberance was one of the reasons she'd connected with Ryan in the first place, they were both dramatic individuals, but right now Ryan had taken it to an SNL level. Maybe he needed to switch to decaf.

"Why don't you email me your layout and a list of the people, marking who they don't get along with. A second set of eyes on it couldn't hurt. And if Mrs. Carlson calls again, give her my number and I'll handle her."

Ryan reached across the table and took her hand in both of his. "Thank you, Merry. I did the vendors last year and it wasn't this bad, but we have fifteen more this year. It's like squishing a bunch of fighting cats into one carrier! I swear, someone put out an advertisement for crazy at a Christmas charity function and everyone responded."

Merry didn't admit that she'd been the one to offer a discounted booth rate to anyone who bought a tree to auction off as well. She'd been shocked by the number of people who'd jumped at the chance to do both, and several businesses had gone halvesies on either a booth or a tree. However they wanted to do it was fine with Merry, as long as it meant more money raised.

"It's no problem. Sometimes people stress out around the holidays and aren't their best selves. We got this."

Ryan released her hand and stacked his napkin on top of his half-eaten Denver Omelet. "I know, it was just a day," he said, followed by a heavy sigh. "Thanks for putting up with me."

"Thank you for being here. I appreciate the extra assistance with this event. Dana didn't tell me about the committee and if you hadn't reached out, I would have been scrambling to get all of it done."

"No offense, but Dana was a mess last year. I don't know how many times I had to tell that woman to breathe and hydrate and I swear there was something more than water in that travel cup she was carrying around."

"That wouldn't surprise me. I'm two weeks into planning this thing, and I'm tempted to walk around with a flask in my purse."

"If you're drinking the good stuff, you'd better share." Ryan checked his smart watch with a click of his tongue. "I gotta get to work, but this should cover my meal…" He trailed off as he pulled his wallet out.

"Don't worry about it. You can buy next time."

Ryan snapped his wallet closed with a grin. "I'm good with that. I'll call you later."

"Please let it be a social call and not more drama," she pleaded playfully.

"Yes, we will make plans for food and margaritas and I will do my best to wrangle the K squad into submission."

"The K squad?"

"The Kyles and Karens of this town. Your support has empowered me and the next time an agent of petty comes at me in a fit of temper, I will level them."

"Can you do it with kindness though? Because we still want their donations."

"Always, but if they push me—"

"Send them to me," she reiterated.

He climbed out of the booth with a nod. "I will if it gets too hairy. Thanks for letting me vent. Enjoy your free day."

"I will, thanks."

Ryan leaned over and gave her a hug before ducking out the front door. Once he walked passed the window, Merry sat back against the bench seat of the booth, sipping on her coffee and enjoying the quiet.

Despite all the hiccups and drama, she was pleasantly surprised with the way people had stepped up this year and she couldn't wait to see all the beautiful trees. At least, she hoped they were all tastefully decorated. The plumbers mentioned something about making a tree stand out of a toilet and she couldn't help thinking *ick*, even though they'd assured her it was brand new.

She finished off her coffee and before she put the phone in her purse, Merry tapped on the MeetMe app. After reading Woodsman27's second message on Sunday, she'd responded, a nagging idea marinating in the back of her mind.

What if the Woodsman was Clark?

She didn't know for sure, and it could be wishful thinking, but she really wanted it to be. Yes, he'd been adamant about not dating, but what if this had been a fluke, like the Woodsman said? He wasn't planning to meet anyone, but once they started talking, he changed his mind?

Not only that, but Clark and the Woodsman both had their brother unexpectedly visit and with the exception of Clark, the Woodsman was the only other man who'd even piqued her interest. There was no way that was a coincidence.

Merry clicked on the newest message from him, imagining Clark's voice in her head.

> Hey KnottyGirl,
>
> Do you ever walk outside and just breathe in the cold? There is something about that crisp air that makes me think of all the winter activities that are about to start. Snow-mobiling, ice skating, sledding, snowball fights...I know I've told you I love outdoor activities, but I am also partial to the cold versus the three months out of the year Idaho warms up.
>
> If you're interested, I've been setting aside a few rounds for more snowmen. I know you said you wanted some and when they're finished, they are yours.
>
> Will you meet me this Saturday at Brews and Chews? Same time?
>
> I hope you say yes.
>
> Yours,
>
> Woodsman

Merry smiled at her screen, her heart jumping into her throat. Should she respond and just ask if he really was Clark? But what if she was wrong and she ruined whatever was going on between Woodsman and her?

No, she could wait until Saturday.

Woodsman27,

I would love the snowmen! And I'll totally pay for them. Name your price! Within reason. ;) I don't mind outdoor activities, but when I get too cold, I want to go inside and curl up in front of the fire and watch a movie. I'm kind of a homebody, I guess.

And yes, I would love to try again. I'm taking the day off from work and will be running a few errands, but I will talk to you when I get home.

Xo,

KnottyGirl25

She hit send and dropped her phone into her purse. Despite the setback with her friend and Ryan's meltdown, Merry was determined to enjoy her day.

Once she paid her check, Merry limped out of the diner and headed down the street toward her sister's shop. Thankfully she'd decided to wear her snow boots, and between the bandage over her stitches and the extra padding inside, her foot didn't ache as much. She didn't want to drive, as parking in the heart of town was limited and besides, it wasn't that far. She wanted to get one of those cute light projectors in lieu of Christmas lights and knew Holly had them last year. Hopefully she had a few hiding in the back to get put out after Thanksgiving.

"Get back here, you stupid son of a bitch!" someone shouted behind her, and she turned in time to see a dirty ball of fluff run right for her legs. Merry dropped to her knees, capturing the fleeing dog in her arms with an *oooofff.*

Brianna Vincent jogged down the street in her animal print scrubs, a scowling elderly man marching several feet behind her.

"Nice catch," Brianna said, kneeling down in front of her. Brianna had worked at Mistletoe Animal Hospital for at least ten years and Merry remembered all the times Brianna snuck Butch treats when she'd taken him in for his annual.

"Thanks, but I'm not sure what I have here."

"That's what you call a Dysapeer." Brianna patted the puppy's side with a laugh. "Great Pyrenees puppy Mr. Olson bought. Only twelve weeks and already a runner."

Merry's arms ached from holding the struggling dog. "Did you say twelve weeks? Geez, he'll be a monster."

"It's a she, which is just another thing that idiot of a breeder screwed up." The raspy voice belonged to the old man, who hovered over them like a menacing cloud. The puppy in Merry's arms trembled at the sound of his harsh tone and every muscle in Merry's body stiffened.

"Will you grab that little bitch for me so I can go about my day?" he snapped, thrusting a red slip leash at Brianna. "I've wasted enough time on this worthless thing. If I'm going to get to Twin Falls today, I need to leave now."

Merry let Brianna lasso the leash over the puppy's head and climbed to her feet, wincing when the skin on the bottom of her feet pulled. The man's deep weathered creases told the story of someone who'd spent many years outdoors and enjoyed keeping his expression in a permascowl. He jerked the rope away from Brianna rudely and it was on the tip of Merry's tongue to call him out. If his dog didn't like him, that said a lot about a person and Merry wanted to pick the poor thing up and run as far and as fast as she could.

As if sensing an ally, the pup looked up at her with soulful dark eyes surrounded by thick white lashes, eyes that begged her: *Don't let him take me.*

"Why are you going to Twin Falls?" Merry asked, keeping her tone light.

"To get rid of her. I can't get the damn breeder to call me back and I have no use for a dog who doesn't listen and pisses all over the place."

"It's a puppy," Merry said coldly.

"It's a lemon, is what it is!"

Brianna's gaze shifted between Merry and Mr. Olson, and spoke up cheerfully, "Pyrs are really great dogs with proper training—"

"Male ones! I've had Pyrs my whole life and I'm telling you, the bitches aren't worth a damn. I told that breeder I wanted a boy or nothing and she shipped me this. Female dogs are for breeding and nothing else."

The puppy did a few acrobatics, trying to escape from the rope leash by biting it. Without warning, Mr. Olson kicked her, and the young dog released a furious series of yelps.

Merry and Brianna gasped.

"Shut up, damn you," he snarled, reeling back to kick her again.

"Hey!" Merry shouted, putting herself between him and the dog. "What the hell is the matter with you? You don't kick animals!"

The man was only a few inches taller and stood nearly eye to eye. "It's none of your business what I do with her, she's my dog."

Merry snatched the leash from him and backed away, keeping the puppy behind her. "Not anymore she's not!"

"You can't go around stealing people's property! I'm going to call the police."

"Go ahead. Brianna and I watched you abuse this baby and I'm sure at least one of the camera phones pointed at you right now caught most of it on video."

Mr. Olson peered into the windows of the diner and down the street, where several people stood around with their cell phones up, watching. His rough hands curled into fists.

"That dog cost me six hundred dollars!"

Brianna, who had been letting Merry take the lead, stepped up. "Pretty sure first offense animal cruelty charges will cost you five thousand, but it goes up from there if you've got priors."

Mr. Olson stabbed a boney finger at Brianna. "I'm going to speak to your boss."

With one last sneer, he marched back toward the veterinary hospital and Merry knelt down to examine the puppy. Her pink tongue darted out to lick Merry's hands as she ran them over the matted fur.

"God, she stinks."

"Not surprising. None of his animals are well cared for. He tried to bring her in to surrender her, but when we told him there was a surrender fee, he changed his mind."

Merry cupped the puppy's cheeks, staring into her eyes. "How could he not want this sweetness?"

"A long list of stupid reasons. He was trying to put her in the car when she took off. Guess she didn't want to go back with him."

"I wouldn't either."

"I better get over there and defend myself. And congratulations on your first rescue."

Merry stopped petting the dog long enough to realize what she'd done. "I have a dog."

"Yeah, you do. Have you ever owned a Pyr before?"

Merry shook her head and Brianna grinned. "Give me ten minutes to square things away at the hospital and come see us. We'll get you prepared as best we can."

Brianna walked away, leaving Merry alone with the panting puppy. Everything happened so fast, and her protective instincts kicked in the moment she'd felt the dog's reaction.

Merry sat down on the sidewalk, pulling the puppy onto her lap as she kept her eye out in front of the veterinary hospital. Several moments later, Mr. Olson tore out of the hospital and climbed into his old Ford pickup, burning rubber down the street toward Merry. He hollered several colorful names as he passed, black smoke billowing out of his tail pipe behind him, and Merry held her breath until the smell dissipated.

When she climbed to her feet with the puppy in her arms, she kissed the side of her head, ignoring the noxious smell in her fur. "The good news is you never have to see that evil man again. The bad news is you're going to need a bath before you come into my house. If you're okay with those terms, give me a sign."

An enthusiastic tongue slurped across her nose and mouth.

"I'm gonna go out on a limb and say that's an affirmative." Merry headed down the street with the dog and Brianna met her at the door of the hospital, holding it open for her. Dr. Turner stood behind the counter, her peppery brown hair cut in a short faux hawk.

"I hear you're the reason Mr. Olson read me the riot act?"

"I apologize for that, but I had to. That man is awful."

"Yes, he's something else." Dr. Turner came around and scratched the puppy on her head. "Brianna says you want to keep her?"

"Yeah, I mean…she licked me, so she's mine, right?"

Dr. Turner laughed. "All right. I'll have her records transferred to you. According to her records, she's up to date on distemper, but she'll need her rabies next month and both boosters in a year. She could also use another deworming."

"I'm good with whatever she needs, but I was wondering if you could clean her up for me while I run a few errands?" Merry said with a sheepish smile. "She's pretty rank."

"We'll make the time for you. Between you and me, I don't think this little girl would have lived to see tomorrow if you hadn't stepped in. I've called with concerns about the animals on the Olson ranch multiple times. I would have waived the surrender fee if I'd been up front when he came in." Dr. Turner took the puppy from Merry. "But this lucky girl had an angel watching out for her today."

Merry's eyes stung with tears and she ran her hand over the puppy's ear. "Thank you. I've been talking about getting a dog for a while. I'm glad I was at the right place at the right time."

"Well, you got quite the dog here. You ever owned a guardian breed before?"

"No, this is my first."

Dr. Turner winked. "Just remember, even when we're at our wits end, God never gives us more than we can handle."

Chapter 11

CLARK

"SON OF A BITCH!" CLARK yelled, shaking out his hand and dropping the woodburning tool onto his workbench. The snowman's face smirked at him crookedly, mocking his clumsiness. Maybe he should have bought some of those heat resistant gloves KnottyGirl25 suggested. Save himself a few scars.

Clark grabbed the burn relief cream off the second shelf to his right, gently applying it over the red skin. He'd only been using the engraver a few months and was still perfecting his technique, but he loved the finished projects. Once he'd covered the burn with a large bandage he picked up the tool and started again, cleaning up the line of the snowman's smile. He wanted them ready by the weekend, before his date.

Three more days and he'd be sitting across from the faceless woman who had been at the forefront of his mind for nearly two weeks. At least in theory, unless something else cropped up.

Everything should be in place, though. He'd booked Erica to hang with Jace from eight to eleven, and Sam had accepted a job at

MistleInk Tattoo Parlor and started this week, so they would both be occupied. Besides the employee pictures for the 75th anniversary of the farm this weekend, he didn't have anything else going on that could interfere.

Suddenly his shop door was thrown open and Jace raced inside, shouting, "Dad! Merry got a dog!"

Clark put the tool aside and turned, but his son was already running out of the shop, presumably to greet the new addition. Jace knew not to pet strange dogs without asking, but he worried enough to hurry along behind his son.

He came around the front of the house to find his brother and son talking to Merry, who held the end of a bright red leash. The dog in question looked like a cotton ball on a rope, wiggling with excitement as it strained to get close to them.

Merry noticed him coming and waved, her face split in that warm, welcoming smile he'd grown accustomed to seeing. Her hair always seemed to be pulled back, showing off her round cheeks and kissable mouth.

Clark pulled up short at the thought. When the hell did he start thinking of Merry's lips that way?

"Hey, Clark."

"Hi. Who is this?"

"I'm not sure yet. We just met today, so we are still getting to know each other."

"Can I pet her?" Jace asked.

"Of course you can! She's three months old, so she's just a puppy."

"Holy shit," Sam said. "She's going to be a big dog."

"You owe fifty cents to the swear jar, Uncle Sam." Jace rubbed a palm over the dog's white, fluffy head. "She's soft."

Merry's face softened, her gaze focused on Jace and the dog. His heart squeezed in response.

"Yeah, she got bathed at the vet. She was pretty stinky."

"Where did she come from?" Jace asked.

"A very bad man didn't want her anymore, so I took her."

"You're such a sweet woman, Merry. Beautiful. Loves kids and puppies. Damn near perfect, don't you think, Clark?"

"Thirty cents, Uncle Sam."

"Shhh, kid, I'm asking your dad a question." Sam crossed his arms over his chest. "Well?"

Merry laughed, brushing a hand against her pink cheeks. "I'm not even close to perfect. If I named off all my flaws, you'd be singing a different tune."

"Everyone has flaws," Sam said. "Only a near-perfect woman would acknowledge hers."

She wrinkled her nose. "I'm not falling for your smooth-talking charm, Sam Griffin."

A flash of jealousy wrenched through Clark's stomach when his brother took Merry's hand and kissed her palm. "Maybe not now, but give me time."

"I think Merry's a wonderful woman," Clark blurted, shooting his brother a pointed look, silently reminding him to stay away.

"Brrr, I think the weather is about to turn. I've got to head to work." Sam dropped Merry's hand with a wink. "Always a pleasure, Merry. And Jace, my dude, I'll pay for my swearing when I get home." He straddled his motorcycle, giving them a little wave. "Have fun, kiddos."

"Get a helmet on!" Clark hollered.

Sam held a hand up to his ear. "Sorry, can't hear you."

"Yes, you can!"

Sam roared away, leaving Clark and Merry standing across from each other, Jace and the puppy playing at their feet.

"Well, that was abrupt." Merry laughed.

"That's Sam. Tact and social grace are not his strong suits. Oh and common sense, another thing he lacks."

"He's a lot like my sister, Holly. She has this YouTube channel where she does all of these high-risk activities and it terrifies me."

"Except my brother is in his mid-thirties and still acts like a rebellious teenager."

"What's rebellious mean?" Jace asked without looking up.

"It means he likes to break the rules and doesn't care about consequences."

"You love him very much, huh?"

"I do. Besides my son, he's the only other family I have."

Merry reached out and squeezed his arm. "Family is more than the people you're related to. If you looked around, I'm sure you'd find a lot of people care about you."

Clark covered her hand with his. "Thanks, Merry."

She dropped her gaze suddenly and pulled away. "Unfortunately, I've got a lot of stuff to unload from the car, so we must go." Merry smiled at Jace. "But you can come over any time to play with her."

"Like now?" Jace asked, his eyes wide and hopeful.

Merry chuckled, catching Clark's eye. "That's up to your dad. You're both welcome to come over for dinner tonight. I was going to do something for just me, but if I have company, I love to cook."

Jace popped up from petting the dog and took Merry's hand. "I love to eat!"

Clark's gaze shifted from his son's pleading expression to Merry's sweet face.

"Sure, we'd love to come to dinner."

"Yes!" Jace jumped up and down. The puppy bounced up in response, planting her paws in Jace's stomach and he wrapped his arms around his middle with a grunt. Clark took a step toward his son, but Merry was already kneeling in front of him, pushing the puppy back.

"Oh my God, Jace! Are you all right?" Merry cried.

"Yeah, but she grazed my noots."

Merry sat back on her heels, her jaw hanging nearly to her chest. She covered the lower half of her face with her hands, still holding her dog's leash, and turned to Clark, her eyes big as the rims on his Jeep.

"Jace, where did you hear that?" Clark groaned.

"Uncle Sam said it. Actually, he said they're called N-U-T-S, but that I'd get in trouble if I said that."

A feminine snort got Clark's attention and he noticed Merry's eyes were shiny, like she was holding back tears. Another noise escaped and he realized she was trying not to laugh. Her barely contained mirth hit him and he bit back a smile.

"Remind me to smack your uncle when he gets home."

"What?" Jace yelped and Merry exploded.

"I'm...so...sorry. I know...I shouldn't laugh but...that was so unex...pected," she gasped between peals of laughter.

Jace watched her with a wide smile, the wheels in his head turning. Clark's lips twitched even as he gave Jace his best *dad* look and his son's smile dissolved.

"While technically it isn't a bad word, I don't want you using it, all right? I doubt your teacher will think it's as funny as Merry."

She got control of herself and climbed to her feet with a little wince.

"Are you okay? How is your foot healing?"

"It's better, thanks for asking." Her hazel eyes were still sparkling as she addressed Jace. "Your dad's right. It's not an appropriate description for mixed company and I shouldn't have laughed."

Clark pursed his lips as another round of giggles bubbled out of her. "Very convincing."

Jace cocked his head to the side. "Am I in trouble?"

"No, buddy. Your uncle is, but you aren't. Just run any new additions to your vocabulary by me before you use them, okay?"

"Okay. Are we still going to Merry's?"

"Sure. What's for dinner?"

"Do you like tacos?"

"Absolutely."

She beamed. "Then that's what I'll make."

Jace held his hand out. "Can I walk the puppy?"

Merry looked to Clark, who nodded. "Sure. Why don't you walk her into the yard while I get the stuff from the car? Just don't let go of the leash until we're done, okay?"

"You got it." Jace grabbed the leash and took off with a whoop, the puppy biting the leash as she tried to keep up.

"I'll help you," Clark said.

"Thanks. It's just a few Christmas decorations, puppy supplies, and a gift or two." She pressed the button and the back of her car lifted and several bags tumbled to the ground. Clark cocked an eyebrow as he studied the packed back of her SUV, noting the folded down seats.

"A few, huh?"

Merry picked up the dropped bags with a groan. "I know. I always do this. I tell myself I'm not going to go overboard and I always do. Someday I'm going to end up like my mother, with a hoarder's closet my kids will dive into whenever they need a last-minute gift, but I love giving presents. And this is my first Christmas in my own place...I want it to be festive."

Clark grabbed the bag of puppy food and bowls, waving her ahead. "Hey, I get wanting to go a little overboard during the holidays. I have a tub of presents for Jace under my bed I've been collecting all year. Sometimes I dip into it if he gets a good behavior award or has a bad day, but I save most of them so that his birthday and Christmas are magical."

"When is his birthday?"

"January 20th."

"And yours?"

"February 16th. Right after Valentine's Day."

"That's better than having a birthday right before Christmas. With three kids, well, technically four with Noel, all born in December, combined birthday presents and sometimes even parties occurred quite a bit. Last year, we celebrated my brother's birthday separate because we hadn't been able to celebrate with him for years while he was deployed, but I have a feeling my mom is planning another joint party this year. It's usually just dinner with family and friends, anyway. Last year was my 25th, so Tara and Sally took me to Vegas to celebrate and that was awesome."

"When is your birthday?" he asked.

"December 10th."

"Coming up quick. Birthdays weren't a big deal with my parents, but I try to make it special for Jace."

Merry held the gate for him until he passed through and then grabbed the front door. As Clark stepped into Merry's home, the scent of Christmas cookies drifted around him, welcoming him into the surprisingly spacious inside. There were two steps to his right that led to an alcove with a U-shaped couch. On either side of the stairs were three shelves of knickknacks and pictures with a cupboard beneath. The kitchen ran along both walls, with a speckled counter top and white cupboards hanging above.

"You can drop that stuff by the stairs."

Clark walked through the kitchen, noting the fridge, dishwasher, and oven were all stainless steel but smaller than normal kitchen appliances. The stairs climbed the left side into a loft bedroom and there were hooks underneath along with what he assumed was her hope chest.

"I like your place."

Her cheeks flamed as she set her bags on the counter. "I am sorry I haven't invited you in before. Not very neighborly of me."

"I didn't ask you either. When we get done carrying in all your purchases, you'll have to give me the tour."

"The only thing you haven't seen is the bathroom and my bedroom, but I don't think I'll be taking you up there. I can't guarantee it isn't a mess."

Clark nodded, his mind occupied with imagining Merry asleep, her plump lips parted, her face relaxed. What did she wear to bed? *Nope, no, dangerous train of thought.*

"Are you coming?" she asked from the front door.

"Yeah, sorry." He jogged down her front steps after her, checking on Jace as he passed through the gate and back to her car. His son was on the ground with his arms up, laughing as the puppy pounced on him.

"I may never get my son to come home with me," Clark said.

Merry stepped out from around the back of the car, loaded down with plastic bags on each arm, and grinned. "I don't believe that for a second. He might want to stay for a while, but you're his home. I was always okay staying with friends for a night or two, but by the third day, I was ready to go home."

"I really hope he feels that way. I've tried—" Clark's voice broke with emotion, and he cleared his throat, trying to get past the lump that had formed. "I've tried to give him the kind of parent I always wanted. You never know if you're making the right decisions, not until they get a little older."

"I think you're doing a wonderful job."

Clark reached out to tuck a stray hair behind her ear, murmuring, "What my brother said about you? It's the truth. Your parents did one hell of a job on you, Merry Winters. You're an amazing woman."

Merry dropped her bags suddenly and threw her arms around him, catching him off guard. He stumbled back, his arms instinctively gripping her waist as she held him tight around his neck.

"Sorry, but you can't say things like that to me and expect me not to hug you."

Clark tightened his embrace, taking a deep breath, traces of vanilla and sugar drifting down his throat. Merry pulled away slightly, her hands sliding down from his neck across his chest. Her warm touch left a trail of heat through the flannel of his shirt and one of his hands skimmed up her back, along her spine, to rest on the back of her neck. Staring into those golden eyes with their ribbons of green, he didn't want to look away, not even as his head dipped.

"I...Clark...I need to ask you..."

His other hand came up to cover hers, pressing it against him, inching closer to her lips. "What do you need to ask?"

"Are you—"

"What are you doing?" Jace asked.

Clark jerked away at the sound of his son's question, horror ripping through him. For the one brief moment, he'd forgotten his son was there. He'd been watching as Clark came seconds away from kissing Merry.

Jace stood on the other side of the fence, his head cocked to the side.

"I was just giving your dad a hug for helping me and he thought he saw an eyelash on my cheek," Merry said easily. "You know you can make wishes on fallen eyelashes, right?"

Jace shook his head.

"Oh yes. Anytime you see an eyelash on someone's cheek, just let them blow it off the tip of your finger and make a wish."

"Do I have any?"

Merry walked over to the fence and peered closely at his face. "I don't see any, but I'll keep my eye out."

"I didn't know you were friends with my dad."

"Sure, we're friends. And we're neighbors, so that means we're even better friends."

He stared at them for several moments and then shrugged. "Okay."

Jace went back to playing. His son would probably have more questions for him later, but for now, he was content.

Merry dropped down and started gathering up the bags from the ground, her motions shaky. Clark kneeled to help her, lowering his voice. "What did you want to ask me?"

Merry met his gaze briefly, before turning away. "Nothing. It's nothing."

Clark's heart fell, wishing he could see inside her head.

"Merry…"

"We can talk about it some other time, Clark. Right now, I've got ice cream melting in the back of my car."

Clark stared at her as she climbed to her feet and walked back through the gate and into the house.

"Dad?"

Clark turned to Jace. "Yeah?"

"Were you really looking for an eyelash?" Jace asked, his face scrunched in skepticism.

No, I was about to kiss a woman I never saw coming.

"Yeah, buddy. What else would I be doing?"

"I don't know but it looked weird."

It hadn't felt weird. Holding Merry had felt incredible.

And he wanted badly to do it again.

Chapter 12

MERRY

MERRY STIRRED THE HAMBURGER MEAT in her cast iron skillet, watching Clark and Jace play with the puppy in the yard. Jace's upturned elf nose was cherry-red with cold, but he didn't seem at all ready to come inside. Clark laughed as Jace ran past him, the puppy a streak of white behind him.

She smiled and set her wooden spoon off to the side of the stove and rummaged through a few of the plastic bags until she found what she was looking for. She stepped outside and held her hands out, a box in one hand and a squeaky hedgehog dog toy in the other.

"Hey guys, I got something for you."

Jace beat his dad to the steps and took the hedgehog with a laugh, squeezing the toy over the puppy's head. She stood up on her hind legs trying to bite the toy, but Jace threw it. The young dog bounced after it excitedly and grabbed it just before Jace caught up, attempting to make her escape. When she tripped over her own paws and fell, Jace gasped and kneeled down, talking softly to her.

Clark came over to her and she whispered, "That is the sweetest kid."

"Thank you. What's that?" he asked, pointing to the box in her hand.

"It's a Christmas scene projector. Instead of hanging a bunch of lights, I thought I'd put one of these up on the fence and it could project a scene on the side of the house. Not like anyone will see it but me, but I wanted to be a little festive."

Clark studied the outside of the box with a frown. "This is cheating."

"It is not! It's the newest trend and it means I don't have to go to the hardware store and grab those little hook thingies. It also keeps me from having to climb a ladder, which I love. Ladders make my knees squishy."

"I can't let you put one of these out. As a Christmas traditionalist, these offend me."

"Then you don't have to look at it." Merry reached for the box but he held it away from her. She placed her hands on her hips with a scowl. "If I didn't have to stir the taco meat, I'd tackle you."

Clark laughed, tossing the box from hand to hand. "Come get me when you're done. I think I can take you."

I would love for you to take me.

She disappeared inside before he saw her blush. The skin on the back of her neck still tingled from the warmth of his hand before, not to mention the desire to grip the front of his flannel and drag him down to her level. He'd wanted to kiss her; she could see it in the deepening of those intense brown eyes. Just a few weeks ago he'd been her parents' foreman, a man who never really smiled except with his son and hardly cast her a glance. Now...

He was the guy she imagined lying next to her when she couldn't sleep at night, holding her close. Kissing her softly. Hands stroking down her—

The door banged open and Clark popped his head in. "Smells good in here."

"Thanks. Twenty minutes until lift off. Is my projector safe?"

"For now," he teased. "I'm running home for a minute, but I told Jace to stay in the yard. Is that okay with you?"

"Absolutely. I'll keep an eye on him."

"Thanks, I know. Just didn't want you to think I ditched my kid with you." He sent her one of those broad grins she was still getting used to. "Really, I appreciate this, Merry. I'm so used to cooking, it's nice to hang up the chef's hat. I can't wait to taste your tacos."

"Hopefully they live up to the anticipation," she murmured.

"I'm sure they'll be delicious. Be right back."

"Okay."

Clark shut the door and walked past the window on the other side of the gate. She'd been so close to asking him about Woodsman27, but then his gorgeous brown eyes gazing into hers chased every thought away until the only thing she could concentrate on was the hardness of his chest beneath her palms. How easy it would have been to close the distance if she'd been a few inches taller. And could he hurry the hell up and kiss her?

Of course, she didn't want their first kiss to be in front of his son, but she hadn't been thinking straight, a reaction she hadn't expected to have. Merry knew what lust was, but that was usually insubstantial and fleeting. This longing for Clark had been building and grew stronger every time she spoke to him.

She turned off the burner and set the meat to the side, grimacing when she lifted her foot and it throbbed. Merry checked the clock and popped another aspirin, then put all the taco fixings she'd prepped out on the counter in bowls and on plates. The last thing she needed to do was fry the shells and warm the beans. And find somewhere for all of them to sit.

A thwack against the side of her house made her jump, further exacerbating the pain in her foot. She limped to the door, worried Jace had hurt himself, and opened it, nearly stumbling down the steps at the sight that greeted her.

Clark stood on top of a ladder, a buckskin tool belt hanging low on his hips. He was reaching up just under her gutters, the bottom of his flannel shirt riding up, showing off the tightening of his jeans against his firm, round butt.

"Merry? Something wrong?"

She swung her gaze all the way up to meet his smiling face.

"What...what are you doing up there?"

"I'm installing light clips for you. I had extra from when I did my house and figured since you were kind enough to make dinner, I'd get you some real lights hung."

"I didn't buy any Christmas lights, though."

"Don't worry about it. I've got you covered."

Just seeing him lean to the side, barely hanging on the ladder, made her lower back clench and her head swim. "Clark, you really don't have to do this. I'm fine with the projector."

"You can still use your projector, but there's no reason you can't have both."

"I don't want you to break your neck!" she cried.

Clark looked down from the clip he was hanging with a frown. "What?"

She swallowed. "I don't like heights, and seeing you up there… I'm worried you're going to fall."

Clark studied her for several moments before he climbed down, but instead of putting the ladder away, he picked it up and moved it farther down. When he closed the distance, he chucked her under the chin. "If it makes you feel better, you can hold the ladder for me."

"I'll hold the ladder, Dad!" Jace raced over, grabbing the bottom of the ladder with both hands, the puppy flopping down between his legs.

"Thanks, buddy." Clark turned back to Merry with a reassuring smile. "I promise I'm like a squirrel on a tree. Sure-footed. I'll be done before you call us inside, and if it really bothers you, don't look."

Merry huffed and marched back inside, shutting the door behind her. *Stubborn man.*

Except she couldn't really be mad at Clark. She loved Christmas lights and the only reason she hadn't bothered with them was because she didn't want her father to get on a ladder to help her and she knew that her knees wouldn't have made it past the third step.

Besides, she'd had no idea a tool belt and a pair of jeans could be so freaking sexy.

She finished frying the taco shells and set everything out on the counter like a taco bar. After carrying the bags of décor and presents up to her loft, she went about setting up the pet cage she'd bought for the puppy. She curled a fleece blanket in the back, with her food and water in the front. Under the cage, she'd lined the floor with newspaper in case she spilled her water.

Merry opened the door but Clark was nowhere to be seen. Spotting Jace and the puppy playing tug of war, she called, "Tacos are ready."

Jace hopped to his feet and hollered, "Dad! Food!"

"I'll be right there. Only a couple more."

Merry took the puppy's leash when she reached the bottom of the porch steps and started to lead her inside, but the dog dug her heels in.

"What are you doing, babes? Come on."

The puppy stared at the front door like it was the opening to hell and Merry frowned.

"Maybe she's never been inside before," Jace said.

"You could be right. You go on in. I'll carry her inside."

Merry lifted the puppy into her arms like a baby and kissed the side of her snout with a smack. "I promise, you're going to like it in here with me."

She carried her past the kitchen to the space across from the stairs where she'd set up the cage. When the puppy thrashed at the entrance, Merry reached in and removed her food and water, spotting trouble.

"Can I start?" Jace asked.

"Sure, sweetie. There is a set of stools on the other side of the counter you can use when you're done."

Once she got the puppy reluctantly situated, she went to the sink and washed her hands and went back outside to get Clark. Merry opened the door and Clark leaned back when she barreled into him. He stepped back, keeping them both from tumbling down, and the position put them eye level with each other.

"Oh crap, I'm sorry!" She scrambled back onto the top step, her cheeks warm. "I was coming to get you and didn't expect you to be standing right there."

"It's all right. I told you I was sure-footed."

"Funny. I seem to remember someone falling on his back when he slipped on some ice."

"That was a fluke."

"Ah, okay." Merry stepped back out of the way. "You can grab a plate and help yourself."

"You mind if I use your bathroom?"

"Of course not. It's the door at the back of the house."

"Thanks."

Merry's gaze drifted to his hips as he passed and she blurted, "Where did your belt go?"

"It's hanging on my ladder. Figured I wouldn't need it inside."

"Too bad," she mumbled under her breath.

"What?"

"Nothing."

"She said too bad," Jace offered through a huge bite of taco.

Merry wanted to dissolve into the floor.

"All right, I'll be right back." Merry didn't need to look at him to hear the laughter in his voice.

"Why did you want my dad to wear his tool belt?"

"My faucet is leaking and I thought he might have a tool that could tighten things up." Merry's skin burned as her excuse played out in a completely different context.

"You should ask him when he gets out. My dad's really good at fixin' things. I busted the head off my robot snake and he snapped it back on and it works fine."

Merry finished making her taco and sat on the couch. Clark came out of the bathroom past the whining puppy and grabbed a plate.

"How's the grub, bud?"

"It's good. Merry needs her pipes plugged. They're leaking."

She choked on her food, grabbing her napkin in case something came flying out.

"She does, huh?" He grinned at her, his eyes electrified with amusement.

"I said...I need them tightened."

"I can look at them after dinner if you'd like."

"No, it's fine, really." She hopped off the couch, squeezing behind Clark to get to the fridge, her chest brushing against his back. "Would anyone like something to drink? I have soda, water..."

"Can I have soda?" Jace asked.

"As long as it's caffeine-free."

"I have root beer," Merry said.

"I love root beer," Jace said, taking the can with zeal.

The puppy's whining had risen to high-pitched wailing and she was shaking the cage with the full force of her body. Jace frowned. "Does she have to stay in there?"

"Only until we finish eating," Merry said.

By the time Merry put the food away, her head was pounding from the noises coming out of the pup.

"The vet said crate training is the way to go, but I don't know if I can take that screaming all night."

Clark came over next to her and took the dishes out of her hands. "You go see to her and I'll clean up."

"You're my guest."

"And you were an excellent host. Besides, I think you should go into the yard and check out the sky. It's gorgeous." He looked out the window with a smile. "The sun is setting fast."

Merry assumed he wanted her to see her new Christmas lights, and she ran her hand along his shoulders as she passed. Once she pulled the door of the cage, the puppy ran for the front door, scratching to go out.

Jace opened the door and she tumbled down the stairs. Merry wanted to see if she was hurt, but she was already up and running. Merry flipped on the porch light, even though the sky was still light enough to watch her new dog do its business. She was going to need to invest in a pooper scooper tomorrow.

Shoot, she had to work tomorrow. What was she going to do with the puppy during the seven hours she'd be gone? She'd have to talk to her dad. Maybe they could keep her up at the house with Butch.

"I don't see anything, Clark!" she called.

"Give it a minute. It's almost time."

Suddenly, LED lights came to life unde the trim of her house, the bulbs blinking in a wave of color. On the wall next to her window, swirling red and green lasers circled around *Merry Christmas* in bold cursive.

"It's wonderful," she said in awe.

Clark came out of the house, his warm breath fogging as it connected with the cold. "Not mad at me anymore for taking liberties with your decorating?"

"I was never mad. I just hate asking for help."

"Well, you should get over that, because I like helping out my friends."

The word "friend" thrust through her like a sword. Was that really all this was? She could have sworn he was feeling this too, but maybe she was imagining it. Their almost kiss...could it have been all in her head?

"We should probably get home and get ready for bed." Clark shut the door behind him and climbed down the steps next to her. "Thank you for having us, Merry."

"Of course. You're welcome any time."

"Jace. Come thank Merry."

Jace's shoulders slumped. "Awww, Dad, do we have to go right now?"

"Yes, you still have homework and I need to do some laundry before tomorrow."

Jace leaned down and hugged the puppy, whispering something to her.

"Thank you for the lights," Merry murmured.

"You're welcome." He stood on the bottom step with her for several seconds, before running a hand down her arm. "Goodnight, Merry."

"That's all I get?" she said.

"What do you mean?"

"Well, if we're friends, then we should hug good-bye." Wrapping her arms around his waist, she pulled him close. He returned her embrace, his hand smoothing over the back of her pony tail.

"You always smell like fresh-baked Christmas cookies?"

"Is that a good thing?"

"It is. It makes me want to eat you up."

Merry shivered.

Clark pulled away, running his hands up and down her arms. "You should get inside. It's chilly. Jace! Come on."

The boy climbed to his feet with a sigh, trudging back toward them.

"Say goodnight, Jace."

Suddenly, the boy ran full tilt into her middle, almost knocking the wind out of her and squeezing her tight. "Thank you for letting me play with your puppy."

"Like I said, anytime you want to come over you can, but I was wondering…what do you think of the name Daisy? When we were making the tacos tonight and I put a dollop of Daisy sour cream on my taco, I thought, now she's white, a little sour, but lovable. Right?"

Jace seemed to mull it over, then nodded. "It could work."

"I'm glad you approve. I'll see you tomorrow, all right?"

"Yeah."

Merry got hold of the puppy before they passed through the gate and the white fuzzball whined as they walked away under the dusky sky. Merry carried her back up the stairs into the house.

Merry put her down in front of her food and water and although she downed half her bowl of water, Daisy didn't touch her food. She wasn't worried about it, as the vet warned her Daisy might not eat today due to stress.

Merry grabbed her phone and sat on her couch, tapping on the MeetMe app. There was a message from Woodsman, from two and a half hours ago.

KnottyGirl25,

I'm counting down the days until Friday. I only hope we get along as well in person as we do here. Are you nervous?

Woodsman27

Daisy scratched at the door, but Merry gave her a firm no. With her head down, she climbed up the stairs and put her big feet on the cushion of the couch but couldn't make it all the way up on her own. Merry lifted her up, smiling as she settled on the cushion with her head in Merry's lap. Merry stroked her fur with one hand and tapped out a reply with the other.

Woodsman27,
    I am nervous for many reasons. What if we don't get along as well in person? Or if there's no chemistry? What if we're both expecting this to be more than just a friendly communication between two lonely people?
    There are so many what-ifs rattling around in my head

and I know they won't go away until we meet and to be honest…there is someone else I have feelings for. It's new and I'm not even sure he feels the same, but I wanted to be honest before we met.

I hope this doesn't change your mind about Friday.

KnottyGirl25

P.S. Do you like dogs or cats better?

Merry's phone rang before she could hit send and she tapped on the talk button. "Hello?"

"Hello, is this Merry Winters?"

"Yes, and if you're calling to talk about my car's extended warranty, I'm not interested."

"No, this is Faith Hagen with Channel Ten news in Twin Falls. I'm calling because we received some footage of you rescuing a puppy today and we'd like to set up an interview with you tomorrow. Are you free?"

CHAPTER 13

CLARK

CLARK DROVE THE QUAD BACK to the office Friday afternoon, his thoughts still as heavy as they were since that morning. Ever since he read KnottyGirl25's message.

He appreciated her honesty, but now he wondered why she wanted to meet him if she was interested in someone she already knew in person. Why not pursue something with him? Like she pointed out, there was no guarantee anything would come of their date.

Should he be honest and tell her about Merry? Not naming her specifically, but that there was someone else he was interested in?

Dating Merry would complicate his life on a professional level as well as personal, but he couldn't stop thinking of her. This morning, he'd been lying in bed, relaxing, and he'd thought about Merry's soft, full lips. Her soft mouth under his, kissing him back as he slowly undressed her, and then rolled her beneath him, coming into her with a sigh.

Clark wanted to get through this first season without a hitch and fantasizing about his boss's daughter was bad enough, but dating her? The woman who would potentially become his boss in the future? It seemed like a recipe for disaster.

Even if she did give the sweetest hugs and made him laugh and smelled like she'd rolled in a basket of Christmas cookies.

Clark stomped into his house to grab a beer and a bag of chips, hoping to get an hour in his woodworking shed to blow off some steam, but his brother caught him as he was walking out the door.

"Clark, I need to talk to you."

Clark stopped in the doorway and turned, his tone coming out harsher than he meant. "Can it wait until later, Sam? I've got a lot on my mind."

Sam sat down at the kitchen table, rubbing a hand roughly over the top of his head. "I do too, which is why I think we should talk."

Clark finally registered the slight slur in his brother's words and the beer bottle dangling from his fingers. "It's five in the afternoon."

"I know that."

"Why are you drunk?"

"It's my night off. I thought I would partake in some debauchery after I unburden my soul."

Clark sat at the table next to him, frowning. "Sam, are you all right?"

"No, my dear brother. I am very much not all right." Sam took a long pull of his beer and swallowed. Hard. "And I don't have anyone else to talk to about this."

"What is this?"

"Why I came back. My life has been dragged through runny shit lately and I can't fix it."

"I thought you had a great life in Oregon. Lots of friends. Girls."

Sam chuckled bitterly. "I did, until I didn't. I trusted the wrong man. Had a handshake agreement with the guy I worked for, known him for years. I was paying him monthly installments to buy the business from him because I couldn't get a loan with my credit. But he sold it out from under me and left town like a coward. I have some savings left, but not nearly enough to buy anything outright. So I came back here, tail between my legs, to be near the only family I have."

Clark pulled Sam into an unexpected hug and thumped him on the back. "I'm glad you told me."

Sam returned his hug, burying his face in his shoulder. "It's humiliating to realize your little brother has his life together and I'm still a train wreck in my thirties."

"Train wreck or not, I want you here. You are my brother and I love you. We can hire a lawyer and go after him, try to get some of your money back—"

"It wouldn't be worth it. Besides, I don't have enough in the bank to fight."

"I can help you. I have money saved—"

"No. Your money is to take care of that boy and I'm not letting you waste it on an asshole like me. I should have never trusted him and I'd bankrupt myself and you chasing him. It will take some time, but I'll get enough saved for a down payment and go through the right channels next time."

"It's my money. And if I want to use some of it to help my

brother realize his dream, then I'm going to do it and you cannot stop me."

Sam chuckled wetly. "I think I can still take you, bro."

"I'm a lot stronger than the last time you tried."

"Fair enough." Sam ran his hands over his face with a deep breath. "You're a good man, Clark. I'm proud of you."

"Thanks, but honestly, don't be too hard on yourself. I've trusted the wrong person before and while it feels like someone threw a pallet of bricks at you, you learn from it and will listen to the little voice telling you to be cautious."

"We're talking about women now, huh?" Sam said with a sheepish grin. "I know you've got a date tonight. You taking out Merry?"

Clark cleared his throat. Even his brother thought there was something going on with Merry. That wasn't good.

"Actually, no. I am meeting a woman I've been talking to on a dating site."

Sam's blue eyes narrowed. "Why would you do that when you have a flesh and blood woman who is completely into you right next door?"

"Merry isn't into me."

"The hell she isn't. That girl watches you with that sweet, sappy look I've only seen in romance movies. She thinks you're it, man, and you're going to ignore that to go out with some woman from the internet? Have you at least seen her picture?"

"No, and she hasn't seen mine. I didn't want her looking into me before we met."

"Are you insane? It is the digital age! There is no reason to go on some virtual blind date when you can video chat and see what this woman looks like."

"Maybe I don't care about her physical appearance. I am more concerned about meeting someone I can see as a serious partner. Have a lasting relationship based on mutual respect and—"

"Sex? Please tell me you were going to say sex."

"No, I wasn't."

Sam shook his head. "You can have the respect and all that, but you need to also admit that sex and attraction are important, especially to a relationship starting out. You have the whole honeymoon phase, where you can't keep your hands off each other, but not if you two have no chemistry."

Clark said with disgust, "I'm an adult male with a child. I'm not going to bring women back to make out on the couch like a randy teenager who can't control himself."

"Good God, what happened to you?" Sam looked ready to tear his hair out. "Just because you're a father doesn't mean you stop living. I get that Patrice hurt you, and in the long term Jace, but you cut yourself off. You could have been dating all this time and found a nice girl to love. You didn't have to be alone."

"I wanted it that way, all right? I didn't want to have to date someone, introduce her to my son, and have her gone the next year. I don't want to jump from one relationship to the next because I made another mistake."

"Are you talking about Jace? As your mistake?"

"No. Jace wasn't and will never be a mistake, but Patrice was." Clark sighed, searching for the right words that would make his intrusive brother back off. "I'll always be grateful to her for giving me Jace, but let's say I dated Merry. She's sweet. She's beautiful. And she likes Jace, maybe she even grows to love him, but then what we have fizzles. Then I'm stuck in an uncomfortable situation. My son is heartbroken because he wants Victoria and Chris to be his grand-parents. That's what he told me when I was tucking him into bed the other night, after one casual dinner with Merry. That he wanted me to fall in love with Merry. That he wanted the Winterses to be our family." Clark sat running his fingers through his hair. "Maybe I shouldn't have let him spend so much time with them."

"Having people in your son's life who love him isn't a mistake," Sam said softly. "We got the shit end of the stick when it comes to parents. But you are an amazing dad, and moving here, you found the Winters family, who as far as I can tell love you like a son and treat your kid like he's their blood. I could not imagine a better blessing. To top it off, if you just tried with Merry, I think you two could be the real deal."

If he was a selfish man, he wouldn't be second-guessing getting involved with Merry. He'd do it because he wanted her, but there were too many hearts on the line to be broken if he made the wrong choice. "She's a romantic, Sam. She believes in true love. In long-lasting love. I love you. I love Jace. But I have never fallen in love with a woman. I'm not even sure I know how."

"You treat her well, you make sure you're fulfilling her needs. It's not that hard."

"Oh yeah? How many times have you been in love?"

Sam shrugged. "A couple, but the difference between you and me is I'm an asshole. I can't be in a relationship because I'm too selfish. But not you. You are the kind of guy women want to find."

"Well, hopefully the woman I'm meeting feels like I'm worth the wait."

Sam sighed, a resigned exhale that worked his entire body. "I think you're wasting your time, but what do I know? Good luck on your date." Sam took a step to leave the room and turned back at the last moment. "I do have to ask...why do you assume you'll fail with Merry? Our parents are still married, as cold as they are. You're built for monogamy. Why won't you at least give her a chance?"

Honesty poured out of Clark like hot soup from a thermos. "Because I want her, all right? I keep thinking about her even when I don't want to. I almost kissed her the other day, in front of Jace. I like her, but it's that attraction that scares me."

Sam laughed. "There may be hope for you yet, little brother."

CHAPTER 14

MERRY

BREWS AND CHEWS BUSTLED WITH the Friday crowd of early evening patrons who were looking to unwind after a long week. The place wouldn't start filling up until closer to ten with the drinkers and dancers. Merry took a breath, her gaze scanning the place for the fifth time since arriving. It was a little after eight, and although her sister had griped at her about arriving for a date half an hour early, Merry needed the time to collect herself. She'd invited her siblings and friends to hang out at the bar. Holly had insisted on driving her—in case things went well and Merry wanted to let him drive her home.

And if it went south, it felt safer to have a group there in case he turned out to be a creep.

Noel, Nick, Sally, and Pike sat at the table next to them since there wasn't enough room. Tara was late, as usual, and Merry couldn't wait to give her the voodoo peen. She hadn't told anyone yet that she'd been oddly inspired by Tara and Holly's request and had a tub of various peens by her bed and was slowly filling another. She was still working on the elf one for Holly, but she'd made a Santa one for fun, with a long white beard hanging from the head and a buckle between the twins. It turned out adorable, but it was one of the main reasons she hadn't wanted Clark climbing up to her bedroom. That very obvious project was facing out against the wall of the clear plastic tub, as if silently screaming *Let me out!*

Merry giggled.

"What are you laughing about?" Nick's longtime pal Anthony Russo asked. He was sitting next to her, relegated to the singles table. At least, that's what he'd grumbled about when he arrived.

"Just nervous."

"It's going to be great," Holly said, winking. "How could he not fall all over himself when he sees you. Don't you think, Anthony?"

"I'm not commenting on my best friend's sister's attractiveness."

Holly rolled her eyes. "You don't have to be a guy about it. Just say she looks nice?"

Anthony turned her way, giving her a slight sweep and nodding. "You look nice, Merry."

"What was that?" Nick asked loudly.

"Fucking Vulcan hearing," Anthony muttered.

Merry laughed, smoothing down the bodice of her flared burgundy sweater dress. The off the shoulder collar folded over, the soft, thick fabric warm inside the bar. Merry knew she looked insane wearing a dress in thirty-degree weather, but she'd wanted to stand out so it would be easier for the Woodsman to spot her.

She checked her phone again. Eight-eleven. Almost time.

Arms wrapped around her from behind and Merry stiffened until Tara dropped her head down to kiss her cheek. "Sorry I'm late."

"You're always late. If you were on time, I'd think there was something amiss."

"Haha." Tara took the seat across from her. The powder- pink wig on her head hung past her shoulders, complementing the black sweater that draped over her slender frame.

"Don't be snarky or I won't give you—" Merry reached into her large purse and pulled out the pink voodoo peen, complete with pins. "This!"

"Oh, my God, he is so cute," Tara squealed, taking it from her.

"What in the fuck is that?" Anthony asked.

Tara swung it at him and he leaned out of the way. "Shut your truck driver mouth. It's a voodoo doll of my ex's penis. I'm going to stab it anytime I think about the jerk."

Anthony stared at the plushie and pushed back his chair. "On that note, I'm going to get a drink."

Holly hollered after him, "Come on, Ant! You don't want to play with it?"

He flipped her off without turning back.

"Play with what?" Noel asked.

Tara held up the peen and suddenly Nick and Pike were alone at the table and Noel and Sally had moved their chairs over.

"What is the hard thing in the middle?" Sally asked, her hands squeezing her way up the shaft.

"It's one of those tubes meant for flower arrangements. I couldn't get the pins to stay without it."

Holly shook her head. "I don't want that in mine. I just want it huggable."

"She's making you one?" Noel asked.

"An elf one!"

Sally handed it over to Noel, so she could examine it. "I want a snuggly one with a red beard and a little bow tie between the balls."

Pike's head swiveled their way. "Do what now?"

"I think a cute Pike peen to snuggle with would be awesome."

"Why would you need that when you have the real thing?"

Holly and Merry both threw something at him, but only Merry's ice cube got him in the chest. Holly's napkin floated over Tara and hit the floor.

"Pick up after yourself, you heathen," Pike said with a devilish smile.

Holly got up to get the napkin, muttering, "I thought getting a girlfriend would mellow you out, but you're still a pill."

"Coming from Nick's baby sister. Ouch."

Nick leaned against Noel's shoulder and made a face. "Please don't get one of those."

"I won't, but I want to stick a pin in it."

Nick stood up. "I can't watch. Pike, let's get drinks."

"Right behind you." Pike leaned over and kissed Sally's cheek, whispering something no one else could hear.

"What did he say?" Holly asked.

"He begged me not to get the stabbing one, too."

Merry snickered as her brother and his friend headed to the bar to join Anthony.

"Oh, he's cute!" Holly said, pointing over Merry's shoulder. "What is your guy supposed to be wearing?"

Merry turned to inspect the man in question, shaking her head. "Blue button-down shirt."

"All right, not him…" Holly scanned the crowd and stopped, her face twisting like she'd smelled burning fruitcake. "Oh no."

"What?" Merry turned, craning her neck to see over Noel and Sally, searching the faces until she landed on Trip Douglas.

In a baby-blue button-down.

"What's wrong?" Noel asked.

The rest of the table turned as Holly hissed, "It's Trip. He's her date."

Tara gagged. "Ew."

Noel groaned. "Can we not *ew* someone I used to sleep with?"

"Why did you have to remind us?" Holly looked a little green and Merry would have laughed if she wasn't so disappointed. She'd really imagined a whole Tom Hanks/Meg Ryan moment where Clark walked in and their eyes met across the room. He'd cross it slowly, as romantic music played above their heads, and he'd stop in front of her, holding out his hand.

"I hoped it was you."

"Merry, what are you going to do?" Tara whispered loudly.

Sally picked up her drink, her eyebrows raised. "I'd put my coat back on and duck out of here."

"I'm with Sally," Noel said.

"No, I'm not going to do that. He may have been a jerk in the past, but he is still a human being."

Holly smirked. "Debatable."

Merry stood up with a resigned sigh. "I'm going to say hello, thank him for his time, and then come back to the table and drink. Please have three shots waiting for me upon my return."

"We've got you," Tara said, squeezing her hand. "I'm sorry he isn't who you thought he was."

Merry startled, wondering how she knew about Clark, but realized her friend meant in general. That Woodsman wasn't the sweet, funny guy he seemed online. How the heck could he be Trip? No morals. Lack of empathy hidden under a smarmy, albeit handsome face. Trip was a non-homicidal version of Ted Bundy.

He was leaning against the bar alone, waiting for Ricki Takini to notice him and take his order.

With a deep breath, she tapped his shoulder. He turned her way, his gaze traveling over her and a lazy smile stretched over his lips, revealing perfectly capped teeth.

"Merry. You need something?"

"Yes. I felt like I owed you a face to face explanation."

"That's sweet." He leered at her, an expression that made her palm itch to smack him. "I like that you got dressed up to do it. That dress makes your rack look hot."

"Thanks." *Why did I think this guy deserved human decency? He really is a pig.*

"Anyway, I know we said a lot of things the last couple of weeks, but you get why this—" She pointed to him and then her—"isn't going to work."

"It won't?"

"No. Even if you hadn't put hands on Noel, we aren't interested in the same things." Trip lost his smile, his eyebrows dropping over his eyes in a scowl. "In fact, it's pretty dishonest to click long term relationship when I doubt those are your intentions with all of this."

Trip straightened up and crossed his arms over his chest. "First of all, I didn't put hands on her like I hit her or something. I just held her arm so we could talk."

"Doesn't make it better."

"And second, I have no idea what you're talking about. I haven't talked to you in months. You've got the wrong guy, babe."

"You don't...like woodworking?"

Trip snorted. "What the fuck, am I eighty?" He chortled at his own joke and Merry stood there, frozen.

"What can I get you, Trip?" Ricki glanced her way, her eyes silently asking what she was doing with Trip. Even the women who slept with Trip knew what a jerk he was, but after his treatment of Noel, most women in Mistletoe wouldn't touch him with a ten-foot pole.

But she'd thought he was Woodsman.

"Have a good night," she murmured, turning away. She weaved back through the people and took her seat again.

"It wasn't him?" Noel asked, pushing a creamy shot toward her.

"Nope."

"Thank the Lord," Sally said.

"So we're still looking for a Woodsman in a blue shirt." Holly rubbed her hands together.

Merry knocked back the shot, the sweet liquor streaming down her throat. "We are."

"Do we know anything else about him? Eye color? Hair?"

"No. I only know details about his personality, his past, his likes and dislikes. I don't know how I could have even entertained the thought he was Trip. The Woodsman is sweet. Intelligent. Funny."

"Huh." Tara was staring at something over Merry's shoulder. "Clark just walked in."

Her pulse picked up speed. "Is he…"

"I can't tell if his shirt is blue because he's got his jacket on."

Merry wiped her damp palms on her skirt as she twisted around, catching Clark's slack-jawed expression. His work jacket was zipped all the way up without a hint of blue in sight, but this couldn't be a coincidence. Clark never went out, especially to the bar, so it had to be a specific reason he'd come out tonight.

Like meeting someone special.

It *was* him. Clark was the Woodsman. Every fantasy she'd had about this moment was about to come true.

Except his expression wasn't right. He looked…hurt. Clark's gaze scanned the table and came back to rest on her, his mouth set in a grim line.

He took a step toward her…

And immediately spun around, heading back through the exit.

Merry sat stunned, like someone had thrown an icy snowball right in her chest and the breath was knocked out of her. Tears stung her gaze and she slowly turned away from the door, her skin rippling with the power of her humiliation, as if at any moment she could come out of it completely.

"Guess he didn't like what he saw, huh?"

"Seriously, who does that?" Sally said.

Noel passed her another shot, brown eyes burning. "Fuck that prick."

Merry saw her brother and his friends coming back to the table and she grabbed Noel's hand. "Do me a favor. Don't tell my brother it was Clark, okay?"

Noel looked like she wanted to protest, but she nodded. "I won't."

"Or Pike." Merry waited for Sally to agree. "Or Anthony."

"We won't tell them, but he deserves his ass kicked," Noel grumbled.

Tara shoved a heart pin into the voodoo peen. "I want one of these for Clark now. He's a douche."

Only Holly remained silent, watching her sadly, and Merry kicked back another shot.

"What did we miss?" Nick asked as he sat back down with the guys at the next table, setting a frosty pitcher of beer and glasses in the center.

"Your sister got stood up," Tara volunteered.

"Guys," Merry mumbled. "Don't."

Nick moved his chair next to her, watching her with his deep-brown eyes. "Are you okay, Mer?"

"I'll be fine, you don't have to make a big deal about it. It was one internet date. He probably wasn't my bag, anyway." Merry swallowed back the lump in her throat and stole Sally's shot. "But I will require more alcohol."

They all put on a happy face, drawing her into their conversations and out of her own head. She couldn't have asked for better people in her life. Even Pike and Anthony, who usually teased her mercilessly, were going out of their way to make her smile.

But after twenty minutes, it still wasn't working and not just because she was hurt. No, she wanted to smack Clark Griffin clear into next week.

Merry replayed the moment he'd walked in to the second he walked out through her head, trying to figure out why he'd been upset. What the hell did she do to deserve that? Even as Merry and Clark, she thought they were at least friendly.

"You know, I'm going to go to the bathroom."

"Want me to come?" Holly asked.

"No, I'm good. This isn't prom, it's a bar. I just have to pee. Be right back."

She weaved through the multiplying bodies and pushed the swinging bathroom door open with a sob. Trying to keep a brave face in place physically hurt and as she sat down in the first of two stalls, Merry shook with every tear. With trembling hands, she pulled out her phone, then tapped on the MeetMe app. There were no new messages, just the last one Clark sent before their date.

I can't wait to see you.

"Bullshit," she sniffled, hitting the reply button with her thumb.

Woodsman27,
　　I thought I knew who you were but clearly, I was wrong.
No wonder I have feelings for you, for Clark. You're one and

the same and just my type. A big, freaking jerk that would walk away from a waiting woman instead of being honest about your lack of interest. You could have come over and sat down. At least had a drink and let me down easy. I treated the biggest asshole in the whole town with more respect than you showed me. You're a coward and I'm sorry I wasted even a moment on you.

Don't bother responding. I'm blocking you after I hit send.

KnottyGirl25

Merry hit send and did exactly what she promised and blocked his ass. She dumped her phone back into her purse and washed her hands before leaving the bathroom, hoping her friends wouldn't notice she'd been crying. God, she wanted to go home, but one of them would have to drive her home and all of them had been watching her with sympathy, as if waiting for her to have a major meltdown. She didn't want anger or pity.

When she exited, she ran smack into Ryan.

"Merry, hey. You okay, lovely? Your eyes are red and puffy."

"I'm fine," she muttered, wiping her wet cheeks.

"Yeah, you look it. Come on, hooker. Let's get a drink and you can tell me all your woes."

"Aren't you here with someone?" she asked.

"Ricki was going to introduce me to the new bartender, but that can wait. Tell me what you need."

Merry's lip trembled despite her brain screaming at her to

hold it together. "I was supposed to meet someone, but he blew me off. I came with my friends, but I don't want to ask them to leave early and have them all feel sorry for me, but I don't want to be here."

Ryan stroked his clean-shaven chin as he studied her, as if weighing a heavy decision. Then he snapped his fingers and pointed at her. "Here's what we're going to do. Tell your friends I'm having a rough night and could use a friend, so we're leaving now. Takes the attention off you and puts it onto me. We'll go to your place. I want to see it and we can pick up drinks and water on the way because hydration is important. Then we'll drink and online shop for the perfect dress that will make him regret every decision he made that didn't end with him worshipping the ground you walk on. Deal?"

"We haven't hung out since high school. Why would you want to tank your night for me?"

Ryan wrapped his arm around her shoulders and squeezed her to him. "Because a long time ago, a very scared kid told his girlfriend he liked boys and not girls and she said 'Me too.'"

"Oh God, did I really say something so stupid?"

"It wasn't stupid. It made me laugh and then I was crying because it was such a relief to tell someone and you know what you did? You hugged me and told me that you were excited to get to know the real me. It wasn't always easy growing up here but my family, you, and a handful of amazing friends made it worth a few narrow-minded individuals." He tapped her chin with the end of his finger, smiling gently. "It's my turn to comfort you."

Merry leaned up and kissed his cheek. "Thank you."

"Now, let's blow this whiskey-soaked sex den."

"We have to swing by my parents' and pick up my puppy."

He clapped his hands. "Oh, I love puppies!"

"Just keep anything you value off the floor. She's teething."

"I'll risk it. My truck is parked in the back so I'll pull around and grab you from the front. All right?"

"Sounds good. Thanks."

"My pleasure."

It took a few minutes of convincing, but her friends finally let her leave without one of them coming with her. As much as she loved them, she wanted someone who hadn't witnessed her humiliation and wouldn't bring it up every five minutes in an attempt to make her feel better about the bullet she dodged.

She stepped outside the bar and took a deep breath, the chilly air reminding her of Clark and how he loved breathing in the cold.

The fucker.

She closed her eyes and leaned her head back against the front of the building, waiting for Ryan. A car door opened somewhere in the parking lot, but she didn't want to say hi or chitchat. Heavy boots crunched on the gravel parking lot, drawing closer, and she opened her eyes when they stopped.

Clark stood several feet in front of her with his hands in his pockets, his expression unreadable. Merry's jaw clenched as he stood there not saying anything, just staring at her like he didn't know what to say.

Well, she knew what to say. She had a *lot* to say.

"Why are you still here?"

"I was waiting for you."

"Why?" she snapped.

"To apologize. I shouldn't have walked out like that. I was just...surprised. I didn't know how to handle the situation and needed a beat to collect myself."

"You could have come back in after you *collected yourself*." Sarcasm oozed from her tone like paint spilling over cement. "I was right inside where you left me."

"What I have to say doesn't require an audience," he said bitterly.

Why does he sound like I'm the bad guy in this scenario?

"If you aren't interested in me, you could have at least said hi and told me that. It would have been less traumatic than you bailing on our date because you were disappointed."

"That wasn't how I felt," he argued, finally pulling his hands out of his pockets and throwing them into the air. "Seeing you waiting for me threw me completely off-kilter. I had no idea you were KnottyGirl25. Not a single fucking clue. I thought you were going to be...well, I had no idea, but not Merry Winters, the darling of Mistletoe, holding court as you waited for some poor sap to walk through the door and fall at your feet."

"If that's your apology, it needs some serious work."

"Maybe so. I know I didn't deal with tonight well—"

"Or at all really."

"But at least I took it seriously. I came alone, because I thought this was a *real* date."

The mockery in his voice made her fingers tingle and she gripped her coat in her fists so she wouldn't hit him. "And I thought you were a *nice* guy who would be fun to be around. Turns out I was wrong. Sucks to be me, huh?"

"Imagine what it was like for me to walk in there and see you and all your friends laughing at me. Loser Clark Griffin actually believed he could meet someone he could connect with. Who actually cared. Who wouldn't…" He didn't finish the sentence.

"Are you listening to yourself? This isn't high school and I am a single woman!" Merry pushed off the wall, her body vibrating with rage. "Did you think I was going to meet a stranger at a bar, *alone*? Even in Mistletoe, I would never do that. If you'd suggested we meet for coffee, I would have had a friend with a newspaper and sunglasses watching every move you made from two tables away."

"One friend, sure, but you had a table full of women!"

"I asked them to come in case the date didn't work out, I could still have fun with my friends, but you even ruined that!" Merry kicked at a pebble, and cried, "Why in the fuck am I explaining myself to *you*? I have never been so humiliated in my life and I've walked in on a guy I was dating having Zoom sex with his high school sweetheart."

"Merry." The way he said her name, as though he was trying not to lose control, grated on her. She wanted him to lose it. Mr. Unreadable. Mr. Cool and Collected, never letting his emotions show. "Did you know it was me?"

"Not for sure. Not until you walked through the door."

"I saw your face and I thought…I thought you'd played me."

"How could you think I would do that?" she asked, breathless with emotion. "Or didn't you mean it all of those times you called me kind?"

"I did, but…I've been wrong about people before."

"If you believed that I could be that cruel, then you don't know me at all. Actually, you never knew me because even in high school, I wasn't a mean girl. I wouldn't hurt you like that." Damn it, she did not want to cry again, but she could hear her voice breaking with every word. "The funny thing is, I thought you, Clark, might like me. That we were becoming friends and I actually hoped…that the Woodsman was you. I wanted you to be the guy because I had feelings for you. I wanted you."

"Merry…" He took a step toward her, the blank expression crumbling and underneath she saw the uncertainty, the vulnerability in his eyes, but she moved away.

"No. I don't want to hear about your parents' indifference. I don't want you to use your intimacy issues as an excuse right now. You intentionally hurt me before I could hurt you. You were irrational and cruel. The man I exchanged dozens of emails with wouldn't do that and neither would my friend Clark. You…I don't know who you are."

"Merry, please…I…I'm so sorry."

She avoided his hand reaching out for hers. "You're going to have to do a lot better than I'm sorry if you want my forgiveness." Ryan's truck pulled around the corner and she wiped at her cheeks. "That's my ride. Don't worry about tonight, Clark. We'll just go back to the way things were and stick to three subjects. The weather, the farm, and your son."

Merry hurried around the hood of the truck and climbed inside.

"Are you all right, sweetie?"

"No."

"Want me to back up and run him over?"

"Just go, please."

Ryan did as she asked, but when Merry turned back, Clark still stood in the same spot she'd left him.

CHAPTER 15

CLARK

CLARK STOOD ON HIS FRONT porch, his head pounding from lack of sleep. He took several sips of his coffee, his gaze straying to Merry's house. He'd left his window open so he could hear her come home, hoping to catch her before she went into the house and try again to apologize. He knew he'd fucked up the minute he walked out of the bar, but he'd been so shocked when he'd spotted that maroon dress, the only one in the place, being worn by Merry. All of her friends staring at him expectantly, watching for his reaction.

He'd panicked. He wasn't proud of it, but it had been too much. Letting people in wasn't natural to him. Online with KnottyGirl25, it was easier. The easiest experience with a stranger he'd ever had.

Except for Merry. Merry, who'd lured him out with laughter. He'd relaxed around her as much as he'd ever done with anyone besides Sam and Jace. He'd wanted her in a way he'd never wanted any woman. It wasn't the rush of lust he'd experienced with Patrice or the need to feel close to someone else for a few hours. His desire to be around Merry had everything to do with her. And taking that step with Merry could have not only jeopardized his job but their budding friendship.

Which was why when the woman he'd been waiting to meet turned out to be the one he'd been fighting not to want, he'd reacted irrationally. Deep down, he knew Merry wasn't cruel. Wasn't the type to toy with a man for her amusement. He'd sat in that parking lot for almost forty minutes kicking himself, the last two weeks playing back in his head like scenes out of a bad romantic comedy and Clark didn't think it was funny. Especially when he'd watched Merry come out and he'd needed to say the right things, but instead everything that came out of his mouth made what he'd done worse.

When he heard the truck that picked her up pull in last night, he'd gotten out of bed and into his boots. He'd planned to walk over after they left and try again. No excuses.

He'd barely made it past the porch when he realized the truck was still there. He'd ducked behind his Jeep when he heard Merry talking to someone, the second voice faint but distinctively male. Clark knew the involuntary flash of jealousy wasn't fair, but that didn't keep him from lying awake half the night, listening for the guy to leave. Now, he could clearly see the other vehicle next to Merry's, a black lifted truck with round headlights. He scowled at the truck over his coffee cup rim, taking another gulp of the bitter brew. Her taste in men hadn't changed at all, but then she'd said as much over email.

God, that last email she sent. He had no right to be jealous of anything she did. He'd been the asshole, an idiot. In a matter of moments, he'd let all of his issues and insecurities bubble to the surface and destroy his own potential happiness.

He'd tried to write all of his feelings down in email form, but had no way to send it. He'd copied and pasted the words into a document and printed them out, tempted to drop them in her mailbox, but there was no guarantee she'd read it and he couldn't blame her.

KnottyGirl25 and Merry. One and the same. How had he never considered the possibility? They'd both made him feel more than any woman had before.

The door opened to his left and Sam blew out a breath. "Brrr. What are you doing out here?"

"Nothing. Enjoying the quiet."

Sam followed his gaze and smirked, holding up the coffee carafe. "Need more caffeine for your stakeout?"

Clark turned his scowl on his brother, who chuckled, pouring the coffee into his own cup. "Fine, not a stakeout. We're just listening to the birds. The breeze through the trees. The—"

"Will you shut...the fuck...up."

"I believe that's a dollar to the swear jar, my dude."

Clark didn't respond, rubbing a hand over his face, the prickles of his unshaven face scratching his palm. "I messed up, Sam."

"I figured, since you're out here alone and there is a big boy toy parked at Merry's. Things didn't go well with your mystery woman?"

"It was Merry."

"What was Merry? Your date?" Sam cocked an eyebrow at his nod. "Then why the hell are you here and not there?"

"I walked out. I saw her, turned, and went back to my Jeep." Clark pulled the letter he wrote out of his pocket and handed it to his brother. "It's all in there."

Sam kept silent as he read, his gaze racing over every line, giving nothing away. Clark tapped his foot impatiently as he waited for him to grunt or scoff. Something.

Instead he folded the letter and handed it back to Clark.

"Nothing to say?"

"I do, but I'm processing."

Clark groaned. "You've never been shy about saying what's on your mind in every situation. Why stop now?"

"Will it help?"

"Probably not, but I still want to hear it."

"Okay." Sam set his mug down on the porch railing and with blinding speed, knocked Clark upside the head. "Are you out of your fucking mind? Who walks away from a woman like that? If you weren't my brother, I'd kick your ass on principle."

"You're telling me you haven't done worse?" Clark rasped, rubbing the side of his head.

"Have I been a complete twat waffle, yes, but even a reprobate like me wouldn't stand up Merry Winters in a crowded bar for any reason. And we were raised by the same emotionally defective robots!"

"And you compensated by charming the pants off every woman you meet, whereas I...can't seem to connect with anyone except you and my son."

"It's all those books you read instead of getting the hell out of that house and meeting people. You got so used to your own company you can't relate to anyone else."

"She's never going to forgive me. I walked away from her as an entire table of her friends watched."

Sam whistled long and low. "Yeah, I don't know how you come back from that." He slapped Clark on the back. "Look on the bright side…at least your hand won't feel neglected."

"You're a dick."

Merry's front door opened and Daisy came trotting down the porch steps first, disappearing behind the height of the fence. Clark couldn't make out the guy's features, but he looked rumpled as he turned at the bottom step in time for Merry to come out. She was bundled up in a purple robe, her blond hair hanging around her shoulders in waves. It was the second time Clark had seen it down, including last night, and he remembered thinking how thick and beautiful it looked. Clark imagined the guy with his hands in her soft locks last night, kissing her neck and—

Hot coffee spilled onto his hand and he released his tin mug. "Fuck."

"Drop now!" Sam hissed, seconds before grabbing Clark and dragging him to the wood planks of the porch.

Pain radiated through his legs when his knees hit the wood, but he gritted his teeth against it. "Did she see me?"

"I don't think so." Sam crawled over to the railing, carefully peeking through a gap. "They aren't looking this way. We're good."

Clark moved across the wood planks until he was next to his brother. "Why did you pour coffee on me?"

"I was just topping you off. I didn't know you were going to move."

"Shhh." Clark peered at Merry and the other man through the

two-inch spaces, and although he couldn't be sure, he thought she was smiling at the guy.

"Bastard."

"Green looks good on you, man."

Clark couldn't breathe, let alone respond, as he watched Merry come down one more step and kiss the man on the lips. His stomach twisted into knots, every urge to say something so strong he caught himself opening and closing his mouth several times, but nothing came. She was already pulling back when Sam hopped to his feet.

"Okay, I'm squashing this shit."

Clark slunk down even lower. "What the fuck are you—"

"Good morning, Merry!" Sam yelled, waving. "Beautiful day, isn't it?"

Clark didn't want to move, in case she noticed the motion. Her laughter trailed across the yard, friendly and warm the way it always was.

"Good morning to you too, Sam. Come on, Daisy Mae."

Sam kept waving like he was in the Miss America Pageant.

"Is she gone yet?" Clark whispered.

"Yes, but he's not."

"What's he doing?"

"Flipping me off."

Clark peeked through the railing. The guy was climbing into his truck and a few seconds later, the obnoxious roar of a tailpipe shattered the tranquility of the woods as he backed out of the driveway out of sight.

"And that is why I panicked and walked away last night,"

Clark growled, gathering his fallen mug from the ground and pouring himself another cup.

"Come again?"

"Merry always dates the jocks. Cocky dickheads that used to toss my books in the trash or trip me as I walked down the halls. That is what she falls for, not me."

"Seems to me you're not exactly the skinny book nerd you were ten years ago."

"Not on the outside, but inside I'm still the same fucked-up, insecure asshole who shafted the world before they could do it to him."

"I notice your language gets downright filthy when you're irritated. I like it."

"I try to watch my mouth around Jace, but I'm tired and pissed at myself." Clark took a deep, calming breath. "I'm going to apologize to Merry for walking out on her, but I'm not giving her the letter."

"Why? Because she brought a guy home after you shattered her self-esteem, maybe even her heart?"

"No, because she said she wanted me and then the minute I disappointed her, Merry fell back on old habits. Assholes in lifted trucks."

Sam covered his chest, his eyes widening mockingly. "As opposed to the asshole in the Jeep who can't even admit he's crazy about her?" His expression went flat, matching his wry tone. "Yeah, I can see how that would be a dilemma for Merry."

"Is that supposed to make me feel better?" Clark snapped.

"No, it's supposed to wake your ass up. You might be all mature when it comes to money and finances, but you're an adolescent with women. Merry doesn't owe you anything and she can sleep with anyone she wants. It doesn't diminish her or that big beautiful heart she carries around on her sleeve. If you can't see that, then you don't deserve her."

His brother picked up the pot of coffee and went back inside, the door shutting with a thwack behind him. Clark leaned on the porch railing with his coffee cup cradled in his hands, the letter in his pocket whispering to him.

Flashes of Merry rolled through his mind like a film reel. Chasing Butch around the yard. Walking among the trees with him. Gazing up at him, her lips parted. Whispering his name.

"We'll just go back to the way things were and stick to three subjects. The weather, the farm, and your son."

The idea of regressing to avoiding each other left him morose.

Clark wanted Merry to look at him with those golden-green eyes again, not with hurt or anger but with that radiant sparkle he'd only experienced when she smiled. He wanted more of her impromptu hugs, the ones that came without warning and chipped away every force field he'd built around his emotions. He wanted to know what it was like to be the best part of her day, not another guy who'd made her cry. Clark wanted to be the man Merry thought he was before last night.

And the only way to do that was to make a move.

Clark left his coffee cup on the railing and strode down the steps, eating up the distance between their homes with urgency.

He burst through her gate, trying to slow his breathing as he knocked on her door. Merry's voice came out of the camera doorbell to his left, the circle camera lit up red.

"What is wrong with you? Banging on someone's door like that?"

"I knocked. I didn't bang."

"You shook my door," she snapped.

"I'm sorry. I need to talk to you, Merry, and I don't want to do it through a door."

"Listening to you isn't on my agenda for today, so kindly remove yourself from my front stoop."

Clark frowned, his gaze boring into the camera lens. "You said I was going to have to do a lot better than I'm sorry if I was going to make it up to you." He pulled the letter out of his pocket, holding it up so she could see it. "I couldn't remember everything I wanted to say so I wrote it down."

Several moments passed and he backed down one step, about to slide the letter in his back pocket.

"Read it to me," she said.

He winced. "Don't you want to do that yourself?"

"No, I want you to read it. I want to hear your voice, so I know it's coming from you and not just something you wrote down because you could pretend to be someone else."

"I never pretended with you, Merry."

"Then prove it."

Clark cleared his throat. Unfolding the letter and stretching it between his hands, he did what she wanted.

"Merry, I know how badly I hurt you and that you don't want any excuses, so I'll start this letter with the facts. The fact is I told you I've only been in one relationship, but it's more than that. I've never been in love. I don't even know if I am capable of romantic love and I know how important it is to you. I love my brother and Jace. I would die for them, but being in love is different, I'm sure.

"Fact: There have been so many times over the last few weeks that I looked at you, at Merry, and I almost said to hell with fears and what-ifs. When you were in my arms, trying to ask me a question, the urge to kiss you was torturous. I have dreamed of you, not because I think you're beautiful or desirable, even though you are, but because of the way I feel when I'm with you."

The door swung open and both Merry and her puppy charged down the steps, but only one of them was focused on him. Her eyes seemed brighter than normal, although the whites surrounding them were bloodshot. She shut the door behind her and stood on the top step, her arms crossed over her chest.

"Go on."

With her eyes trained on him, sweat trickled down his temple and along his neck despite the chill in the air as he continued. "When I'm with you, Merry, the world slows down. I smile easier. I laugh louder. I play, Merry, something I've only ever done in the safety of my home with Jace. You bring the best out in me. Being around you makes me feel alive and it scares the hell out of me. That's why I break eye contact. Why I pull away. I've never felt like I deserved you, Merry. You were too much and I didn't think that you could ever keep your shine with someone like me."

"You didn't think you deserved me?" Merry came down one step, her face flushed. "When? In high school when you thought I was shallow? Or last night when you thought I'd set you up for a laugh?"

The hurt in her voice twisted his gut in knots. "I knew deep down I'd made a mistake. It's why I couldn't go home, but you were right. I was a coward. The thought of going back into that bar with your friends and admitting I'd been a colossal asshole spun me so hard, I couldn't sift through all the chaos in my head."

"Is there a word bigger than colossal? Mega? Gigantic? Massive?"

"All of the above."

The lines of her face had eased slightly and she nodded toward the letter in his hand. "Is there more?"

"Yes, there's another paragraph."

"I'd like to hear the rest."

"All right." He took a deep breath. "I really want you to forgive me, Merry, but more than that, I want another chance to be your friend. To be the guy you thought could be more. I want to earn back your respect and trust, to show you I'm not damaged beyond repair. If you want me to stand up in front of all your friends and tell them what an idiot I am, I will."

"Oh, they know," Merry said.

Clark's mouth twitched, but he kept going. "If you want me to go on the radio and tell the world that I made a huge mistake, I won't hesitate."

"I think you're more likely to go viral on TikTok. The radio is so dated."

He laughed, meeting her eyes. Her arms were no longer crossed but stuffed into the pockets of her robe.

"I will do anything you ask of me, Merry. I'll even give up the last piece of apple pie."

Her eyes narrowed. "Your favorite flavor is pumpkin."

"You remember that?"

She sighed. "Unfortunately, I remember everything about our conversations, both online and off."

"Unfortunately?"

"Yeah, unfortunately. It's really annoying to have all these funny, wonderful messages and conversations in my head and then that one ugly moment tarnishing them."

"I really am sorry. I wish I could take it back."

"Which parts?" she asked.

"All of last night."

"What about the rest?" Her voice was barely above a whisper. "You said you were trying not to like me."

"Because if things go bad between us, it doesn't affect just one aspect of my life. If I get involved with a woman, it's not only me I have to think about. It's Jace."

Merry's eyebrows snapped down. "I adore your son and he likes me." She said it firmly, almost defensively.

"I know he does and that is the scary part. This place, your parents…I have never seen Jace so happy. He loves it on this farm. You're connected to my work. Where I live. If you were someone across town who I could avoid if things didn't work out, it would be one thing, but if I start something with you, I could lose everything. I don't want to be responsible for taking away my son's joy."

Her expression softened. "I would never let that happen. No matter what, I know how much you love him. It's one of the first things I noticed when you came back, what an amazing dad you are. No matter how I felt about you, I would never let that affect your position here."

"I know that. Now."

"Well, you should have known it last week, too."

Clark fought a smile at her sass and continued sincerely, "I know I should have. It's difficult for me to trust people, but that's my insecurity, not yours."

"Damn right it is," she said, bending over to pick up her disobedient puppy. "Last night, I thought you were a dense, inconsiderate, judgmental douche canoe."

Clark put a hand out against the house, stopping her from walking away. She turned with exasperation tightening the space between her eyes, Daisy cuddled in her arms mirroring her expression.

"What do you think now, Merry? Is there anything you see worth forgiving?"

Merry leaned against the house, her expression undecipherable. "Today, I see a contrite douche canoe."

"I am. I may be the biggest douche canoe you have ever met, but I don't want to be one." He noticed the twitch of her full lips, even though she wasn't meeting his gaze, and he pressed on. "I am an idiot, Merry, especially where you're concerned. With the exception of your mom, you are the kindest person I have ever met. You surprise me, you make me laugh. Being around you lifts a weight inside me I didn't know was there. I loathe myself for hurting you. I would have told you all this again last night, but you had company."

She met his gaze then, narrowing her eyes. "What was that?"

"What?"

"That tone."

"What," he asked innocently. "I just said you had company."

"Yeah, but you said it like, ewww, company…like you were sneering at it."

He scoffed. "I did not. I just didn't want to disturb you when you had a guy over."

"Ah-ha!" Merry cheered, pointing a finger into his chest while keeping an arm around her squirming dog. "How did you know it was a guy?"

Clark cocked his head. "The big truck?"

"Women drive big trucks too."

"Sam mentioned it."

"Liar." She laughed, bending over and letting Daisy wiggle back down to the ground. "I thought I saw you on the porch this morning, but I was sure I was imagining things. Because why would someone who was so obviously not interested in me be on the porch, spying?"

"I wasn't spying. I happened to be on the porch enjoying my coffee when you walked outside."

"And you hid?"

"I mean…I didn't want you to think what you already do, so I may have moved out of sight."

"Uh-huh."

Her body language had relaxed, and he bent his elbow to lean closer, drawn to her walls lowering. "You don't believe me?"

"Not even a little bit."

His gaze dropped to her smirking, full lips. "What do you think?"

"I think you're jealous."

"Of a monster truck?" Clark scoffed.

"It's a lifted Chevy."

"I'm definitely not jealous of that."

"My mistake," she said airily, ducking under his arm.

She opened the front door and he cleared his throat. "Is there a reason I should be?"

Merry reached inside and came back with some dog treats, rattling the bag. Daisy's head lifted at the sound and she rushed to her mistress, following the bag inside.

"If you're telling the truth about wanting forgiveness so we can be friends again, then no. There's not a single solitary reason."

"And if I want more?"

Merry didn't answer him, simply held her hand out. "May I keep the letter?"

Clark held it between his hands. "Are you going to post it on the internet?"

"No, Clark, I'm not. But if you don't trust me..."

He placed the letter in her hand. "I do. Does this mean you might forgive me?"

"I'm considering it." She shut the door without saying anything more and Clark stood there, realizing he hadn't gotten the answer he wanted but she hadn't completely shut him down.

"Have a nice day, Clark," she said through the intercom speaker.

Clark was done fighting his feelings. He wanted Merry all to himself. The biggest challenge would be convincing her he meant it.

"You too, Merry."

CHAPTER 16

MERRY

MERRY WALKED UP THE HILL to her parents' Sunday, Daisy pulling ahead of her, tightening the leash in her hand. The entire Winters family and the farm employees were meeting this morning to take pictures for the 75th anniversary Christmas cards. Her mother decided since the photographer would already be at the farm, they might as well do family pictures. Something Merry was thankful was happening today, instead of yesterday when her face looked like she'd gone several rounds with a boxer.

Of course, she'd still ended up on camera, anyway. She'd agreed to the News Ten interview, and after her story ran about rescuing Daisy Thursday night, her plug about the farm's anniversary had brought people from all over yesterday. They'd ended up with nearly a hundred prepaid trees to be delivered the day after Thanksgiving, which was still eleven days away. With the exception of the pre-cut delivery and the Festival of Trees, it was the largest order they'd seen in years. Four more papers and news stations had shown up throughout the day, catching her on the worst day, but she'd smiled and told the truth. That everything happened so fast and she'd only done what her parents raised her to do: the right thing. They'd seemed excited about it.

Halfway up the hill her tummy rumbled unhappily. She should have made an omelet like she'd planned, but when she'd found a box on her doorstep with a whole pumpkin pie inside, eggs and vegetables didn't sound as good as a slice with whipped cream on top.

The note on top read: *Forget the last piece, you can have the whole pie. Forgive me yet?*

Not completely, but he'd scored a few points with that one.

When she rounded the front of the house, Jace burst out of the door, wearing a Christmas plaid flannel and blue jeans. His hair was spiked up, like someone had run a bucket of gel through the short, golden strands.

"Hey, Merry. Daisy!" At his high-pitched greeting, the puppy yanked with all her strength until she could reach his face with her tongue.

"You look nice, Jace. New clothes?"

"Victoria bought them for me for family pictures. We're all supposed to match. She has something for you too."

"Of course she does."

"Can I take Daisy inside to see Butch?"

"Sure." She handed off the leash to him and he jetted back up the porch steps. When she walked into the living room, Nick and Clark were changing their shirts, but her gaze locked on Clark's open flannel, framing a set of washboard abs too pretty to cover up.

"Hey, Sis," Nick said, jerking her attention away from Clark's six-pack.

"Hi." She cleared her throat, afraid to look at Clark again. "Where is Mom?"

"She's in the back getting changed."

"Great, thanks." Merry stole a glance at Clark, wondering what he was thinking. They'd left things up in the air when she'd shut the door on him, but she'd needed time to think about where they went from here. If he wanted her, he was going to have to stop all this back and forth. If he wasn't all in, then she was out.

"Good morning, Merry," he said with that warm rumble she loved.

"Hey, Clark." She hoped her voice was cheery and not a nervous pitch. "Nice to see you."

"You too."

Clark's fingers worked over each button, keeping his gaze on her, and she noticed he'd messed up a few.

"Your shirt's not lined up," she said.

He looked down with a laugh. "You're right. Guess I got distracted."

He was teasing, his voice laced with seduction and temptation and...

Nope, she wasn't falling for it. He had more groveling to do.

"Excuse me, I better get dressed."

"Bye, Merry," he called after her, but she was already halfway down the hall.

Merry had spent the last year learning her worth, and as much as she liked Clark, he had messed up big time. It was going to take some major effort if he wanted her, and she would not let him back in with anything less. No sexy tone or sweet nothings were going to work. He needed to be open to her, not shut down whenever something got too intense.

She knocked on her mother's door and it swung open, her mother posing in a red cowl-neck sweater and leggings the same plaid as the men's shirts.

"Oh good, your clothes are in the bathroom hanging up."

"Are we all wearing red?"

"No, you and I are wearing red and Holly and Noel are wearing green. And with Jace and Clark, we have equal boys and girls for family pictures. They are family, so after we do the big farm photo, we'll do family pictures with us. I booked the photographer for the whole day so the employees can also have family photos taken. It's a thank-you for how hard they work."

"That's wonderful, Mom. And I agree about Jace."

"Not Clark?"

Clark can be family, but not in the gross, incest kind of way.

"Clark too."

"Thank you, now get changed! She'll be here any minute. Are you going to wear lipstick?"

Merry laughed, talking to her mom through the door. "Would you like me to wear lipstick?"

"I thought a matte red would look lovely with the sweater, but it's up to you. If you want to wear it, the tube is on the counter."

"Thanks." Merry changed her clothes and ran the lipstick over her upper and lower lip, smiling to make sure there wasn't any on her teeth. She fluffed her blond waves before stepping out. Usually she liked her hair back and out of her face, but with the slouch neck of the sweater and her lips, having her hair down made her feel beautiful. Sexy.

Her mother came over and cupped Merry's face in her hands. "You're so beautiful, Merry, inside and out." Merry beamed for a half second before her mother playfully pushed her out of the way. "Now, I need to finish putting my face on, so skedaddle!" She went into the bathroom, holding the door slightly open so Merry could see her wink. "Tell your father I need ten minutes, so if the photographer shows up, stall her."

Her mother shut the door before Merry could reply.

Shouting in the living room traveled down the hallway.

"What in the heck! What's going on?" Merry called as she hurried into the living room just in time to watch Nick run out the door, slamming it behind him. Merry opened the door to find Holly and Noel standing on the porch, snickering.

"What are we looking at?"

Holly pointed toward the trees, where Nick, Clark, Jace, and their dad were running opposite ways through the maze of trees, like the characters in a Scooby-Doo cartoon.

"Your puppy slipped her leash and the guys are trying to catch her."

When Daisy flashed between the rows with Clark chasing her, bent over with his arms outstretched, she smothered a laugh.

"Damn that sneaky brat."

Merry ran back into her parents' house, rummaging through the cupboard until she found a bag of jerky. She brushed past the other women down the steps and stopped at the edge of the trees, shaking the bag contents with a three-note whistle.

Suddenly, a dirty-white Daisy came barreling out of the trees toward her, her mouth open and her ears pinned back as Nick gave chase. He stopped when he noticed Merry, and stood up straight with his head back, chest heaving.

"That...dog...is quick...for a baby."

"Yeah, she is! Good girl!" Merry spoke in an excited voice, shaking the bag with a grin until the pup skidded to a stop.

"She is not a good girl," Clark grumbled, coming up alongside Nick.

"But she's a cute girl and you gotta praise her when she minds." Merry put her hand up and Daisy plopped her butt down in front of her. She pulled out a piece of jerky and gave it to her, snatching the collar in her other hand before Daisy got any ideas about bolting again.

All three men had emerged from the trees, bent over and sucking in air like they'd run a half marathon.

"You all right?" Merry asked.

"That pup is going to give me a heart attack," her dad croaked. "And you're feeding it my good jerky?"

"I forgot her treat bag at home. I read up on emergency recalls for Pyrs online and apparently if you combine their favorite treat with a noise or word, they will come running most of the time. Ours is the bag shake and a special whistle."

Jace ran out of the rows, holding Daisy's leash out to Merry with tears streaming down his cheeks. "I am so sorry. I didn't know she could wiggle her head out when it was too loose."

"Hey, hey, I'm not upset with you." Merry slipped Daisy's leash on and pulled Jace into her arms, holding the sobbing little boy. "Jace, do you know how many times she's gotten away from me or my parents since I brought her home?" He shook his head against her and she smiled. "Too many and I haven't even had her a week. She's wily." She kneeled down so they were eye level, her hands rubbing his shaking back. "But maybe until I've taken her through obedience training, I'll keep her in my grasp when we're outside the yard. Would that be okay?"

He nodded, wiping his face with his hands.

"Should we go inside and get you some tissues and clean Daisy up for pictures?"

"Yeah."

"Let's do that," she said, taking his hand.

Leading Jace and Daisy back toward the house, she heard footsteps behind them. Clark caught up to them and took Jace's other hand.

"I can help so we're not holding things up for everyone else."

Merry smiled at his uncertain expression, as if waiting for her to tell him to get lost. "Thank you."

"Thank you, Merry."

Those three words, spoken with a tender electricity that zipped through her chest like a lightning bolt, left a tingling heat in their wake.

Noel passed by them on the sidewalk, and when her eyes met Merry's, she nodded toward Clark with a thumbs up, silently asking if they were good. All the girls had witnessed the dramatic events of the disaster date, but Merry had begged them all to leave the guys out of it. Merry knew it would be hardest for Noel, who genuinely considered Nick her best friend, but considering her brother hadn't knocked Clark into the dirt, she assumed Noel kept her word.

As they neared the porch, Holly's gaze shifted from Merry to Clark, her eyes narrowing. She opened her mouth as if ready to give him a piece of her mind, but then she looked down at Jace and shut it. Even though she'd told Holly about their encounter yesterday, her sister still wasn't ready to forgive and forget.

Her mom opened the front door as Merry reached the top porch step, her frazzled smile dissolving as she took in Jace's tears and Daisy's dirt-streaked fur.

"Oh no! What happened?" Victoria cried.

"Daisy decided to go for a little jaunt," Merry said, squeezing Jace's hand reassuringly. She didn't want him blaming himself anymore. "And Jace was upset about it, but there's no harm done that a little soap and water won't cure. We'll get her cleaned up, wash our faces, and get back out here."

"I'll take Jace, while you work on the troublemaker." Victoria gave Daisy her angry mom look, complete with wide eyes and a deep frown. Daisy backed up a few paces and pressed against Merry's leg.

"Come here, baby," her mom called and Jace dropped their hands, running full tilt into Victoria's arms, who picked him up like he weighed nothing at all. "We'll get that face washed, but first, how about a cookie?"

"Mom, shouldn't you ask his dad if he wants him to have a cookie?" Merry asked.

"I pretty much let Victoria do whatever she wants with him."

He said it with affection. Like all of her mom's children, he'd resigned himself to going along with whatever Victoria wanted.

Victoria bounced Jace on her hip. "And we want cookies, because they make everything better, right?"

"Right!" Jace laughed, already happier.

"So, Merry, mind your business and get that dog cleaned up. She has an outfit too."

Merry shook her head as the two of them disappeared inside and she smirked. "You've created a monster."

"Me? What did I do?"

"You brought that adorable child into our lives and made everyone, especially my mother, fall in love with him. I'm just saying I don't think there is anything you could do that would get rid of her."

"I don't want to get rid of any of you," he whispered.

"Yeah, right." Holly snorted from behind them, but Merry ignored her, her heart keeping up with the rapid tempo when he stepped closer, his hand coming up to rest against the side of her neck, his thumb running along her jawline. Bells jingled in the distance, like some kind of musical soundtrack to this charged moment, growing louder as he leaned over so only she could hear.

"Can we—"

A loud bay made Merry jump and she looked down as Butch stopped between them, wearing a plaid dog sweater complete with a red leather collar dotted with bells. Daisy jumped on Butch, grabbing his long ear in her mouth, and the other dog tolerated her gnawing.

"Merry! Get your dog washed!" Victoria hollered from inside.

"Do you still want help?" he asked.

"That's okay. We can talk later when we have more privacy," she said, shooting her sister a lethal look.

"All right, I'll see you out there."

She covered Clark's hand with hers, releasing a heavy sigh. "One thing."

"Yeah?"

"If I ever try to dress Daisy in ridiculous outfits, please stop me."

"I promise," he said.

CHAPTER 17

CLARK

CLARK COULD FEEL HOLLY HOT on his heels the instant he stepped off the porch and he knew this moment was coming. If he was going to win Merry over again, he was going to have to prove to her sister and friends he wasn't the douche they most likely thought he was.

"Hey, you!"

Clark stopped at the edge of the walkway, waiting for Holly to catch up.

"Hi, Holly."

She was shorter than Merry by a few inches and while their features were similar, Holly's eyes were a deep brown and narrowed, her mouth pursed mulishly.

"You hurt my sister."

"I know and I'm—"

"Shhh, no, I am not done. Merry acts tough, but she is as soft and squishy as a stuffed animal. And while she seems to be on her way to forgiving you for your deplorable behavior, I'm going to need more."

"More than…?" Had Merry told her about the letter and the pie?

"An apology. I need to know what you're doing to make

things up to my sister. Do you actually care about her or are you still sticking to 'we can't date because I work for your parents'?"

"It's a valid reason. They could fire me and kick me out if I underperform or break their daughter's heart."

Holly crossed her arms over her chest with a huff. "Are you planning on doing either of those?"

"No."

"Do you care about my sister?"

"Yes, but—"

"Eh, no buts. You either do or you do not."

Why did he feel like he was sitting under a hot light being questioned by a CIA operative? "The but is important."

She released a skeptical grunt. "Let's hear it then."

"I've never been in love with a woman, and Merry believes in all of that romance and happily ever after. What if I can't give her what she needs?"

"You'll break up and she'll get over it. Unless you're a total dick bag, there is no reason for all of this added stress. Merry is an adult. You don't need to ask our father's permission with fifty goats as compensation to date her. Stop trying to crunch the numbers and plot out everything that can go wrong."

"How do you know I do that?"

"Because my dad does it and so do I. It's what makes us good at business. The difference is you don't seem to be able to leave that at the door and instead bring it into your personal life. Just relax and let things happen. If she'll give you another chance, that is. I wouldn't."

Before Clark could process all this, Victoria came out of the house and waved a shirt at Clark from the front porch. "Oh, Clark! I forgot I bought an extra shirt in case I mis-sized anyone. Is your brother around?"

"Yeah, I think he's watching TV. The tattoo parlor isn't open on Sundays. Is Jace okay?"

"Yes, he's finishing his cookie." Victoria came down the steps, spryly eating up the walkway until she stopped next to him. "Merry will bring him out when he's done, but your brother..." She slapped it against his chest. "Go tell him to put this on and get his behind up here."

"He's not an employee, though."

"These are family shirts. Chris and I have paid for a full day of family photos for all the farm employees. He is your family and you need some pictures together."

Clark looked at Nick and Chris, who'd been joined by Martin and his wife and several other employees. All of them were wearing red or white, except the Winters men. They wore plaid, the same plaid Victoria bought for Clark, Sam, and Jace.

Emotion crawled up his throat, making it difficult to swallow. "Thank you."

Victoria patted his cheek. "You are so welcome. Now hurry. I want you back here in a few minutes for the big farm picture."

She breezed farther down the sidewalk, leaving Clark befuddled.

"Your mom is something else."

Holly smiled proudly. "Yes, she is."

"I better get Sam," Clark said.

"You didn't finish telling me about your intentions. Are you going to keep pulling away from Merry? Or are you going to do your very best to make her happy?"

Clark ran a hand through his hair, searching for the right answer. "I tried staying away from Merry and it didn't work. If she'll give me a chance, I'm going all in."

"All right then."

"That's it?" Clark prodded.

"If Merry still wants you, then I'm satisfied."

"Thank you, Holly."

"Don't thank me. I won't sway her one way or the other, unless you let me get your brother. Then I might put in a good word for you."

Clark raised an eyebrow. "I'm trying to get on your sister's good side. Letting you near my brother isn't conducive to my mission."

Holly wrinkled her nose. "I don't need another protective person in my life."

Clark shrugged. "Well, you got one."

Jace and Merry came out of the house, leading a slightly cleaner Daisy. She slowed down when she saw them, eyeing her sister warily. "Everything all right?"

"It's great. I have to grab my brother for pictures, so I'll see you in a bit."

"Do I have to come?" Jace asked, his attention on a few boys stick-fighting within the growing group of employees and their families.

"No, I've got your uncle. Just don't get into any trouble until I get back."

"I'll keep an eye on him," Merry said.

"No, I will keep an eye on him. You two...converse." Holly held her hand out for Daisy's leash and when Merry handed it over, she nodded to Jace. "Come on, little man. Let's go see what kind of trouble we can get into."

Jace took off with Holly, who struggled to keep up with the boy and the puppy straining after him.

"Look, whatever my sister said to you, I swear you're fine. We don't even have a wood chipper."

Clark burst into surprised laughter. "She didn't mention a wood chipper."

"I'd be concerned she didn't outright threaten you."

"Maybe she already knows I'm aware of my mistakes and is giving me a chance to make it right."

"And are you?" she asked lightly.

"Making it right?" She nodded and he took a step toward her. "I'd like to. If you'll be patient with me, I was hoping we'd start with a date. No secret identities. No surprises. Just us."

Her blank expression made his stomach swirl, bubbling with nervous nausea.

"I'll think about it and get back to you," she said airily.

"No problem, take your time."

As if sensing his disappointment, she reached out and rested a hand on his arm. "It's just that it's the last week of school before Thanksgiving break, and I've got festival planning meetings, and I don't want Daisy to spend too much time with my dad or he may try to steal her."

"I don't think your dad wants that pain-in-the-ass puppy."

"Ha, that is what he wants you think, but he was the same way when my mother brought home Butch, who was supposed to be *her* dog. When I went to pick up Daisy from them Friday night, my dad was leaning back in his recliner, sleeping, with Butch at his feet and Daisy stretched out from his lap to his chest, her face buried in his neck." She shook her head with a laugh. "Such a softy."

"He's a good man." Clark cleared his throat. "You'll let me know? About that date?"

"Absolutely."

"Clark! Get your brother!" Victoria hollered.

Merry chuckled. "You'd better get going before she starts counting to three."

"Sounds terrifying." His hand brushed hers as he passed. "I'll be right back."

"I'll be here."

He cut across past the garage and headed down the hill to the house, thinking about Holly's analogy that he treated everything, including his personal life, like he needed to prepare for every potential disaster. When Patrice got pregnant, he researched scholarships, financial aid, and grants, anything to help keep him in school. Then she'd left and although he hadn't expected it, he'd been able to handle it because he'd assumed they'd both be returning to college after Jace was born and would need daycare. He'd been one step ahead, analyzing the pros and cons. Completely prepared for whatever life could throw at them.

Except Merry. She'd come out of nowhere, and he'd been overwhelmed by his feelings for her, playing them down even in his own mind.

When she was a faceless woman on the computer, there hadn't

been the stakes until she became a flesh and blood person. She wasn't the superficial princess he'd imagined her to be in high school. People wanted to be around Merry because of her caring, open heart, spreading warmth like the sun to the trees.

Man, when did he start waxing poetic?

He walked through the door and his brother turned his head against the back of the couch to look at him, a day's growth on his cheeks, chin, and above his upper lip.

"I thought you were getting pictures taken?"

"I am, but so are you." Clark tossed him the plaid. "Hurry up and shower, shave, and put this on with a pair of jeans. We'll be up by the trees to the left of the main house waiting."

"When did you buy us matching shirts like we're some Pinterest-perfect family?"

"I didn't. Victoria did. The Winterses are giving their employees family pictures for Christmas, and you and Jace are my family so she bought us all matching shirts."

Sam got up and held the shirt in front of him. "Three guys in one picture wearing the same shirt? We're going to look stupid."

"I don't care," Clark growled, ready to choke Sam. "I'm wearing the shirt and so are you because we're not hurting her feelings. And although I always get Jace's picture taken this time of year, this will be the first one as a family. So can you just put aside all that *too cool for this* attitude and look like a dork for your little brother?"

"Fine. But only because I never like to disappoint a beautiful woman and Victoria—"

"Whatever you're about to say, don't."

Sam grumbled his way to the back room and Clark left the house with a sappy grin on his face. For the first time in his life, he really felt like he was part of something. Not just a family, although Chris and Victoria definitely did that for him and Jace, but that he belonged here. On this farm. In Mistletoe.

Maybe even with Merry?

As he crested the hill, the photographer, Bonnie Rickets, had all the employees squished together with Victoria and Chris in the center, the rolling hills of Christmas tree rows in the background.

"Clark!" Chris called. "Come over here by Merry and Jace."

Clark jogged up next to Merry and Chris, Jace leaning back against him. Chris put his arm around Clark and shook him. "I'm glad you're here, son. Thank you for all your hard work."

"You're welcome, sir. I'm grateful I saw your ad."

"Me too."

"All right, squeeze together," Bonnie ordered. "Clark, put your one hand behind Merry and the other on your son's shoulder."

Clark did what she asked, resting his hand against Merry's lower back.

"Perfect, here we go!"

Merry leaned into him, whispering, "I checked my schedule. I'm free this Saturday."

He turned her way and she met his gaze, smiling. "That's awesome, because so am I."

When the photographer yelled at everyone to look at the camera, he didn't have to fake a smile.

CHAPTER 18

MERRY

FRIDAY AFTERNOON, MERRY TOSSED HER pilgrim's hat on the desk and slipped off her boot to scratch the bottom of her foot. She'd gotten her stitches out yesterday and the damn thing still itched. It was the last day before the week-long Thanksgiving holiday Idahoan schools enjoyed and she was beyond ready for it. As much as she loved her job and the kids, she was looking forward to vegging out with her yarn in front of the TV, watching Christmas movies with Daisy. Eating good food on Thanksgiving. Maybe sharing the last piece of pie with her sexy neighbor.

That was if the date tomorrow night went well.

When he'd walked her home Sunday after pictures, he'd put his number in her phone and they'd been texting every chance they could and talking on the phone after Jace went to bed until one of them fell asleep, usually Clark. He'd been working long hours with the truck drivers, making sure the pre-cut trees were loaded properly and wouldn't be damaged, getting home with enough time to eat something and tuck Jace in. He'd told her long days were why he left his last job, but knew it was only certain times of the year. That the flexibility and everything he'd been able to save made this week worth it.

Then last night, whew. She had no idea what got into him, but their conversation took a sexy turn.

"Do you know I lie in bed every morning, half asleep, and the first thought I have is you?" Clark's deep voice murmured.

Merry replied in a flirty tone, "Oh yeah? What am I doing?"

"Kissing me."

"Where?" She'd slapped her hand over her mouth, but Clark chuckled, a deep throaty rumble that shot straight to her center.

"Do you really want me to answer that?"

"I think I do." Her voice dropped to a hushed whisper, her hand slipping under her comforter and across her stomach. When her fingers dipped lower, she let out a little moan.

"Merry…"

"Yeah?"

"Do you know what you're doing to me?"

The ringing phone burst through her memory and she grumbled under her breath as she picked up the receiver and pressed line one.

"Mistletoe Elementary, how may I help you?"

"Merry? Is everything all right? You sound out of breath."

Leave it to her mother to notice. "Hey, Mom. Yeah, it's fine. I'm just tired and ready for vacation. What's going on?"

"I hate to ask, but can you bring Jace home? I'm stuck in road construction on 84 and your dad and Clark are overseeing the last of the pre-cut shipments."

"Sure, I'm here anyway, so that's no problem. I don't leave until three-thirty though."

"That's all right, I'll let Clark know. Thanks, honey. Tell Jace I'll see him when I get home."

"I will, bye." Merry took a deep breath. A group of kids ran past in paper turkey hats, giggling and chatting, and Merry held her finger over her lips, silently telling them to speak softly. The kids put their fingers over their mouths until they disappeared down the hall and the chatter resumed.

Merry couldn't wait to get home and prepare for her date tomorrow. The dresses she'd drunk-ordered with Ryan last weekend arrived and he'd agreed to come over and help her pick one out. Maybe after Ryan went home, she and Clark could have a repeat of last night, preferably without Daisy trying to attack her busy hand through the covers and making her laugh.

Since Jace would be at her place for a while, she'd make dinner for Clark too. Ryan wouldn't be there until closer to nine because of his date with the hot bartender he'd blown off to help her, so they had time for dinner and to talk. The last thing Clark had said to her last night floated through her mind like a dream growl.

"I cannot wait to kiss you, Merry. It's about time, don't you think?"

She knew it wouldn't happen with Jace around. They'd had a long talk on Sunday about how they needed to proceed with discretion until he was ready for Jace to know. Merry understood, since this was Clark's first real attempt at dating anyone since Jace's mom. She could empathize with Clark's hesitancy, especially because Jace was so attached to her parents, but she'd made a promise. If their relationship ended, the fallout wouldn't bleed over to affect Jace's home or Clark's job and she meant it with every fiber of her being.

She logged into her computer and searched Jace's name. Tapping the extension on her phone, she waited for his teacher to answer.

"Hello?"

"Hi, this is Miss Winters in the office. Can you let Jace Griffin know to come down here when school is over? He's going home with me."

"No problem, I'll let him know."

"Thank you." Merry ended the call and went about her end of day duties. There was only a half hour left in the school day, and it went by in a blur of phone calls, last-minute paperwork, and a quick run to the restroom.

The bell rang and children filled the halls, bursting out the front doors past her office. Jace came around the corner and pushed through the door of her office at a snail's pace, his back pack dragging across the floor.

"Hi," he said.

A paper pilgrim's hat covered Jace's sandy hair, his cheeks flushed. He set his backpack on the bench against the rear of her office and sat down next to it. He made a noise and rubbed at his neck, frowning.

"Hey, you okay?"

Jace shrugged. "My throat hurts."

"Oh, are you thirsty? Hang on." Merry grabbed a bottle of water from the mini fridge under the counter and opened it for him. "Here you go."

"Thanks." He didn't take a drink, just stared down at his shoes.

Merry ducked her head, trying to catch his eye, and he looked up at her. "If you're upset about something, sometimes it helps to talk about it."

His forehead knitted in a scowl. "Harvey Trent said that Spider-Man was stupid."

Merry almost laughed, thinking about Clark's outrage over her not watching *Game of Thrones*. "Oh man. Who does Harvey like?"

"Batman," Jace said, rolling his eyes.

Merry held her amusement in check. She knew enough from her brother and watching superhero films that there were two kinds of fans and it was obvious what comic book camp Jace came from.

"But...Marvel is better than DC."

Jace's head jerked up, his whole countenance perking at her statement. "I know! I said that and he told me I was stupid too."

Irritation lit through Merry like a surge of electricity. "What did you do?"

"I told him that's not a nice word, and he laughed at me."

Merry put a hand on his shoulder, hating the hurt in his small, soft voice. "While I don't think that Harvey should be name calling, his opinion on Spider-Man is just that: his opinion. Everyone has one, and sometimes it's just better to ignore them. But if he keeps calling you names, you should tell Mrs. Hill, all right?" Jace nodded. "Now, I need to wait here for a little bit until all the kids get picked up. Do you want to color? Or watch a movie on my phone?"

Jace beamed at that. "Phone, please."

She pulled out her phone, tapped on the streaming app. "Here. This is the kids' section, so just scroll through and pick whatever you want."

"Thanks."

Merry didn't have time to say anything else before several kids came up to her office window, asking to call their parents. By the time the last child left, it was almost three-forty-five.

"All right, ready to go, Jace?"

Merry noticed he was lying down on the bench now, his arm dangling over the side and his pilgrim hat on the floor along with her phone. Merry picked up both and slipped the phone into her purse, smiling at the flushed little face. His lips were puckered into adorable fish lips and she ran a hand over his forehead.

Hmmm, he feels warm.

"Hey Jace, you ready to go home?"

He groaned and sat up slowly, his eyes half-closed. "I don't feel good."

She frowned, worry knotting her stomach. "What's wrong?"

"My throat. And I feel like I'm going to throw up."

Merry grabbed the forehead thermometer from the cupboard and knelt down, running it over his forehead.

100.1. Crap.

She fought down the panic bubbling inside. She may not have ever taken care of a sick kid, but she knew the basics, starting with medication.

"I'm sorry you feel crappy, kiddo. Sit here and I'll get you some medicine." Merry checked his file for allergies and there were none, so she grabbed the liquid children's Tylenol from the locked medicine cupboard. She knelt in front of him and poured some of the thick, pink liquid to the measurement line. "Drink this and we'll get out of here." Jace knocked it back and Merry took the cup, wiping it out with a sanitary wipe and replacing the medicine. "I'm sure you want to be all tucked in at home with your blanket and favorite movie." When Merry returned to Jace, she picked up his backpack and put it over her shoulder. "That is what I like when I'm sick. You ready?"

Jace nodded and reached up with both arms. At first, Merry wasn't sure what he wanted and then she realized he was silently asking her to carry him.

"Poor guy." Merry bent over and wrapped her arms around him. "Up you go," she grunted, lifting him. She'd expected him to be heavier, but she was able to keep him on one hip with just an arm around him. Merry slipped her purse over her free shoulder and called a good night to the janitor, Mr. Johnson. The teachers and principal were in an after-school meeting down the hall and she didn't want to disturb them.

"I want my daddy," Jace moaned.

Merry rubbed his back soothingly, her purse and his bag slipping down her arm. "I know, honey. I'm going to see if I can get ahold of your dad."

By the time she got to her car, her arms were burning in protest at the extra weight. "All right, Jace, I need to set you down while I unlock the door. Can you stand?"

He nodded against the side of her neck before she slowly dropped him to his feet. Once she had the door open, she set his bag on the floorboard and helped him climb in. She buckled the seatbelt over his lap in the middle seat, she smiled, fighting back the worry at his peaked appearance. "All right, you ready?"

"Yeah," he mumbled weakly.

Merry shut the door and got into the driver's seat, her heart hammering as she turned the ignition. She'd never taken care of a sick kid before, never even babysat a healthy one. She assumed everything that was happening was normal, but she'd rather be sure. As she backed out of the parking space, she pressed the phonebook button on her steering wheel, trying Clark. It didn't even ring, just went straight to voicemail. At the beep, she glanced in the mirror at Jace, who stared out the window blankly.

"Hey Clark, it's Merry. I have Jace and he's not feeling so great. He says his throat hurts and he feels nauseated, so I'm taking him home to your place and going to stay with him. I'll see you soon."

She ended the call and tried her mom, but after three rings, it went to voicemail. She could be going through the mountains and out of service range or on another call, but Merry didn't bother leaving her a message.

In a last ditch effort for some reassurance, she dialed Noel.

"Hey, Mer."

"Hi, what do you do if a kid has a 100 degree fever once you've given him Tylenol?"

"Huh? Whose kid?"

"Clark's. Mom isn't answering her phone and Clark is at work. I called you because you're a nurse and I'm a bit out of my element."

"Don't panic, first of all."

"I'm not panicking."

"There is a high-pitched note at the end of your sentences, so yeah, you are, but you don't need to. His fever isn't too high. How long has he had it?"

"I don't know. He seemed a little lethargic and flushed when he came into my office fifty minutes ago, but then he fell asleep and when he woke up, he was hot. He says it's his throat and stomach."

"Could be any kind of virus. Schools are a petri dish of germs. He was probably feeling punky before his little nap."

"He did mention his throat was hurting then, but I thought he was thirsty."

"Mmm, might be strep then, which he'll need antibiotics for."

"I think I'll wait for Clark before I rush him off to the doctor."

"Good call, since he doesn't sound critical, just miserable. When you get him home, make him comfortable. You gave him meds?"

"Yeah, Children's Tylenol."

"Good. Sometimes a warm compress on his forehead and the back of his neck can help too. Make sure he gets plenty of liquids, but if fever goes over 104 or he has trouble breathing, take him straight to the hospital. And Merry?"

"Yeah?"

"Breathe. It's most likely just a bug. They come on quick sometimes with kids. I'm sure he's going to be fine."

"All right, thanks, Noel."

"Call me if you need me."

"I will."

Merry pressed the red phone on the screen and checked on

Jace in the rearview mirror. He was staring out the window with a grimace.

"How you doing?"

"Sick."

"Aw, sweetie," Merry said, feeling helpless. She took the left into the gravel driveway that led to both of their houses. She looked for Clark among the trees but he was nowhere to be seen. She parked next to Clark's Jeep, hoping to see Sam's motorcycle, but he wasn't there either.

Merry turned the car off and got out, then opened the rear passenger door. She hated the pallor in his cute little face as she unclipped Jace's seat belt.

"Come on, honey," she said, lifting him out of the car. "We're almost there."

He looped his arms and legs around her, his body shivering. "Merry..."

"Yes?"

Merry knew what was coming the minute the tiny body in her arms convulsed and retched.

Hot liquid splattered against the side of her neck, sliding over her shoulder and down her back under her jacket. The noxious smell of bile and sour food filled her nostrils and she closed her eyes, breathing through her mouth in an attempt to keep her own nausea at bay.

"I'm sorry," he cried weakly.

"Shhh, it's all right, Jace. You don't have to be sorry. Let's get you cleaned up."

Merry carried Jace into the house, happy to find the door

unlocked. It had been several years since she'd been inside the place and although most of the furniture was the same, all of the animal heads their former foreman had loved were gone.

Merry set Jace on the toilet and looked in the cupboard under the sink for a washcloth. Except for some vomit on his chin, he'd missed the rest of his body completely. Based on the wet strands of her hair sticking to her neck, he'd gotten most of it on her.

"I w-want my d-dad," he stuttered, his teeth chattering.

"I know, honey. He'll be here soon."

She found a stack of washcloths in the hall closet just outside the bathroom and got one wet, cleaning Jace's chin gently. "I'm going to run and get you a glass of water. Which room is yours?"

"First room."

"Can you head in there and change into your favorite pajamas? I'll be in there in just a moment."

Jace nodded, sliding off the toilet and stumbling across the hall.

Merry went to the kitchen first and after opening a few cupboards, found the glasses. The back of her shirt was sticking to her skin, but she tried to think of anything else except the smell of Jace's puke. She grabbed two plastic Spider-Man cups, filled one halfway full from the tap, but when she walked into Jace's room, he was lying on the floor in his jeans and no shirt.

"You didn't make it very far, huh?" She sat down next to him and held out the water cup. "Sit up for me. That's right. Now, I want you to put a little bit of this water in your mouth, swish it around and spit it out into this cup, okay? Don't swallow it." Jace did as she asked and she praised him. "Nice job. Do you need to do it again? That taste in your mouth can be gross."

He shook his head and she put the dirty water cup off to the side of his dresser on the hardwood floor. She got to her feet and set the clean cup next to his bed so he would have it if he got thirsty. Jace laid down again looking dazed, while Merry opened his dresser drawers until she found a matching set of superhero pajamas.

"Can you get dressed by yourself or do you need help?"

"Help," Jace said softly from his fetal position on the floor.

"Help it is."

Merry got him out of his jeans and into the pajamas. Once he was tucked into his bed, she ran a hand over his sweaty mussed hair. "I'm going to get cleaned up, but I will be just down the hall if you need me."

Jace nodded, his eyes already drifting shut.

Merry left his door open and stood in the hallway, debating. She could probably make it home for a change of clothes and back, but in case Jace woke up while she was gone, she didn't want to leave.

She went to the kitchen and dumped the dirty water cup. After going through several more cupboards, she found a plastic mixing bowl, and set it by the side of Jace's bed quietly. His eyes remained closed, his breathing coming heavy and a little raspy. She looked at the clock next to his bed. Four-thirty. Hopefully Clark got her message and could get home before the after-hours clinic closed.

Merry padded down the hallway to the master bedroom, feeling a little weird about being in Clark's room without asking. The dark wood bed matched the side tables and dresser, and the room was neat, the brown bedspread folded back and smooth.

She went through his drawers, pulling out a T-shirt and a pair of sweats. She stepped into his bathroom and undressed, wadding her soiled clothes into a ball as she removed each piece. When she pulled out her wet ponytail and her hair touched her bare back, she realized it really had gone everywhere and the thought almost sent her head-first into the toilet.

The front door opened and closed with a hard snap. "Merry? Jace?"

At the sound of Clark's voice, Merry wrapped the towel around her and ran out of the bathroom, *shhhing* the whole way. He was coming down the hallway when she came through the open doorway of his bedroom and he stopped in his tracks when he saw her.

"Shhh, hey. I put him in his room to rest. I would have taken him to my parents, but I thought he would be more comfortable at home"

His eyes widened as they traveled over her from the top of her head to the toes of her feet. Clark took a few steps forward and looked through the doorway of Jace's room, his face tight with concern.

"What happened?"

"My mom called and asked if I could bring him home. I can't leave until every kid gets picked up and when he came to my office, he was a little down, but I thought it had to do with a mean kid in his class."

"Someone's being mean to him?"

"It's not a big deal, he can tell you about it later. He fell asleep in my office while I finished up and when I woke him up, he felt warm, so I took his temperature and it was over 100. I gave him

Children's Tylenol but then he threw up as I was getting him out of the car to bring him inside, so I got him cleaned up and tucked in, but I didn't give him the meds again because my mom wouldn't ever give us meds when we were vomiting." She paused long enough to take a breath and continued, "Oh! And I am sorry but I got out some of your clothes to change into because I didn't want to leave him and—"

Clark moved so fast, she didn't have time to react. His arms wrapped around her in a fierce hug, his mouth hovering over her right ear.

"Thank you."

Merry felt his body trembling against hers and hugged him back. "Of course. I was a little out of my depth, because I don't have a lot of experience with kids. I didn't know a fever could come on like that, but I just kept thinking about what my mom did for me growing up when I got the flu."

Clark pulled away, just far enough to look into her face.

"You did fine."

"He was asking for you."

"I'll go in and check on him." Instead of releasing her, his arms tightened. "Thank you for caring."

Merry blinked up at him. "Why wouldn't I care? I did what anyone else would have done for him."

"That's not true. I can't remember either of my parents taking care of me so well. They'd give me medicine and send me to my room, but they didn't stay with me. Sam was the only one..." He took a shaky breath, running his hands over the towel at her back. "Thank you for being you."

The way he looked at her as though she'd walked over hot coals and dived through the depths of hell when all she'd been was a decent human being tugged at her heart strings and tears pricked her eyes.

"You're welcome," she whispered, her voice husky.

His eyes dropped to her mouth and before she could blink, his lips covered hers. Merry's breath caught in her throat as his lips pulled at hers, and her mouth opened, allowing Clark to deepen the kiss. She closed her eyes, her hands gripping his arms as she kissed him back, flames spreading along her skin, tightening the peaks of her breasts. The towel slipped without her hand on it, but she was pressed so hard against him, it didn't fall far.

Clark kissed her desperately, like he couldn't get enough of her, and she melted into his body until suddenly he broke the kiss and rasped, "What is that smell?"

It took Merry a second to muddle through and pinpoint exactly what he was talking about and then it hit her.

He had his hands in her hair. Her puke-saturated hair.

Merry groaned, resting her forehead against his chest. "Your son vomited all over me, including my hair."

Clark coughed, covering a low rumble that sounded a lot like laughter, and her eyes narrowed, pretending to be offended even as Merry forced back a smile.

"You think this is funny, huh?"

Merry could tell he was biting the inside of his cheek, but sputters of mirth kept escaping through his lips.

"You do know it's probably all over your hands."

"I think I missed it by a hair." This time, he threw his head back, his hands falling away from her, and she pursed her lips.

"Very punny."

"I'm sorry. I swear, I'm not laughing at you. I'm laughing because you tried so hard to take care of Jace and you got vomited on as thanks."

Merry adjusted the towel around her. "And a really great kiss. Well, until my stench interrupted it."

Clark smiled softly, the tender look in his dark eyes giving her goosebumps. No one had ever looked at her that way.

"Go take a shower and borrow anything you want. Mi closet is su closet."

Merry kept a tight grip on the towel as she went back to Clark's bathroom, shutting the door behind her. Her heart pounded in her chest and her lips tingled like crazy.

His kiss had come out of nowhere, but wow. Just...wow.

CHAPTER 19

CLARK

CLARK SAT ON THE SIDE of Jace's bed, watching his son sleep. He remembered the first time Jace came down with croup when he was barely a year old. Clark had been a wreck, unable to sleep while his son coughed so hard his little body convulsed in his arms. Clark rushed him to the ER, where they'd treated him for pneumonia and kept him for several days. Every time Jace got sick, that memory of watching his son struggling for every breath popped up and fear churned in the pit of his stomach.

When he'd heard Merry's message, he'd taken off across the farm, imagining the worst, and then she'd come out of his bedroom, shushing him like a scolding schoolteacher. Wearing nothing but that skimpy towel and rambling the events off to him as though she was waiting for him to get mad at her for choosing to stay with Jace rather than look after her own comfort.

The raw emotion bubbling inside him when he heard the worry in her voice made the need to have her in his arms unbearable and he couldn't stop himself from hugging her, from taking comfort in her soft, warm body. If it hadn't been for the smell of Jace's vomit getting to him, he would have kissed her just a little bit longer.

Jace stirred on the bed and opened his eyes blearily. "Dad…"

"Hey, buddy. I heard you were feeling pretty crappy. Can I get you anything?"

"Thirsty. Merry gave me a drink, on my nightstand. Can you give it to me?"

Clark picked up the cup next to the bed and handed it to him. "Here you go. Do you still feel sick to your stomach?"

Jace took a drink from the spout and shook his head, but stopped suddenly with a wince. "My head."

"Anything else hurt?"

Jace motioned to his neck.

"Your throat?"

"Yes."

"I'll get a flashlight so I can check things out."

"Is Merry still here?" Jace rasped.

Clark smiled. "She's just getting cleaned up. Want me to send her in when she's done?"

Jace set his cup on the nightstand and gave a small nod, but stopped with a groan.

"Try not to move if it hurts. I'll be right back."

He got up and left the room, nearly colliding with Merry coming down the hall. He caught her by the shoulders, giving her a once-over. She looked adorable in his baggy shirt and sweat-pants, her wet hair in a knot on top of her head.

"Hey, he was asking for you. Do you mind sitting with him while I get the flashlight?"

"Of course not." She took a step toward the room, but he clasped her hand, squeezing it in his.

"You look cute in my clothes."

"Thank you. They're comfy. I may have to steal them."

"They're yours if you want them." *And so am I*, he thought.

Merry returned his squeeze and released his hand. Clark watched her take his place on the side of Jace's bed, brushing his son's hair back. Merry spoke too softly for Clark to hear, but whatever she said to Jace made him smile.

Clark pulled a flashlight from the hall closet, wondering if she was regretting the way their first kiss came about. It wasn't exactly romantic, with his sick son in the next room and vomit dripping down her back, but he'd been caught up in the rush of emotions her actions and babbling created and he couldn't help himself. He could still feel the heat of her mouth under his and he wanted to do it again. Only they'd agreed to take things slow as they built trust and open communication, plus being sure about what they both wanted before they brought Jace into the mix. Every encounter he'd had with a woman started out hot and fast, fizzling the minute he walked out the door. He wanted more from Merry.

Merry started to get up when he came back in, but Clark waved her down. "You're fine there." Clark clicked the flashlight on, and put his hand on the bed next to Merry, leaning over his son. "All right, buddy, open up."

Jace opened his mouth wide and stuck out his tongue. "Ahhhh."

Clark studied the red, angry spots at the back of his throat and grimaced.

"Welp, looks like we're going to the doctor."

"Noooo," Jace whined, hiding under his blankets. "I don't want a shot."

"No shots, I promise, but I think you have strep which means you need different medication."

Jace didn't budge from under the covers and before Clark could tell him to come out, Merry touched Jace's knee. "I hate the doctor too. I had to get a shot a couple weeks ago and the doctor sewed up my foot afterwards."

Jace poked his head out so only his eyes showed. "Did it hurt?"

"A little pinch, but if you're going to Doctor Hofstetter, he was my pediatrician when I was growing up and he is very nice. He even lets you pick a prize from the treasure chest."

Clark had completely forgotten about that when he'd set Dr. Hofstetter up as Jace's primary physician after their move. His face split into a grin.

"He was my pediatrician, too."

"Small town problems, right?" Merry smiled.

"What kind of prizes?" Jace asked, dropping his blanket completely.

"One time, I got a giant yo-yo from the box."

Jace turned his gaze to Clark. "Can we go there?"

Clark winced at the hope in his son's face. "It's after five, Jace. They may be gone for the day."

Merry stood up and touched his arm. "Would it be okay if I made the call while you stay with him? I might be able to work some magic."

Emotions warred inside Clark as his first instinct was to tell her no, because up until they'd moved back to Mistletoe, he'd handled everything for them. Being here on the farm, he'd slowly learned that having a village of people to help wasn't such a bad thing. It took trust, and Clark trusted Merry.

"That would be great. Thanks."

Merry left the room and he heard the front door open and shut. She must have left her phone in the car.

He could tell that, to the Winters women, taking charge was just in their nature. They didn't think anything about donating their time and caring for others, and it was humbling to witness. Harder to accept.

Especially when having her there made everything better and he didn't want to lose that.

"You okay, Dad?"

"Yeah, sure." Clark leaned over and kissed his son's forehead. "I just hate when you're sick."

"Me too." Jace settled down into his bed and pulled the blanket over him. "Merry took good care of me."

"I can see that."

"Can we keep her?"

Clark's heart thumped. "What?"

"Can Merry be a part of our family, like Uncle Sam and Victoria and Chris?"

"You mean I don't have to marry her to get you new grand-parents anymore?" he teased.

Jace shook his head. "Victoria told me that she took in Noel when her parents died and that she thinks of Noel as her daughter. That families don't have to share blood to show love and that she will always consider me her family. And you too."

Clark's vision blurred and he wiped his eyes with a little laugh. "She said that, huh?"

"Yeah, so I was thinking. You don't have to marry Merry if you don't want to, but I like her."

"I know you do, buddy."

"So can she be our family, too?"

"If you want her to be family, then she is."

"Thanks, Dad."

"Hey, speaking of Merry, she mentioned a mean kid in your class. What happened?"

"He said I was stupid for liking Spider-Man. That Batman was better."

"I don't know who this kid was raised by, but calling someone stupid is wrong. Besides, Marvel is way better than DC."

"That's what Merry said."

Jace's tone overflowed with approval and Clark laughed, thinking *Forget food. The way to a boy's heart is through his favorite superhero franchise.*

The front door opened and closed again and he heard Merry thanking the person on the call. "We'll be right there." She leaned around the doorway, grinning. "Good news. Dr. Hofstetter said he'd stay for us, but we have to leave now."

Clark pulled the blanket off Jace and lifted him into his arms. "You hear that? I think Merry might be a superhero all on her own."

"I'll take that compliment. Can I borrow your washer before we go? I'd like to throw my clothes in while we're gone."

He stopped just before the door, his jaw hanging. "You want to go with us?"

"Is that okay?"

Clark looked at Jace, who nodded.

"All right. I'll meet you at the car," she said, disappearing down the hall.

Clark carried Jace outside, his fleece Spider-Man blanket clutched in his little hand, and considered the craziness of the last few weeks. He'd thought about Merry but never imagined she'd become this person he couldn't wait to see. For the first time, Clark could envision a future that included someone else in their lives and it gave him a rush of exhilarating hope, something he'd thought long dead for him.

He was climbing into the driver's seat when Merry came out wearing one of his hooded sweatshirts that hung down to nearly her knees, and nervous energy raced through him. Taking his kid to the doctor wasn't exactly a date, but he found himself hopping out of the car to meet her on the passenger side.

She cocked her head with a puzzled smile. "What are you doing?"

Clark pulled the handle and held the door for her. "Being a gentleman."

Merry covered his hand for a second before getting in. "I appreciate the consideration, but less chivalry and more speed racer."

He shut the door with a chuckle.

The drive into town was quiet. Clark kept glancing into the rearview mirror at Jace, who was nodding off. He reached out and touched Merry's hand lightly.

"Hey," he whispered softly.

She turned toward him with a smile. "Yeah?"

"I'm glad you stayed."

"Me too."

Clark grumbled the whole way up the steps to the house. Jace was sacked out like a fifty-pound bag of potatoes in his arms.

"Are you still complaining that he picked slime for his treasure chest prize?" Merry asked behind him, her voice laced with laughter.

Clark turned as he opened the door and scowled at her. "You do not understand how awful that stuff is. He will leave it everywhere and I will find it fused with the furniture or the floor or the drain."

"You could have said no."

"Not with him giving me that pitiful face. Not to mention you and the receptionist giving me identical expressions of disapproval when I tried, like I was some kind of evil dad monster."

"I did not!" Merry giggled. "I just didn't understand what the big deal was until you explained it for the entire fifteen-minute drive home from the pharmacy."

"You asked."

"Yeah, I won't make that mistake again."

Clark chuckled, carrying his son down the hallway to his room. Although Jace hadn't enjoyed the throat swab, he'd been a relatively good patient for the doctor and nurse. Clark tucked him into bed and took the white pharmacy bag from Merry. "I hate to wake him up, but I want to get this into him so it can work its

magic. Good news is this medicine does taste like bubblegum."
He measured out the dosage and shook Jace gently. "Bottoms up,
buddy."

Jace sat up sleepily and tipped it back with a gulp. He handed
his dad the measuring spoon and snuggled down into bed. "Night."

"You want some soup?"

"No, thanks."

"All right, I'll be out here if you need me." Clark hugged him.
"I love you, buddy."

"Love you, too." Clark got out of the way as Jace reached out
a hand toward Merry. "Night, Merry."

Clark leaned against the door frame and watched as she took
his hand and leaned over to kiss his son's forehead. "Good night,
Jace. I hope you feel better tomorrow."

"Me too. I'm sorry I threw up on you."

Clark smothered a laugh with his hand, but Merry didn't even
look at him as she addressed Jace. "It's okay. We can't help that
kind of thing. I'm sure I threw up on my mom a time or two."

"I bet she didn't get mad either."

"Not a bit." Merry held up the slime in her other hand, waving
it at him. "Where do you want your slime?"

"On my nightstand. Don't let dad take it when I fall asleep,
okay?"

"I'll kick his butt if he tries."

"Hey!" Clark protested.

"I mean it," she said, shooting him a wink as she set the slime
on Jace's nightstand. "Back off his slime."

Clark held his hands up in surrender. "Consider me backed."

Jace's eyes drooped as he murmured, "I love you, Merry."

Clark's heart contracted as she took a beat to respond. "I love you, too. Sleep well, Jace."

He cleared his throat in an attempt to dislodge the emotional lump there, but his voice still came out hoarse. "Can you pull the cord on the lamp for me?"

She turned on the lamp and Clark tapped the light switch. When she joined him in the hallway, Merry pinched the back of his arm lightly. "I heard you laughing about the puke, you jerk."

"Ow!" Clark laughed. "I tried not to."

"Not very well."

"I'm sorry," he said, tucking a strand of hair behind her ear. "I love your hair. It's so soft."

"I have to use a really good conditioner or it becomes a rat's nest of knots."

"Is that why you picked the name *Knottygirl?*" he teased.

"No, smart-ass. My mom used to say I was a whiz with knots." Her eyes danced as her hands demonstrated. "In yarn or cords or chains, give me enough time and I could untangle anything."

"Quite the set of skills." Clark caught himself leaning into her, and blurted, "Do you want to stay and watch a movie or something?"

"I should transfer my clothes to your dryer before—" Her phone rang and she held up the screen. "Mom."

Clark whispered, "I'll get us something to drink."

"Thanks. Hi, Mom. Yeah, we got back from the doctor a little bit ago and he's all tucked in. You and Clark were right, strep throat. We stopped by the pharmacy and got meds. Clark gave him the first dose." Merry chuckled. "I am sure he'd love some of Dad's magic soup." Merry paused another moment and when she finally let out an exasperated sigh, Clark laughed softly. "Elderberry, zinc, some vitamin C, I have all of that. Why do I need to stay healthy?" When Merry released a guttural groan, Clark swung around with the sodas in his hands, thinking she'd hurt herself. "Oh, Mom, can't you be Mrs. Claus for the Parade of Lights float?" Merry went to the washer and pulled the wet clothes out of the front loader. "How can I say no to the woman who gave me life?"

"Good answer," Clark whispered loudly and Merry turned from transferring laundry to roll her eyes.

"Well, you do take care of my dog, so it's only fair. You tell him that's my dog, not his dog, and I will be up in a bit to get her." Merry started the dryer and crossed the room to stand next to Clark. "Thanks, Mom. I'll remember that. Bye."

She slipped the phone in her pocket and Clark handed her the soda. "Thanks, My mother says she wants you to take zinc and she'll be sending down some soup and more vitamins in the morning."

"I don't have zinc. I'm not even sure I know what that is."

"I've got some at my place, I can grab it."

Clark reached out for her hand, catching her when she started to leave. "Wait, Merry—"

Her phone blared in her back pocket again and she pulled it out with a wince. "I'm sorry, hang on." Clark let her go and Merry pressed the talk button. "Hi. It's okay, Ryan." Clark's eyebrow arched and she shook her head. "You go have fun. I'm sure I can pick out a dress without your input. Tell Mr. Bartender I said hello and call me tomorrow. I want to hear everything." Merry looked up at Clark, her lips tilting into a smug smile, and he really wanted to know what it meant. "Funny, I was thinking the same thing. Talk to you later."

She slipped the phone into her back pocket and wrapped her arms around his shoulders. "Sorry. That was my friend, Ryan. With the monster truck."

Clark's eyes narrowed, fighting back the bolt of jealousy. "I see."

"You remember Ryan Welsh?" she asked innocently. "He was in the same grade as me."

It took several minutes, but Clark's eyes widened and he laughed. "That's who was at your house?"

"Yep."

"But you kissed him..."

"Ah-ha! Spy!"

Clark shrugged sheepishly. "I couldn't help myself."

"I figured, and I may have told Ryan I saw you watching. It was his idea for me to kiss him."

His free hand cradled her face, his thumb stroking her cheek. "So...there's no other guy then?"

She covered his hand and shook her head. "I would have told you there wasn't if you'd asked."

"I'm sorry. I acted like a jealous asshat."

He waited for her to say something, but she smirked. "Did you think I was going to argue?"

"Fair enough." Lacing his fingers through hers, he tugged gently. "Come on. I want to show you something in my shop."

"What about Jace?"

"He'll be all right for a little bit."

"What about Sam?"

"I sent him a text about Jace, but he's at work until ten and will probably head out afterwards, since he agreed to stay home tomorrow while we're out." Clark led her out of the house and around to his shop, his breath fogging in front of him.

"I understand if we need to postpone."

"Not just yet. Let's see how Jace feels after those antibiotics."

"If you don't feel comfortable leaving him, we can do a low-key date. You could come to my house for dinner and a movie. Then if there was an emergency, you would be close."

Clark stopped just outside the shop doors and wrapped his arms around her. "Are you sure?"

"Yeah, of course. Plus I'm a little concerned about leaving Daisy with my dad too much. I think he's got designs on her."

"Maybe you could share her," Clark teased as he opened the door to his shop.

"My dad doesn't..." Her voice trailed off as Clark flipped on the light and they stepped inside. "Share. Clark...they're beautiful."

Pride charged through Clark as Merry stared at the oversized rocking chairs in the corner, each head board engraved with a tree line. In script above the trees were the words *His* on the left and *Hers* on the right.

"They're for your parents. For Christmas. I thought they could put them on the porch instead of that patio set."

"You made these?" she asked in a hushed whisper.

"Yeah. I've been working on them since August in between other projects. I also made you a few things."

"You did?"

He pointed to the far workbench. "I know you don't have a lot of space in your house, but I thought these guys were the perfect size."

The trio of wooden snowmen were no more than two feet high, all wearing adorable wood hats, with smiling faces engraved into the heads. Christmas scarves adorned their necks and a pointed orange cylinder wooden nose stood out from the middle of the flat face. Black wooden buttons in sets of three trailed down their torsos and their big bottom sections sat on a flat platform of wood.

"They're adorable. I love them." She turned and threw her arms around his neck. "Thank you."

"You're welcome," he murmured into her hair, his fingers curling against her, fighting the urge to push her against the wall of the shop and kiss her until she writhed under his mouth.

With strength he didn't know he possessed he released her slowly, pressing a chaste kiss on her forehead. "Let's go inside and watch that movie."

"Sure," she said softly, taking his hand. "What are you in the mood for?"

You, naked on my bed, with my mouth tasting every inch of your body, he thought.

"How about you pick?" Why did his voice sound so high?

"Probably nothing scary, since I'm a screamer."

Clark jerked, studying her face as they rounded the porch. "Come again?"

"The jumpy parts. They make me cling and squeal, and we

don't want to wake up Jace." She reached for the door knob, giving him a saucy grin. "I know you're not into romance, but I know a really funny rom-com I think even you will enjoy."

Merry burrowed against him as close as she could get would not be copacetic to his resolve, so he nodded.

"Great. There are a couple of sex scenes, but we can just mute them," she said before disappearing inside.

Clark groaned. *This is gonna hurt.*

CHAPTER 20

MERRY

MERRY WALKED DOWN THE GRAVEL road with Daisy's leash looped over her wrist while clutching the handle grips on each side of a plastic tote filled with penis plushies. It hadn't snowed for a few days, but several inches still covered the ground, and according to her weather app it would be coming down non-stop from Monday to Thanksgiving. Thank goodness she didn't have anywhere she couldn't walk to, because she hated shoveling the stuff.

Daisy weaved in front of her and Merry stumbled, barely catching herself before she went down, and looked around the tote at the puppy. Daisy seemed to have doubled in size in just ten days, and although her leash manners were improving, she still tried to do her own thing.

"Hey, watch what you're doing down there, sister. I've got a date tonight, and I cannot be walking around with torn up knees 'cause you can't stay in your lane."

Daisy looked up at her long enough to pretend like she was

acknowledging Merry's existence and stepped out to the right, giving Merry more room.

"Thank you."

Last year, she hadn't worried about anyone seeing her legs, since she'd been on a dating hiatus, but in preparation for her first official date with Clark, she'd shaved, exfoliated, and plucked any and all areas that might be seen. She'd narrowed down her date dresses to two and folded them inside the tote so she wouldn't drop them on the slushy ground by accident. She'd snapped a few pics for Ryan this morning with no response and wanted a second opinion from her mom. She'd already started asking her questions last night during their brief phone call about Clark, and Merry expected she'd slide a few more into the conversation today. Once Merry brought her into it, her mom would want all the details about her and Clark.

Which so far consisted of sexual tension, a night best left out of the conversation, some groveling, more sexual tension, and one fabulous kiss. Well, two kisses, but the other one wasn't as... intense and zingy. They'd sat on the couch at an acceptable close-ness in case Jace woke up, her fingers entwined with his, and he'd actually laughed a few times during the movie. It wasn't as though she'd expected him to make out with her the entire time, but she wouldn't have minded a few kisses throughout.

After the credits rolled, Clark put the snowmen in her back seat and bent down to give her a sweet, lingering kiss, but broke it before her toes finished curling. Bewildered, she'd climbed into her car as Clark held the door for her and said goodnight. She'd been so distracted thinking about those kisses, Merry almost forgot to grab Daisy from her parents. Luckily, her mom was already in bed when she arrived and she was able to escape with a mild inquiry from her dad.

As she curled up in bed, stroking Daisy's fur, she'd replayed each kiss in her mind. The first kiss caught her by surprise, unexpected and passionate. The second was controlled and chaste. It was the Jekyll and Hyde of kisses and she worried he was pulling away again.

Was that just Clark? She'd only ever seen him fired up twice, the night at Brews and Chews she'd rather forget, and the morning after their failed meet-up. When he'd put his arm against the side of her house, she'd imagined for a moment he might push her against the wall and kiss her slippers off.

But he didn't. In the past, men hadn't been shy about kissing her, even when the timing was completely wrong, but not Clark. Last night, she'd been the one to initiate the kiss, standing up on her tiptoes to kiss him, and he'd met her halfway but she could feel him holding back and she needed to know why. Clark's mouth on hers warmed her like a cup of spiked cocoa and she wanted more of those smooches.

Clark's house came into sight and she slowed down to rest, setting the tote on the ground in front of her. It wasn't heavy, but awkward and her hands were cramping. Clark was probably inside with Jace and she didn't want to drop by unannounced, especially since they were keeping things low-key around him.

She picked the tote back up and kept walking. She heard a faint *thunk* echoing through the trees and swiveled her head, searching for the origin of the sound.

Merry heard it again and she eyed the pines warily. It sounded almost like something moving through the underbrush, breaking limbs, and it wouldn't be the first time a bear wandered onto the farm. Her heart galloped rapidly and she felt the pulse on the side of her neck flutter. Any second she expected a large animal to burst through the trees and Merry was ready to drop the tote and curl her body around Daisy to protect her puppy. Her gaze darted every which way, searching for movement, but all was quiet. Merry sighed as she passed by Clark's porch, relaxing as she turned to head up the hill.

Twack. Merry jumped, spinning toward the sound, but stilled when she heard a deep male grunt, followed by another crack. Curious now, Merry followed the noise around to the back of the house and the sight that greeted her stopped her in her tracks.

Holy hot lumberjack.

Despite the chill in the air, Clark stood with his back to her in a gray T-shirt and jeans, raising an axe over his head. Her gaze traveled over Clark's shoulders and back as he swung the axe down, two halves of wood flying in opposite directions. The muscles of his arms bunched under his skin as he picked up the wood and tossed it onto a growing mound outside his workshop.

Clark leaned his axe against the stump and grabbed his water bottle off the ground near his shop opening. Merry's mouth went dry as he took a long drink, his neck muscles working as he chugged, and little rivulets of water escaped his lips, racing along his jaw and down to soak the collar of his T-shirt. The temperature under her coat went up ten degrees and she set the container at her feet, about ready to shrug out of her jacket when Daisy barked, bouncing back on her haunches.

Clark twisted her way, and his eyes lit up. "Hey. How long have you been there?"

Merry cleared her throat. "I probably shouldn't answer that, as I may incriminate myself."

"Oh yeah?" He picked up his flannel shirt and wiped the sheen from his face, before tossing it to the side with a grin. "Now who's spying."

"Me, absolutely me, and I will do it again if you want to keep chopping, perhaps with your remaining clothes off?"

Clark chuckled. "I can imagine what my brother would say if he came out to see me swinging my axe naked. 'Don't cut off anything important.'"

"That is excellent advice, I suppose." She cleared her throat, needing to get off the subject of nakedness and important body parts. "How's Jace feeling?"

"His throat hurts still, but his fever broke this morning and he came out asking for a smoothie. He sucked down half of it, watched *The Avengers*, and went back to sleep."

"He probably needed the rest. What about you? Did you sleep well?"

"I passed out as soon as you left, and only woke up once to get Jace some more Tylenol." Clark stopped in front of her and kissed her cheek, his hand squeezing her hip. "I'm glad I got to see you before tonight. I was missing the sound of your voice."

"Me too. I mean I was missing you, not my own voice."

"I knew what you meant." He knelt at her feet and rubbed all over a wiggling Daisy. "Hi, pain-in-the-ass dog. Are you out for a walk with Mommy?"

"Yes, and besides one trip-up, she's not doing too bad on the leash. She'll have this heeling thing down soon."

"I know you're talking about the other kind of healing, but how is your foot?"

She flexed her foot in the air, twirling it like she was ready to do the hokey pokey. "Stitches are gone and I've learned to stop chasing dogs while barefoot."

"An important life lesson." Clark stood up, his dark eyes locked on hers. "Where are you walking her to?"

"My parents' to show my mother something. I took a detour when I heard you chopping wood, which I actually thought might be a bear stomping around in the trees."

"Damn, was I making that much noise? I thought I'd kept my growling and snarling to a minimum."

"It was my overactive imagination." Merry eyed the fully stocked woodshed around Clark's shoulder. "Why are you doing that? Are you a secret survivalist, preparing for the end of the world?"

"No, but I needed to work out some frustrations."

"Oh?" Maybe he was confused too and wasn't sure how to bring it up. "Why were you frustrated?"

"I'm only teasing."

Clark stood back up, even as Daisy tried to jump for his hands. "Daisy, stop."

The puppy flopped down with a disgruntled sigh.

"Maybe there's hope for you yet, pup," he said.

"You were telling me why you were frustrated?" she prodded.

He leaned over her without touching, his gaze on her mouth.

Her heart ricocheted against her breast bone as he whispered, "I guess frustrated isn't the right word. But there's this girl...woman, actually, and I cannot get her out of my mind."

Merry blushed, a small smile teasing her lips. "Oh yeah?"

"Yep. I even have a date with her tonight."

"What are the two of you going to do?"

"I don't know. She won't tell me."

"What do you want to do?" she asked softly.

"Dinner? Maybe curl up and watch another movie?"

"That's it?" she said sharply.

Clark's eyebrows shot up his forehead. "What?"

"Nothing." She stepped back and bent over to grab her tote, but Clark took her hand, pulling her and her dog to him.

"Merry, if you don't tell me what I've done, I can't fix it."

"It's what you're not doing."

Clark frowned. "I don't follow."

"We were alone in your shop last night, and then during the movie, you didn't..."

"I didn't what?"

"Kiss me."

Clark's eyes brightened and he slipped his arms loosely around her waist. "I kissed you at the car."

"I mean...the way you did yesterday. In the hallway."

He leaned closer, grazing her cheek with his, his mouth resting against her ear. "You liked that?"

"I loved it," she answered breathlessly.

"Merry..." His lips pressed against the side of her neck. Merry sighed, melting into his embrace.

"When I asked if we could take things slow, it wasn't only because of Jace. I knew I'd hurt you and I wanted to take my time and show you how special you are to me. With Patrice, we'd fight and then make up, but I never really knew her and I lived with her for seven months. And every girl since, it was about sex, not intimacy." He cradled the back of her head and kissed her cheek. "I didn't want you to think that's all I wanted from you. I plan to do it right this time, but yesterday, after you were there for Jace, I couldn't not kiss you. And last night, it took every ounce of control not to set you up on my workbench and kiss you until you begged me to stop."

Merry released a husky laugh. "Yeah, I'm going to go out on a limb and say that is never going to happen. I think I could kiss you all day, every day."

"That's why I've been behaving," he murmured, trailing kisses along her jaw. "Because once I really get started kissing you, touching you...I'm not going to want to stop."

"Well, I'm telling you there is a difference between slow and glacial, and right now I'm like the Titanic waiting for impact. So if you want to pick up the pace a bit, I promise I won't mind."

Before she knew it, Clark took Daisy's leash from her, leading the dog toward his workshop. "Where are you going with her?"

Clark stopped outside the doorway with a crook of his finger. "Luring her mistress into my lair."

Merry trailed after him, excited laughter escaping as he shut the door behind her. A pellet stove glowed orange in the corner, the air around them crackling with heat, and he dropped Daisy's leash. Merry shrugged out of her jacket and tossed it onto the workbench behind her, anticipation pulsing through her like electrical currents. Clark's eyes dipped to the vee of her low-cut long-sleeved top and he closed the distance.

"How does forty knots sound?" he said, lifting her onto the workbench.

"What is that?"

His stepped between her legs, his fingers gripping her hips, and he ground against her. "It's a ship term for speed."

Breathless laughter rushed past her lips. "Why do you know that?"

"I read a lot." Clark's mouth took hers, his tongue rolling inside, and she held onto the bench with one hand, the other threading through his hair, curling into the strands. He circled his hips into her, the friction against her open center creating a steady pulse with every thrust.

Merry arched her hips, matching his motions, as his mouth left hers and feathered kisses along her throat.

"What about Daisy?" she gasped.

"There's nothing she can get into in here." Clark cradled Merry's face with his hands, his gaze boring into hers before his mouth covered hers again. Merry sighed, her hands at his shoulders and traveling down his chest, memorizing every plane and groove through the soft cotton of his T-shirt and coming to a stop on his sides. The muscles under her palms tensed and flexed as his tongue swirled against hers. Flames of need sparked and danced through her body, tightening her nipples and licking farther south to her pulsating pussy. Every one of her senses came to life as Clark's hands traveled down her neck, holding there in a gentle circle all the while he continued to devour her mouth. When his fingers grazed her nipples, she moaned, and suddenly both of his hands were covering her breasts, squeezing and teasing, tweaking her pebbled peaks until she arched her back, his name rushing past her lips in a hushed plea for more.

After being celibate for over a year, she couldn't think straight. She wanted to rip his shirt off and lick her way down his body. To be naked, now, under him, and her fingers went to his belt with urgency. He caught her hands with his and put them back on the bench, holding them there as he pressed a soft kiss to her lips.

Wait, was he stopping?

"I'm the captain here and you're my ship. I'm going to take my time learning every curve," he murmured, releasing her hands. His left hand followed the line of her hip, skimming across her thigh and stopping in between, the heat of his palm cradling her pussy as he rubbed her through her jeans. "Explore every cabin."

"God, yes," she whimpered, closing her eyes as he teased her.

"I want to know everything above deck." His lips nibbled her neck, sucking her skin gently into his mouth as his hands found the buttons on her jeans, all five of them, and she cursed herself for buying the stupid things. Her body screamed for his bare hands on her skin and she used her feet to push her boots off.

"Look, no hands," she teased as the second boot dropped to the floor.

"I had a feeling you were magic." He knelt down to pull her jeans and underwear down her legs, tossing them on the workbench beside her, his mouth wasting no time making its way up. With his palms on her thighs, he pressed them wide open, his smoldering gaze staring at her, his flushed cheeks covered by a dark shadow of stubble and she reached out to run her hand over the rough whiskers.

"O Captain! My Captain!"

In answer, his lips teased the sensitive skin of her inner thighs, and she closed her eyes, running her fingers through his soft hair. Her hips arched involuntarily at the first stroke of his tongue along her seam, slow and thorough, sending shock waves deep within her. Her muscles clenched and he spread her legs further until they ached, but when he deepened the pressure, his tongue circling her clit in frenzied laps that left her panting and trembling, on the cusp of—

"Oh, holy fuck," she cried, her legs jerking as he picked up the tempo with his mouth. Clark's raw enthusiasm created fireworks between her legs and as her body rolled with a new shock wave of pleasure, her bones seemed to evaporate. Mush and moans were all that remained of her. He'd called her magic, but the way he touched her, kissed her, worshipped her...that was spellbinding.

Limp with satisfaction, she leaned back against the wall behind the bench, catching her breath. "I don't think I can walk."

Clark kissed her lower stomach. "Fine by me."

Merry laughed softly. "I mean ever again. You may have to carry me around from now on."

"Hmmm, people might ask questions."

"Just tell them your oral skills have side effects, including but not limited to tremors, sudden outbursts of praise, followed by any and all curse words, and possible bone-melting pleasure."

"I have a feeling you'll be experiencing all of the above quite often, because your belowdecks—" Clark wrapped his arms around her waist and brought her to the edge of the bench. "—is my favorite area to plunder."

Merry snorted. "I have no idea why, but your nerdy ship talk totally works for me."

"I think that's because I work for you."

Merry brushed his hair back from his forehead and kissed him. "You definitely do that. I haven't felt this good in forever."

"I made you happy then?"

"I'm sorry, did the very vocal sounds I emitted and this smile on my face not give that away?"

Clark's fingers brushed against her right cheek. "It gives me a clue."

"Then let me spell it out for you." She pressed her lips to his softly, before winding her arms around his shoulders. "Y-O-U M-A-K-E M-E H-A-P-P-Y."

"Knock, knock."

Sam's voice on the other side of the shop door made Merry scream and fall back against the shop wall, the back of her head connecting with a *thunk*. "Ouch."

Clark's hand went around to cradle it as he helped her straighten up. "Shit, Merry, are you all right?"

"Yes, but your brother might not be when I get outta here," she muttered darkly.

"I heard that," Sam said.

Clark rolled his eyes and lifted Merry off the bench, keeping an arm around her waist. "Sam, how long have you been out there?"

"I just got here. Why, did I miss something?"

The amusement in Sam's voice was all too telling and Merry covered her hands with her face. "Oh, God. He heard everything."

"No, he didn't, because that would make him a perverted asshole," Clark said loudly.

"I heard nothing, except that my brother makes you happy. Congratulations."

Merry moaned, burying her face in Clark's chest.

"Is there something you need, Sam?" Clark asked through gritted teeth.

"Yes, my nephew is awake, hungry, and asking where his father is."

"Can you tell him I'm working on something and will be in momentarily?"

"I can. Do you need a hand with that...something you're working on?"

"No, but you can make Jace a smoothie until I get in there."

"All right, geez. Just trying to help."

Merry listened for Sam's retreating footsteps as she gathered her clothes. Underwear. Jeans. One boot...

"Where's my other boot?"

Crunch. Crunch.

Merry squatted down and stared. Daisy was lying under the workbench with Merry's other boot in her mouth, holding the brown shoe in place with her paws.

Clark crawled down next to her, his voice laced with laughter. "What was it you said about nothing on the floor she could destroy?"

"I guess I should have said nothing of mine."

Merry grabbed her boot from Daisy, who chased the shoe

all the way out from under the bench. She set the pair up where the puppy wouldn't get them and dressed, aware of Clark's gaze watching her every move.

"My mother is going to wonder what happened to me. I told her I would be up in a few to show her potential date outfits."

"You told her about us?"

Merry stilled, looking up from tying her boots to study Clark's expression. "I told her I had a date, but I haven't told her who with. Not yet at least. Is there a reason I shouldn't?"

"No. In fact, after tonight, I was going to have a talk with Jace about you and me."

Merry continued tying her boots, keeping her face down until she finished so Clark wouldn't see the wide smile. "What made you change your mind?"

"This week." Clark took her hands and put her arms around his neck. "Between your work, the farm, and the festival, I barely caught a glimpse of you. It was like we were back to being the Woodsman and KnottyGirl, but over the phone."

"And a PG-13 upgrade," she teased.

"Yeah, I didn't mind that at all, but it got me thinking. Next week is going to be crazier starting Friday, and every week after until Christmas. I don't want to sneak around just to steal moments with you."

"Are you worried about Jace being upset?"

"I'm more concerned he wanted us together too much and if things changed, he'd be heartbroken."

"But you're not concerned about things changing anymore?" she prodded.

"Not on my end. How about you?"

Merry kissed him fast and hard, before dropping her arms from his neck. "I'm good."

Clark bent down to grab Daisy's leash from the floor, chuckling. "By the way, what's in the tote outside?"

"More plush penises. It's become a hobby of mine."

"Plural penises, huh?"

"Uh-huh. I'm considering turning it into a side hustle. What do you think?"

Clark climbed to his feet, holding out the leash with a smile. "Does it make you happy?"

"Yes, it does," she said, their fingertips connecting as she took it.

"Then I think it's a great idea."

Chapter 21

MERRY

MERRY SET HER TOTE ON her parents' front porch and opened the front door, trying to be as stealthy as possible. She'd attempted to repair the damage Clark's hands wreaked on her hair, bringing it forward to cover any possible whisker burn to her neck. Her body still hummed at the memories of his mouth and hands, and his dirty talk, well, *nerdy talk* was an unexpected turn-on.

And while she appreciated him wanting her to feel special, Merry was seriously considering skipping dinner tonight and going straight for dessert. Eating pie off of Clark's stomach sounded like a delicious activity and she couldn't wait to try it.

She managed to get Daisy and the container over the threshold before Butch let out a hair-raising bay, his toenails clattering down the hallway.

"It's just us, Butch, calm thyself."

Daisy yanked on the leash the minute she saw Butch, her front paws flying through the air excitedly. Merry shut the door firmly behind them and slipped the leash over Daisy's head with a laugh.

"All right, get 'em!"

The minute she was free, Daisy pounced at Butch, who took off back down the hallway with the white puppy hot on his heels. Merry realized that the laundry room door could be open and sprinted after the dogs. The last thing she wanted was another runaway puppy debacle.

"Butch, come here, Butch!"

The hound stopped and leaped over the lunging puppy to get to Merry. She slid past him and sighed happily when she spotted the closed laundry room door.

"Okay, false alarm. Play."

Her parents' bedroom door opened and her mom poked her head out. "Merry? What's going on out here?"

"The dogs creating a ruckus. Were you taking a nap?"

"I might have been," she said, yawning. "What time is it?"

"One-twenty."

Her mother leveled her with a suspicious look. "I thought you were on your way an hour ago?"

"Something came up. Where's Dad?" Merry asked, casually changing the subject as she followed her mother down the hallway and into the kitchen. Butch and Daisy were chasing each other around the living room, a long orange rope hanging from Butch's jowls.

"Your father went to Twin Falls this morning to get whatever he needs for his weekend project." She stood on her toes and pulled two cups from the cupboard. "Want some coffee?"

"It's the afternoon, Mom, you remember?"

"And obviously I need another cup if I'm sleeping the day away." Victoria snapped the top of the single-cup coffee maker down and pressed a button. "I also have chai, if you prefer. I ordered one of those assortment boxes online."

"I'll just take a regular cup of joe." Merry drummed her fingers over the counter nervously as she added, "I can't be falling asleep during my date tonight."

"Ah yes, the mystery date you're modeling for. Where are the dresses?"

"They're in my tote."

Butch ran into the back of Merry's legs as he raced past.

"Damn it, that hurt!"

"Put them out through the laundry room."

"I can't, Daisy will take off."

"No, she won't. Nick came over with Pike and Anthony and helped your father put three chain link kennels together so the dogs could have a little yard. It's only temporary until the ground thaws, but at least this way they aren't knocking over everything wrestling through the house."

Merry walked down the hall to the laundry room and opened the back door. Both dogs came barreling through, sniffing along the straw covered ground, the kennels pressed against the house with the open gate where the larger back steps were. A narrowed set of stairs was in its place and she smiled as Daisy grabbed Butch's rope toy and hopped away playfully.

Merry returned to the kitchen in awe. "I don't know when Dad found the time. Clark's been working fourteen-hour days."

"Clark handles a lot of the invoicing and bookkeeping, so your dad doesn't have to work long hours at his age, which I appreciate."

The mention of her father stepping back stung, especially

when he'd been so adamant about not being ready. "You know, I told Dad that I want to be trained to run this place, but he doesn't seem like he wants to give me a chance."

"It's not that," her mother protested. "With Clark, he doesn't have to give up any control. Your father still questions Clark on things and will double check the books, but Clark takes it all in stride."

"I'm not controlling! I just want to help," Merry muttered.

"I know that. Clark does what your dad wants, nothing more or less, because he works for him, but this is your home. This is your future. Would you just do what your dad asked, or would you want to try out some of your ideas to make this place better, the way you've done with the festival?"

Merry hesitated, imagining what life would be like if her dad gave her the keys to the farm. It would be like when he taught her to do anything: he'd hover. She could see it in her head. Not because he didn't believe she could do it but because he was a control freak.

"You may be right, but he's going to have to accept that I need to learn at some point."

Victoria squeezed her hand. "If you really want something, Merry, you don't sit back and wait for it to come to you. You fight to make it happen and you don't take no for an answer."

Merry smirked. "My mother wants me to push my stubborn as hell father into retiring?"

"I didn't say that. Your father will not retire unless he wants to, but at least with you here to really take the helm, I can buy an RV and drag him off on vacation. I want to enjoy being an empty-nester, and when you own a business, you can't relax and shut

down when you're always worried about what's happening here."
Her mother handed Merry her coffee with a light chuckle. "We're
not getting any younger."

"How old are you guys this year?"

"You don't know how old your parents are?"

Merry held up one hand in defense. "I'm drawing a blank, geez."

"He's fifty-three and I'm fifty-one. I want to explore and travel
before I can't hike anymore."

"Sounds like you're the one who needs to talk to your husband."

Victoria threw a kitchen towel at Merry. "Smart-ass."

"I'm saying if anyone can get around Dad, it's you."

"I've tried, but like you said...stubborn." Her mom sighed.
"Oh well, whatever will be, etc. Are you hungry? He's bringing
home The Wrangler when he passes through Fairfield. There's
probably still time to catch him if you want to text him your order."

"No, that's okay. I stopped to check in on Jace, and Clark
made us smoothies for lunch."

"So, you're an us?" her mom asked slyly.

Merry snorted. "I just mean us as in the three of us. It's not a
title."

"Really?" She picked up her own cup of coffee with a frown.
"Because I think there's something going on with you and Clark."

"There might be something going on, but it's too soon to talk
to my mother about it."

"That's your opinion." Her mother drank her coffee silently,
watching her with narrowed eyes.

"That's it? You're not going to torture me with fire pokers
until I confess all?"

"I've decided that you're an adult and if you don't want your mother's insight, then I'll just mind my business," her mother said airily. "Even though I am older and wiser, so you could benefit from my expertise and years of life experience, but I won't press you if you really think you have things under control."

Merry's eyes blinked rapidly. She was completely bewildered. "What kind of sorcery are you working, woman?"

Her mother took another sip of her coffee innocently. "I know not of what you speak. I am simply allowing you to live your life without any interference from me."

After several beats of waiting for her mother to crack a knowing grin, Merry clapped her hands. "Wow...you're good. You have me itching to spill my guts to you. Well played." Merry took a drink of her coffee and set the mug back down on the counter. "But I'm not gonna."

Victoria sighed dramatically. "You don't have to tell me anything, but I am going to give you unsolicited advice."

"I knew it. You just can't help yourself."

"I'm your mother and that doesn't stop when you turn eighteen," she said firmly. "So I'll just say this...Clark is a good man."

Merry was expecting a lot of things, but not the obvious. "I know."

"But he's closed himself off from everyone and it's hard to break down walls like that unless he wants to let you in. Even now, he doesn't know quite what to do with your father and me, and we aren't seeking a romantic attachment to him. Tread slowly with him, all right?"

"Whoa, wait a second. Are you warning me off?"

"No, honey," her mom said gently. "I would love for you to find a man worthy of you. But when you date a single parent, it isn't just about you and him. It's about you, him, and his children. If things get serious but don't work out between you, Jace's heart will be broken."

Merry's stomach twisted in knots. "Clark's told me the exact same thing."

"He's an excellent father, so that isn't surprising, but even good people make mistakes when emotions are involved and I don't want you getting hurt either."

"I know that," Merry said reassuringly.

"Then I'll let you be."

They sat down in silence, drinking their coffees as Merry worked up the nerve to openly talk about her concerns. She was afraid if she voiced them out loud, her mother would confirm her insecurities.

"Mom, you had Nick when you were twenty-three."

"Uh-huh."

"We're you ever worried that you were too young to be a mom?"

Her mother cradled the cup between the tips of her fingers, holding Merry's gaze. "Are you asking because of Jace?"

"If you want to be uber insightful, then yes."

"To answer your question, no. I never thought I was too young, but it was almost thirty years ago." Her mother paused a beat, raising her cup to her lips as she added, "I was scared, though."

"You were?" The words rushed out like a hopeful sigh.

"I was in charge of raising a tiny person into a functioning adult. Some days I thought I would break down, it got so difficult, especially when there were three of you under the age of six! It is humbling to be a parent and you question every decision." Her mom leaned over and grabbed Merry's nose in a gentle grip. "But I think I did all right with you guys."

"I don't know about Holly, but Nick and I are pretty solid."

"Your sister is fine!" her mother shouted.

"She's certifiable."

"Maybe so, but I'm proud of all of you. You carved your own path in this world."

"Maybe Holly and Nick did, but sometimes..."

Victoria frowned. "What, honey?"

"I don't know. I went away to college and kept searching for my passion. Nick has his dream job and Noel, and Holly became an internet sensation and opened her shop. And I came home to Mistletoe."

"Baby, if you don't want to run the farm, you don't have to. You kids can sell it when we're gone."

"No way!" Merry protested. "I love this place. I want it. But with two extraordinary siblings, I feel like my dreams are too simple for this family."

"Just because a dream isn't elaborate doesn't mean it isn't extraordinary. I wanted to marry your father."

"Mom..." Merry groaned.

"What? It's true. We didn't share a circle of friends in high school because he was two years ahead, but I held such a torch for him. When we ran into each other in college, I gave him a run for his money, but this math geek—" Her mother pointed her thumb at her chest. "—got the guy."

"Don't sell yourself short, Mom. You were a smoking hot math geek. I've seen pics."

"Your dad still thinks I'm sexy."

Merry wrinkled her nose. "Mom!"

"When I put on my reading glasses and go into CPA mode with my calculator, it drives him crazy."

"What is wrong with you? I'm your daughter!"

Victoria laughed so hard, her eyes teared. "Ahhh, your face."

"Gross." Merry giggled.

Her mom wiped her eyes, her mirth subsiding. "I love torturing my children. That's good parenting right there."

"Holly hasn't forgiven you for threatening to tell her where she was conceived."

"Serves her right. I love my wild child, but she gives me all the gray hair. Except this section over here," she said, pointing to her left temple. "That's your brother, and when I part my hair to the side, this whole line is you."

"I don't see any gray hair."

"That is because I refuse to age gracefully and visit my stylist every six weeks."

Merry smiled, her heart bursting as she watched her beautiful mother across the table. She was the kisser of ouchies, the baker of cookies, the surgeon of injured stuffed animals, and never said no to one more story or a hug from her children. Merry hoped someday to be half the mom she'd had.

Merry got up from the table with tears in her eyes. "Thank you, Mom."

"What are you thanking me for?"

"For being the best mom in the world."

"Awwww, my baby." She held her arms out and Merry went into them, sitting on her mom's lap and hugging her hard. "My sweet girl."

"Do you think I'd be a good parent?" Merry sniffled.

"Absolutely. Not a doubt in my mind. But do you want to know the secret to being an amazing mom is?"

"Sure."

"You love all your children equally, no matter how your relationship came to be. Noel is as much my daughter as you and Holly and I would never want her to feel less than mine."

Merry sat up with a laugh. "I just realized my brother is one of those semi-incestuous in-love-with-his-stepsister relationships I used to hate on teen dramas."

"Oh you!" Her mother playfully pushed Merry off her lap and to her feet. Merry returned to her seat, trying to get a handle on her guffaws.

After several ticks, her mirth subsided and she asked, "In all seriousness, what do you think about me and Clark?"

"I think Clark is a hardworking, trustworthy man and a fantastic father. I think that you two would be great together. The question is, what do you think of Clark?"

"I really like him, Mom, but there is so much to unpack," Merry said slowly, trying to put her thoughts and concerns into the right words. "He's never had anyone want to love him, or maybe it's that he hasn't let anyone get to that point. I don't have the best track record with men, mostly because I pick the wrong ones, but Clark is...different. We've had a couple of hiccups and a huge speed bump, but we're taking things slower and seeing where this can go. Thus the first date tonight and I really want it to go well."

"Who is going to stay with Jace while you go out?"

"I think Sam."

Victoria huffed. "He could have come up here."

"Mom, I am pretty sure Clark doesn't want his date's parents knowing how late he's out with their daughter."

Her mother's face flushed and she stammered, "Oh! Um... right. So, you two..."

"We've only kissed," Merry said, leaving it at that.

"You didn't kiss in front of Jace, did you?"

"No, of course not."

"I don't know why I asked. You've got a good head on your shoulders."

"Thanks, Mom." Merry reached across the table with her palm up and her mom placed her hand in hers.

"All I ever care about is that my children are happy and loved."

"And to tell you all of our secrets?" Merry teased.

"Most definitely." Victoria grinned. "Are the two of you going to talk about what you want in the future? Because I don't know if you want more children, but it is important to discuss that before you get too close."

"What happened to no more being said on the matter?"

Her mother set her coffee cup down and held her hands up. "It's a hard habit to break, getting to the bottom of everything."

"I'm sure it is, and yes, I want more than one child. As for Clark, I'm not sure, but I appreciate the advice."

"I'm always here if you need me. Or when you don't *think* you need me."

The front door opened and Holly burst in, slamming it behind her as she danced into the kitchen.

"Guess whose voodoo peen went viral on Instagram?"

"What?"

"Okay, don't be mad and I know you didn't ask me to do this, but...I created a new Instagram for you and posted a pic of your voodoo peen from the bar last week!" Holly waved her hands in the air excitedly. "I shared it on my account from yours and people are going nuts!"

"What is a voodoo peen?" their mother asked.

"Oh God." Merry covered her face with her hands.

"Do you want me to show her?" Holly asked, pulling out her phone.

"No, I've got it." Merry hesitated, finally meeting her mom's puzzled gaze. "I need to show you something."

"All right," she said slowly.

Merry got up from the table, leaving her coffee behind as she picked up her tote and carried it over to the table. With a deep breath, she set it at her mother's feet and lifted the lid, removing her date dresses so her mother could see the contents below.

Her mom's eyes widened. "Merry, are those..."

"Penises?" She released a dry laugh. "Yeah. I've made quite a few the last two weeks. All of the totes I've been stacking in my old room? Penises in a variety of styles and sizes."

Holly picked up the dresses, holding them in front of her. "What are these?"

"Her date outfits," her mother murmured, distracted by a Christmas tree peen she'd picked up.

"Huh. I like the blue one. By the way, where is my elf?" Holly asked.

Merry scowled at her. "It's in there, but you're never getting it."

"That's rude, considering I was trying to help you."

"I'm still confused," their mom said, pulling out the Pike peen she'd made for Sally, complete with bow tie on the balls. "Why did you make these?"

"It started as a goof. I crocheted one as a voodoo doll for Tara after the last guy broke up with her."

"This is it," Holly said, pulling up the picture on her phone.

Her mom burst out laughing, covering her mouth. "Oh my!"

"Then I started making them at night when I was winding down. The small ones take about forty-five minutes. Before I knew it, I had a tub full. Then two."

Merry bit her lip, waiting for her mom to say something about how inappropriate or crazy this was, but she just picked up another plushie, her brow furrowed.

"How much would you charge for them?"

"Nothing. I've just been giving them away."

"Why? Sounds like people are excited about them. Excited people usually pay." Her mom turned to Holly, holding up the Pike peen. "How many people have commented on the post?"

"One hundred and eleven thousand people liked the post and there are thousands of comments from people asking how to order them. She has eight thousand followers now and growing."

Merry nearly fell over. "Did you say eight thousand?"

"Yes!" Holly squealed.

She stood shell-shocked, her hand holding the counter for balance. "I can't believe it."

"Holly, get my calculator and my computer from my bedroom," Victoria said, ignoring her daughter's reaction. Holly slid down the hallway out of view, while her mother started pulling the peens out of the tote and lining them out across the table.

"What are you doing?" Merry asked.

"Looking through your inventory. We need to make a spread sheet that lists your costs and time, and then upscale that by forty percent plus shipping."

Holly came back with the computer and calculator stacked on top of each other, placing them on the table in front of their mom. "I can make a pre-order sheet online and a link tree."

"Don't you have to go back to the shop? It's only three," Merry said.

"I put up a sign. Family emergency." Holly sat down next to Victoria and pulled out her phone, thumbs flying across the screen.

"But...I don't even know if I want to do this."

Holly scoffed. "Then why are you filling Mom and Dad's place with inventory?"

"Because I was bored?"

"Then let's turn your boredom into money," Holly said, shooing her. "Go put on your dresses and model them for us while we work on this. Oh!" Holly looked up from her phone screen to address their mom, who was typing away on her laptop. "She's also going to need an ecommerce site and I'll have to teach her how to take pictures with her phone."

Merry's gaze shifted between her mother and sister, concentrating on their screens and talking about her as if she wasn't there.

"You're not upset with me?" Merry asked, her gaze locked on her mom.

Her mother looked up, confusion knitting her brow. "Honey, as long as you aren't doing anything illegal or that would hurt others, I don't have a problem with how you want to live your life. You might get some push back from internet prudes, but you've always loved crafting and if this is what sets you apart, I am going to support you. I'll also need to teach you how to do your taxes if you're going to be a small business owner."

"What about Dad?"

Holly snorted and their mother shot her a look. "Your father... well, he'll probably need a minute or two to acclimate."

"I figured as much," she said with a laugh, holding up the dresses in her hands. "I'll go try these on."

"Do the blue one first!" Holly hollered after her. "Oh, and Merry?"

She braced herself for another slightly embarrassing announcement. "Yeah?"

Holly beamed at her. "I got Declan Gallagher to buy a tree."

Merry blinked several times. That put them at seventy-five trees in town and five more from neighboring rescues and businesses she'd recruited.

"I take back every mean thing I ever said about you. You... are my hero."

Her sister went back to looking at her phone screen, but Merry could see she was grinning from ear to ear. "I'd believe it more if you sang it, but that will do."

Merry sang the chorus of "Wind Beneath My Wings" down the hallways until she slipped into her old room and closed the door on her family's laughter. The room still held her old dresser, bed, and nightstand, but when she'd built her tiny house, she'd helped her mom clean it out. Since the room had gone unused for months, Merry had asked if she could store some things in it. Four large blue totes were stacked in the corner of the room, containing blankets, teddy bears, hats, and peens. She'd never imagined anyone would want to buy her crafts until Holly asked her if she could put a few in her shop. She'd idly thought about an online store, but this was the first time she'd believed it was her path. The reactions of her sister and her mother...they believed in Merry.

The front door opened and slammed shut and she heard her dad's voice. "What's going on here?"

Oh my God. Her dad was home and there were yarn penises all over the table, in plain sight!

Merry scrambled to get her dress on and zipped, racing for the door of her room. She'd barely cracked it open when her mother answered, "Your daughter's new side business."

Could this day get any more embarrassing?

Merry entered the kitchen in time to see her mother holding up the Christmas tree peen, making it dance in the air.

Welp, there's no going back now.

"There is a switch in the balls that makes the Christmas lights turn on," Merry said.

Her dad stared for several moments, then shifted his glance between Merry, Holly, and his wife.

"I could have gone my whole life without seeing that."

Her mom burst out laughing. "People love them."

"People are weird." Her dad set the bags of food on the counter and Merry twisted her hands in front of her.

"Dad...are you mad?"

Her dad sent her a quizzical look as he pulled out a tray of tater tots. "Why would I be mad? If someone wants a stuffed johnson to play with, who am I to judge."

Holly let out an excited cry. "Johnsons! That's what you should call them."

"That's a cute name. What about Jolly Johnsons by Merry? Adult-themed plushies and crafts," her mom said.

Merry's cheeks warmed, getting caught up in their enthusiasm. "I love it!"

"And I love that," Holly said, pointing at her dress. "Don't even bother with the other. That is the one."

"I agree," their mom said.

Their dad picked up a dick plushie with a grin. "Do I get royalties for the name?"

"I'll tell everyone who asks that my dad came up with my business moniker."

"Nah, you can just leave me out of it," her dad said, kissing her forehead. "You girls have fun plotting more wacky products the world doesn't need. I'm going to find a place to eat my burger that isn't covered in bow tie-sporting wieners."

Chapter 22

CLARK

CLARK SHRUGGED INTO HIS SUIT jacket and left it hanging open, his white shirt and red tie pressed and smooth. Merry didn't know it yet, but he'd booked reservations at the Mistletoe Lodge right after the family pictures last Sunday. She'd suggested they stay in at her place so he could be close by if Jace needed him, but something made him hesitate to break the reservation, and now that Jace was on the mend, he was glad he hadn't.

He walked out of his bedroom and when he cleared the hallway, Sam and Jace turned away from their movie and his brother whistled.

"Whew, you clean up purty. Do a spin for us."

"I'm not doing that," he said with a laugh, slipping his phone into his pocket. "What are you two watching?"

"*The Nightmare Before Christmas.*"

"Ah, not sad about missing that one."

"My dad doesn't like all the singing," Jace clarified.

"But the tunes are so catchy." Sam belted out a bar and Jace giggled.

"Can you pause it for me so I can talk to my son?"

Sam climbed to his feet. "Sure, I gotta piss anyway."

"That's fifty cents!"

"What? Piss is a bodily function. Not a bad word."

"You said b-a-l-l-s earlier and you just said the p-word again. Three words at twenty-five cents is seventy-five cents. Don't make me charge you a penalty tax."

Sam dropped three quarters in the jar as he passed. "Penalty tax, where did he come up with that?"

"Victoria." Clark smirked.

"Corrupting America's youth." Sam shook his head and left the room.

Clark sat down next to Jace on the couch, resting his arm on the back. "How you feeling, buddy?"

"My throat feels better."

"I'm glad. Are you mad at me about going out tonight?"

"No. You should go out and make friends."

Clark quirked a brow. "That doesn't sound like you talking."

"Well, Uncle Sam said it first, but I agree."

"I love having my brother and son discussing how I should live my life."

"We only worry 'cause we love you."

"Hey, don't turn my own words against me," Clark said, tickling Jace's ribs. He giggled and squealed for several seconds and broke into a fit of coughing.

Clark stopped tickling, cursing himself for forgetting Jace was better, not healed. "Sorry. I'll get you a popsicle before I leave, but I wanted to talk to you because I decided to ask Merry to have dinner with me. And she agreed."

"Tonight?" Jace clarified.

"Yes."

"Awesome!" Jace jumped on him, and Clark froze for a split second, the hour he'd spent washing and ironing his clothes flashing through his mind. But a hug from his son would be worth whatever stickiness or wrinkles he left behind and he squeezed him back.

"It is awesome, but we need to talk about what's going to happen moving forward, so sit back and look at me so I know you're listening." Jace did and Clark smoothed the front of his shirt. "What happens with Merry and me is between us. So even if we don't end up being anything more than friends, Merry and the rest of the Winters family will continue to be a part of your life. Daddy will still have a job and we'll live in this house until we buy a place of our own. You got it?"

"Okay. But you're going to try, right? To keep her?"

"I will do my very best."

Someone knocked on the front door and he ruffled his son's hair as he stood. "You're a good egg, Jace."

"I get it from you."

Those words hit him right in the feels and he coughed, fighting the urge to cry. "Don't think because you're a great kid I'm going to let you watch scary movies with your uncle."

"I know," Jace said, settling back into the couch.

Clark opened the door and found Chris on the porch, holding

a box in his arms. Surprise swiftly followed by panic zipped through Clark and he squeaked embarrassingly. "Chris! I thought we were taking the day off."

"We are, but I brought this down from the wife and me. It's my magic healing chicken noodle soup and a bunch of vitamins Victoria thought you needed." Clark took the box from him and Chris called over Clark's shoulder, "How is the boy feeling?"

"Jace, Chris is here and brought you some things."

Jace got up from the couch and stopped alongside Clark in the open doorway. "Hi. I'm feeling better."

"You eat all of this soup and you'll feel like Superman."

Jace made a face at the DC superhero and Clark nudged him. "Superman is pretty cool, huh?"

Jace took the hint and nodded. "Thank you for the soup."

"You're welcome, Jace. You can go back to resting."

"Do you want to come in?" Clark asked.

"No, you look like you're getting ready to head out."

He cleared his throat nervously. "I am. I...Merry and I are going to dinner."

"I know, her mom told me. Thought you were staying in?"

"I made reservations last week at the Lodge, so my brother is going to stay with Jace."

"Hello!" Sam hollered from behind him.

"Hey, Sam. Well, you have fun at dinner. We've got her demon dog up at the house overnight, so at least you won't have to worry about rushing back to let her out."

"That's good." What an awkward conversation to be having with his boss and his date's father. "We won't be out too late."

"Relax, Clark. I'm not here to bust your balls. I came to drop off the box and let you know you've been a tremendous addition to this farm. I'm glad you're here. What you do in your personal life is none of my business. As long as you treat my daughter with respect, I won't get involved."

"I will, sir."

"Then have a good time. And free piece of advice, be sure to tell her how nice she looks."

"I will, thanks." Clark stepped back into the house and set the box down on the table. "I'm going to put the soup in the fridge for Jace, all right?"

"I got this," Sam said, waving without turning around. "Have fun on your date."

Clark called a goodbye to Jace and Sam and when he stepped out onto the porch, he noticed Chris hadn't crested the bottom of the hill. While every fiber of his being cautioned him to mind his own business, he jogged to catch Merry's dad.

"Sir, hold up a moment." Chris stopped, waiting for Clark to pull up alongside him. "At the risk of overstepping, I think Merry wants to have more involvement with the farm. She went out with me to check the north sector one afternoon and wanted to know all about what I did and specific things to look for. She could be an asset if you gave her a chance."

Chris stayed quiet long enough to make Clark squirm, and admitted, "She said something along those lines before you got here, but she hasn't brought it up since. I figured she liked her job at the school and her interest in learning the ropes here was just a passing fancy."

"I think the school job gives her a steady paycheck, but her heart is set on following in your footsteps one day."

"And she's told you this, huh?"

"More or less."

"I'll talk to her." Chris grinned. "You're a brave man."

"Why do you say that?"

"Dating a woman who will be your boss one day." Chris chuckled, taking a few steps up the hill. "Have fun tonight, Clark."

Clark straightened his tie nervously as he walked the distance to Merry's house. Every excuse he'd been using to keep his distance had been blown to smithereens. The Winterses knew, and Jace was on board. The rest was between him and Merry.

He stepped through the gate and, taking the front porch steps in one monster stride, knocked on the door.

Merry opened it slowly, a vision in a tight sapphire-blue velvet dress that hugged her curves, enhancing her round hips, and his fingers curled against the urge to splay his hands there. The dress was v-cut, her breasts rounding over the neckline, and her arms were bare thanks to the tank sleeves. Her hair was pulled over her left shoulder in an intricate braided coronet, the ends free and curling. She looked elegant and classy.

Maybe I should have canceled that reservation and stayed in after all.

"Wow, you look nice," she said, her gaze stopping on his empty hands with a frown. "I thought you were bringing take-out?"

"Merry..." He climbed the remaining steps until they were at eye level, afraid to touch her even as every fiber in his body wanted to push her back into the house and wreck that perfect, gorgeous hair so it flowed through his fingers while he kissed her.

"Clark?"

He leaned close, his mouth teasing the shell of her right ear. "I can't think of a word strong enough to describe you."

Merry turned her face, her lips mere inches from his, and smoothed her hand over his tie. "I never thought you'd be one for cheesy lines."

He kissed her then, his arm hooking around her waist and fitting her body to his. She tasted and smelled sweet and while he'd never considered himself a lover of sugary things, he'd make an exception for Merry.

She broke the kiss with her hands on his chest. "What was that?"

"In lieu of words, I tried to show you how amazing you look."

She laughed breathlessly, patting him. "You can keep trying to come up with the right word while you explain where the food is. I'm starving."

"We're going out to dinner after all."

Merry's brow furrowed. "What about Jace?"

"He's going to be fine with my brother for the night," Clark said, pushing an escaping hair behind her ear. "I have my phone on me if there's an emergency and your parents are just up the hill. I want to enjoy this evening with you. Our first official date."

"That sounds wonderful. Why don't you come in while I get my shoes and jacket?"

"I'm worried if I go in there with you, we won't be going anywhere."

Merry rolled her eyes. "I am too hungry to let you distract me, so stop being silly and enter."

Clark followed behind Merry and took a seat on her couch as she continued toward the back of her house to retrieve her shoes. Clark's gaze scanned her house, noting all the little touches she'd added since he'd last been there. The snowmen he made for her were perched in the window at the end of the house, twinkling white lights hanging above. Christmas throw pillows and blankets adorned the gray cushions and back of her couch. Every surface or shelf had a touch of Christmas décor, from the Santa Claus hand towels to the reindeer cookie jar on the counter.

"I like what you've done with the place."

Merry smiled from the alcove under her bedroom loft, slipping on her heels. "You ain't seen nothing. I ordered dishes, sheets, and bathroom stuff. I am so ready for the day after Thanksgiving."

"Maybe you can come decorate my place. We do a tree and I've got my lights on the outside of the house, but that's it."

"I can do that, but I'll require a credit card and creative control."

"Whatever you need. Can you wear that dress while you do it, though?"

Merry pulled her jacket off the hook and he stood to help her put it on. "I don't know what's gotten into you tonight, but I love it."

"You've gotten into me, Merry," he whispered, pressing tiny kisses along the side of her neck. "There's something about you and I just can't resist doing everything in my power to make you smile."

She twirled slowly to face him, stretching up along his body, and he dropped his mouth to hers, holding the back of her neck with one hand. Merry's hands rested on his sides above his hips, her touch burning through his shirt and racing straight to his groin.

He groaned, giving her one last soft kiss. "I knew I should have stayed outside."

Merry giggled. "You act like you're some barbarian about to lose control any moment and ravage me."

"Don't think it hasn't crossed my mind, although it would be a consensual ravaging."

"It most definitely would," she murmured, tugging on the end of his jacket before letting him go. "Are you going to be warm enough in just this?"

"I'll be fine." Being around her had him so revved up, he could almost do without the jacket. "We should get going before we miss our reservation."

"Where are you taking me?"

"It's a surprise."

She told her Alexa goodbye and Clark kept hold of her hand as he helped her down the porch steps. As they passed through the gate, he cursed himself for not driving the Jeep over to pick her up, but he hadn't been thinking after his run-in with her dad.

"Sorry, you okay?" he asked when she wobbled a bit and gripped his hand tighter.

"Sure. Just that heels and gravel don't mix well."

Without further explanation, Clark bent over and lifted her up into his arms, cradling her against his chest. "I'm an idiot. I meant to bring the Jeep over to your place and I got distracted."

"Hey, I'm not hating this at all," she said, looping her arms around his neck.

"You're saying that because you want to know what the surprise is."

"Maybe, but being carried to the car like a princess doesn't suck." She curled against him, placing her cheek to his chest with a purr. "Now, shhh, let me enjoy this."

He laughed as he came around the side of the Jeep, lowering her gently to her feet.

"Thanks for the ride."

Clark opened the door for her, leaning against the inside of it. "Anytime."

Merry hiked her leg to climb inside and her skirt rode up her thigh, exposing the creamy soft skin. The sight sliced through his body and his already aching cock stiffened further, straining against his boxer briefs and slacks. Unable to resist, he rested his hand on that bare skin once she was situated on the seat, sliding it farther under her skirt and around to graze the inside of her thighs. Merry's breath hitched as his fingers skimmed higher until they traced the edge of her lace panties.

"You get as many rides as you want tonight."

Merry's gaze jerked up to meet his, blinking at him.

"Ummm...did you mean that the way it came out?"

His mouth stretched into a wicked grin as his finger dipped inside, tracing the length of her seam. "I don't know. Why don't you explain it to me?"

"Clark," she whimpered, her eyes closing as her head fell back against the seat.

God, he wanted to press on, to make her come in the front seat of his Jeep and listen to her cry out his name again, but instead, he removed his hand slowly, stalling to give her knee a squeeze.

"Does that answer your question?" Clark teased.

Merry blinked several times before his words clicked and she shivered. "You're evil."

"What can I say?" Clark said, grinning wolfishly. "You bring the devil out of me."

Chapter 23

CLARK

"IT BLOWS MY MIND HOW it takes so long to prepare for Christmas and all the events, yet once Thanksgiving is over, December flies by." Merry took another sip of her wine, her cheeks flushed with the heady effects of her second glass. Normally she didn't drink wine, especially not red, but being in the beautiful dining room of the Lodge made her feel like the awkward teenaged girl dreaming of this moment and she'd wanted a little something to take the edge off. Especially when Clark continued to throw her off balance with every flirty quip and smoldering look.

"You mean it isn't even December yet?" Clark nodded to the corner of the room, where a twenty-foot Christmas tree stood fully decorated.

"Don't be a Declan Gallagher," she said, pointing her fork at him.

Clark chuckled. "What does that mean?"

"Declan and his father treat Christmas the way single people treat Valentine's Day. With total and utter contempt."

"He can't be all bad," Clark said, scooping potatoes onto his fork. "He gives me a discount on tools and supplies."

Merry rolled her eyes. "That's good for business, not because he's helping out his fellow neighbors. I don't think he's a bad guy. I'll just be using his name in lieu of Grinch or Scrooge from now on."

Clark sat back in his chair, making a time out gesture. "Wait a second, I thought you weren't a mean girl?"

"I'm not, but…is it mean if it's true?"

"Yes."

Merry huffed. "Oh, fine. I won't do that. I simply can't understand how people can hate Christmas. Bright lights. Catchy music. It literally gives me a happy thinking about it."

"I didn't think girls got *happies*," he teased, using his fingers for air quotes.

Merry almost tossed her napkin at him, but she didn't want to get banned from the Lodge now that she'd tasted its heavenly delights. "You're terrible."

His foot brushed hers under the table playfully. "In a good way though."

"If you say so," she said noncommittally.

Clark placed a hand over his chest as if she'd wounded him. "Wow, I see you. You do have a little bit of a mean streak. It's tiny but there." She stuck her tongue out and he chuckled. "As to your confusion as to why some people might not be thrilled for the holidays, not everyone looks at them the same. People of different religions and cultures celebrate their own holidays, not to mention Christmas is extremely commercialized, and shoved down our throats even before Halloween is over. I can understand how other people may get sick of it all."

"I will give you that," Merry conceded. She enjoyed that Clark didn't just agree with her because he thought that's what she wanted to hear, but seemed to relish debating various points. "I remember walking by the craft store right after Halloween and she had this sign that read HAPPY HALLOWTHANKSMAS and I thought that was so accurate because really, we make a big deal about Halloween, then Christmas stuff comes out in stores, with a sprinkle of fall and Thanksgiving décor, and once that day is done, Christmas is everywhere. When I was a kid, it seemed like December 24th took forever to arrive, but as an adult, time flies."

"I didn't have that problem, since we didn't celebrate. My mother didn't change the house décor for holidays unless they were having friends over, and my dad thought Christmas lights were a ridiculous energy suck."

"Your dad is definitely a Declan."

He chuckled. "Maybe it was their lack of love for the holidays that made me such an advocate for them. Jace and I start planning for Halloween after the Fourth of July. Did you see our costumes?"

"No. I didn't know you even dressed up."

"Oh yeah." Clark pulled out his phone and scrolled through. "We do family costumes every year. The one year Sam visited for Halloween, we all went as pirates." Clark handed it to her. "This year, Jace was Spider-Man and I was Dr. Octopus."

Merry awwwed at the picture of Jace crouched down with his wrist up and Clark standing behind him in a brown leather jacket with tubes coming out the back. "How did you make the tentacles?"

"Bought some duct tubing at the hardware store."

She returned the phone to him. "That is very creative. My mom made our costumes until we got a little older and asked for store-bought ones. I think she still has all of them. She hates to throw anything away in case we need it later. They have two storage sheds and I think my dad will need a new one before spring."

"I'm not handy with a needle at all. Jace wanted to learn to sew and I bought him this kids' machine for his birthday. I almost took my finger off with it."

"You did not!" Merry chuckled.

Clark grinned sheepishly. "No, but when he saw my stitching, he told me he'd just look up tutorials on YouTube."

"Ah, the joys of the computer era. If Dad doesn't know, ask Google."

"Exactly. That's why I don't have an Alexa in the house. Especially with my brother living with us, Jace would be asking her what everything meant and there are some things I'm not ready to explain."

Merry choked on her wine and covered her mouth with a napkin until she finally swallowed. "Oh God, you better watch out for my mother. She had an open-door policy with us and she would answer any questions we asked. She watered down some answers depending on how old we were, but yeah, he'll learn all kinds of new things."

"Like penalty taxes on tip jars?"

"What?"

"When my brother questioned his practices on swear word fees, Jace threatened him with a penalty tax."

Merry held her glass up in a toast. "He will make an excellent banker. Or CPA. My mom will probably buy him his own printing calculator for Christmas if she hears that story."

"Your mother is great. Really, both your parents are. Your dad brought by chicken noodle soup and vitamins for us tonight right before I walked over to your place."

"I'm assuming he didn't run you off since you're here," she murmured.

"He didn't talk about us dating except to say I will treat you with respect. I promised I would."

"I feel very respected, so you're safe. For now," she deepened her voice to a creepy whisper.

"Yikes, consider me scared." He finished the last bite of his steak and set his empty plate off to the side, rubbing his stomach with a groan. "I think I ate too much."

"That is why I ordered the salad instead of the baked potato. Leaves room for dessert."

"You're on your own for dessert, I'm afraid."

"I'm not talking about here. I bought your favorite dessert and it is waiting for us back at my house."

Clark grinned. "Oh man, you are killing me."

"We'll have to figure out something to do to work off this meal. Can't have you going into a food coma on me." Merry's gaze strayed to the dance floor, where several elderly couples shuffled to an instrumental Frank Sinatra tune. "How about a dance?"

Clark studied the other dancers and took a deep breath as he stood, holding his hand out to her. "Do you think we can keep up with them?"

"I'm willing to give it a try." She climbed to her feet and took his outstretched hand, following him out onto the dance floor. Clark twirled her out and ducked under her arm to catch her against him. She spluttered with surprise as he gracefully swung her around, his face split into a smug smile.

"Where did you learn to dance?"

"I took a ballroom dance elective in college. Turns out I was a natural."

"I'll say." She held onto his shoulders as he lifted her up while he turned below, smiling as he lowered her down the front of his body.

"You are an enigma, Clark Griffin. Just when I think I've got you figured out, boom. Curveball."

"Gotta keep you on your toes."

The music slowed and Clark pulled her in close, his palm spread over her lower back. He held her hand in his as he led her in a slow waltz, humming along with the melody.

"I didn't know you could sing," she whispered, resting her cheek against the front of his jacket.

"I can hum. Far cry from leading a rock band."

"I wanted to be in a rock band when I was a kid. Well, a country music band."

"As a singer?"

"No, I play the drums."

"Really? You have a drum kit?"

"In my parents' basement. Nick, Holly, Noel, and I performed at the Christmas concert last year, but I have since retired from the rock and roll lifestyle. Noel's got a gorgeous voice and has a TikTok dedicated to singing, but she does it for fun. I keep waiting for some big record mogul to try to woo her away from all this, but I think she's happy with my brother."

"Seems like it," Clark murmured.

"Can I tell you something kind of weird?"

"Sure."

"I think that Christmas is more romantic than Valentine's Day."

"Because of all the mistletoe?"

Merry looked around. "Where?"

Clark pointed to the exit. "We missed it when we came in."

"Well, that's a pity." She smiled up at him as she looped her arms around his neck. "Good thing you don't need a dead plant as an excuse to kiss me."

"A very good thing." His lips sought hers, and she breathed in the heavenly scent of cedar, cradling the back of his neck in her hands.

Someone next to them cleared their throat and they broke apart to find an elderly couple dancing close. The woman smacked her partner with a laugh. "Leave the young people alone, Walter."

"I was only interrupting them in case they wanted to take it elsewhere," he said with a wink.

Merry's face burned as she buried it in Clark's jacket front.

"Maybe we should get the check?" Clark said.

"Yes, please."

They paid their check and Merry finished off the last of her glass of wine. Clark spun her through the doorway and pulled her in close as they walked to the Jeep. "What time is it?"

Clark pulled out his phone. "A little after nine."

"It didn't seem that long." While he unlocked the Jeep door, Merry leaned back against it, giggling. "I may have overdone it with that second glass."

"That's all right, you were having a good time, which is exactly what I wanted."

"What about you?" she murmured, taking his tie in between her thumb and forefinger. "Did you have fun?"

He caged her in with his arms on either side of her head against the Jeep, smoothing her hair back with both hands. "This was the best night of my life, Merry. Thank you."

She took hold of his hips and brought his body flush with hers, arching against him. "Wanna make it better?"

He groaned, resting his forehead to hers. "Merry...I think we should wait until you sober up."

"I'm tipsy, not drunk, Clark." She turned her head, her lips so close to his, but he held himself just out of reach. "Kiss me," she whispered.

Clark pressed her into the side of his Jeep, crushing her mouth beneath his. Her heart flipped, the intensity of his kiss sending ripples of electricity from her mouth to her pussy. Like a roaring fire on a winter's eve, every sweep of his tongue licked like flames along her skin, urging her closer.

When his hand moved down to her knee and climbed up the outside of her thigh, she didn't care if someone walked by and saw them. He could take her right here, against the side of the Jeep with her skirt hiked up and her heels locked around his waist.

Clark broke away with a deep, trembling breath. "Get in the car, Merry. Please."

He dropped his hand from her thigh and grabbed the handle, opening the door for her. She climbed inside, wriggling in the seat to ease the ache between her legs, but it only made the throbbing intensify. She was so turned on all she could think about was stripping him out of that suit and making him lose control.

Clark got in and started the car, his hand curving around her thigh as he left the Lodge parking lot. Before they even cleared the stop sign, Merry twisted in the seat and pressed lingering kisses along his neck.

"Merry..." He groaned as her hand slid over his leg and cupped his rigid cock. His grip on her thigh tightened as she rubbed him, her other hand undoing his belt buckle. "What are you doing?"

She freed the button of his slacks and pulled the zipper down slowly as her teeth grazed his ear.

"Just watch the road."

Clark took his hand off her thigh as she stretched across the middle console, listening as his breathing grew ragged above her when she shimmied the elastic of his boxer briefs and pants down his hips, thankful that he lifted up without being asked. Wrapping her hand around his shaft, she pulled him from the confines of the boxer briefs, sweeping her tongue across its head and down along the corded length.

"Fuck, Merry."

The rough edge in his voice rushed through her like a drug as she took him all the way in, sucking him while the pulse inside her beat faster, remembering his mouth on her. His hands. They way he'd looked at her. The sounds of his pleasure urged her on, and she imagined his smile, the way he stroked her face and took her hand. Her body cradled in his arms as he carried her.

He trembled under her as he came, her name erupting from his lips like a prayer. Merry raised up slowly when Clark pulled onto their road, studying his face in the flashing Christmas lights as he pulled in front of her house. His breathing was harsh, his mouth parted, and a wave of powerful longing rolled through her, the need to be close, to touch him too much to resist. She unbuckled her seat belt and kissed him. She kissed along his jaw, his neck. When the car finally came to a stop, she curled against his shoulder as he sighed, his lips pressing against her forehead.

"That was amazing," he said, setting his pants and belt to rights.

"I'm glad you thought so," she murmured, flattening her palm against the front of his shirt. "Do you want to come in for dessert now?"

"I want to come in and hold you properly."

"We can do that too," she whispered.

Clark cupped her chin and lifted her mouth to his in a soft, chaste kiss. "Thank you."

She giggled. "You're thanking me for an orgasm?"

"No, I'm thanking you for everything. For caring. For saying yes."

"It's my pleasure."

"Not yet," he rumbled.

Merry's jaw dropped and anticipation zinged along her skin as she let him help her out of the car.

In the dark, the vibrant shine of her Christmas lights lit up the area like a strobe light. Her pulse kicked up speed the second they stepped over the threshold, Clark following her through the kitchen to the back of the house. She slipped the coat down her arms and he took it from her with one hand, hanging it on the hook while the fingers of his other hand trailed lightly up her arm, leaving streaks of heat across her skin.

His mouth skimmed the side of her neck and she sighed, leaning to give him better access, her hand circling to cradle the back of his head. Clark's big hands traveled along her body lightly, reaching the bottom of her dress and gathering it slowly, exposing her legs an inch at a time. She stepped out of her shoes one at a time and he chuckled against her skin.

"Trying to get away from me?"

"My feet were sore."

"We can't have that," he whispered, turning her by her hips until she faced him. She held on tight as he lifted her against him, wrapping her legs around his hips as he carried her to the couch. He lowered her onto the cushion with his mouth on hers, divesting himself of his jacket in jerky motions, while her hands worked on unthreading his tie. Merry slid the tie off, unconcerned with where it fell, and went to work on his shirt buttons, the need to touch his bare skin riding her.

Clark found the zipper on the back of her dress, racing it down her back as his hand slid down the opening, rough palms leaving frissons of delight along her bare shoulder blades. Every touch of his hands lit a passion in her she'd never experienced. She'd been felt up. Pawed at. But this slow sensual dance with Clark was something entirely different. He pulled the straps of her dress down to her waist, exposing her red lace demi bra, and she swung her feet onto the floor to shimmy the dress over her hips to the floor, holding his hungry gaze with hers.

Their actions ramped into a frenzied need. His shirt dropped along with the dress and he reached for her, tracing the edges of her bra strap with first his fingers and then his mouth. Merry closed her eyes as his callused hands grazed the soft skin of her arms, skimming around to unhook the clasp of her bra. Their mouths met once more as Merry blindly removed his belt.

Clothes were discarded everywhere. The counter. The floor. The doorknob. Clark sat on the couch to pull off his shoes, watching her slip her bra down her arms and throw it over the top of the snowmen. The flashes of Christmas lights illuminated the hunger burning in his eyes and she smiled coyly, her hands traveling down over her hips, hooking her thumbs in the lacy strap of her thong. Clark pulled a condom from his wallet, rolling it over his dick with his hand grasping his width as he watched her strip.

"I guess I should take these off," she said, turning to the side and bending, sliding them to the floor.

In a flash, his hand was between her legs, his finger teasing the lips of her seam and she gripped the other side of her u-shaped couch with a moan. His lips traveled over the globes of her ass as his fingers played with her, twisting and pulling. Merry dropped her forehead to the cushion and cried out when Clark's tongue joined his fingers, sucking her, thrusting his tongue inside while he rubbed her clit, faster, the pressure building until she cried out her pleasure.

With a gentle tug he brought her onto his lap, one arm wrapped around her middle as his other covered her breasts, his hard length flexing against her, so close.

"I want you inside me," she moaned, rolling her ass against his stiff cock.

Clark took her hips and lifted her, the head of his cock finding her entrance, inch by inch, stretching her, and she leaned back against him, trembling as he used his hands on her to thrust all the way inside. With one hand on her stomach and the other squeezing her breast, he rocked her, like a ship riding along the ocean waves. His finger slipped between her folds to stroke her clit, kissing her neck and squeezing her breast as he spoke in that deep timber.

"Fuck, Merry, I could be inside you forever. Tell me this is good for you."

"Yes," she gasped, her legs shaking as his circles quickened on her sensitive nub, his cock sliding in and out, matching the speed of his hand.

"Don't leave me," he whispered against the back of her neck, his lips pressed against her skin. "Please, don't leave. Ever."

The raw emotion in his voice tore at her heart and she turned her head to meet his lips, cupping the back of his head. The air was charged around them, humid with sex, and when his thrusts intensified, she gasped against his mouth. "I'm not going anywhere. Do you understand? I'm yours."

Clark's hand came up to cradle her face, his kiss messy and desperate, and Merry broke, a rush of heat flushing her skin, and she shook with every aftershock. Clark convulsed beneath her, his mouth opening around hers as he called her name.

Long moments passed, their bodies slick with sweat as she leaned against him, his arms clasped across her middle. Merry's eyes fluttered open, and she pivoted her neck to watch the lights on his skin. "So...you ready for dessert yet?"

Clark laughed, falling onto the couch with her curled up in front of him. "Maybe for breakfast."

"Wait, are you...staying?" she asked hesitantly.

"I think I can sneak back into the house before they wake up. Just gotta move my Jeep." He kissed her shoulder, running his rugged palm down her arm. "Don't move, okay? I'm going to clean up and drive it over."

Clark got up and headed for the bathroom. When the door closed, she pulled the blanket down from the back of the couch, covering herself. The windows of her small living room were opaque with steam and she yawned, considering whether it was worth climbing the stairs to her bed.

The bathroom door opened with a click, and she glanced at his approach blearily, doing a double take. "What are you doing in my robe?"

The lavender flannel hung open over his chest, closing just above the belt at his waist. "I'm just going to move the car. I don't want to get all these clothes back on for that."

"What if your brother sees you running back across the road in my robe?" She laughed.

"He'll know what's going on and give me shit in the morning." He put his shoes on and grabbed his keys from his pocket, pausing to take a bracing breath.

"You're going to freeze your ass off."

"Good thing I'll have you to warm me up when I get back." He ducked out the door, slamming it as she shouted, "I'm not a space heater!"

Merry got up from the couch, listening to his Jeep rumble and the crunch of tires on gravel. She went to the bathroom, removing the pins and rubber bands from her hair and finishing her nightly routine.

She'd reached the top step when the door opened and Clark came back in, dancing from foot to foot. "Fucking cold!"

Merry watched him from the loft with a smirk. "Don't think you're coming to bed and putting cold hands all over me."

Clark opened the fridge and pulled out the pie. "What if I bring dessert?"

She pursed her lips, pretending to consider. "You may join me on one condition."

"What's that?"

"Don't forget the whipped cream."

CHAPTER 24

MERRY

MERRY PUT THE GIANT POT of potatoes on the stove and turned on the burner, wiping the back of her hand over her forehead. Her mother was on the other side of the table slicing the yams, slapping Holly's hands when she went for another round of mini marshmallows.

"Why didn't you eat before you came to help?" their mother grumbled.

"I did eat, but there's always room for marshmallows."

Another sharp smack. "Stay out of them or I won't have enough for the yams. Make yourself useful and check to see if the rolls are rising."

Holly rolled her eyes. "I know what that means. You're telling me I'm in the way without telling me I'm in the way."

"You are in the way," Noel teased, sipping a glass of wine.

"I don't see you helping out!"

"I brought the green bean casserole per the boss's" —she tipped her glass toward Victoria—"specification and I brought the rolls. What did you bring?"

"I brought roasted Brussels sprouts and wine."

"One of those was helpful." Noel snickered.

"I'm sure your dish will be wonderful, baby," Victoria said.

Merry winked at Noel as she poured herself a glass of wine. "Mom, don't lie, it will only encourage her."

"You know what? I'm tapping out. I'm going to see what the boys are up to." Holly slammed out the front door.

"The boys are freezing their asses off trying to fry a turkey in the snow." Noel raised her glass. "Here is hoping no one gets burned and needs to go to the ER."

Victoria's gaze widened. "They won't, will they?"

"It's their first time frying a turkey, so I wouldn't be surprised. I told Nick to treat it like a spectator sport."

Her mom got up from the table and opened the front door, hollering, "Hey! Do not hurt yourself. You get me?"

Merry heard her dad grumble something along the lines of "Woman, we got this." And she shut the door in a huff.

"I swear, why he didn't just want to cook the turkey in the oven is beyond me. Merry, check the ham. I hope it's big enough to feed everyone if the turkey doesn't turn out."

Noel poured another glass of wine and handed it to Victoria. "You need this. It's just Thanksgiving. We eat, we laugh, we say what we're grateful for, and then it's over."

"Yeah, Mom, why don't you go put your feet up and have a rest. Noel and I got this."

Victoria's gaze cut to the couch hesitatingly. "But the yams. I need to finish them."

Merry picked up the cutting board and baking pan like she

was brandishing weapons. "I've got the yams, and then it's just putting everything we've prepped in the oven at appropriate intervals and mashing the potatoes."

"And feeding your other daughter's side dish to the dogs," Noel joked.

Victoria wagged her finger at Noel. "Don't you dare. I'm going to be right over there, so no funny business."

"No promises, Mom." Merry stole a marshmallow from the bag with a smirk.

The front door burst open and Jace ran right for Victoria. "Happy Thanksgiving!"

She caught him in her arms, picking him up off the floor. "Happy Thanksgiving to you! Don't you look handsome."

Jace made a face. "I'm choking to death with this thing." He pulled at the top of his shirt and the tie came off with a snap. "Oops."

"Here, give it to me." Her mom clipped it back into place. "Now, go get the chess set while these two do all the work."

"Hey! I don't get a hello?" Merry called.

He stopped running toward the closet and cocked his head to the side. "I just saw you this morning."

Merry's face flushed, feeling Noel and her mother's eyes on her. "Fine, I didn't want your stinky hug anyway."

He laughed, danced his way over, and wrapped his arms around her neck tight.

"Thank you." He pulled back and she held out a handful of marshmallows. "When you act sweet, you get treats."

Jace popped the whole mass in his mouth and smiled, his cheeks puffed out like a chipmunk.

"Ugh, go get the chess set. Gross." He took off for the hallway, chortling. Merry caught Noel's smirk and scowled. "What?"

"Nothing," Noel said, coming over to sit next to her. "Last I heard, you'd forgiven Clark for walking out of the bar, but I didn't know we'd moved on to brown chicken brown cow."

"Will you stop? My mother is listening to every word."

"I'm not listening to you. I'm going to play chess."

"See?" Merry kicked Noel's foot with hers, fighting back a grin. "I didn't stay the night. I got up and made cinnamon rolls with them this morning."

"Ah. So, none of the other."

Merry ducked her head, slicing through an orange tuber with a smirk.

"I see that smile!" Noel hissed.

"All right, stop. We can talk about this later, when tiny ears and moms aren't in the next room."

"Fine."

"Where's Daisy?" Jace asked.

"In the laundry room with Butch," Victoria said. "Miss Daisy stole the first batch of rolls this morning when no one was looking, so she cannot be trusted around food."

"Can we let her out later?" Jace asked, his tone laced with hope.

"Once all the food is put away, absolutely."

Noel held her hand out to Merry. "Why don't you pass the torch to me and go say hi to your honey?"

Merry grinned, handing her the knife. "Thanks."

"You tell Clark I'm waiting in here for my hello," her mom called over her shoulder.

"If you want something, Mom, you gotta go after it." Her mother turned, giving her an arch look as Merry laughed her way out the door.

Clark, Nick, and her dad were standing around the fryer talking, but when she stepped onto the porch, Clark smiled at her tenderly. Butterflies erupted in her stomach and she wanted to walk over to him and snuggle into his arms but she wasn't sure how Clark would feel about PDA in front of her family.

"How's the turkey?" Merry asked.

"Coming along," her dad called. "This is going to be so good. It takes a quarter of the time and gets a real crispy skin."

"How do you know? You've never fried a turkey before," Merry said.

"They did a demonstration when I was in Twin Falls last week. That's where I got this baby."

Merry eyed the fryer warily. "Maybe you should let Nick get the turkey out, in case there is grease splatter."

"I've got my gear over here." Her dad held up his black-gloved hands and adjusted the goggles over his eyes. "I'm ready."

"I've never even cooked a turkey, why would I be better at frying one?" Nick asked.

"Because you're young. You'll heal faster."

Nick glared at her. "I feel used and kinda expendable."

Clark clapped him on the back. "I'd miss you, Nick."

"Thanks, Clark."

Holly and Sam were off to the side having their own conversation. Sam gave Merry a wave as she sauntered by on her way to Clark, but when she pointed to Holly and made a scissor motion, he scrunched his face in discomfiture.

"What do you need cut?" he teased.

"Don't test me, Sam. I'll come for you."

"Why are you threatening my brother?" Clark asked, his hand brushing hers when she stopped next to him. She took the invitation and laced her fingers with his.

"He knows why."

"I'm being unjustly threatened," Sam protested.

Chris leveled him with a dry stare. "Son, I've known you a short time and if my daughter is threatening you, it's with good reason."

Everyone laughed but Sam, who held a hand over his chest. "Damn, Chris. That hurts."

"Why don't you go in and help Noel with food prep?" Merry shot Sam a pointed look.

"Hey, now, I don't want Sam anywhere near my girl," Nick argued, smoothing down the front of his collared shirt. "He's prettier than me."

"Thanks, Nick. It's the hair," Sam said, flinging his head back.

"Come on, Sam. Let's go inside where it's warm." Holly stuck her tongue out at Merry when she glared at her sister.

"Dad, can I murder Holly?" Merry asked.

"You people do what you want." Her dad squatted down, checking the fryer gauge. "I'm busy."

Holly and Sam disappeared inside and Clark whispered in her ear, "Happy Thanksgiving."

"Yeah, you may want to go tell my mother that. She said she's not coming out to get her greeting from you."

"Sounds like I'm in trouble. Excuse me." To her surprise, he kissed her cheek before heading into the house.

Nick's gaze landed on Merry, his eyebrows raised. "So...when did that happen?"

"Mind your own business, son," their dad said without looking up from the temperature gauge.

Merry sneered. "Yeah, Nick."

"Geez, can't even ask a question around here. I'm going to see what my girl is doing. Have fun turkey watching."

Left alone with her dad, she hopped up on the porch railing. "About Clark..."

"You don't need to tell me anything. Like I told him...as long as he treats you with respect, you are adults and can do whatever you want." Her dad climbed to his feet and lifted the goggles up, his gaze serious. "I'm glad we have a moment to talk."

Merry swallowed. "About what?"

"It's gonna be busy tomorrow with the season opening and the big anniversary. I thought you'd like to get up and hang with me for the day. See what I do and help me keep things running smoothly."

"I've helped out on opening day before, Dad. I know it's all hands on deck."

"I'm not talking about hauling trees. I want to go over all the projections with you and make sure orders get filled. Oversee things." He cleared his throat. "I know you weren't happy when I brought Clark on board and your mom said you might feel like I don't want you running the farm when I...retire." He said the last like it tasted bad. "I'm just not ready to admit I'm getting old."

"You aren't old, Dad."

"Tell that to my back in the morning."

Merry laughed. "I just mean that I'm not going to push you out, but I want you to know that I love this place and I will help you take care of it. That's all."

Her dad crossed the porch and hugged her, the rubber of his gloves squeaking as he patted her back. "When did you grow up on me? You and your sister...you have your own lives, and I still see my gangly little girls with missing teeth, playing hide and seek in the trees." He released her, his voice stern with authority. "Go to bed early tonight. I want you up here at five-thirty for coffee and breakfast."

"The farm doesn't open until ten!"

"And there's a lot that goes into getting it ready, and with this being a big anniversary year, it will be a madhouse. If you don't want to learn..."

"No, I'll be here," she said, hopping down. "Thanks, Dad. And for the record, I still feel like that awkward little girl sometimes."

Holly poked her head out of the door. "Hey, Mom wants you in here so she can force all of us to share what we're grateful for."

Merry groaned. "Seriously?"

"I don't make the rules. So hurry your butts up."

Holly closed the door and her dad shrugged.

"Your mother likes all of the sentimental stuff. Best to humor her."

"It's just awkward with Sam and Clark here."

"Why? Aren't you grateful for them?"

Merry shot her dad a disgruntled look. "Yes. I'm not sure how much to say though. Clark is...well, he hasn't dated anyone in a long time and I don't want to scare him off."

"Honey, I like Clark a lot, but if you pour your heart out to a man, and he runs? He wasn't the guy for you and I say good riddance." He pulled his gloved and goggles off, curling his arm around her shoulders with a tight squeeze. "If it's any consolation, I think Clark will stick around."

"Thanks, Dad."

"I love you."

"I love you too."

"Good, now, let's get in there before your mom comes looking for us."

Merry followed behind her dad and the minute she shut the door, her mom stared barking orders.

"Oh good, get a glass of something to drink. We can't do a proper toast without something to drink."

Holly handed her the glass of wine she'd poured earlier and Merry went to stand next to Clark and Jace. Clark took her hand in his free one and to her utter delight, Jace leaned back against her, sipping on a glass of bubbling cider.

"All right, everyone has a drink?" Her father held up a glass of amber liquid and Victoria smiled in approval. "Excellent. Now, we are going to go around the room and say what we're grateful for." Merry and her siblings, including Noel, groaned and their mom narrowed her eyes. "I'll start. I'm grateful that my family is good-natured enough to go along with all of my traditions, no matter how tedious they may seem. I am grateful for my husband, although that may change depending on how his turkey turns out." Victoria kissed Chris, sliding her arm around his waist. "I'm only kidding, darling." She raised her glass, her eyes scanning the room warmly. "My children, who have grown into wonderful adults, for the most part. Clark, thank you and Jace for coming into our lives. And to Sam…thank you for making me laugh."

"It's been my pleasure, Victoria," Sam purred, waggling his eyebrows.

"Be careful how much you charm my wife, pretty boy," Chris deadpanned.

The adults chuckled.

"Can I go next?" Jace asked.

"Sure." Victoria smiled fondly. "Then we'll go around the room clockwise after you're done."

Jace pulled at his collared shirt, his tie having gone by the wayside. "I'm grateful my dad and I can have fun together again. In California, he worked really hard and his head hurt all the time, so he didn't want to play as much. But since coming here, he smiles more and he wants me to be his mate again when we cook. He has the best pirate voice I've ever heard."

"Jace," Clark groaned.

"What?"

"Keep going, Jace," Merry said, giggling. "What else are you grateful for?"

Jace looked up at his dad, his expression bewildered. "Can I?"

"Go ahead, buddy."

"Okay. I am grateful for Victoria and Chris, all the friends I made at school. And I am glad my dad likes Merry, because she is really nice and I want her to stay with us forever. Amen."

Tears in her eyes, Merry dropped Clark's hand and hugged his son from behind, kissing his cheek. "Thank you, Jace."

"It's your turn, Clark," Chris said. "Although I don't know how you follow that."

"I don't know how I do either." Clark cleared his throat. "This is the first Thanksgiving we've had where it wasn't just the two or three of us. I'm grateful to be here today with all of you. Victoria and Chris, I can never repay you for everything you've done for us. You have the biggest hearts, opening your home and your family to my son and me and I see that goodness in your children."

Merry watched her siblings smile as they listened to Clark. Merry's arm was still around Jace, his little hand holding hers against his chest.

"Sam, I am so lucky to have you for a brother. Thanks for being there for me," Clark said, slapping his back.

Sam gave him a one-armed hug. "Same goes, bro."

"Merry." Clark turned her way, his smile sweet and loving. "Getting to know you has changed my life. Thank you for giving me a second chance to make a better first impression."

"You're very welcome," she murmured.

"And that's what I'm grateful for. Cheers!" Clark took a drink from his glass and then leaned over to kiss her cheek, his arm slipping around her waist.

"Guess that means I'm up," Sam said, holding his beer bottle in the air. "Thank you for good friends, good food, my family, and my health. Salute."

"Salute."

Clark's mouth moved to her ear, his voice barely audibly, "I have more to say, but it's not appropriate in front of your family, but I'll tell you the rest later."

Merry blushed, leaning into him. "I can't wait."

The remaining speeches were short and sweet, even Chris's, who finished his by asking when they could have dessert before dinner. Before Merry finished them off, someone knocked at the front door.

"Who could that be?" Victoria asked.

"I got this," Clark said, letting Merry go to answer the door.

Martin stepped inside, shaking Clark's hand. The two men spoke quietly, until Merry's dad barked, "What is going on, you two?"

"Sorry." Clark grinned sheepishly, holding the door open. "Martin and some of the other farm employees helped me with a surprise for you and Victoria. I know it's not Christmas, but I couldn't wait. If you'll all join us outside?"

Jace wiggled out of her arms to follow his dad, with Merry trailing at the end of the group. She heard her mother's gasp of surprise and a smile spread across her face when she realized what Clark had done.

She stepped up next to Clark and watched her parents sit down in the rocking chairs Clark made for them.

"These are beautiful," Victoria murmured, her hands gliding over the arms. Tears spilled down her cheeks and she dashed at them with a laugh. "I can't believe you made them."

Clark waved a hand towards Martin and the other men scattered down the steps of the porch. "I did, but they are from all of us."

"He's being humble. We didn't even know about them until he asked to borrow my truck Monday," Martin said.

Merry's heart raced as she watched Clark blush when Martin

patted his shoulder. Clark created beautiful rocking chairs for her parents and gifted them early because he couldn't wait. He included the other employees, even though the gift was really his. He played pirates while cooking with his son, and took his brother in when he had nowhere else to go. With the exception of her father and brother, he was the best man she knew, and she'd fallen irrevocably in love with him.

"We're going to get back to our families," Martin said, waving. "Happy Thanksgiving."

"Happy Thanksgiving," Merry and the rest of her family chorused. When the men disappeared around the corner, Chris got up from the rocker and approached Clark, taking his hand and bringing him in for a backslapping hug.

"This was very generous of you, Clark. Thank you." Her dad pulled away from a stunned Clark and waved at her. "Merry? Don't you still need to tell us what you're thankful for?"

Merry looked around at her family, joy coursing through her as she spoke from the heart.

"I'm grateful to be home, living my dreams and discovering new ones. I'm grateful for my family and their unwavering love and support. To Sam." Her gaze landed on him in the corner next to Clark and grinned. "It's like having another annoying brother around and I love it. Jace, the greatest kid in the entire world." He'd climbed up into her dad's rocker and stalled his motions when she called out to him. "Thank you for keeping my dog entertained."

Jace beamed. "You're welcome, but Chris said she was his dog now."

"I said no such thing, you scamp," Chris growled, picking him up out of his chair and dropping him in Victoria's lap as the boy squealed with laughter.

When the ribbing died down, Merry turned her gaze on Clark, a tender smile on her lips. "And to Clark, who came out of nowhere. I look forward to more surprises and a lot of happiness in our future."

She watched his face for panic or uncertainty, but there was none. To her delight and amazement, he drew her into his arms and kissed her softly, in full view of her family, and her heart flipped.

"To our future," he murmured.

CHAPTER 25

MERRY

MERRY FOLLOWED BEHIND HER DAD as they headed for the flocking tent, ready for a nap and it was only two in the afternoon on Friday. When they'd gone over the books that morning, she'd been shocked to realize how delicate the profit margins were on the farm. One disaster and it could take years to recover, if it didn't bankrupt them. She'd discovered the only thing that kept them afloat after a bad crop was her mom's income and none of them, not Nick, Holly, or herself, knew.

She paused just inside the trees, her eyes scanning the hills of green firs covered in the several inches of snow that had fallen this week, but even though the temperature hadn't risen above twenty today, the sun was shining and the farm was celebrating.

Especially Merry. Her dad was finally including her in the day to day of the farm. Daisy scratched on the door to be let out, instead of having an accident. And she'd enjoyed a very hot, sexually explicit wake-up call with Clark before he'd gone home to get ready for the day. And even though Merry was one hundred percent sure she'd fallen in love, she decided not to say anything until he did. There was plenty of time for heartfelt confessions, and the fact that he'd toasted to their future in front of her family gave her a level of confidence he was feeling it too.

Tires squealing in the distance disrupted her happy thoughts and an old blue car fishtailed into their private driveway. Spraying gravel as it skidded to a stop in front of the house, the car took out her mother's white planter. Soil and snow exploded on the other side of the car like a land mine and Merry gasped, bursting through the trees. What the hell were they thinking? At least he hadn't pulled into the Christmas tree parking lot where all of the customers were.

The driver's door opened and Merry hollered, "Are you out of your mind? This is a family farm and there are children!"

A familiar old man climbed out, slurring his words. "Remember me, cupcake?"

"Mr. Olson. What are you doing?"

"I came to congratulate you. Celebrate the big hero! Savior of unwanted dogs and destroyer of lives!"

"Merry, are you all right?" her dad puffed, coming up behind her. "Olson?" Her father looked beyond to the shards of white wood littered across the snow and shouted, "You destroyed my wife's planter!"

Mr. Olson squinted past her. "I could give two shits about your wife's planter, Chris Winters. I'm here to talk about your kid!" Mr. Olson stumbled, letting out a trembling whistle. "You raised a gem here. Your daughter doesn't mind her own business. Do you know what she cost me?"

"I know that you were caught on video kicking a dog," her

dad said coldly. "It was on every local news channel. Maybe you should have kept your temper in check."

"I'd been scammed! I was the victim and your daughter" —he spat the word at her—"added fuel to the fire."

Merry shook her head, watching the keys in his hands. If he tried to get back into that car, she would tackle him. He was so drunk he could barely walk, let alone operate a vehicle.

"Mr. Olson, whatever happened to you isn't my fault. If you'll give me your keys, we can go up to the house and get some coffee and talk."

"I don't want any of your damn coffee," he said, floundering back with his keys held high. "You want my keys? Why? So you can take my car too?"

"No, I want them so you don't try to drive again," she said patiently, taking another step toward him. "You could hurt someone."

"I haven't hurt nobody, you're the one hurting people! The sheriff came out with those damn animal people and took my sheep. My dogs. Gave me a fucking court date!" he screamed, pulling a piece of paper from his pocket and waving it at her. "Said I had to make an appearance or they'd double my fine."

The old man opened his back door and bent inside. Merry saw her dad on the phone and she took a few swift steps until she saw the dog crate.

"They didn't get everything though," Mr. Olson muttered.

Panic surged through her at the scrape of the metal gate opening. If he released an aggressive dog with all of the people in the trees…families…

Jace. He liked to follow his dad around and help out.

"Mr. Olson, don't!" she screamed, grabbing his shoulder.

He spun around suddenly and knocked her off balance. She fell to the ground on her butt and threw her hands over her face, waiting for a raging animal to come flying out of the back of the car.

A black blur flew overhead, squawking in outrage, and Merry lowered her arms, staring at the fat, beady-eyed chicken as it landed and took off.

"They didn't get my chickens!" Mr. Olson crowed, clapping his hands. "You wanna take everything from me? Here!" He threw another red chicken in the air and it flapped frantically toward her. It landed a few feet behind her and hopped along after the other. "Have another!"

Her dad lifted her to her feet from behind. "You okay, honey?"

"Yeah, but I think Mr. Olson is off his rocker."

"You're right about that." Her dad ducked another screeching bird and hollered, "Olson, knock it off! We don't want your damn chickens!"

"Your daughter does! I'm just giving her what she wants." He opened the trunk and a dozen more birds poured out.

When two hens hopped out of the back seat and casually pecked the ground around her feet, Merry burst out laughing.

"Merry?"

Her dad watched her guffaw as though she were the crazy one and she wheezed, "You gotta admit,"—she gulped for breath— "as far as revenge plots go, it could have been worse."

Her dad's mouth twitched. "I guess you're right, although the little bastards are going to poop everywhere." When Mr. Olson went to the other side of his car and opened the front seat, her father ran around to stop him. "For the last time, Olson, stop releasing chickens."

"Why? You don't like chickens?" He opened another cage before her dad reached him and the two wrestled around for a moment before Olson got loose and staggered away, falling to the ground by the trunk. He frowned over the car as Merry laughed harder. "Why are you laughing? I'm ruining your great celebration!"

Merry managed to get ahold of herself and walked over to where the old man's keys had fallen. "No, you didn't, Mr. Olson," she said, picking them up off the ground.

He scrambled after her, crawling across the gravel. "You can't take my car."

"I'm not, but I'm making sure you can't either."

She checked that all the animals were out before she closed the trunk and the rear passenger door. "Dad, will you make sure there aren't any more chickens inside?"

"We're good," he said, shutting the front passenger door.

Mr. Olson managed to get back on his feet and followed behind her with an unsteady gait, his arms reaching for her like he was auditioning for *The Walking Dead*. "Where are you going? Gimme my damn keys!"

"Not until you sober up, Mr. Olson."

Her mother came running out of the house, Jace right behind her. "What in the world is going on?"

"Mr. Olson executing his revenge against us. Well, against me." She handed the keys off to her dad, but Mr. Olson was too busy retching to worry about snatching them anymore.

"Chickens!" Jace cheered, running after a Rhode Island Red hen, who took off down the hill.

"How many?" her mom asked.

"Mr. Olson? You wanna tell us how many chickens you brought us?"

"Don't know for sure," he heaved. "Whatever I could catch."

"Close to twenty, I think," her dad said. "I'll let the guys know and we can start gathering em up."

"Are they hens?" her mom asked.

"Mr. Olson?" He'd stopped vomiting and Merry prodded him on the shoulder. "Are all the chickens you brought hens?"

"Yeah. I ate the rooster. Annoying bastard."

Her mother clapped her hands. "Well, happy birthday to me. Jace! Baby, stop chasing them! If you scare them, they won't lay any more eggs!"

"Oh no," Merry's dad said firmly. "Victoria, we are not keeping these things."

"That's where you're wrong, honey." Her mother's voice was sweet as sugar, with a hard edge that brooked no argument. "I've been asking for chickens for years—"

"And I was adamantly against them! I hate chickens."

"But these were a gift." Her mother walked over to Mr. Olson and patted his dazed face. "Gordon! Wake up."

"What?" he muttered.

"I want to thank you for the chickens."

He squinted at her in confusion. "Thank me?"

"Yes. Thank you. I know it wasn't your intention, but we appreciate them."

"Victoria, we don't have any place to put them!"

Merry grinned sheepishly. "Didn't you buy an extra dog kennel?"

Her dad's brows snapped into a murderous scowl.

"Don't look so constipated, honey," her mom said, kissing his cheek. "You'll love having fresh eggs, I promise."

Resigned, her father grumbled, "I'll get Nick. Merry, can you stay with Mr. Olson until the police arrive?"

"Yes, I can."

"Tell everyone not to hurt my chickens!" her mom called after him.

"Mom...why do you want chickens?"

"For the eggs, dear, like I said." Lowering her voice, she added, "And only slightly to annoy your father."

"I thought you were supposed to love, honor, and obey your husband?"

Her mom scoffed. "Not since the dark ages. Wedding vows now state wives are to love, honor, and annoy their husbands. Keeps them on their toes. You'll learn when you get married."

Merry rolled her eyes. "I might elope to Vegas when I decide to tie the knot."

She didn't even cast Merry an outraged glance. "You wouldn't dare break your mother's heart like that." Cupping her mouth with her hands, Victoria shouted, "Come on, Jace. Let's finish the cookies." Jace raced back up the hill and her mother patted Merry's arm. "Stop by the house after you're done with Mr. Olson. You look like you could use a cup of coffee."

"Thanks, Mom."

"Bye, Merry," Jace called as he ran past both of them. When

she was all alone with Mr. Olson, she leaned against the car and listened to the old man snore. If only she had her phone, she could at least scroll through Instagram as she waited and answer messages. She'd already been able to fill all the generic pre-orders from Holly's online form and had half a dozen custom orders she needed to work on that were due before Christmas. She could be working instead of drunk-sitting and she looked toward the sky, silently asking why her day went to hell.

Merry heard a car and whirled around, expecting to find a sheriff's deputy rolling up the drive. Instead, a white Ford truck stopped alongside her. A woman leaned over the seat and waved, her voice carrying out of the open window. "Hi. You all right?"

"Oh yeah, just waiting for someone to pick up this chicken flinger."

"I'm sorry, what?" she asked.

"Sorry, long story. Can I help you?"

The woman appeared to be in her early thirties, with russet-brown hair and a dainty silver ring in her nose. "I'm looking for Clark Griffin. His folks told me he works here."

Merry paused, taking a step closer to the truck. "He does. If you go out onto the main road and turn right, the next entrance will take you to the farm. He should be there."

"Thanks. I appreciate it."

"You're welcome." Merry's curiosity got the best of her and she asked, "Would you like to give me your name? In case I see him first."

"It's Patrice," she said with a small smile. Merry stiffened and the woman released a bitter laugh. "Guess he's told you about me?"

"Not a lot," Merry hedged.

"I'm sure what he did mention didn't cast a flattering light on my character. I put that man through the ringer." Patrice laughed bitterly, and Merry got the feeling she was fishing for a confirmation. "Probably won't be happy to see me."

Merry cleared her throat and leaned against the door. "If you think that's the case, maybe you should wait. I don't want to overstep, but he's at work and there's a lot of people down there today. He might not have time to talk."

"You two involved?" The question wasn't rude, simply curious.

"We are."

"Do you...how is my son?"

While her voice remained passive, Merry saw the pinch of sadness in her eyes and softened.

"He's a great kid."

"So, nothing like me," she joked.

"I...sorry, I don't know how to respond to that."

"It's all right. Let me give you my number." She pulled out a card and Merry leaned in to take it. "Tell Clark I'll be waiting for his call."

"I will. Patrice?"

"Yeah?"

You missed out? You shouldn't have left? What can I say that she doesn't already know?

"Take care."

"You too, hon." She rolled up her window and turned around, passing by the sheriff on her way out. Merry watched her turn the corner away from the farm entrance, her breath whooshing out in relief. At least Patrice took her advice not to approach Clark at work. She wasn't sure how he'd react seeing her after all this time. He said they always fought, but she was still the mother of his child.

Jealousy zipped through her veins, not because she didn't trust Clark, but they did share a child. Even if she signed away her rights, Jace was still hers biologically. What if she'd changed her mind? If things ended so horribly between them, why would Clark's parents tell her where to find them? So many questions and each one ticked her anxiety up another level.

She flipped the card over and saw the neat print on the front.

Patrice Neilson. Massage therapist.

The sheriff's deputy parked on the other side of the blue car and Merry slipped the card into her pocket, shaking the old man awake. "Mr. Olson, your ride is here."

He sat straight up in a panic, his head craning around. "Ah, shit. You called my wife?"

"No, sir. You can do that when they get you back to the station."

By the time the cops got Mr. Olson and his car off the property, it was well past three. The business card burned a hole in her pocket and Merry headed down the hill to Clark's place. She knew he was most likely on the grounds helping people, but she didn't want to hand it off to him while he was working. In all honesty, Merry didn't want to be the one to give it to him at all.

She saw Sam's motorcycle under its cover and climbed the porch steps, knocking furiously. Sam answered with his tooth-brush hanging out of his mouth, his hair wet and slicked back like he was just out of the shower.

"Hey, Merry. I'm getting ready to go to work. You cool?"

"I, um...no, not really." She pulled the card from her back pocket and held it out to him. "A woman came by and dropped this off for Clark. Can you make sure he gets it?"

Sam took the card and read the name. "Fuck me," he said, removing the toothbrush. "She was here?"

"Yeah. She was headed to the main house. I was standing out front when she stopped and asked me about Clark."

"Bitch," he snarled. Merry winced and he patted her shoulder reassuringly. "Sorry, but I never did like her. I only met her once and I thought she was using Clark." Sam held the card out to her. "Why are you giving this to me when you can hand it over yourself?"

"Because I don't know how he'll react."

"And, what, you think he'd shoot the messenger?"

"Something like that."

Sam shook his head. "If you leave this with me, I'll burn it. I don't want that woman anywhere near Clark or Jace." He took her hand and slapped the small white rectangle into her palm. "I promise you that no matter what happens, this will not affect the way he feels about you. Now scoot. I've got places to be."

"Thanks a lot," Merry muttered as she trudged up the hill, making a sharp right toward the flocking tent.

It took her longer than normal to reach the covered area, dread weighing her entire body down. She spotted Clark coming back from the parking lot, a dark beanie pulled over his ears, and when he spotted her, his face split into a jaunty grin.

"Hey, you," he said, jogging the remaining distance to meet her. "What's this I hear about chickens?"

"You mean the most bizarre form of warfare I have ever seen? Yeah, that was a trip, but there's something pressing we need to talk about first."

"Mer, can it wait? I've got four people waiting for me to load 'em up and I'm short your dad and brother."

Merry swallowed and held the card out to him. "I have to give you this. She dropped it by about an hour ago."

Clark took the card, his eyes shuttering. When he simply stared at the card without saying anything to her, she turned to give him a moment alone.

"Whoa, wait a second," he said, putting a hand on her arm to stop her. "Did she show up at the house?"

"Yeah, but she didn't get out of the truck. She was going to come down here to see you, but I told her you were busy. She said she'd be waiting for your call."

In one swift jerk, he ripped the card in two and dropped it at his feet. "There is nothing I have to say to her."

"Don't you want to at least find out what she wants?" Merry prodded.

"Why would I extend her a courtesy that she never once considered giving me?"

"Because she's Jace's mother," Merry said softly.

"Not according to the court system." He cupped the back of her neck and kissed her forehead roughly. "I gotta get back to work."

The kiss lacked his usual tenderness and he walked away from her without looking back, his stride eating up the ground and putting more distance between them. Her chest ached as she watched him go, imagining all the memories, the pain he'd thought long buried rising to the surface, and for the briefest moment, she hated Patrice for coming back and hurting the man she loved all over again.

Maybe she'd come here to make amends?

The thought hovered at the back of her mind as Merry picked up the pieces of the card and put them in her pocket. For two more hours, she carried trees out to the parking lot, handing out door prizes, and taking payments, jumping in wherever she was needed. By the time the last car pulled out of the parking lot and the gates were shut, it was after five and Clark was nowhere to be seen.

Merry walked by her parents' house and headed straight home. She didn't feel like talking to anyone at the moment. Her mother would take one look at her and know something was amiss and it wasn't her place to share Clark's troubles, even if they affected her too.

She noticed Clark on her front step when she'd almost reached the bottom of the hill, his elbows resting on his knees and his head down. Her stomach flipped on itself nervously as she picked up the pace.

"Hi," she said when she reached her fence. He looked up then, his expression ragged, and her chest squeezed. "Clark."

Merry came through the gate and he stood up, crushing her to him. Her arms went around his waist, resting her cheek against his chest.

"I'm here," she whispered.

"I hate her, Merry. I don't even hate my parents, but I can't stand the thought of seeing her. And if she asks about him…"

"She already did."

"What?" He pulled away, his eyes blazing. "What did you say?"

"She asked what he was like. I said he was a great kid and she said, 'Nothing like me, then.'"

"You shouldn't have said anything." His voice broke over the words and she shook her head.

"Maybe not, but I wanted her to know she screwed up." Merry's fingers dug into the muscles of his back, her voice shaking with anger she hadn't realized had been simmering under the surface for hours. "That she left an amazing man, who raised an extraordinary kid. I promise I didn't tell her anything more than that and I said it with the best of intentions."

"I'm sorry, Merry. God, I'm sorry."

"Hey, stop." She pulled him down onto the step with her and he buried his face in her neck.

"I don't think I can do it, Merry. You don't know the hell she put me through. And when she left...she left him all alone in the room. Who does that?"

Merry kissed his cheek, her arms looping around his shoulders. "I don't know. The only person who can answer that question is Patrice. And you're right, you don't owe her anything."

Clark lifted his head, a small smile tilting his mouth. "I sense a but coming."

"I'm a little scared to overstep."

"Merry..." He cradled her cheeks, his gaze boring into hers. "Your opinion matters to me. If we're going to have a future, then I want you to be a part of my life, even the messy sections I'd rather forget exist."

Merry kissed his lips, happy tears stinging her eyes despite the stressful situation they found themselves in. "But, I think if you don't talk to her, it could make the situation much worse. Who knows, she may surprise you."

CHAPTER 26

CLARK

CLARK SAT IN THE BACK of Brews and Chews on Monday night, peeling the label off his beer bottle. The normally rustic bar ceiling sparkled with tiny white Christmas lights, the same lights interwoven into the green garland secured around the front of the counter. The moose head on the far side of the room had Christmas wreaths looped over its antlers, and above every doorway, including the one to the bathroom, were sprigs of green mistletoe.

It had taken him three days to call Patrice and when he had, she wouldn't tell him what she wanted over the phone. He'd agreed to give her an hour of his time and nothing more. It was more than he got when she left. He'd tracked her down three years ago, dipping into his savings to hire a private investigator and a lawyer to draw up the paperwork to give up her parental rights. When she'd told his lawyer she would sign for a price, he'd done it, nearly depleting his retirement. He'd have sold his kidney to get the money if it meant keeping Jace's heart safe from her manipulations.

Clark noticed Nick and his friends sitting across the bar,

chatting with ease, and he winced, wishing Merry was with him tonight. He knew she would have offered if he'd asked, but he wasn't sure Patrice would tell him the truth about what she wanted if he brought Merry with him. Merry hadn't pushed him to call or made a big deal about it.

In the short time they'd been together, Merry understood that he needed to contact Patrice in his own time. She'd become more than the woman he was dating. Merry was the person he wanted to talk to at the end of a frustrating day. The voice telling him it would be all right. He missed her Christmas cookie scent while he was working. He wanted to hear her laugh every day of his life or watch her play video games with Jace, screaming at the TV when she got killed and tickling Jace when he told her he'd done it. She'd become more than a lover. A friend. His best friend.

Patrice walked into the bar wearing a long trench coat and wide-legged jeans, her once dirty-blond hair a dark copper. It didn't take her long to spot him, but she took her time coming over. She went to the bar first, chatting up Ricki while she waited for her beer, and Clark's fist clenched around his own glass bottle. What game was she playing?

When she finally slid into the chair across from him, Clark glanced at his phone. "You've wasted fourteen minutes of your hour."

"I was just getting a drink. I noticed you already had one and thought I would join you." She took a pull from her bottle and set it down, her blue-eyed gaze taking him in. "It's good to see you, Clark. You look well."

"Thanks, Patrice. You look like you're healthy. Now, what do you want?"

"Help."

That took him by surprise. "You want my help? With what?"

She straightened her shoulders, her tone defensive. "I don't know if that PI you sent to find me told you anything, but I've... made a mess of my life. I didn't mean to, but I got involved with some bad people and I need a fresh start."

"Here?" he asked incredulously.

"No, I wouldn't do that to you."

"After everything you have done, that's where you draw the line?"

She sat forward and hissed, "I know you hate me for leaving, but I couldn't stay. We weren't right for each other, Clark, and you know it. We carry our baggage around like battle shields and all we did was clash. When I found out I was having a boy, I just...I knew."

"You knew what? That you were going to leave me alone with a newborn with no fucking clue what I was going to do?"

"Looks like you did all right for yourself. Cushy job. Cute girlfriend. She seems sweet."

"I've worked my ass off to take care of my son."

"I'm not saying you didn't. But you're in a better position than me."

"Let's cut the bullshit, Patrice, and tell me what you want."

She pulled a folded envelope from her bag. "I have a letter for Jace I want you to give him."

"What's in it?"

"Excuses, mostly. A few regrets." She held it out to him and he took it.

"That's it? Just the letter? That's the help you need?"

"No. There's one more thing." She pointed. "If you flip it over, you'll see an amount. That's what I need. It will get me far enough away for a fresh start."

Clark leaned back against the back of the seat, staring down at the numbers for several ticks. Finally, he dropped it onto the table and collected his thoughts. "Three years ago, you told my lawyer you wanted five grand and if I gave you that, you'd sign over your rights. Our business is done. Why would I give you another cent?"

Patrice shrugged. "I'm still the mother of your son. Has he ever asked about me?"

"Once or twice."

"If I don't get out now, I'll be dead," she whispered, the edge of desperation attached to every word. "What are you going to tell him, when he finds out you could have saved my life and didn't?"

"I don't have this kind of money."

"Really? Because I think you do." Her cool mask slipped slightly and Patrice pulled down the collar of her trench coat, revealing purple finger bruises on her throat.

Clark's breath hissed out. "Who did that to you?"

"It doesn't matter." Patrice let the collar fall back into place.

"Why don't you go to the cops instead of coming to me?"

"Because he owns the cops. Even if I got a restraining order, he'd make me disappear before they gave him a slap on the wrist. And I won't leave my daughter alone with that monster."

"Your...daughter?"

"Jillian. She's two." Patrice pulled out her phone and slid it over to him. "Look for yourself."

Clark tapped the gallery icon and scrolled through pictures of a little girl with white-blond curls and the same nose as Jace.

He slid the phone back to her. "Where is she?"

"Back at the hotel I'm staying at. The owner's daughter is sitting with her until I get back."

Even with the bruises, Clark might have been able to tell her to go to hell, but he'd taught Jace to be kind, to help those in need. If something terrible befell Patrice and Jace found out Clark could have helped, he'd never forgive him. And that little girl didn't have anyone else but Patrice. What would happen to her?

There was no other choice. "It will take me time to liquify some of my assets. I can get you most of what you need by Friday. Are you good to stay in town until then?"

"I'm…I paid for the hotel through tomorrow, but I'm almost out of money. We left in a hurry."

"Which hotel?"

"Mistletoe Motel. Room 15."

"I'll call and take care of it." He pulled some bills out of his wallet and handed them to her. "This should be enough to get some groceries and whatever else you need."

"Thank you. You could have told me to fuck off, you know."

"No. I've hated you for a long time, Patrice, but you aren't wrong about how my son would feel if I didn't help you. I hope you really are going to make a better life for your daughter. I just have one more question."

"What's that?"

"You said once that you couldn't have a boy. Why?"

Patrice smiled bitterly. "We all have our traumas, Clark."

"Is that what you're going to leave me with? You had a rough childhood, so you abandon your child because you were hoping for a specific gender?"

Her expression hardened. "I know your mom and dad didn't love you enough, but my step-dad? He loved me too much." She finished her beer and set it to the side. "You can judge me all you want, Clark, but the truth is you never really knew me. I saw a cute, shy guy at a party when I was on a bender, burning away my past one shot at a time, and I used him to make myself feel better. You wanted love so badly you were willing to settle for a broken, borderline alcoholic. You were sweet, but I would have made you miserable. I knew when you told me you wanted him that you would take care of our son. That he'd be safe and loved. That's all any parent wants."

"Don't play the martyr, Patrice."

"I'm not. You may hate me for leaving, but imagine if I'd stayed. Can you say for sure that...Jace would have been better off if I'd stuck around?"

Clark sighed. "I guess we'll never know."

"Your friend said he was a great kid."

"I know, she told me." He drained his beer and put her letter in his back pocket. "She's the other reason I came tonight. She thought I should hear you out."

"Well, thank her for me."

"Goodnight, Patrice." He stood, took a step, but turned back to her. "When you get to where you're going, let me know, all right?"

Her lips tilted up in a small smile. "Didn't think you cared, Clark."

"No one deserves what's been done to you. I hope you and your daughter get your fresh start."

"Thank you." She climbed to her feet and touched his arm briefly. "You're a good man."

"I'll walk you to your car and call the motel on my way home."

"Hey, Clark," Nick said as he approached them, his hand held out in greeting. "What are you doing?"

Clark took Nick's outstretched hand and shook it, noting the hard squeeze. "Just came out for a beer."

When Nick's gaze shifted to Patrice, she offered her hand to him. "Hi, I'm Patrice Neilson."

"It's nice to meet you. You from around here, Patrice?"

"I'm just passing through and thought I'd catch up with an old friend. I appreciate the offer, Clark, but I think I can make it to my car in one piece. It was nice to meet you, Nick."

"Good to meet you."

"I'll be in touch later this week, Clark. Thanks again."

"Be safe." Clark gave Nick one of his closed-mouth smiles. "I was heading home."

"Alone?" Nick asked.

"Back to my son and brother, but yes."

Nick's brown eyes bored into his. "Look, as a rule, I tend to stay out of my sisters' dating lives, but I'm confused. You two were pretty cozy last week, am I right?"

"Yes."

"Then who the fuck is that?" he asked gruffly.

"My son's mother."

Nick whistled. "Does Merry know she's here?"

"She does."

"All right, well, sorry to assume, man, but...she's been through a few assholes. Noel told me you were the one who stood Merry up before, but from what I gathered, it was an emotional cluster-fuck that worked itself out. Then I saw you here with *her* and... it wouldn't be the first time someone fooled me." Nick clapped Clark on the back. "Glad to know I was wrong. Come on, join us for a beer and tell us all your worldly troubles."

"I should get home. Merry is waiting for me to tell her how it went—"

"Shoot her a text. You've been working for my family for months and now that you're dating my sister, I want to get to know the kind of man you are."

Clark followed Nick back to his table, assuming he didn't have a choice. He pulled his phone out of his pocket and texted Merry.

> Your brother caught me as I was leaving and wants me to stay for a drink. Will text you when I get home.

He replaced the phone as they reached the table, where Nick's friends Pike and Anthony were waiting. He'd met them a few times at the Winters home but had only spoken to them in passing.

"Clark's going to join us," Nick said, taking a seat between his friends and Clark sat across from Nick. Pike leaned back in his chair, watching Clark over the rim of a martini glass covered in red sugar, sucking on a red and white straw that resembled a candy cane. He released it with a pop and an "ahhh" of satisfaction.

"Welcome. Would you like a taste of Santa's Lap?"

"I think I'm good," Clark said with a laugh.

"No one wants to drink after you, Pike." Anthony held out a hand, the big man's paw swallowing Clark's. "How's it going, man?"

"Along a curvy creek without a paddle. Sorry to crash the party."

"The more the merrier," Pike said, taking another suck of his straw. "I have no idea why I hated on delicious drinks like this for so long. I could down a dozen."

"And fall flat on your face, you lightweight. Speaking of which, I need another." Anthony snapped his fingers in Clark's direction. "Clark, you want a drink? What's your poison?"

"I'll take a whiskey. Thanks." His phone buzzed and he checked the message.

Don't let my brother bully you. I'll be waiting.

Nick leaned over and whispered something to Anthony, who grinned. "Coming right up."

Clark noticed Nick and Pike exchanging sheepish looks. "What did I miss?"

Nick chuckled. "If Anthony offers to buy you a drink, it means he thinks you're good people and he's about to get you very, very drunk."

"I can't, I gotta drive."

"Eh, if you get shit-faced, we'll call my sister to come get us," Nick said.

Pike finished off his drink and burped. "Can she come get me too?"

"What happened to Sally?"

"She's pissed at me over something stupid."

Nick shook his head. "If she's angry with you, just admit you're wrong and apologize."

"What if I'm not wrong?" Pike asked.

"Clark, back me up here," Nick said. "He's wrong."

Clark wasn't sure how to respond, especially when Pike didn't seem in any mood to take advice from him.

"I don't know his relationship, so..."

"Yeah, but I know you've pissed Merry off at least once! What did you do to get back into my sister's good graces?"

"Groveled. Gave her a pie. Groveled some more."

Nick leaned forward, pointing at Clark. "See, this is a man who understands women." Nick's smile dissolved swiftly into an eerie expression. "But if you hurt her again, I'll take you to the top of Soldier Mountain and leave you there for the wolves."

Clark stared at Nick, his stomach churning.

Nick burst out laughing. "You should see your face. I'm just kidding, man."

"One Hold Onto Your Sleighbells for Clark." Clark jumped when Anthony set a tall glass of green liquid in front of him.

"Did you make sure they put that something extra in it?" Nick asked, winking at Anthony.

"Oh yeah. He's going to love it."

Clark eyed the drink warily. "I thought you were getting me a whiskey?"

"There's whiskey in there," Anthony said.

"I'm a little worried you're trying to poison me."

Pike snorted. "Eh, we'd never do that. If we were going to kill ya, we'd make it look like an accident."

From their expressions, he wasn't a hundred percent sure they weren't serious.

CHAPTER 27

MERRY

MERRY GROANED AS *"JOLLY OLD St. Nicholas"* blared from her phone, which was dancing across her nightstand obnoxiously. She picked it up and saw the time. Twelve eleven? Pressing the green talk button, she tried to roll onto her back, but Daisy was sprawled out on her bed sideways. With a gravelly voice, she answered, "You'd better be maimed and bleeding out."

"Little sister, did I wake you up?" Nick asked cheerfully.

"Hanging up now."

"No, don't do that. I need a ride. Clark and I had a little too much to drink and Noel is at work."

Merry sat up in bed and mumbled, "Alexa, turn on the bedroom light."

Blinded for several beats, she closed her eyes. She heard Daisy groan behind her, obviously as happy as she was to be disturbed.

"Since when is my man one of your drinking buddies?"

"Since he's had a rough couple of days and I thought a few festive drinks at Brews would do him good. So, come get us, will ya?"

It wasn't that she didn't want her brother and Clark to get along, but Clark wasn't much for getting drunk and it worried her.

"Give me fifteen."

"Thank you, sister, you are fant—"

She hung up on whatever else Nick said and threw her legs over the side of the bed, opening one eye and then the other, blinking rapidly. She'd fallen asleep waiting for Clark to get home and opened her texts with him, scrolling through the half dozen he'd sent.

> Your brother and his friends may be trying to kill me.
> If I don't come home, Nick did it.
> I may be a little drunk.
> I miss you.
> I love your scent on my sheets.
> I'm ned to sleop in ma car. Sorry.

As she got up and threw on her clothes, Merry's heart hammered. She'd never seen him drink more than a beer, but if he'd been kicking back drinks with Nick and his pals, then Patrice must have really spun his head. She'd wanted to be there with him for moral support, but respected his decision to go alone. Now her mind raced with what the heck that woman said to him. As much as she'd wanted to give Patrice the benefit of the doubt, Merry wouldn't allow her to hurt Clark or Jace again.

"Come on, Daisy," she said, grabbing her leash from the hook by the front door. The puppy hopped down each stair slowly, giving Merry a disgruntled look. "Don't blame me. You can tell it to Uncle Nick."

After Daisy went potty, Merry led her to the car, loading her into the back seat. She couldn't believe she'd actually fallen asleep, especially with how keyed up she'd been waiting for Clark to finish his meeting with Patrice. Maybe it was the late night and early morning romps with Clark or the stress of knowing Patrice was in town, but she'd obviously needed the rest.

She pulled into the Brews and Chews parking lot, stopping right outside the front door with her foot on the brake. She dialed Nick, waiting for him to answer.

"Hello, dear sister."

"Your Uber is here."

"We're coming out."

"Hurry up. I want to go back to bed."

The call ended and Merry watched the door open and Nick and Clark came pouring out, talking animatedly like they hadn't a care in the world. Merry's eyes narrowed as Nick grabbed her passenger door and held it for Clark. "In you go, pal."

"You two look like you had a jolly good time."

"We did, sister." Nick shut the door with a snap and Merry's foot itched to hop from the brake to the gas and leave him.

"Sorry he called you, Mer," Clark murmured, leaning across the console to kiss her cheek, but Daisy intercepted his lips with her tongue. "Ack, no, Daisy, that kiss was for Merry, not you."

"There will be no kisses until you explain a few things, sir," Merry said, with only a hint of sternness. "First, why did my brother call for a safe ride and not you?"

"I thought I would sleep it off for a few hours in the Jeep and drive home. I didn't want to wake you up for that."

Nick opened the door as she added, "I would have rather heard your deep voice than Nick's annoying one."

"Hey, now, that's not very nice." Daisy jumped Nick as he slid across the seat, fighting off doggy kisses. "Damn it, why did you bring the demon?"

"Because she goes nuts when I leave her alone."

"Doesn't she have a crate? She's lying across my lap and she's not exactly a Yorkie."

"She hates her crate and I like her a whole lot more than you right now and didn't want to upset her. She chews things when she's upset. So you can deal."

Clark reached across the console for her hand, bringing it to his mouth. "We appreciate you coming to get us."

"I mean, I love getting out of bed in the middle of the night… on a Monday."

"Technically, it's Tuesday," Nick said.

"There is no arguing with me during this ride. This is going to be a drive of quiet reflection to think about the poor choices you both made tonight."

Nick huffed. "Damn, you sound like Mom."

"Not my mom." Clark laughed. No, wait. It was higher than a laugh.

Did he just…giggle?

"What the heck did you drink?" Merry asked.

"It's called a Hold the Jingle Bells. It was tasty." When she didn't respond, he kept talking. "Anthony bought it for me. He was trying to make me feel welcome 'cause he likes me. Nick just wants to kill me."

That caught her attention. "Come again?"

"He's exaggerating," Nick said.

"You said if I hurt Merry, you were going to do me in."

"But he gave Pike advice on how to get back into Sally's good graces, so I decided he could live...for now."

"Whoa, wait, what did Pike do to my Sally?"

"Mind ya bidness, sister," Nick said.

"You are very annoying." She pulled up to Nick and Noel's apartment and spotted Noel's car. Merry spun around in the seat to glare at her brother. "You!"

"What, you were going to come out to get Clark anyway and Noel has to work early. No sense in waking you both up." Nick dodged Merry's attempt to whack him with a grin. "Remember, fratricide is frowned upon. See ya, Clark." Nick opened the back door, holding Daisy at bay, and dived out like he was afraid the puppy or Merry was going to follow.

"Next time your Uncle Nick comes over, Daisy, eat his shoes," Merry grumbled. She took the turn out of the parking lot and onto the main highway, glancing at Clark. "Did you fall asleep?"

"No, I was thinking," he said.

"About what?"

"Do you know what I thought the first time I ever saw you?"

"Not a clue."

"That your smile could light up the whole world if the sun went out."

Merry smiled reflexively. "That's sweet."

"I realized something tonight while I was waiting for Patrice to show." His hand settled on her thigh as he leaned in, his lips tickling the shell of her ear. "I love you, Merry."

Her throat tightened. "Really? The first time you drop the L-bomb you do it drunk?"

"I remember you telling me once you were tipsy, not drunk and I'm saying the same thing to you. I didn't feel right driving, but I was already sobering up when Nick called you. I know exactly what I'm saying, because I realized it before I had a single drop of alcohol."

"Right, that's why you were giggling with my brother and saying ridiculous things."

"I didn't giggle."

"Yeah, you did."

"Regardless. I mean every word. I don't have very many people I consider friends, but you are so much more than that. I want to spend my days and nights with you, to hear about your day and tell you about mine. I love you with all my heart."

Tears welled up in her eyes and she turned in her seat. "If you really feel that way about me, it would have been nice if you'd have called to tell me so earlier, instead of getting drunk with my brother. I fell asleep waiting for you."

Clark cupped her face in his hands. "I'm sorry. It was nice to hang with guys my age, you know? I haven't done it in years, and after Patrice left, it felt good to blow off steam. I didn't mean to stay so late."

As disappointed as she was about his timing of *I love you*, Merry realized she was being bratty. "Clark, I'm sorry. You should be able to go out and have fun without me carping at you. About Patrice..." Merry put her hand on his arm. "Are you all right?"

"It's a lot to unpack, but you were right. I did need to see her. It's going to cost me, but I feel like I got some closure."

"Why will it cost you? Is she trying to get Jace back?"

"No. She asked me for money."

"What?" White-hot rage burned through her. "Why?"

"Because she needs help and has no one in her corner. I understand a little bit about that. If it wasn't for your parents, Sam, and a lot of others over the years, I wouldn't have been able to finish my education, let alone provide for my son. Patrice may be a lot of things, but people deserve the chance to better themselves if they are willing to try."

"You told me that if she was here, it wasn't good. That she wanted something, but I'd hoped that maybe she'd prove you wrong. I wouldn't give her a cent."

Clark chuckled. "Yes, you would. If you'd been there, you would have bent over backwards to help her because you're an amazing, generous person. And as much as she's hurt me, I want to be the kind of man who deserves you, Merry, the kind of man my son can look up to. If something happened to Patrice because I didn't help her, I wouldn't be able to look my son in the eye."

"I am glad you feel good about helping her, but I don't like anyone taking advantage of you."

Clark took her hand, bringing it to his mouth. "Thank you for looking out for us. It means so much to have you in my life."

"Thank you. When are you getting her the money?"

"It will take me a few days, but hopefully by Friday. I didn't even tell you the craziest part. She has a daughter."

Merry hesitated a few moments, bringing his hand to her chest. "That must have been rough to hear."

"More surprising than rough, but whatever happened to

Patrice growing up…it's bad. I just hope she'll take the money and do better for herself and her little girl."

"All you can do is have a little faith, I guess." Daisy whimpered in the back seat and Merry pulled her hand away. "I should get her home."

"Merry…I know you think I'm saying things because my inhibitions are down, but the truth is, not telling you felt worse than saying it out loud at the wrong time. I know I'm not romantic and I have bungled things with you more times than I can count, but I love you. I wish you'd been with me tonight and I regret not bringing you along. If you're willing, I'd appreciate having you there when I give the money to her Friday."

Merry's heart swelled. As far as romantic gestures went, this was huge and she regretted giving him such a bad time about his tipsy I love you.

"I'm more than willing. I wouldn't be anywhere else but by your side." Clark's smile lit up the cab and he cupped her face. Merry's mouth met his and her heart kicked up with every sweep of his tongue, every brush of his hand against her skin. Their relationship may have started a little rocky, but she believed that he loved her. *Not telling you felt worse than saying it out loud at the wrong time.*

Clark's hand moved over her waist, yanking her closer and Merry realized too late her foot had slipped off the brake and they were rolling. The car jerked and the sound of metal crashing to the ground sank in. She broke away, slamming her foot back over the thick pedal in a panic.

"Oh shit!" she cried. "Please don't tell me…"

Clark covered his mouth with his hand, his wide eyes locking with hers. "I won't tell you."

Movement beyond Clark's Jeep caught her eye and she watched in horror as Sam stepped into her high beams, staring down at his motorcycle. Slowly, his furious gaze traveled up, staring into the windshield at her.

"Both of you—" He pointed at them with two fingers. "Out of the car. Now."

Merry put the car in park and unbuckled. "I think your brother means business."

"You did run over his pride and joy."

"Hey, it's your fault too! You distracted me with your mouth and tongue and your hands."

Clark laughed. "I didn't realize the car wasn't in park."

Merry gripped the door handle, pausing. "This may be bad timing, but I think you need to know something."

"What's that?"

"I love you, too."

Clark's face broke into that wide, joyful smile she adored and before she knew it, his hands were tangled in her hair, pulling her in for another kiss. Sam tapped on the hood, hollering, "I said no more of that! Front and center."

"Do you think if we ignore him he'll go away?" she murmured.

"Probably not." Clark pulled away with a sigh. "I'll take care of him. You go get some rest. I've got big plans for you tomorrow."

CHAPTER 28

CLARK

CLARK GOT OUT OF HIS Jeep Tuesday afternoon and headed into Mistletoe Elementary, an invitation and a hot coffee in his hand. Sam had taken him to get his car that morning, bitching the whole time about the scratches on his bike, exacerbating Clark's already throbbing head. Clark had promised to pay for any repairs and buffing the motorcycle needed, but Sam hadn't let up until Clark reminded Sam who he was living with rent-free.

Two Tylenol and a greasy breakfast later, he'd felt better and asked Chris for the afternoon off so he could grab Jace early from school. Chris told him to get out and have a good time and he'd taken off.

He had a plan to repair the damage he'd done to his relationship with his son and in addition show Merry he was serious about everything he'd said last night. Now it was time to put it in motion.

He pushed through the main door and saw Merry sitting at her front office desk in a red sweater dress, her blond hair pulled back with a scrunchie that looked like sparkling red tinsel. Clark pressed the buzzer, smiling widely when she looked up. She gave a little wave, and her hand went for something on her desk. He heard the door click open and he stepped inside.

"Hey there."

She got up and came around her desk to the front counter, her forehead knitted. "Hi. What are you doing here?"

"I'm picking up Jace a little early and giving you this." He handed her the coffee and the white envelope, which she took hesitantly, befuddlement in her eyes.

"Well, thank you. I needed an afternoon pick-me-up. Are you taking him to a doctor's appointment or something?"

"Or something."

"Okay, I'll stop being nosy and I'll call down to his teacher."

"Thanks." Clark leaned against the counter as she placed the coffee cup on her desk and made the phone call. He noticed her tights had little holly sprigs all over them when she returned, and he grinned at the adorable touch.

"All right, he's coming."

"You're awfully Christmassy today."

"Is that a compliment?"

"It is."

"Then thank you. I got a multipack of holiday stockings and I'm determined to wear every pair before Christmas." She held the envelope up and waved it. "Can I open?"

"Absolutely. It's time-sensitive."

Merry ripped the top and pulled out the white invitation, reading it aloud. "Clark and Jace Griffin request the honor of your presence for a very special outing. Please dress for cold weather and be ready to leave promptly at four-thirty pm. Dinner and hot cocoa will be provided." She looked up from the invite, bemused. "Exactly where are you taking me?"

"It's a surprise. I know it's last minute, but I promise fun."

"And food, which I'm a fan of." She smiled coyly. "I suppose I can put a pin in any other plans for the man I love."

"I appreciate that." He leaned against the counter and lowered his voice. "I really wish I could kiss you right now."

"Dad?" Jace called, his brow furrowed.

Clark stood straight, noting Merry's red face and grinned. "Hey, buddy!"

"Why are you picking me up?"

"Because we have an appointment. You ready?"

"I guess." Jace looked at Merry with his head cocked to the side. "Do you know what's going on?"

"Not a clue. You gotta sign him out before you can take him," Merry said, sliding the sheet toward him.

Clark filled it out, tossing her a wink. "We'll see you in a couple hours."

"I'm looking forward to it. Bye, Jace."

"Bye." Jace walked ahead of him out the door. "Are you going to tell me what we're doing?"

"Let's get to the car and I'll explain."

When they pulled out of the parking lot, Clark started talking. "I've got something fun planned for Merry and the two of us tonight, and there's a couple of things I need your help picking out."

"Like what?" Jace asked.

"I was thinking about some flowers."

Jace made a face. "Flowers are boring."

"Women like flowers."

"Fine, but can I get her something else?"

"With what money?" Clark teased.

"Swear jar money."

Clark laughed. "Hey, it's yours to spend, but I thought you were saving for a new game?"

"Nah, I'd rather get something for her. I shouldn't buy anything for myself this close to Christmas, anyway."

Clark took a left and parked around the back of Kiss My Donut. "I think Merry's birthday is next week. Do you want to save it for then?"

"Sure. Can we get a donut?" Jace asked.

"I guess. It's five am somewhere, right?"

"Huh?"

"Never mind, just a dad joke." Clark held the door open and let Jace pass through first. The display case was decorated with snowflake glass clings and on the counter next to the register sat a stuffed snowman eating a donut.

His son jumped in line behind a woman in a green beanie and sweatshirt, holding her child on her hip.

"Can I get two?" Jace wheedled.

"That would be a no. We're having cocoa later with Merry."

"Okay. What about a chocolate bar with sprinkles?"

"You can get whatever single donut you want."

The woman in front of him turned and he found himself staring into Patrice's startled blue eyes. The breath whooshed out between his lips and he shot a panicked look from her to Jace, who was craning his neck to see the donuts better.

"Hi," she said.

"Hey." His gaze drifted to her daughter, who sucked on a pink binky furiously. A fuchsia winter hat with cat ears covered her blond hair and she watched Clark warily with her mother's blue eyes.

"I..." Patrice swallowed, staring down at Jace, her expression unreadable.

"This is my son, Jace." There was no other option but to play it through and his mind raced for an explanation for their acquaintance. "Jace, this is Miss Neilson. I helped tow her car out of a ditch last night."

"Nice to meet you," Jace said, holding his hand out without questioning Clark's introduction. When Patrice stared at him blankly, Clark cleared his throat, and Patrice seemed to come out of her trance with a jolt, taking Jace's hand in hers.

"It's nice to meet you, too. This is my daughter, Jillian."

The little girl ducked her face against her mother's shoulder.

Jace smiled at Jillian. "Hello. I used to be shy when I was little, too."

"Were you?" Patrice's voice sounded strained, like she was fighting with her emotions. The cashier called out for whoever was next, and she stepped forward.

"Hi, can we get a pink snowflake sprinkle donut, a chocolate custard, a small coffee, a milk, and whatever the gentleman behind me and his son would like."

Clark stiffened, his eyebrow arched.

Patrice held Clark's gaze, playing along. "It's the least I could do after you helped me out of that ditch."

"Right. Well, thank you." He almost laughed out loud that she was using his money to pay for their donuts, but he refrained. Clark gave the cashier their order and they stepped to the side.

"Thank you for the donut," Jace said.

"You're welcome. You take care of your dad."

"I do."

The man behind the donut display held out two pastry bags and a drink carrier. "Here you are."

"Thanks." Clark grabbed the drinks and the bags, setting them on an empty table. "Here are your drinks and your donuts. And these are ours."

"All right. Well, it was nice to meet you."

"Do you want to just sit together?" Jace piped in. "No reason to dirty two tables, right, Dad?"

Clark nearly choked on his coffee.

"That's very nice of you, Jace. We're actually going back to where we're staying to eat. But thank you for the invitation."

"You're welcome."

"Be safe," Clark said, waving at the little girl, who gave him a dirty look.

"Thank you. Good-bye." Patrice's gaze lingered on Jace for a moment longer before they turned and left the donut shop.

Jace sat down with the donut bag in front of him. "Uh-oh. Some of my chocolate got on your glaze."

"That's all right, that just makes it better." He took the donut from his son and said, "Hey, Jace?"

"Yeah?"

"I'm proud you're my son."

"Why?"

"I just am."

"Okay," Jace said, taking a bite of his donut. "You're weird."

"Maybe so, but you know what? This weirdo thinks you're the best thing that's ever happened to him."

"Thanks," Jace said, his mouth full of donut. "Where we going next?"

"Flowers and whatever you want to buy Merry. Then we'll go home, put the cocoa in the thermos, get cleaned up and grab her."

"Can Daisy come?"

"No, buddy, we're going ice skating."

Jace's mouth dipped into an anxious frown. "But I don't know how to ice skate."

"It's okay, you'll learn. It will be fun."

"Does Merry like ice skating?"

Clark froze. "You know, I'm actually not sure."

"What if she hates it?"

"Then we'll pick another activity."

"Like what?"

"I have no idea. Now finish your donut. We got places to be."

CHAPTER 29

MERRY

MERRY STEPPED OUT HER DOOR at 4:29 p.m. wearing her snow boots, blue jeans, and a blue sweater under her jacket. The invitation had said to dress warm, so with gloves and a knit cap in her pocket, she was prepared for whatever the Griffins had planned.

Clark was backing out of his driveway and made a circle, stopping behind her car. Before she could reach the door, Jace hopped out of the back and got it for her.

"Good afternoon," he said in a lofty voice.

Merry laughed and climbed inside. "Thank you for opening my door."

"You are welcome."

Clark sat behind the wheel with a large bouquet of red roses in his lap. He handed it to her, leaning over to kiss her cheek. "Hello, beautiful."

"What's all this?"

"We're taking you out," Jace said from the back seat.

"I can see that, and you got me flowers and opened my door. I feel like a queen."

"Let's hope you still feel that way when you see where I've taken you."

"Uh-oh, I'm a little scared," Merry said, turning to look at Jace with an exaggerated expression of panic. He giggled.

Clark pulled out onto the road and reached across to take her hand. It was the first time they'd done so in nearly a week and she'd almost forgotten the sense of home his hand in hers created.

"Merry, guess what?"

"What, Jace?"

"I got you a present. I used the money from the swear jar to buy it. Well, technically, Dad bought it with his card and he is going to take the money out of the swear jar. He said I should wait until your birthday to give it to you but I really want you to have it now."

"Breathe, buddy," Clark joked.

"I think waiting for my birthday is a fantastic plan, although I am really excited and can't wait to see what you got me."

Clark squeezed her hand. "So, Jace brought up an excellent question I didn't even think to ask. Do you like ice skating?"

"I love it."

"Good, because that is where we are taking you."

"I've never done it before, but Dad says it will be fine."

"You will be, but your dad…" Merry hesitated, shooting Jace an unsure expression. "I'm a little concerned about him. I've seen your dad go up against a patch of ice and he lost."

"Hey, that ice came out of nowhere."

Merry laughed. "Keep telling yourself that."

"Merry, guess what we had this afternoon?" Jace jumped in, changing the subject as only a kid could, but his excitement was infectious and Merry turned, her voice high with exhilaration.

"I give up!"

"We had donuts. I got a chocolate bar. What is your favorite?"

"Hmmm, I like buttermilk bars. The glazed kind."

"Dad likes the apple fritters, but I think they look like brains."

"They do kind of look like brains, don't they? Maybe that means your dad's a zombie."

"Argh, grr, ahhh," Clark groaned, making his son and Merry crack up. Clark's whole body seemed looser, as though he'd left all his worries at his house and Merry wondered what had changed since last night.

He caught her staring and smiled. "What?"

"Nothing, I just like looking at you."

"Why?" Jace asked from the back.

"'Cause your dad is pretty."

Jace sat forward and turned his head to the side. "Eh, he's okay."

"Hey, sit back and watch it!" Clark barked with mock ferocity. "If my girl wants to say I'm pretty, then I'm pretty."

"Grownups are weird."

They took Main Street through town, the rows of street lamps wrapped in green garland and festive red bows finally in place. A large bow made out of wood with red lights hung below the Mistletoe town arch. They'd constructed the arch in the spring as part of the initiative to restore and update to attract tourists.

"I love driving down Main Street when everything is lit up."

"I wish it was Christmas today," Jace said.

Merry turned in her seat again. "Speaking of Christmas, what do you want?"

"I want some video games. A few Lego sets."

"You'll have to get me a list with things you haven't told anyone else."

"Okay."

Clark pulled into the parking lot of Mistletoe's outdoor ice rink and Merry hopped out before Jace could get out and grab her door for her.

"Hey," he griped.

She wrapped him up in a bear hug and kissed his head. "Don't worry about getting my door, kid. I've been doing it a long time, so I can manage."

"It's my job though." He frowned.

"Here, I got a new job for you," Clark said, pulling his wallet out. "You take this card and give it to the guy behind the glass. Say it's for the three of us."

"Cool!" Jace took off for the booth while Merry and Clark hung back.

"Your girl, huh?"

Clark smiled sheepishly. "Sorry, that was presumptuous of me. We haven't discussed labels, although I thought maybe the whole exchanging I love yous sealed the deal."

Merry pursed her lips, fighting a smile. "You're not too far off base."

"Oh yeah?"

"I was calling you mine before last night, so yeah," Merry said, leaning against him. "I guess we're together."

Clark waved when the guy behind the glass looked up at them. With a furtive glance at his son, he leaned in and whispered against the shell of her ear, "Sounds like you may need further convincing later tonight."

The urge to turn her head and meet his lips coursed through her body, but Jace was already heading back to them with wristbands.

"He said we go through the gate for our skates."

"Awesome," Merry said.

Clark took the wristbands from Jace and once they'd secured them, Merry slipped her hand into Clark's. To her surprised delight, Jace took her other hand.

The burly man behind a long counter waited for them, only a few of the cubbies on the wall empty.

"What size skates, folks?" Burly Guy asked.

"Men's twelve, two in kids', and—" Clark pointed to Merry.

"Size eight in women's."

"Coming right up."

"Can I go watch?" Jace asked.

Clark nodded. "Sure, we'll be right there."

Jace ran off to the edge of the rink. There were a few families and couples on the ice, some of them shuffling awkwardly while others glided with ease.

"I'm assuming you've been ice skating before," she said.

"A long time ago, so you may be holding both of us up on the ice."

"I'll hold your hand unless you try to take me down and then you are on your own."

He lowered his voice. "What if I promise you can land on top of me and cushion your fall?"

Merry's cheeks burned. She glanced at Burly, but he was at the other end of the counter. "I'd say you are too hard to be a cushion and also there are kids at this rink. People will talk."

"They'll talk about how much I like you on top of me?"

She pushed him playfully, watching Jace run back to them. "Behave."

"Hard ask when all I can think about is getting you home."

Is he asking me back to his place again?

"There are real little kids skating out there," said Jace.

"I told you it will be fine," Clark said.

Once they collected their skates and handed over their shoes, they sat down on one of the benches to put them on. Jace got his skate over his foot and held it out to Merry. "Can you tie them?"

Clark snorted. "You can tie your own skates."

"I want Merry to do them."

"Want me to do the other?" Clark asked.

"No, you tie them too tight."

"Well, geez, I see how it is." Clark shot Merry a bemused smile as she tied the skates.

"There. Bunny ears are beautiful and you are ready to rock."

Jace got to his feet, his legs wobbling a little. A teenaged girl in a Mistletoe Ice Rink sweatshirt stopped in the opening of the rink with a wide, welcoming smile.

"Hi there. Is this your first time skating?"

"It's his first time," Merry said.

"Would you like a free lesson to get you started?"

Merry and Clark looked at each other and Clark shrugged. "Sure. That okay with you, buddy?"

"Are you a professional?" Jace asked her skeptically.

The girl grinned, skated back from the wall and spun in a hard fast circle that turned her into a blur. She skated back and held out her hand. "What do you think?"

"You'll do," Jace said.

Clark shook his head. "Geez, my kid is a smart-ass."

Merry stepped onto the ice and sailed forward. "Don't act innocent, I'm sure he didn't come by that gift naturally."

"Are you calling me sarcastic?" He sounded outraged, but she had to turn around to be sure.

"Maybe a little—ooof." Merry caught herself before she fell, glaring when Clark laughed.

"That's called karma for being sassy," he said, catching up.

"You're the sassy one. What's gotten into you today?"

Clark took her hand and they skated forward. "You. Isn't that enough?"

"Hey, I love flattery, but I don't think it's that I said yes to skating that has you all light-hearted and sunny. Even on your best day, you're mildly broody."

"Damn, you're saying I'm a lot of fun to be around, then?"

"I like all your quirks, including your seriousness."

"Today's just been a good day. Jace looks like he's having a good time," he said, nodding toward his son, who was working on his glide. "I'm here with the most amazing woman I've ever met and I can't believe you love me as much as I do you."

Merry skated closer, dropping his hand so she could slide her arm around his waist. "But I do. I want to build something with you, partners on equal ground, so that maybe someday you'll be making us matching rocking chairs like the ones you built for my parents."

Clark held her to him and murmured, "I want that too."

"Excuse me!" Another teenager waved at them. "You need to keep skating!"

"Sorry!" Merry called, taking Clark's hand again. "Anything else happen today?"

"Yeah, it was strange. We bumped into Patrice and her daughter at the donut shop."

"With Jace? Did he recognize her?"

Clark shook his head. "We never had any pictures printed and everything digital I deleted a long time ago, so he doesn't know what she looked like."

"What did she say?"

"We both stared at each other with identical expressions of horror and then I just kind of threw out that I pulled her out of a ditch. He chatted with her, because that's just how he is. That kid will get a job dealing with the public, I swear. He even invited her and her daughter to join us, but she said they were going back to their place. After that, she thanked us and left."

Merry frowned. "I can't understand not wanting to be a part of her child's life. I know she signed over rights, but she is missing out on so much."

"I asked her why she left and she didn't give me details, but maybe she isn't the narcissistic monster I've painted her to be. I'm not excusing her behavior, but people aren't black and white, good or bad. Sometimes they make poor choices because it's what's best for everyone involved or maybe just for them, but either way, I hope Patrice finds a way to heal."

"Did you think about telling Jace the truth?" she asked.

"No. It's not what she wants and there is no reason to put him through an emotional upheaval for someone who doesn't want to be involved in his life. She gave me a letter for him and when he is ready, I'll give it to him. If he wants to find her and try to connect with her, I'll support him, because his happiness has always come first."

"You're an amazing father, Clark. I know that because I was raised by one."

Jace skated toward them, the instructor skating along next to him.

"Look at you go," Merry cried, holding her free hand out to him.

"Joy says I'm a natural."

Clark pulled out his wallet and gave Joy a five. When it was just the three of them again, Merry in the middle, they skated along. They passed below a speaker playing "Winter Wonderland" and Jace sang along, loudly and off key.

"We should build a snowman after this!"

"I think it's going to be too dark by the time we leave, buddy. But we can do it another day."

"Will you help us, Merry?"

"I'd love to. I haven't built a snowman in years, so you may have to help remind me how it goes."

"You should watch tutorials on YouTube so you know what you're doing."

Merry's laughter was cut short when Jace lost his balance and fell, nearly taking her down with him.

Clark came around in front of her to help his son up. "You okay, buddy?"

"Yeah," Jace grumbled.

"Let's skate it off."

They made it another few laps before Jace said his knee really hurt and they skated to the side and sat down. Clark rolled up Jace's jeans and tsked. "Oh man. This leg may need to come off."

"Dad," Jace groaned, but his lips kicked up in the corners.

"You wanna go get food and then take Merry to our next surprise?"

"Yes!"

Clark returned the skates, leaving Jace and Merry sitting on the bench together.

"Are you going to marry my dad?" Jace asked abruptly.

Merry started, staring down into his earnest eyes. "I don't know. We only started dating a few weeks ago and while I care about him, he hasn't asked."

"I think he will. He is definitely happy with you. I've never seen him hold anyone's hand before. And he talks about you a lot to Uncle Sam."

"You probably shouldn't eavesdrop on conversations between your dad and your uncle."

"I know, my dad tells me to stay out of adult conversations, but he told my uncle he didn't want to lose you and my uncle told him to get off his bad word for butt and tell you how he feels."

Jace lowered his voice as Clark approached. "I just wanted to tell you, if you want to marry him, I'm okay with it."

Merry's heart hammered in her chest and she took her shoes from Clark wordlessly.

"Who's ready for fries and chicken strips?" Clark asked.

"You know it, boy!" Jace said, dragging out the *oy*.

"God, it's started. Pretty soon you're going to start calling me *dude* and *bruh* like that kid Westin I work with."

The two went back and forth on the way out of the skating rink gate, while Merry pushed down the spark of giddiness bubbling in her stomach. Jace probably didn't even realize how touching it was that he'd given her permission to be with Clark and join their family. She blinked back happy tears as he raced ahead and opened her door, but Clark shooed him into the car, studying her face with concern.

"Hey, everything all right?"

"Yes, it's perfect. This date is perfect." She kissed his lips softly. "Thank you for this."

"You're welcome, but it's not over yet. We're going to sit down for some food and then head over to Evergreen Lane to walk through the neighborhood."

"And after that?"

"I'll take you home, unless...you want to stay over."

Merry kissed him, aware Jace was probably watching and eavesdropping.

"I've got to get Daisy from my parents, but just so you know, I'm getting closer to saying yes."

Clark smiled. "Guess I'm doing something right then, huh?"

"Tens across the board."

CHAPTER 30

CLARK

CLARK PULLED INTO THE MISTLETOE Hotel Friday evening and parked, sitting in his Jeep for a few more moments with Merry in the passenger seat. He took her hand in his, drawing on her strength.

"You doing okay?" she asked.

"As well as can be expected." He pulled the thick envelope out from under his seat, the weight of it matching the sinking sensation in his stomach. "It's not all of my savings, but a large chunk of it."

"You don't have to give her anything. Or at least let me help. I can give her some—"

"No," he said firmly, softening the blow with a kiss. "I love you and I want to share my life with you. But this is my past to deal with." He brushed his lips against the knuckles of her hand. "I promise, any future problems will be one hundred percent a *we* thing."

"I guess we better get this done and get me to the parade."

Clark knew he had to do this, that it was the only way he could look his son in the eye. "I'm ready."

They climbed out of his Jeep and joined hands when they

reached the sidewalk, heading slowly across the cracked cement to room number 15. Clark knocked and waited with nervous energy coursing through him until he heard the door chain being removed.

Patrice opened the door, her gaze widening when she saw Merry by his side. "Hello. I didn't know you were bringing someone."

"I'm only here for moral support," Merry said.

"Well, come in. We are watching cartoons while we wait on food to get here."

Clark stepped over the threshold first, taking in the king bed and open suitcases in the corner. Jillian sat on the bed, watching cartoons on the TV, ignoring them.

"What's your daughter's name?" Merry asked.

"Jillian."

"Would it be all right for me to say hi?"

Patrice glanced at her daughter hesitantly. "Sure, but she doesn't really warm up to strangers."

"That's cool, this guy is the same way," Merry joked, squeezing his hand. She released his hand and walked over to the edge of the bed, speaking softly to Jillian, who shot her a suspicious glance.

"Is she really that nice or is it an act?" Patrice asked in a low voice. Clark's lips pressed in a thin line and she sighed. "Sorry, trusting people is not my strong suit."

"We have that in common," he said, holding out the envelope. "Here is what you asked for."

Patrice took the manila envelope, turning it over in her hands. When she looked inside, her brow furrowed.

"What's in here?"

"Picture copies I thought you might like to have. I know you have your reasons for the choices you've made, but he is a part of you."

Patrice's hands trembled as she pulled the pictures out, sliding one behind another as she looked through them.

"Why did you do this?" she whispered.

Clark's ire rose and he reached for the pictures. "If you don't want them—"

"Why did you have to make this so hard?" She held the pictures away from him and put the money envelope in his hand. "Keep your money."

Merry got up from the bed. "Is everything all right?"

"It's fine, Mer. We're just talking." Clark kept his hard gaze on Patrice. "I don't understand. I thought you needed it."

"I can't take that money. What is it, his college fund?" She dropped the pictures on the bed, covering her face with her hands for several ticks and then she brought them down and Clark saw the tears in her eyes. "I didn't want to see him."

"That was an accident."

"I know. And I'm not saying I suddenly want a relationship with him. Merry wasn't wrong, though," Patrice said, shooting Merry a trembling smile. "He's a great kid. Kind. Considerate. He deserves everything you can give him, which is why I can't take that."

"I pulled it out for you. It's done."

She shook her head. "Put it back, then."

"What about her?" Clark asked. "You said you had nothing left. If you don't take this, how are you going to find a safe place for you both?"

"I'll figure something out."

"Patrice, I'm glad to see that you have a soul. I may have compared you to a heartless demon a few times over the years." She chuckled quietly and he smiled, holding the money out. "You are going to need money for car repairs, first and last month's rent, utilities, gas, groceries... I made you a budget spreadsheet. If you follow it, you should be able to make it a few months comfortably until you can find a job. I also put an investment outline for whatever is left after things settle down. If you continue to add ten percent of your income to it, it will grow at a steady rate." Clark lowered his voice so Jillian wouldn't hear, although she seemed preoccupied naming off all the ponies on the screen for Merry. She really was the kid whisperer. "Christmas is also in the budget, including a tree."

Patrice pulled out his budget sheet and before he knew what she was about, she'd counted out what he'd told her to invest and handed it back to him. "I'll follow your advice, but I don't want to take more than what we need."

"If that's what you want," he said.

"It is. Thank you for this. I will try to pay you back."

"Honestly, Patrice, consider it a gift. Just text me when you get to wherever you're going so I know you're safe."

"I know I don't deserve it, but thank you, Clark."

"You're welcome. When are you leaving?"

"Tomorrow. I'm thinking somewhere East of the Mississippi. I hear Kentucky is pretty."

"Safe travels then. Mer, you ready?"

Merry got up from the bed. "Goodnight, Jillian. Thank you for letting me watch ponies with you."

"Night." The little girl gave her a smile, but when she caught Clark watching, she looked away.

"I guess you have the touch with kids, huh?" Patrice said.

"She's a sweetheart." Merry reached out to Patrice and took her hands. "It was nice to meet you. I hope you have a merry Christmas and you take really good care of each other."

"Thank you."

Clark held his hand out to Merry and she slipped her smaller one into his. The hotel room door closed behind them as they walked back to the Jeep in silence, the wad of cash burning a hole in his hand.

"If it's any consolation, I think she's already changing for the better," Merry said softly as he got into the driver's seat.

"I think so too. I'm going to go deposit this in the bank before we head over to the Parade of Lights."

"Fine by me, but don't dawdle. Mrs. Claus cannot disappoint her subjects."

"Why is Mrs. Claus British and talking about herself in the third person?"

"Because I know that was really difficult for you and I wanted to make you laugh."

Clark leaned over and kissed her, his hand cradling her cheek with a smile. "Thank you for being here tonight."

"I love you," she whispered.

"I love you, too." He headed up the road to the bank and deposited it into his savings. He could decide where best to distribute it Monday, but right now, he needed to get downtown for the Parade of Lights.

His phone pinged with a notification, but he couldn't check

until he parked a mile outside of the square of town. Families streamed down the sidewalk, finding free spots to watch. He weaved his way to the start where the Winters Christmas Tree Farm float was parked in front of the tire shop on the end of 4th street.

Merry unbuckled the moment his engine shut off. "Hurry, before my mother has a cow."

"We've got time, Mer. The float is parked right over there."

"Yes, but I still need to change into my Mrs. Claus outfit and there is a lot of fluffing and molding to do or my boobs will look crooked."

Clark let her drag him across the dirt parking lot, grinning from ear to ear. "I have no idea what you are talking about, but sounds like something I could help with."

"Clark, Merry!" Victoria yelled, waving her arms as she rushed to meet them.

Merry waved back. "Hey, I'm here."

"Where's Jace?" Clark asked.

"Chris took him to get hot cocoa. Now, I need you both to get changed."

"Both? Mom, what are you talking about?"

Victoria huffed. "Didn't you get my texts? Nick is sick and Martin's wife went into labor, so I need to fill float positions. You're going to be Santa—" She pointed at Clark. "And your brother agreed to be our other elf."

"Um, wait, my brother agreed to that?"

"Yes, so will you please help out? Chris can't get in and out of that float with his knees and we'll keep Jace with us so he can see the whole thing."

Clark nodded. "Of course I'll help."

Victoria clapped her hands gleefully. "Wonderful. Now, both of you head past the float and into the back of the tire shop. The door is open. Hurry."

Merry led the way past the Winters Family float. It was the same float they'd used for the last five years, with a little refreshed paint and props. The trailer was hooked to the back of a 1954 cherry-red Ford truck, with green wooden trees lit up by a spotlight in the back of the truck. The trailer was covered in white cotton fluff, with thousands of white Christmas lights woven throughout. Two wooden boxes painted to look like presents sat on either side toward the front, a spotlight on each to illuminate whoever sat inside. Pre-lit Christmas present yard displays were randomly placed and stacked at the feet of the brown wooden reindeer, held to Santa's sleigh by reins of Christmas lights and golden bells. More trees took up the rear behind Santa's sleigh and a sign for the farm twinkled with green and red lights.

Clark crossed the rough parking lot behind Merry and to the double doors. They opened as he was reaching around Merry to open them and Sam stepped out in an elf costume that was obviously meant for a much shorter man. The ruffled legs stopped mid-calf on Sam and Clark coughed, covering his laugh.

"Not a word."

Merry giggled. "You look adorable, Sam."

"Hey, you better watch it, missy. You're still on my naughty list."

"Please, your bike is fine. I'll see you in there," she said, kissing Clark swiftly. Almost as an afterthought, Merry kissed

Sam's cheek. "I am really sorry about hurting your motorcycle, Sam. Forgive me?"

Sam gave her a wicked grin. "Maybe for a real kiss."

"Hey!" Clark protested.

Merry laughed, blowing them both a kiss. "Sorry, Sam, but these lips are taken."

"You hear that? Taken."

Sam ruffled his hair. "I was only playing, brother, although it would have made me feel better about this get-up."

Clark laughed as Sam danced a jig in the pointy bell shoes. "How did she get you to wear it?"

"Mentioned I'd been staying in their foreman house rent-free."

"Well, you look adorable."

"Fuck you. Did she con you into riding on the float or are you just here for shits and giggles?"

"I'm going to fill in for Nick as Santa Claus."

"I should have been Santa! I'm older. Wanna trade?"

Clark slapped Sam on the back. "Not a chance. I'll see you out there, though."

Sam muttered a few colorful names as he stomped away and Clark grinned, enjoying his older brother's discomfort. It said a lot about the Winters family that Victoria could get Sam to potentially embarrass himself after some prodding. While his brother would always be the real rebel, maybe Sam had found a little of what Clark discovered being here. A place to belong.

Clark walked in to Merry adjusting a white wig with a perfectly circular bun on her head. She turned away to look at him, spectacles perched on her pert nose.

"Is that you, Santa Claus?"

Clark burst out laughing. "What are you wearing?"

"You don't like my dress?" The red number was trimmed on the collar and sleeves with white lace, with a black buckle belt secured below an enormous chest, and ample hips.

"I mean...your boobs are a little bigger than I remember them."

She picked a garment bag off the desk and handed it to him, rising up to give him a kiss. "You wanna feel 'em?"

"Is it weird if I say yes?"

"No, they crinkle." She put her hands over her chest and squeezed, creating a crackling sound. "Mom bought this bra years ago that was a G cup or something, sewed it to a girdle and created pockets filled with newspaper. She puts more in every year to keep it fluffy."

"Not gonna lie, that's a little hot."

"None of that, or Mom will come looking for us." Merry hopped up onto the desk, watching him change. Clark unzipped his jacket and tossed it over the desk next to her, followed by his shirt, holding her gaze. "So, no peeking under Mrs. Claus's skirts?"

"Absolutely not. We can't be late for our big debut."

"You've never ridden in the parade before?" Clark kicked off his boots and went for the buckle of his belt.

"I have, but as an elf. My mom used to be Mrs. Claus, but when she got her new glasses prescription, the motion makes her sick." When he dropped his jeans, she made an appreciative sound in the back of her throat. "I like what you're wearing right now. Maybe you could get away with just the beard."

"I'd freeze off everything you like and then some." He opened up the garment bag and pulled out the Santa jacket. "Wow, it's Sherpa lined."

"So is my dress. It's like wearing a cozy blanket." Clark buckled the jacket into place and Merry booed him.

"Stop making all that noise or your mother is going to come in here to see what we're doing."

"Which is nothing. I'm just enjoying the view."

Clark secured the pants and put his boots back on. "Should we get going?"

"You gotta have the hat and beard on from the time you leave until you get back here in case there are kids around."

"Got it." Clark secured the hat and fastened the beard in place. He turned to the mirror and struck a pose. "This is me."

"Will you come on?" Merry giggled, taking his hand. They walked out the door and across the parking lot to the float. When Victoria saw them, she clapped her hands.

"Oh, you two look wonderful. Now get up there. It's going to start in a few minutes."

Clark climbed up first and took Merry's hand, leading her across the trailer bed to the sleigh. Clark caught sight of his brother scrunched in one of the wooden boxes in the front of the sleigh and waved. Sam flipped him off in return.

"Sam!" Victoria barked. "There are children present."

Clark snort laughed as he climbed into the sleigh next to Merry. She covered them with a blanket and picked up a thermos from the floor. "The parade lasts a little over an hour, so Mom made us some of her special hot chocolate." She took off the lid and handed it to him.

He took a swig and cocked his head. "Is that...coconut?"

"Yeah, she puts rum in it. Just enough to keep us warm."

He took the cap from her and screwed it back into place. "This is my first time riding in the parade. You'll have to tell me what to do."

"Pretend you're Santa. Wave to the crowd. Stroke your beard. They can only see us from the waist up, and fair warning, the only songs that play on this float have to do with Santa and Christmas trees, so it will wear thin. Oh, your gloves. Are they in your pocket?"

Clark stuck a hand in and pulled out black leather gloves. Merry wore white ones and when he took her hand, he wasn't happy that he couldn't feel her warm skin on his.

The sound of the mayor's voice in the distance announced the start of the parade and Clark waited to move, but the float sat still.

"Why aren't we moving?"

"There's a lot of floats and we'll be going maybe five miles an hour. It takes a while. I do want to tell you that I'm proud of how you handled things with Patrice. How do you feel?"

"Like I'm ready to put a lot of things behind me and concentrate on all the good in my life."

"Like Jace and Sam?"

"Are you fishing?" he teased.

"I am not. I am waiting patiently."

Clark released her hand to cup her cheek. "And you. Always you, Merry."

She met his kiss and he slid his hand behind her neck, cradling it as he ignored the irritating whiskers of the beard above his upper lip and got lost in the taste of the woman he loved.

After twenty-seven years, he'd fallen in love for the very first time with Merry Winters and he planned to do everything he could to make sure she was the one he spent the rest of his life with.

Something bonked him over the head and he broke away with a startled "Hey!"

Holly stood over them with a three-foot-long candy cane, smirking. "Mom says stop making out. There are kids."

"I know there are kids, but Santa should be allowed to kiss his wife!" Clark laughed.

"Santa doesn't use his tongue on Mrs. Claus." Holly giggled.

"This one does," Merry quipped, her face turning red.

Holly waved the candy cane at them. "Don't make me come back here."

As Holly swished back to her box, Clark grumbled, "Did I just get kiss-blocked by an angry elf wielding a candy cane?"

"I think you did."

"Your sister is getting coal for Christmas."

The float rolled forward slowly and the speakers blared with "Up on the Housetop". It was so loud that Clark could barely hear himself think. When they came up on the start of the crowd, Holly and Sam tossed handfuls of candy. Clark waved at all the excited kids, but after ten minutes, his arm ached from holding it up.

Merry took a discreet sip of hot cocoa and leaned over. "Having fun?"

"I thinking my arm is going to fall off."

"Use the sleigh edge to rest your arm on. That's why it's padded."

Clark did what she said and the instant relief made him sigh. "Why didn't you tell me before?"

"I wanted to see how long you could keep it up."

"There's that little mean streak again."

Her gaze softened and she leaned over, giving him a long, lingering kiss. "I promise to kiss all your aching muscles better."

"Is that right," he murmured against her lips.

"Hmmm mmmmm." When Merry pulled away, she pointed to the front of the float. "We're in so much trouble."

Clark turned to find Holly glaring at them, smacking her candy cane against the palm of her hand angrily.

"She's an angry elf," he said and laughed.

"Did you mean to do that?" she asked.

"What?"

"That's a line from the movie *Elf*. I thought you may have remembered it was my favorite from our messages."

Clark smiled sheepishly. "I forgot. I'm sorry."

"It's fine, really. Funnily enough, I went onto the MeetMe app a few hours before our first date. I logged in to reread our emails and your profile was gone. I was wondering if you did it the first night we were supposed to meet."

"No. I did it after."

"When?"

"After our first kiss. When Jace was sick. I hadn't been on since I read your final message anyway, but after we kissed, I knew I didn't want anyone else."

Merry smiled wide and cupped his face. "Aren't you going to ask me something?"

He stared into her eyes tenderly. "Merry, will you please come home with me?"

"I'd love to."

CHAPTER 31

MERRY

WHEN THE BLARING BEEP OF an alarm clock went off Saturday morning, Merry groaned as she looked around Clark's room blearily for the source of the obnoxious sound. She smacked the top of the clock on his nightstand and blinked a few times, trying to make out the red numbers. Nine thirty-one.

Merry sat straight up in bed, holding the sheet to her naked chest. It was Saturday. She needed to be at the community center to set up for the Festival of Trees in less than thirty minutes.

Jumping out of Clark's bed, she started gathering her clothes off the floor. She borrowed a T-shirt from Clark's drawer and got dressed in a hurry, throwing her hair up into a messy bun as she rushed out of his room with her boots and socks in her hands.

Sam and Jace were sitting at the kitchen table, a tray of giant cinnamon rolls in the center. Jace held one in his hand, his face a mess of frosting.

"Good morning, Merry," Sam said, picking up his cup of coffee. "How did you sleep?"

Merry glared at him. "Bite me, Sam."

"Is bite me a bad word?" Jace asked.

"No, but it's rude."

"I stand by my rudeness this morning. Now, I'm late." Hopping from foot to foot she got on her socks and shoes and then came around the back of the kitchen and kissed Jace on top of his head. "Have a good day."

"You too."

She grabbed a cinnamon roll, shrugged, and kissed Sam on the top of his head. "You have a good day too."

"Thanks, I will."

She skidded to a halt before the door. "Wait, where is Clark?"

"In his workshop," Sam said.

"And my dog?"

"With my brother."

"All right."

"Are you going to have this kind of energy every morning?" Sam called after her. "Because if so, I am going to need to mentally prepare myself to live with you."

Merry slammed the front door without responding, because really, she didn't know what the future held. Only that her future included Clark and Jace. After the parade ended, they'd gotten changed and headed home. She'd grabbed Daisy from her kennel and walked her the several hundred feet to Clark's place. Jace had wanted Daisy in his room, but they'd vetoed the idea due to her destructive nature. He'd been disappointed until they'd agreed to let him hang in Clark's room and watch a movie. Clark carried him to bed when he fell asleep, and after...

Well, Merry had tried to be very quiet, but based on Sam's smirk, she hadn't been successful.

Merry trekked down the hill, calling Clark's name. She was reaching for the handles on his shop door when he opened them and stepped out, Daisy following along beside him.

"Good morning." He kissed her long and lingeringly, making her shiver.

"Hey, what are you doing in there?" she asked, craning her neck.

"Nothing, just woodwork. Did you sleep okay?"

"A little too good. Sorry, I'm borrowing a shirt because I am so late." She kissed him again, fast and hard. "Would you mind taking Daisy to my parents' for me?"

"Yeah, I can do that."

"You are a life saver." One more kiss and then she took off up the hill, waving. "I'll see you soon. I love you."

"I love you too. Good luck."

Merry didn't slow as she booked it across town, even when a sheriff's deputy flashed his lights when she passed. Her phone rang as she took the left into the community center parking lot and she pressed the green phone on her screen.

"Hello?"

"Are we still having your launch party in January?" Holly asked.

"Yes, that is the plan."

"I'm only checking because your pre-sale Christmas numbers are excellent, so if you wanted to open early…"

"Holly, with Clark, the Parade of Lights, the festival, my job at the school, and learning the ins and outs of the farm, I cannot launch until after the new year. I closed the pre-order sheet because it was getting out of control and there was no way I was going to get all those orders done if I kept it open."

"All right, but if you want to lighten your load, I would put in your notice at the school. And have you seen how many new followers you've gained?"

Merry grinned as she parked next to Ryan's monster truck. "Twenty-one thousand as of last night, and depending on how sales go over the next six months, I may just do that."

"You've got two thousand more this morning and—"

Suddenly her car door jerked open and Ryan reached in and pulled her out. "Why are you late?"

"I am not—one minute! I am one minute late."

"But you are never late!"

"What's going on?" Holly hollered.

"I gotta go, sis! Duty calls. Love you."

"Love you."

Merry grabbed her purse and shut her car door, listening with half an ear as Ryan continued his rant. "You are always ten minutes earlier than everyone else and I thought you were dead, bloody in pieces on the side of the road."

"I overslept, not a big deal." Merry squeezed his arm. "Breathe, Ryan. It's all going to be fine."

"How can you say that? I already broke up one fight between a couple of crafters!"

"Maybe next year we'll set up a sparring ring and take bets."

Ryan looked at her like she'd been replaced by pod people. "Why are you not freaking out?"

"Because we've done our best to make this event spectacular and I am not going to stress a hiccup or two." Merry thought about Clark and all their hiccups. They'd been uncomfortable at the time, but led to something better, stronger.

"Okay, you are freaking me out, but if you want to channel some kind of Zen que será, será bullshit, who am I to squash it?"

"That's the spirit," Merry joked.

"Oh, and someone else bought a tree so now we have to shift the rows. I called your dad to get another one delivered, but he didn't pick up."

"Wait, someone else bought a tree? Who?"

Ryan looked down at his phone, tapping the screen. "Ummmm, Pumpkin Pie Designs? I don't know, but what do you want me to do about the crafters auditioning for their own reality show, the Real Craft Karens of Mistletoe?"

Merry grabbed the door and winked. "Don't worry, I've got this."

The community center was bustling with life, people setting up booths and tree stands. Merry stepped onto the top of one of the tables set up in the food section, put her fingers into her mouth, and whistled. When the chatter stopped, she projected, "All right, everyone, listen up! I appreciate all of you being here and want to thank you. Your support for this amazing charity event has raised the most money in five years." The room clapped and Merry held her hands up. "That being said, this is a Christmas event. I want cheery dispositions and neighbors helping each other. I hear about any fighting or bickering and you will be asked to leave the event without a refund. I don't want to do that, but I will if people cannot get along." Merry clapped her hands. "Excellent. Now that's out of the way and we can talk about the trees. I need them shifted into rows of nine. If you've got upper body strength, meet me over at the tree area and we'll move them around. Thank you."

Merry hopped down, smiling at Ryan's slack-jawed face. "How was that?"

"Like I'm expecting burly enforcers to show up any minute and start dragging people out."

"Perfect, exactly what I was going for."

"Okay, you have got to tell me what happened to you, because you are like yourself but supercharged."

"I thrive under pressure. Now, enough jabbering. We've got work to do."

They got the trees reassembled into a nine by nine square with pathways between so people could see all of the trees and their ornaments. Each tree had a box where raffle tickets could be slipped inside with the name of the business on the outside.

The hours flew by in a sea of faces all asking her questions. She was working on stringing lights through the food court when Jace came running up.

"Hey, Merry, I'm here to help."

"Awesome, I can use a go-getter like you," she said, giving him a big hug. "Is your dad here?"

"Yeah."

"Perfect. All right, I need you to bring me those tablecloths and we're going to cover every table."

The ten folding tables were covered with red vinyl tablecloths with green Christmas tree confetti scattered on them and the centerpiece was a pop-up paper tree.

"What do you think?"

Jace stroked his chin thoughtfully. "It will work."

Merry laughed, ruffling his hair. "Let's go find your dad."

"Uh, no!" Jace yelled.

"Why not?"

"He's...busy," Jace stammered.

"Okay, is there something going on you want to tell me about?"

Jace shook his head vehemently.

"You're being weird, kid, but I'm going to let it go for now. We'll check out the booths and make sure everyone has what they need and then you can tell me all about what your dad is up to."

After an hour of Jace shadowing her every move, she knew that Clark had told him to keep her away from him, but wasn't sure why. She passed by Holly on a step stool, putting a Christmas star made from plastic tools on the top of one of the trees.

"Hey, is that yours?"

"No, this is Declan's tree."

"Why are you decorating it?" Merry asked.

"Because that was the deal. He buys. I decorate."

Merry held her hands up. "Whatever, your deal, not mine. Have you seen Clark?"

"He was over—what?" Holly was looking beyond Merry, her brow furrowed. Merry turned and Jace smiled innocently.

Merry arched a brow. There were definitely games afoot.

"You know, actually," Holly said, standing on her tiptoes to hang a wrench ornament, "I haven't seen him. And please tell me you're going home to shower and change, because you are smelling a little ripe, sis."

Merry lowered her nose toward her armpit and scowled. "Fine. I'll just find Ryan and tell him I'm running home really quick."

"I can tell him for you," Holly said brightly. "Honestly, it's better if you don't expose too many people to it."

Merry's gaze shifted between Holly and Jace, waving her fingers at them. "I don't know what is happening here, but this better not be a prank."

"Good Lord, will you trust me and go get pretty? Come on, Jace. We don't have to stand here and suffer her slander."

"What's slander?" Jace asked, following behind Holly.

Merry shot Ryan a quick text and headed home. After six hours of sweat and grime she agreed with Holly's assessment of her hygiene. It was strange Clark hadn't come to find her when he arrived. Her birthday wasn't until next week, so she didn't think they'd be planning a birthday surprise today.

Maybe he was irritated with her for rushing off. Had she been overtly inconsiderate? She sent Clark a text to clear the air.

> Hey, I'm sorry about this morning. I ran home to get cleaned up, but I'll be back in a bit.

When she pulled into her driveway, he'd read the text but hadn't replied.

By the time she got out of the shower and hadn't heard from him, she was worried. Her phone beeped finally as she was tying her boots.

> Don't worry about it. The place is looking great. See you when you get here.

The text was pleasant but perfunctory and not at all like him. Merry got back to the community center a little after five and went in search of Clark. The doors opened at five-thirty, and she didn't want to wait three hours to talk to him about why he was avoiding her.

She found him over by the food court, talking to her brother Nick and his friends. She came up alongside him and touched his arm. "Hey."

"Hey, there you are," he said, wrapping his arm around her shoulders. "I missed you today."

"Really? Because every time I tried to find you, your son would steer me in the opposite direction."

"That's because I didn't want you to see my surprise before it was done."

"What surprise?"

Pike chuckled. "Do you notice her change in tone? At first she was irritated. Now she's all sweet and eager."

"Shut it, Pike," she said mildly, letting Clark lead her away.

"The place looks great, Merry," he said, lacing his fingers with hers.

"Thanks, but Ryan did a lot and all the volunteers helped."

"I know, but you also kept things organized. Ryan told me you threatened to kick out anyone who caused trouble. I'm sorry I missed it."

"He was shocked. I don't think he knew I had it in me." Merry pointed to the Gallaghers' tree. "Did you know that Declan had my sister decorate his tree for him? I mean, it was nice that he bought one, but Holly has enough to do. He must have paid her well, 'cause she can't stand the guy."

"Where's Holly's tree?"

"Oh, I don't have my spreadsheet. I think it's in the corner."

"Should we take a turn before the crowds get to them?"

"Sure, but I want to see your surprise."

"It's in the trees. You won't have to look far."

Merry shook her head at his cryptic message, strolling down the first row. Holly's tree was three down on the right and a mix of silver and gold ornaments and a gorgeous porcelain angel with a silver dress, gold wings, and halo.

"Silver and Gold Treasures by Holly Winters. She really outdid herself. Everyone did. Even the plumbing company's tree is fun and festive."

They found her parents' tree on the next row. In lieu of a star, a green plaid bow was tied to the top. Matching plaid bulb ornaments and various red trucks carrying Christmas trees adorned the green branches. A photo ornament with the entire farm staff hung front and center with *Merry Christmas from Winters Christmas Tree Farm* written in gorgeous script on the red frame.

"Come look at this one," Clark called from the end of the next row.

Merry stopped next to him, frowning. "Where is the ticket box?"

"Maybe it's spoken for."

She bent down and read the custom wood sign. "Merry and Bright by Pumpkin Pie Woodworking and Designs. Display only."

The tree was wrapped with bright LED lights, with bulbs the size of a dime. The topper was a simple wood star with holes throughout, and streams of white light shining through.

There were several ornaments of a white dog in various poses and Merry reached out to touch one of the pup hiding behind a Christmas tree.

"Clark…is this your work?"

He slipped behind her, his arms circling her waist. "Yes."

"They're beautiful." There was an ornament carved to look like a slice of pumpkin pie. Another of two interconnecting rocking chairs with HIS and HERS engraved on the backs of them. Tears pooled in her eyes and she turned in his arms.

"You haven't even seen the best ones." He took her hand and led her around back. There was a couple dancing. A pair of ice skates. Santa's sleigh. Her name. A dog with a—

"Clark!" she gasped, grabbing the ornament off the tree and shoving it into her pocket.

He burst out laughing. "What? This tree chronicles every moment I've spent with you. I couldn't leave it out. Or this one."

Clark showed her another ornament of a man carrying a woman in his arms.

"You painted these?"

"Actually, I carved and Sam painted."

"I want this tree."

Clark hung the ornaments back on the tree, except the one of Butch, and he took her face in his hands. "I figured you would say something like that, but if you want it, there's a price."

"Name it."

"I want forever with you. I want to spend a lifetime making wooden memories of us. You. Me. Jace. Your demon dog. Your family. Sam." He kissed her lips, whispering, "I love you, Merry. My first love. My only love. You can have the tree if I can keep your heart."

Merry sobbed, wrapping her arms around his waist. "Yes, my heart is yours. All yours."

He kissed her again, deepening it, his hands tangling in her hair.

"Dad! Merry!" Jace yelled.

They broke apart in time for Clark to catch Jace on the fly.

"Did she like the tree?"

"I love the tree," Merry said, running her hand over his hair.

"Can I give it to her now?"

"There's more?"

Clark reached into his jacket pocket and handed the box to Jace. "He really didn't want to wait until your birthday."

"Just like his dad. Has to give the best gifts early."

Jace handed the box to Merry and she opened it. It was a white gold necklace with three colorful gemstones embedded in the center of a heart.

"It's our birthstones. Blue is you, red is me, and purple is dad."

"I told him it might be too much," Clark said nervously.

"No, it's not." She unclasped the chain and closed it behind her neck. "I love it so much. And you..." Merry kissed Jace's cheek. "I love you."

"I love you, too." He lowered his voice to a stage whisper. "I did okay keeping her away?"

Clark grinned. "You did excellent, buddy."

Merry tickled him until he squealed. "I knew you were distracting me, I just couldn't figure out why."

"Dad wanted everything to be perfect."

"It is," Merry said, hugging them both. "Everything is absolutely perfect."

Acknowledgments

I want to thank Corrine's Craft Shop and her adorable Peters for being the inspiration for Merry's crafty side hustle.

To my readers, especially my ARC team, my amazing Lattes, and the thousands of BookTokers who brighten my days, I freaking adore you!

Writing my beloved books wouldn't be possible without my wonderful husband and children, who share love and laughter with me daily. Thank you for letting me work in peace (mostly).

For my amazing agent, Sarah, who has made my publishing journey a whirlwind of possibilities. You have helped me achieve so many of my dreams and I appreciate you.

To Allison...thank you for helping me bring Mistletoe and all its residents to life. My humble thanks to Deb, Jessica, and the fantastic team at Sourcebooks for polishing Merry up and making her shine. And to their design and marketing teams, for the adorable covers that make very pretty Instagram pictures.

For Tina, my sounding board and biggest cheerleader. I love you!

Special thanks to my dear friend, Erica, who helped me bring Merry's story to life by asking all the right questions.

My extended family, for being proud of me and sharing my books.

To my dear friend, Tammy, for telling perfect strangers I write books with "all the words but one." And to all the authors who have answered my never-ending questions. We are a family and I am so lucky to be a part of it.

ABOUT THE AUTHOR

Codi Hall loves writing small-town romances with big feels. As a Northern California native living in Idaho, she fell in love with the big sky, amazing people, and brisk winters. She enjoys movie marathons with her family, snuggling with her fur babies, creating funny TikToks to share with the world, and snuggling under a blanket with a good book! She also writes contemporary and paranormal romance under the pen name Codi Gary. Readers can get in touch via her website authorcodihall.com.

NICK AND NOEL'S CHRISTMAS PLAYLIST

This Christmas, two best friends play their way into each other's heart.

Nick Winter can always rely on his best friend, Noel Carter, and her endless supply of Christmas tunes to lift his spirits. A night of fun together on his family's Christmas tree farm is just what Nick needs to forget about the ex who cheated on him. But one thing leads to another and… Did he and Noel just kiss?

If Noel can turn Nick's Blue Christmas merry and bright, she'll make sure this is the Last Christmas Nick spends with a broken heart. This year, they'll be Rockin' Around the Christmas Tree as a couple—as long as Nick's ex doesn't go standing under any mistletoe.

"Codi Hall always knows how to bring all the feels."

—Monica Murphy, *New York Times* bestselling author

For more info about Sourcebooks's books and authors, visit:

sourcebooks.com

MISTLETOE AND MR. RIGHT

In this quirky holiday romance by Sarah Morgenthaler,
Christmas is the perfect season to fall in love, as long
as a Grinch-like moose doesn't get in the way...

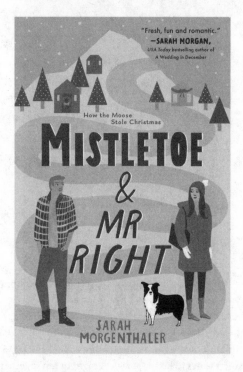

Lana Montgomery is Rick Harding's dream girl. Unfortunately, the socialite
businesswoman has angered the locals with her big dreams and good intentions.
When a rare (and spiteful) white moose starts destroying the holiday decorations
every night, Lana, Rick and all of Moose Springs, Alaska, must work together to
save Christmas, the town...and each other.

"Fresh, fun, and romantic."

—Sarah Morgan, *USA Today* bestselling author of
A Wedding in December

For more info about Sourcebooks's books and authors, visit:

sourcebooks.com

THE HOLIDAY TRAP

One change-up will change their lives.

Greta Russakoff loves her tight-knit family and tiny Maine hometown, even if they don't always understand what it's like to be a lesbian living in such a small world. She desperately needs space to figure out who she is.

Truman Belvedere's heart is crushed when he learns that his boyfriend has a secret life including a husband and daughter. Reeling, all he wants is a place to lick his wounds far, far away from Louisiana.

Enter a mutual friend with a life-changing idea: swap homes (and lives) for the holidays. For one perfect month, Greta and Truman will have a chance to experience a whole new world...and maybe fall in love with the partner of their dreams. But all holidays must come to an end, and eventually these two transplants will have to decide whether the love (and found family) they each discovered so far from home is worth fighting for.

"An irresistible queer romance."

—*Publishers Weekly*, Starred Review, for *Better Than People*

YOU'RE A MEAN ONE, MATTHEW PRINCE

Find a little joy to the world? Not today, Santa.

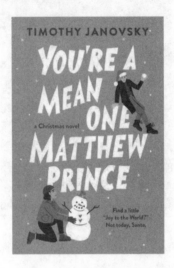

Matthew Prince is young, rich, and thoroughly spoiled. But after one major PR misstep, Matthew is cut off and shipped away to spend the holidays in his grandparents' charming small town hellscape. It's bad enough he's stuck in some festive winter wonderland—it's even worse that he has to share space with Hector Martinez, an obnoxiously attractive local who's unimpressed with anything and everything Matthew does.

Just when it looks like the holiday season is bringing nothing but heated squabbles, the charity gala loses its coordinator and Matthew steps in as a saintly act to get home early on good behavior...with Hector as his maddening plus-one. But even a Grinch can't resist the unexpected joy of found family, and in the end, the forced proximity and infectious holiday cheer might be enough to make a lonely Prince's heart grow three sizes this year.

"This book made my queer heart so very full and deeply happy."

—Anita Kelly for *Never Been Kissed*

For more info about Sourcebooks's books and authors, visit:

sourcebooks.com